From the darkest reaches of the Wild West comes a terrifying band of desperados bent on a course of destruction and revenge. Led by a vicious outlaw with half a face, they are called Dark Riders, neither alive nor dead, trapped in a world of eternal night. They descend upon the 7HL ranch in a fury of flashing fangs and ruthless bloodlust, leaving the compound littered with bloodless bodies.

When Chris Durrin, a man stalked by death and nightmares, returns to find his uncle and all cowhands murdered, he soon realizes the devil has come to claim his due—a devil named Milus Clint.

A devil he killed six years previous.

Before the night is over he finds himself locked in a desperate struggle between the world of the living and the realm of the undead. Can he overcome the menace before he too becomes another in a long line of victims of The Dark Riders?

THE DARK RIDERS
by Howard Hopkins

First print edition: March, 2007

Ebook editions published by Atlantic Bridge Publishing, 2002

Cover art by Judith Huey

ISBN 978-0-6151-5007-9

Published by Golden Perils Press
www.lulu.com/goldenperils

Printed in the United States of America

THE
DARK RIDERS

by

Howard Hopkins

ONE

The sun dripped into the horizon in a blood-colored blaze, bringing death—and Dark Riders.

Scarlet fire stained the rippling ocean of buffalo grass and mesquite, which spring had recently transformed from miles of topaz plains to emerald graze. Scarlet faded to darkening hues of violet to shady blue. With a glimmer all light vanished and shadows danced, concealing creatures that slithered through the blades with whispers of sound. But it couldn't hide the far more deadly creatures who shunned the daylight and devoured souls.

The inky maze of night brought an evil to the grassy sea of the Texas Panhandle, an evil inhuman and cruel, calculating and directed. An evil on horseback who had hungered for this moment in the soulless depths of countless nights, dwelling on the time his revenge would begin.

An evil named Milus Clint.

Milus Clint sat his horse in a grassy swale, ten men reining to a halt to either side of him. Fixated on the elliptical spread of a ranch a mile distant, he barely acknowledged their presence. His cold buzzard eyes surveyed the outbuildings: blacksmith, carpentry and storage sheds; a bunkhouse, flanked by a combination cookhouse and dining hall; scattered corrals and holding pens for branding cattle; a windmill to pump water to gravity pipes within the main house's attic.

A half-smile touched the remains of Clint's face. Eyes narrowing beneath a battered felt hat, his gaze locked on the main house, a large building of planed boards and brick with a veranda running end to end, shaded by cottonwoods. It was a solid house, fine and befitting a man of Clem Durrin's stature, and Milus Clint was pleased.

It would make taking it away from the boy so much sweeter.

Murky sulfur light filtered from a window, swabbing the veranda and lawn with a sickly glow that melded into darkness a few feet farther on. Milus Clint felt a twinge of yearning. It was one of the few forms of light left to the likes of a man such as he: moonlight, firelight, a firefly sparkling in the velvet night, but never sunlight. For that the boy would pay dearly.

Starting tonight.

Milus Clint laughed, an unnatural, strained sound that crawled up from the place inside where his soul used to be. The other Riders, poised expectantly beside him, awaiting his word to strike, shot glances at one another, knowing the foolish wisdom of disturbing Milus Clint when he took to these moods, when the darkness living inside him played with his thoughts.

A breeze stirred the grass, moonlight skittering within the blades, and plucked at the scraggly reddish-brown locks that stuck out from beneath his hat. Milus lifted his head, letting the bone-glow of the moon wash over his mottled features. His fingertips drifted over the scarred mass of flesh covering three-quarters of the left side of his face. He traced the gristly peaks and deep depressions. Inside him fury burned at the thought of it. Beneath the lizardy hide studded with clumps of bristle, throbbed the memory, and he swore he still felt the lead embedded within his brains ache. He knew it was impossible, but he felt it all the same. And recollected who had put it there.

His eyes grew colder, more distant, the hunger-frozen orbs of a creature of prey, devoid of sympathy or remorse or anything else remotely human. For an instant his eyes darkened, a sheet of blackness sliding across them, jagged flashes of blue-black arcing like obsidian lightning within.

"Milus?" asked Emmet, the Rider closest to him. "Shouldn't we be gettin' on with it? You wanna strike a'fore that kid gets back we best move now."

"Yeah." Milus nodded, blackness draining from his eyes as his gaze lowered back to the ranch. "Yeah, best we had." He glanced at the others one by one, centering a spell longer on the one named Billy. A thought pricked his mind, a wonder. He could afford no mistakes, and that one, Milus Clint had become increasingly certain, was like to make one.

His gaze traveled through the rest of the men, strong men, better'n the band he'd rounded up those years back in New Mexico Territory. They were a motley crew of desperadoes, each as vicious and bloodthirsty as the next. All as he, Dark Riders. Not a one had glimpsed the sunlight in years.

Milus's gaze stopped on the last man, who nodded.

"Jeters, head for them Injuns—you know what to do." Milus half-grinned.

"Injun blood always tastes sweeter, 'specially them squaws." Jeters laughed and reined around, spurring his black horse to the left.

A lonesome howl tore through the night and Milus's head rose. On the horizon the shadowy shapes of coyotes skittered about.

"Soon, my friends..." he whispered. A scattering of colorless images streaked through his mind and he saw what they saw, heard what they heard: glimpses of two men on horseback, one of them a boy. The link dissolved and the images vanished.

"*Yah!*" Milus yelled, gouging his bootheels into the horse's sides and sending the black into a gallop. The rest followed and the sound of thunder boomed over the ghostly quiet of the Plains.

The wind whipped at Milus Clint, tearing back the folds of his duster and for a fleeting moment he felt almost human again. Almost. A luxury, that feeling, one in which he seldom indulged. But tonight, with the taste of revenge so sweet on his tongue, he savored it.

A sudden veering off of one of the men shattered his mood and vinegar rose in his veins. He yanked on the reins, bringing the huge black to a stop, the other Riders charging on ahead before jerking up short, circling back.

"What's a'matter?" the Rider called Hascan asked.

Milus spat and made a disgusted grunt, nudging his head to the side as he watched the break-away Rider bolt into the night.

"What's that damn fool up to?" Milus's cold buzzard eyes narrowed to a squint. For an instant, their color blackened, glitters of blue-black sparkling within.

"Goddamn Billy again!" Hascan snorted. "Think he's headin' for them longhorns bunched yonder?"

Milus paused, fury riding him, the thought flashing in his mind that Billy would have to be reprimanded for runnin' off that way.

"Shoulda left him in Fort Sumner that night." Milus peered at Hascan. "Go get 'im. Make sure he's with us when we finish with the old bastard."

Hascan jerked a nod and swung his horse around, riding off in the direction Billy had taken.

"Any of the rest of you got a notion to go steer chasin'?" Milus asked without humor, peering at each man, who shook his head to signify he did not. "Good. I ain't like to take much more from the sonofabitch. I got a limit to my patience and it ain't a goddamn big one." The men remained stone-faced and when Milus uttered a chopped laugh at his own joke they let loose with whoops of their own.

With shouts, the Riders set their mounts in motion, nine outlaws arrowing towards the cattle ranch, now less than a mile away.

They passed the outer corrals and men angled off in different directions, the largest group descending upon the lighted bunkhouse. One man headed towards a corral filled with horses, while two others set about damaging the fences and outbuildings. Milus and two men stayed on course towards the sprawling main house.

The lone Rider reached the corral, leaping from his mount and scrambling to the gate. He flung it wide, screeching and hissing at the startled horses within. The animals neighed in fright, stamped about, began to rear.

The Dark Rider scurried away from the opening as the terrified horses bolted *en masse* from the corral in a tumult of beating hooves and billowing dust. The Rider hissed, lips curling back from razored incisors. He leaped straight up, balancing on a corral rail and flung himself into space. He timed the move perfectly, catching the last horse, a sorrel, as it went towards the opening. The sorrel jerked to a halt, humping its back and springing up like a let-go spring, trying to throw off the parasitic creature clinging to its neck.

The Rider uttered a high-pitched giggle, sensing the beast's terror, savoring it, leeching it. He could smell its rushing blood and drool slithered from the corner of his mouth.

His fingers dug into the animal's silky coat and rippling slabs of muscle. The sorrel, unable to shake him, grew more panicked. It bleated a pathetic tortured sound as the Rider plunged his fangs deep into the huge vein throbbing along its neck.

At the bunkhouse, four Riders reined up, dismounting and charging for the door. A man in long johns, obviously attracted by the commotion, froze in the doorway, paralyzed at the sight of the four outlaws coming towards him. He broke the shock almost instantly, jumping backwards in a herky-jerky motion.

The four men stamped across the porch and filled the doorway.

Within the bunkhouse, seven men sat around a long table, on which silver dollars and greenbacks were piled high, each clutching what he thought was the winning hand. Their gazes jumped to the door. Their faces waxed from looks of wonder to sudden fear.

The lead Rider grabbed the long johns-clad man's face and yanked him close. The Rider's mouth opened, saliva-smeared fangs glinting with lantern light. Dull hazel eyes faded to shiny black arcing with blue-black streaks. The cowhand gasped, mouthing silent pleas.

The Rider hissed, twisting the cowhand's face up and sideways, and sank his fangs deep into the man's neck. The cowhand struggled frantically, vainly, beating at the Rider's head, kicking at the Rider's knees.

The blows had no effect.

The Rider held him fast, grinning, blood dripping from his mouth. He plunged his fangs into the cowhand's neck again, drinking, draining. The man's struggles weakened, ceased.

At the table, the seven cowhands sat spellbound in terror. Their eyes locked first on the Rider, then on the broken body of their companion. In unison they sprang from their chairs, cards flying from their hands, scattering across the tabletop and fluttering to the floor. Some raced for their gunbelts hanging over bunkends, while others bolted for the windows.

The Riders swarmed into the room, two attacking the men lunging for weapons. One cowhand made it to his gunbelt, pulling a Colt .45 from its holster and swinging it around. He jerked the trigger. A shot blasted and a flash of flame and blue smoke turned the air acrid. The shot, hurried and ill-aimed, went wide, lead plowing into a wall. The Rider leaped at him. Dark eyes glittering, the outlaw wrenched the Colt from the ranchhand's grip and flung it. With a flash of gouging teeth, the Rider tore away the man's throat.

The remaining cowhands fell quickly. Ones scrambling to the windows were hauled back, hurled about like ragdolls, one thrown so hard he rebounded from the wall and left a splatter of crimson where his skull had caved under the impact.

Then it was over. Four Riders fell upon the five cowhands remaining. The sounds of screams and tearing flesh stained the night, dying as the Riders fed.

TWO

Clem Durrin was dying.

Nothing on God's green earth could stop that. Cancer had spread through his lungs like wildfire. He felt it devouring his tissue, swallowing his innards. He knew he stood damn little chance of living long enough to see this year's herd of cattle reach Dodge. For the first time he could recollect, he wouldn't make the drive. He would miss the satisfaction of seeing months of hard work pay off, of tasting the grit and salty tang of sweat on his tongue; he'd miss the ragged weariness of trail-worn muscles and the easy camaraderie of cowhands plowing north through the blazing Texas sun.

But worse than that, he wouldn't see Chris reach his twenty-seventh birthday, the day Clem had planned to turn over the 7HL ranch to his adopted son.

Sickening regret rose in his heart. Missing that birthday bothered him more than dying. Dying was nothing compared to living, and Godamighty he'd lived through some hard times.

But to miss Chris' day, the one Clem had planned for all these years, pained him more than the agony that gripped his chest with each spasm of coughing. *That* goaded him. They'd been through so much, and to be robbed of that special moment was just south of intolerable.

Oh, he suspected Chris had an inklin'—how could he not? Chris heard the coughing spells, saw the weak turns that sent him stumbling, ones he would pass off as too much sun and plain old age. Chris knew better, but said little of it, and Clem was glad for that. But in those times Clem saw the sadness that stained his son's eyes, saw the haunting shade of death fluttering about on his face whenever he looked at his old man.

A cough shuddered through Clem's body and he uttered a strained laugh, though God knew he saw nothing funny in it. With large hands that carried a trace of a tremble, he selected a fine cigar from the humidor atop the mantle. After biting off the end, then striking a Lucifer on his fingernail, he sucked the cigar to a glowing red. He inhaled deeply, savoring the flavor and fragrance. He'd be damned if he'd give that up, despite the doc's warning. God might deny him future pleasures, but the taste of a fine cigar, no siree.

To look at him, no one would have guessed his deteriorating condition. In fact, the ranchhands, except possibly Windy, thought Clem Durrin to be as fit as a fiddle. Six months back, Clem had straddled his sixtieth birthday as if he'd climbed onto a familiar old cowhorse.

An ironic laugh touched his lips. Everyone told him he was built along the lines of the galldamned longhorns he had spent his days raising: rangy, slab-sided and still powerful as a bull. Hell, he bet he could still hoist a damn stump clean out of the ground just by wrapping his ropy arms around the trunk—not that he'd dare try it at this juncture. He didn't need Mrs. Tulber giving him jesse again. He swore the old housekeep treated him like a goddamned child at times, fawning over him the way she did.

Clem paced in front of the fireplace, sucking in a deep drag of the cigar and puffing smoke rings. Staring into the flames, a sigh escaped his lips. He saw no putting it off; he had to tell Chris tonight. The boy needed to know his future was set out for him. Windy, too. Windy deserved a piece of the pie for all the dedication, hard work and sweat he'd put into the outfit over the past few years. And with that scalawag Shinn possibly rustling cattle they would need the authority to make instant decisions. The way Clem saw it, some dark times might be ahead and Chris and Windy would need to deal with them.

Dark times.

Clem had dwelled on those far too often since the doc told him the news.

But what about Chris? How can you leave him, the way everyone else in his life has? Can he face that again?

Clem gave a slight shake of his head. Deep down, the thought that Chris had lived through hell and tragedy enough for two lifetimes consoled him in a small way. If Chris had fought the Devil and survived, he would survive an old man's passing.

Why couldn't he convince himself of that?

Clem Durrin sighed a weary sigh and shuffled over to the windows, peering out into the night. A strange apprehension crept over him, like the feeling of being stalked by a grizzly while riding a trail. Beyond the swatch of light bleeding out from the lantern on the table, he saw shadows dancing from shading cottonwoods, swaying to the rhythm of the breeze. He searched those shadows, eyes still sharp as a hawk's. He saw nothing. The outside air had turned crisp with the sweet scent of early spring nights. Moisture beaded on the windows like little drips of diamonds.

Something's coming...

The thought hissed in his mind and he quickly gave it up; something about the notion made him damned uncomfortable, though it was nothing he could pinpoint.

Shaking off the sense, Clem moved back from the windows, only to stop short as a sound reached his ears.

A mournful sound, a funereal yowl pregnant with lonesomeness. It rose and fell, at once part of the night, yet separate.

Clem listened to the grim baying, transfixed by it, then went back to the windows and peered in every direction until he thought he glimpsed skittering dark shapes on the horizon.

A footfall behind him caught his attention and when he turned, he saw Mrs. Tulber had come from the kitchen. The older woman filled the doorway to the dining room, hands clasped and bleached, face pallid and eyes wide as eggs. A heavyset woman north of her mid-fifties, built as if from large ovals stacked one atop the other. She looked like a big ol' winter moon fell to Earth, Clem always teased, and she would chuckle and all her parts would jiggle at once.

"Prairie wolves," Clem said hastily, before she could start on one of her scolding tirades.

"The Indians say those coyotes bring warnings when they get this close, Mr. Clem." She shook her head and her cheeks quaked. Clem saw she was actually frightened of something; he reckoned the coyotes weren't entirely responsible.

He frowned. "Well, them Indians don't know all there is to know, do they, now?" His voice held less conviction than he would have liked.

"You feel it, too, Mr. Clem. Something else is out there." A snippy edge clipped her tone and she gave a jerky nod for emphasis.

"Something else?" Clem's voice went distant as a burst of dread took him. "What in God's name are you jawin' about?"

"Not be just coyotes, Mr. Clem. Something else, something awful and dark."

"You ain't makin' sense, Gladys. Nothing's out there but buffalo grass and longhorns and a bunkhouse full of cussin' card-playin' ranchhands."

"And coyotes."

"And coyotes. But so what? Ain't the first time we've seen 'em of late."

The old woman worked a plump frown and deep creases lined her face. "They've come here every night for the last week, Mr. Clem, sometimes one, sometimes more. They keep getting closer, scaring the buffalo."

"Dammit, they're longhorns, Gladys! I keep tellin' you that!" It was their personal joke, one Gladys Tulber, no matter how distressed, always nettled him with. When she had first come to the ranch, she had mistakenly called the longhorns buffalo, thinking that's what they were. Clem had set her straight but she found some personal amusement calling them that ever since. He supposed he did, too.

The old woman smiled, as if the common exchange had put some solid ground of reality under their feet.

A sharp burst of howling came from the distance, two, three coyotes, at least, Clem judged.

"They're gatherin'..." he muttered, scratching his chin. "They'll booger the steers for sure. We'll have a goddamn stampede if this keeps up. 'Prised they ain't boltin' already."

Another sound grabbed his attention: Hoofbeats. A number of horses from the sounds of it, thundering in from the distance.

His brow crinkled. Odd, that many riders heading this way. He'd only expected Chris and Windy, but they wouldn't make so much noise riding in.

Clem glanced at Mrs. Tulber, as he turned back to the windows and peered out.

There! Charging in at full gallop! A cloud of riders, a dark cloud. He wasn't sure how many at this distance, but they arrowed for the ranch. He shuddered, knowing instinctively they were coming for no good. He watched them draw closer, transfixed as they careened across the field, the very darkness seeming to part before them.

A few broke away and rode towards the bunkhouse, two others looping towards the outbuildings and another heading for a corral. Clem's gaze followed the last, seeing the man dismount and throw wide the corral gate, loosing the horses. Cold horror swelled in his heart as he witnessed the rider fall upon one of the animals and bring it down.

Christ...

He tore his attention from the morbid sight and centered it on the three lead riders reining to a halt before the house.

Clem jerked away from the window, gaze flashing to the old housekeep, but barely seeing her. From the shadowy well of his memory rose a face he thought he would never see again.

"Judas Priest...Clint..." he whispered.

"I told you there was something awful out there!" Mrs. Tulber bleated. "I told you!"

Clem steeled himself against the bloody images flashing through his mind, scenes from another time, of death and of things thought buried. It was impossible for Clint to be riding up to the ranch, yet he was.

"Dammit, you old nag, get the hell upstairs! Grab a gun and barricade yourself somewhere so they can't find you. Anybody comes at you, blow their balls clean off—now!"

Mrs. Tulber shook her head violently. "I can't leave you—"

"Do it, old woman, or by God I'll fire you!"

Clem lunged for the far wall, upon which a loaded scatter-gun rested on pegs pounded into the brick.

Propelled inward by a powerful kick, the front door burst open, ripping loose from one of its hinges.

Mrs. Tulber, having reached the second step of the flight leading to the upper rooms, screeched and jerked around.

Three men, their faces wild beneath battered hats, swarmed in like buzzards swooping on prey. The two Riders behind Milus Clint leaped across the foyer and grabbed Mrs. Tulber, yanking her from the stairs and throwing her to the floor.

"No!" Clem shouted, fury boiling in his veins as he reached for the scatter-gun and pulled it down.

The two Riders tore at the old woman's garments, shredding her blouse and exposing a large fleshy breast. One Rider giggled insanely, eyes turning coal black, sparkling with blue-black arcs of light as he fondled her.

The old woman mewed, tried to push him away, but one Rider forced her down while the other bit at her breast.

The first Rider's lips curled back, baring long canine teeth. He plunged them into her throat as he forced back her head.

Clem whirled, swinging the shotgun around. A look of utter horror and resolve swept over his face at the sight of the Riders mutilating the old woman. He'd felt hate before, but never as cold and clean as he felt it now, and by all that was holy he'd send the bastards straight to hell.

He triggered both barrels. The recoil kicked him back slightly but he held his aim steady.

The blast took the advancing leader in the chest. Shot ripped through the outlaw's shirt, shredding it and the flesh beneath , sending him stumbling backwards. A measure of satisfaction swelled in Clem at knowing this time he had killed Milus Clint for sure.

The satisfaction was short-lived.

The outlaw leader stopped his backward stumble. A half-grin oiled his disfigured features. Across his chest, where the shot had peppered his flesh, an inky fluid boiled from the wounds. Like a living creature, it flowed across the broken skin, sealing the wounds and sinking into the flesh until no trace of the injuries remained.

"You can't hurt me, old man." Milus's voice came low and somber as he came forward again. "But I can surely hurt you, and I surely will."

Milus swept back the fold of his duster, revealing the blacksnake whip coiled at his right hip. "Remember this, Durrin? Had me a fondness for it the first time we met. That didn't leave me in death."

Clem Durrin made a strangled sound, shock cemented on his face. The man before him shouldn't be alive by all rights, yet somehow he was.

"No, it ain't possible. Chris killed you, he must have."

A guttural sound escaped Clint's throat. "There are different ways to die, old man. Some die fast; them's the lucky ones. Some die slow; them's not so lucky. Others, they die like me." Milus's hand drifted to the blacksnake, fingers curling around the thick handle.

Clem's gaze darted to the gruesome form of Mrs. Tulber and immeasurable sadness raged in his heart. By God he'd finish the bastard somehow for that. He flipped the scatter-gun around, intending to use it as a bludgeon.

At the same instant, Clint swept the blacksnake upwards and snapped it out. Pain lanced Clem's cheek as the frayed tip struck him, splitting the skin. The scatter-gun flew from Clem's grip and clattered on the floor across the room.

His gaze rose to meet the outlaw's. All thought of his injury vanished as he glimpsed something in their depths. This was no longer the same man he'd ridden posse after six years ago. Clint was no longer human; he was something else, something fashioned of bloodshed and darkness. He would have no chance against the outlaw; he felt sure of that, but he didn't care. He was going to die soon anyway. Clint would almost be doing him a favor by killing him.

Clem stared spellbound at the blackness that swallowed the color from Clint's buzzard eyes. Blue-black light arced deep within the black orbs, beckoning Clem, luring him.

"You ain't human," Clem muttered.

Milus Clint's gaze focused on the bleeding gash on Clem's cheek with a look of hunger. He took a step closer. "No, I ain't 'xactly."

Clem decided to take a desperate chance. He couldn't shoot the outlaw, but perhaps he could kill him with his bare hands. He still had the strength of a grizzly and if he went down he would go down fighting.

With a sudden roar he flung himself at the hardcase. Grabbing Clint's throat, he pressed his fingers deep into the outlaw's Adam's apple. The leader's skin felt cold, dead as a rain slicker and Clem suddenly knew he had made a mistake.

His last.

Clint's hands came up, fingers locking around Clem's wrists like steel bands. Clem's features turned with shock as Clint squeezed. Bones cracked and pain shot through his hands.

Clint gave a half-grin and hurled the rancher backward. Clem felt his feet lift off the floor, felt himself slam into the wall and slide down, air exploding from his lungs, senses reeling. The impact seemed to numb every part of his body at once. The room tumbled, the disfigured face of Milus Clint swooping before his vision, laughing, grinning, taunting.

The sting of a whip lashing his chest stopped the whirling and Clem looked up, blinking, stunned.

"You're dyin', old man. I can feel it. You ain't got much time left, less now." Milus Clint snapped the whip again and another gory slash opened on Clem's opposite cheek.

The rancher shuddered with a spasm of coughing that tore a chunk from his lungs. He felt a liquidy warmth in his chest and knew something was bleeding internally. He almost laughed. The shock of hitting the wall had merely hastened the inevitable; for that maybe he was thankful. If the outlaw walked away now, Clem reckoned he might live another hour, maybe more, maybe less, and he would have a chance to warn Chris. Something told him that was what Clint had come for, to deliver a message to the boy.

The outlaw stepped closer and knelt, forearm resting across one knee. Clem could smell his foul breath, like the stench from a rotting steer carcass.

Clint's voice lowered to a hoarse whisper. "I got a message for you, old man, one for that no-good bastard boy you got with you. Tell him I aim to take everything he has and do it nice an' slow so he suffers as much as I have. And when I'm done, I'm gonna take his goddamned soul."

Clem's eyes glazed as he stared at the outlaw, vision blurring. Clint's face wavered in and out. He suddenly doubted he'd live long enough to warn Chris, but prayed he would. It was the boy's only chance.

The outlaw spat at Clem and straightened, backed off. The Riders stooping over Mrs. Tulber's body came up and trailed Milus Clint from the house.

He's gone...

Silence fell heavy in the sallow light of the parlor, broken by hoofbeats that quickly faded and the muffled stuttering of his heart. He felt it begin to wind down, knew it wouldn't be long, now.

A gurgly sound escaped his lips at the thought, and again he prayed he could hold on until Chris got back.

In the distance he heard the haunting howl of a coyote and knew that somehow he would have to.

THREE

Billy couldn't rightly say what made him break away when he spotted the longhorns bunched half a mile to his left. It just came over him, way it always did. He couldn't rightly explain it, never cared a diddly damn to try. It simply was and that was all the nevermind he gave it, 'cept in odd moments when specters from his past came a'hauntin'.

Something about those rangy slab-sided beasts, as wild and unpredictable as Billy himself was wont to be, attracted him like the scent of a two-bit saloon gal. Wild, like him, but never truly free, for there always came an end to the trail, and a railhead to whisk them to slaughter, as there had for Billy not so long ago.

Way it was before Milus Clint had Jeters turn him into what he was now.

Billy shot the black horse towards the bunch, enjoying the brisk caress of the dark wind on his face and the feel of the rippling muscles of the demon horse beneath him. For a spell, a sense of freedom swelled in his heart. He bellowed in glee and a lopsided grin came to his lips. His light-brown hair fluttered and flapped where it stuck out from beneath his beaten hat. His trail-worn duster whipped back, snapping like a flag in the wind, revealing a pearl-handled Colt at his right hip. He was the only member of Clint's gang who bothered carrying a gun, but it was, like the vicious specimen of a whip Milus felt partial to, a nod to the past, to what had been, a fragment of humanity for a boy who no longer considered himself as such.

Sometimes he forgot he had been a mere boy when he died. Sometimes he forgot the winks and coy smiles the gals would give the downy-cheeked, buck-toothed man-child who had grown in legend much beyond his scrawny five-foot-three stature. But he remembered how his guileless grin could always fool men into taking him lightly, allowing him to seize the advantage.

Carefree times, those, before fate had shoved him down a trail he had never wished to follow. After that, lonely times, cast out from others, from the simple nurturing emotions he so desperately craved, where Fate saw fit to snatch away any and all he became close to.

No use frettin' over it, was there? Always had been that way and he hated Fate powerfully for it.

Billy laughed. He s'posed he had been predestined to the life he had led and what he had become. Hell, he was damned if he even knew his real name, but William was good as any. He couldn't tell a body where he hailed from—some whispered back East, born to a woman with countless names and moods and a father who died before he could get the chance to know his son or his son him.

Thoughts of those times came as blurs and glimpses of images. When he was fourteen, his mother up and died and every day became hand-to-mouth, until the cattle business adopted him, changed him.

Well, he reckoned maybe not totally changed him, for the seeds had been planted, waiting to be nurtured by blood and murder and the fury of a boy who never truly understood where he belonged.

Sometimes his life seemed merely a series of misadventures and escapes. He'd escaped the first time in Silver City by shimmying up a chimney when falsely accused of stealing a bundle of clothes; he'd escaped jail by shooting dead a deputy with a ferreted gun left for him in an outhouse by an unknown ally. In a final master-stroke, he'd even escaped the death delivered by the bullet lodged in his chest. Thanks to Milus, who saw the irony of having a legend ride with him. A legend whose very reputation for bloodthirstiness only stood to be magnified by the inhuman thing he had become.

Now, Billy wondered if he didn't wish powerfully to escape that.

There was times, oh, yes, there was times a-plenty when the longing for the simple days of tending herd threatened to overwhelm him, when the escape fever grabbed him by the balls and told him to go. He would catch himself staring at the moon sometimes, reveling in the spell that would wander over him. It would take him, lead him back to the daylight hours filled with sweltering heat and choking dust. The erotic touch of warm river water flowing across his naked body. The same feeling that gripped him now, as he charged towards those steers. Free and almost alive.

The longing proved fleeting usually, often spoiled by the intrusive images of times when the blood fever surged through him and murder-lust hazed his vision. The times the darkness inside had driven him to acts of violence and death.

The times that should have come to an end that night in a darkened room at the hands of a so-called friend, but it hadn't.

Thanks to Milus Clint.

Billy's thoughts went to the outlaw leader and the grin dropped from his lips. Clint stood to be downright pissed he'd bolted off like this on such an important night. Billy knew Milus burned for revenge, had waited, schemed, years to exact it. But that wasn't Billy's quarrel, was it?

He had noticed the way Milus Clint looked at him of late, the way men used to, as if he couldn't be trusted, and maybe they, and Clint, were right. Billy had given lots of thought to striking out on his own again, returning to

New Mexico, to the old haunts. He reckoned Milus sensed it, and probably wouldn't put up with it a whole lot longer. Billy would deal with that when the time came.

For now only a taste of the past sweetened his tongue. The lopsided grin returned to his face, the grin that came when he laughed, when he grieved, and when he killed. He reckoned he had been born with it.

Billy slowed his horse as he approached the bunch, five steers huddling close. They acted nervous, probably weary of the coyotes on the horizon and the sense that something inhuman had invaded their lush graze world. He watched them shift feet and, as he drew closer, the specter of fright danced in their glassy black eyes.

Reining to a stop, he peered at the beasts, cooing a comforting note that seemed to transfix them. He had that way with animals. They was wild, them critters, as wild as any beast put on God's green earth. They'd been known to stampede just for the hell of it.

They was also good eatin'.

Attracted by the sound of an approaching rider, Billy's head jerked up. Twisting in the saddle, he half-expected to see a furious Milus Clint thundering up to him, but it was only Hascan, so he relaxed.

"What the hell you got in mind, goin' off like that, Billy?" Hascan blurted, drawing up beside him. "You know how Milus feels about this raid. He's powerful sore you took to runnin' wild like that."

Billy shrugged, the smirk widening on his face, but didn't say a word.

"What the hell you grinnin' for?" Hascan removed his Stetson and scratched his head. "Milus sees that and he just might take a notion to wipe that smile off'n your face."

Billy chuckled and Hascan shook his head. "Ain't you never had the urge to just ride free again, Hascan?" Billy eyed the other Rider, the look on his face a mite more serious now. "Ain't you never wanted to feel the wind whippin' at your hide and the sap risin' in your veins just one more time?"

Hascan shrugged, looking confused. "Reckon once in a spell, but I never let it get to me. Goddamn, I'm glad for what Milus done for me. Otherwise I'd be crawlin' with gizzard worms 'bout now."

Billy spat a disgusted sound. "You ain't got no imagination, Hascan. You follow Milus 'round like a galldamned puppy dog and let him plan ever'thing out for you. You got power, now, Hascan. Can't you feel it? Power like you ain't never had when you was alive. You let him corral that power."

"So?" Hascan's look of perplexity deepened and Billy knew why Milus had chosen the man: Hascan wasn't a thinker, a dreamer. He was roped and branded and would follow wherever Milus led.

"Don't you understand? There's so galldamn little for us, now, Hascan. We can't cross a damn stream and we can't watch a sunrise. We can't trail a herd or court a gal at a county fair. What we can do, you let Milus take away from you."

"What you mean, Billy?" Hascan's brow crinkled.

"Milus gave us power and we don't use it. Only he uses it while we slurp up the scraps like his galldamned pets. We got the power to make a whole wide world of us, Hascan. Make ever'body like us, make the night tolerable. Then we can do things just like we used to. We can ride herd to the railheads and we can stroll the moonlit night with the fillies!"

"I don't foller."

Billy shook his head in disgust. "Milus wants to hoard the secret he gave us, what we are. He wants to keep it for the few he chooses and kill the rest. I want to share it, spread it until the whole goddamn world is full of our kind. That's the only way we'll ever be normal again, Hascan. Milus wants his revenge, and I got some revengin' to do myself, too, but after that, what? We're alone, 'cept for the few of us. What kind of life is that?"

Hascan gave a slight shake of his head and Billy knew the man had never considered the notion, didn't really care to, now. Like most of Milus's gang, he thought for the moment, thought of what he could get and not of what happened after it was gone.

"You best not let Milus hear you talkin' that way, Billy. He wouldn't be likin' it and you know how he can get when he's all fired up."

Billy chuckled again. "Yeah, I do. But I know some things as well, and Milus, he ain't the last word on ever'thing. I got me notions, Hascan. I got me notions about the future."

Hascan frowned. "You best keep 'em to your ownself, then."

"Maybe I will..." Billy grinned wider and eyed Hascan mischievously. "Then again, maybe I won't."

With a sudden whoop, Billy leaped from his saddle, boots lightly touching the ground as he landed catlike. He felt rich grassy earth beneath his feet and felt the breezy stirrings of youth within him. He scooted towards the longhorns, cooing and clucking with an insane light on his face.

A beast eyed him and shifted on its hooves, letting out a nervous bawl. Billy yelled, skipping around the lead steer, reveling in the carefree sensations of the past that sent his mind reeling.

Just as quickly something changed. He felt the darkness inside him shift, grow, hunger. Fever rose in his veins. The feeling took him suddenly and completely; he couldn't even begin to fight it. It intruded on his blissful reverie like a sheriff raiding a whorehouse and that made him all the more angry.

Viciousness on his features, now, he eyed the stupid ugly beast before him. Darting in, he suddenly poked the animal in its glassy eye. That broke any spell Billy had held over the animal. The steer bleated and lunged at him, rangy slabs of muscle bunching and rippling. It charged and Billy hooted, throwing himself sideways as the beast tilted its head, sweeping its horn in a scooping hook of a movement. The razor tip grazed Billy's coat, tearing a shred from it. Only his inhuman quickness saved him from worse.

Billy, going with the momentum, hit the ground and rolled. He'd been lucky; he knew that. The steer's horn spanned about four feet—some ranged past six; had it been any longer he might have made a grievous miscalculation and been gored. He cursed the uncontrollable anger that made him do foolish things, knowing it wouldn't be the last time. He cursed the hunger that made him scent the steer's rushing blood.

He climbed to his feet as the steer charged off into the night in the opposite direction. The other longhorns, boogered by the actions of the first, launched into motion.

A shout from Hascan grabbed Billy's attention.

"Hey, Billy, you best not be doin' that to 'em! You know how wild them critters are, for chrissakes!" Hascan was stepping down from the saddle as he spoke. He took a few tentative steps towards Billy, unheeding of the longhorns already charging.

With a thunder of beating hooves, two of the animals broke in the direction of the first. The remaining two steers had more sand. Their huge muscles propelled them straight at Billy and Hascan, single-minded terror driving them to attack the two puny creatures antagonizing them.

Billy whooped and sidestepped like a matador. The steer didn't turn for another try when it missed; it whisked off into the night.

Hascan, intent on Billy, wasn't so lucky. He didn't realize the threat until the last instant and by then he had no time to get out of the steer's way.

The longhorn bore down on him, wielding a five-foot span of razor-tipped horn. The steer crooked its blocky head, flashing the curved rapier of a horn, hooking.

The point penetrated Hascan just below the ribcage, plowing through the soft part of his belly and tearing out through his back.

"No!" Billy let out a keening wail.

Hascan's mouth burst open. Black fluid gouted from between his lips and spurted from his belly. The steer twisted its head and Hascan was hoisted into the air, impaled on the animal's scything horn.

Billy watched helpless as Hascan's arms and legs flailed in a useless attempt to free himself from the beast.

The steer skidded to a halt, jouncing its head back and forth, side to side in an effort to throw off Hascan's ragdoll figure.

Hascan was hurled forward and sideways. He slammed into the ground, face a distorted mask of agony and shock, black fluid pumping from the crater in his gut.

Not many things could hurt them, Billy knew. Guns, knives and the lot had little effect on the Riders. Being gored by a longhorn was something they was vulnerable to; Billy knew that when he taunted the animal, knew he was wily enough, fast enough, smart enough to avoid harm. To escape.

Hascan didn't know cattle and he didn't know longhorns. But now he knew death.

Rage boiled in Billy's innards and he bellowed at the steer, shaking his fists, stamping his feet. He charged after the animal, who had balls enough to turn on him and lunge.

Billy relaxed, concentrating, waiting, timing the steer's charge.

The steer canted its head for a second go at goring a Rider.

Billy danced sideways, whirling half around as the animal careened past, razor-tipped horn passing an inch from his chest. He leaped, the bull-like strength that came with being a Dark Rider thrusting him a good ten feet through the air to slam into the animal's back near the base of its massive neck.

The steer jolted in its step, as if momentarily confused, then began struggling to fling Billy off, throwing up grass and clods of soil as it kicked out, humped, twisted. He held on, fingers gouging into the rippling leathery hide. His fangs gnashed at the steer's muscle-slabbed neck, tearing away raw flesh. Blood geysered from the severed artery.

The longhorn bleated a frightened bawl and madly bucked, arcing its back, vaulting straight up as it uncoiled like a loosed buggy spring.

Billy's grip slipped. He flew backward, crashing to the ground.

The steer, blood gushing from its open neck, hurtled forward in blind terror.

Billy, spitting dirt and steer blood, gained his feet and brushed off his clothes. He watched the animal's gait slow fifty feet on, falter to staggering steps. Twenty feet later the beast collapsed, making pitiful mewing sounds as its limbs spasmed, then grew still.

"You goddamn ornery sonofabitch!" Billy screamed, stamping about and shaking a fist at the fallen longhorn. "Why'd you go an' do that? I only wanted to have me some fun, galldamn you!"

Billy's anger raged for the better part of five minutes. Slowly he felt his fury calm and he spat again, trying to get the gritty taste of dirt and blood out of his mouth. Longhorn meat was fine and dandy, but longhorn blood was something that had never particularly appealed to him, though he would drink it when the hunger got the best of him.

He gathered up his hat, which had flown off during the tussle with the steer, and walked back to where Hascan had fallen. He stared at the charred area of grass roughly in the shape of a man's body. Shaking his head, he watched puffs of black smoke curl from the ground. Nothing else remained of Hascan. Maybe Hascan was the lucky one, he thought. Maybe he was free from the night, now.

The Dark Riders sat their horses at the border of the 7HL ranch and Milus Clint's cold buzzard eyes took in the moon-streaked surroundings. As he surveyed the damage his men had done to the corrals, bunkhouse and outbuildings, satisfaction swelled within him. In his mind he saw the old man, Durrin, sprawled dying on the floor within the main house and remembered the old days, when it had been his men gasping their last breaths.

Part of his revenge was complete, and now the second part could begin. When the boy returned to find the carnage and felt his torment howl inside him, Milus Clint would savor every moment of it. He had waited countless nights for this time, and he relished the thought of dissecting the Durrin boy in degrees, until at last he made the boy suffer the fate he'd brought upon Milus. Whoever said revenge was best served cold was mistaken; it was best served hot and bloody. And Milus would serve it to the boy in spades.

"Where are they?" a Rider, Clint's right-hand man, Emmet, asked, breaking Milus's reverie.

Milus twisted in his saddle to glance at the man, then stared off into the darkness as a sound reached his ears. "Comin' now." His eyes narrowed, vision as acute as an owl's, picking out the shadowy form of one Rider leading a second horse. Dark light glinted in his eyes and a prickle of irritation went through him.

The Rider came on at a comfortable trot, seemingly in no hurry, and Milus's irritation moved a notch towards anger.

"Looks like Billy." A frown creased Emmet's lips.

"So it does..." A hint of bitterness laced Milus's tone. Billy was alone, leading Hascan's horse. Milus didn't like that one bit. Hascan was a good man, took orders without questions, and Milus would have preferred to have seen him riding back with Billy's horse in tow, instead of the other way around.

Billy drew up beside Clint, for once, Milus noticed, his face devoid of that infernal grin.

"Where's Hascan?" Milus kept his voice level, tinged with threat. More and more Billy got on his goddamn nerves. He was starting to wish he'd left the kid to the worms.

A nervous tick jittered Billy's cheek, but quickly the cockiness came back into his manner. "Skewered by a goddamn longhorn," he said, matter-of-factly.

Milus sucked in a deep breath, tenseness gripping his muscles, back arching. "How the hell'd that happen?" His voice was strained as he drilled the young Rider with his buzzard gaze.

Billy canted his head towards the horizon, avoiding Clint's stare by peering off into the darkness. His voice lowered. "Got careless, I reckon."

Lying. Milus could tell. Something Billy had done had caused Hascan's demise. But for now he chose to let it go; his satisfaction with the attack on the Durrin compound was still fresh and dealing with the kid now would only sour it. But there would come a time when Billy would try Milus' patience at the wrong moment...

"See that *you* don't get careless, Billy. Careless folks have a habit of gettin' dead."

"I'll be sure to take that advice into account." Billy continued looking straight ahead. Milus didn't care for the note of polite arrogance riding Billy's tone, not one bit. The kid had taken some notion into his head and Milus would have to keep a wary eye on it. Billy reckoned he had all the answers, Milus could tell. But Milus knew questions Billy hadn't even dreamed of askin', and if the kid kept on the course he was headin', he'd damn sure learn 'em soon.

"Where's Jeters?" Billy asked, changing the subject, as if he had guessed the course of Milus' thoughts.

Milus shook his head. Another prickle of irritation took him. Jeters should have returned from the Injun camp by now. That he hadn't...

"Ain't come back yet." Milus' tone turned sarcastic. "Reckon he got careless, too." Milus waited to see if it had any effect on Billy, but saw none.

Nevertheless, Milus wouldn't let the loss of Hascan and Jeters spoil his mood or deter him from his path of revenge. He hoped Jeters had at least carried out his part of the plan before dying, but wouldn't dwell on that at the moment, either. They could always rectify that later.

Milus swiveled his head to look at the other Riders. "It's started, boys. We hit that boy hard and now we'll wait a spell. Meantime, there's a whole town of pleasure waitin' on us. Let's get to it!"

Milus let out a yell and shot his black forward. The others followed suit, Billy lagging at the rear.

FOUR

Dark Cloud held up a hand as he and Speaks No More approached their camp. A strange dread wandered over him as they neared the cluster of tipis. He'd first noticed it a few miles back, when the day had blackened and the moon rose, as though the black eyes of the Great Cannibal Owl stared down upon them.

Were the dark spirits angered with him and his cousin tonight for some unknown reason? Would that anger be manifest?

The ride from the Comanche reservation had tried Dark Cloud's mood. The sun had beaten down upon their faces and bare chests like the breath of fire gods. But that did not try him as much as the sight of his beaten-down people residing on the reservation, where the white man had seen fit to tuck the remainder of the Comanche after the white demon, Mackenzie, and his pony soldiers drove the last of the *Nermernuh*, "the people", from Palo Duro Canyon. Led by the great chief, Quanah Parker, they'd resigned themselves to a life of confinement and compliance, poverty and destitution, never again to roam the vast Plains, the wind-swept grassy ocean of the *Llano Estacado*, and hunt buffalo. It saddened Dark Cloud to know what his people had surrendered themselves to, but he could do nothing about it. He would be imprisoned there himself if not for Durrin, the only white man Dark Cloud had any trust in or respect for.

Although the ride back had been soul-wrenching, with thoughts of what the once Lords of the Plains had been reduced to, it paled to the dread that had come as the night had fallen and the eyes of the great Cannibal Owl turned upon them. Exhaustion had given way to something worse: fear.

Fear was something that came unnaturally to the Comanche. Yet now it crept along his spine like the cold breath of Winter Man.

Why had the spirit of the Great Cannibal Owl grown angry with them? What had they done? All had been done to them, had it not? Yet surely that was what it had to be. What else could explain it?

He felt the dark spirits reaching for him and shifted in the Comanche saddle, the pony beneath him snorting, a tenseness hobbling its gait. The beast felt the spirits as well, perhaps more acutely than Dark Cloud himself.

Dark Cloud glanced at his cousin, who stared stoically ahead, towards the distant stream and their camp. Did he feel it, too? Speaks No More seemed oblivious to the breath of darkness that blew in with the night. Or perhaps he chose to ignore it.

Dark Cloud turned his attention ahead. A whisper of breeze chilled this bare chest and ruffled his breechclout. He felt the comforting bulge of his medicine bag nestled at his loins and said a prayer to the spirits that all was well at the camp and with his wives.

In the distance he heard the gurgle of water and the singing of katydids, peaceful sounds, yet still fear lived within him. His brow crinkled and he stiffened in the saddle.

A howling broke his thoughts and he twisted to see dark shapes skittering across the horizon. Coyotes, a number of them, close to the ranch in the opposite direction. Strange. He felt the coldness clawing at his back dig deeper.

Then, turning forward, he saw a flash of flame ahead and knew his fears were well-founded. Twisting fingers of fire came from one of the tipis, blazing high and falling. Dread lanced his belly. They were too late to stop whatever had happened and regret burdened his mind. Perhaps if he'd hastened his departure from the reservation, perhaps if he had ignored the weariness and ridden like the wind...

Yet he knew not what had happened, only that something had, and that it was dreadful.

He looked over to see Speaks No More glancing at him, concern etched deeply onto his dark face. Speaks No More made sign talk and Dark Cloud nodded.

"Something is wrong. The Great Cannibal Owl has turned his wrath upon us."

Speaks No More made the sign for "Why?"

"I do not know. He needs no reason." Dark Cloud drew in a long breath, expanding his deep wide chest and digging his Plains Moccasins into the sides of his pony. He galloped towards the camp, Speaks No More in motion a beat behind. They rode hard, eating the distance, slowing as they reached the edge of the camp.

The blazing tipi had turned into a skeleton of poles. Great plumes of smoke billowed into the darkness. Lashing tongues of yellow-orange swallowed the remaining shreds of buffalo-hide covering and devoured cedar poles. As the structure collapsed, Dark Cloud felt a churning sadness gather in his heart. For the lodge belonged to him, and within it were his two wives.

Next to him, Speaks No More uttered a raspy squawk, the only sound of which he was capable, and pointed.

The camp was in disarray, pots and utensils given to them by the white man scattered about, hides of buffalo and deer littered helter-skelter, along with bone picks and awls, scraps of food and arrows and beads. Dark Cloud paid it little attention. His eyes settled on the black horse tethered to a nearby cottonwood, then on a body sprawled in the dirt at mid-camp. The horse, black as night with soulless eyes, was a sign from the Great Cannibal Owl that this camp had been invaded and the unclean spirit had lingered, awaiting them. The body belonged to the wife of Speaks No More, Tay-kan-na.

Dark Cloud gathered his courage and stepped down from the saddle. Speaks No More, face stricken, dismounted beside him and they slowly walked into the camp. The acrid odor of burnt hide and scorched wood assailed his nostrils. He detected another scent, one that shook him with grief—the scent of burned flesh. Sadness welled in his heart as he gazed at the blackened remains of his lodge, the breeze stirring the ashes and sprigs of flame.

A sharp squawk from Speaks No More and Dark Cloud saw his cousin's finger jab towards where the body of his wife lay. A coyote appeared there, standing beside the lifeless form of Tay-kan-na. Its eyes glittered like evil black jewels slashed with sizzling blue-black veins.

Dark Cloud stopped a few feet from the coyote. The animal's mouth curled back to bare razored fangs and the hair along its back bristled. Its muscles bunched as if it intended to lunge.

Dark Cloud's hand eased to his back, freeing the bow of dogwood and plucking an arrow from his quiver in almost the same move. He set the arrow to the buffalo-sinew string and drew it back.

"No!" Speaks No More signed violently, grabbing Dark Cloud's arm. "It is coyote. You must not kill it!"

Bitterness turned Dark Cloud's features. "It is not coyote. It belongs to the Great Cannibal Owl, an unclean spirit. No coyote has eyes as black as the night."

Dark Cloud centered his aim and the coyote snarled, fangs flashing as it sprang at him.

The Comanche let the arrow fly. It glided through the air in a perfect line, meeting the leaping coyote in mid-jump. The coyote yelped and twisted in mid-air, crashing to the ground, thrashing, whimpering.

As Dark Cloud was about to draw back another arrow, something stopped him. His eyes narrowed, glittering with surprise.

A swirl of blackness formed around the coyote, elongating, shrouding it completely. The blackness solidified, changing shape, and where the animal had been lay the form of a man. He let out a throaty curse and tried to rise, but fell back into a sitting position. The arrow protruded from his shoulder, black fluid bubbling out around it.

"Goddamn Injun!" he barked, gripping the arrow and wrenching it free. The arrow came out, its barbed end rending the flesh as it did so.

THE DARK RIDERS

Dark Cloud's mouth parted in amazement and fear, his claim of the Great Cannibal Owl's anger confirmed before his eyes. Only the dark spirits could have sent something as inhuman as this.

Forcing his astonishment down, he drew back another arrow and let it fly.

The Rider started up, lips curling back from curved razor fangs, and hissed. But he couldn't move fast enough. The arrow burrowed into his heart. He dropped to the dust, body twitching.

Dark Cloud leaped forward, squatting, examining the fallen Rider. A spark of dark life still burned within the man, and Dark Cloud was glad for it. Now, he would savor his retribution.

He plucked his knife from the hide sheath at his breechclout and pushed aside the Rider's hat. Grabbing a handful of the man's hair, the Comanche sawed at the scalp, cutting a patch of it loose and holding it up. He let out an angry cry.

The cry was cut short. For Dark Cloud suddenly felt the scalp quiver and squirm. He dropped the gory patch of flesh and hair and watched as it wriggled and twisted, turning into thick black worms. He stared in disgust and vague awe.

Dark Cloud's attention jerked back to the prone Rider, whose life was trickling way. With swift skillful chops he hacked off the Rider's hands and feet, last cleaving off the manhood parts. No blood ran from the wounds; only a viscous black fluid, which Dark Cloud attributed to the magic of the Great Cannibal Owl.

Dark Cloud skittered back suddenly, alarmed as a spark of blackness jumped from the Rider's gaping mouth. He knew the unclean spirit had departed, that the Rider was dead. He watched in morbid fascination as further sparks leaped from the body, igniting into a sheet of sizzling black flame. The flame consumed the Rider, as well as the dismembered parts and scalp. In seconds, nothing remained but singed patches in the dirt.

For long minutes Dark Cloud remained frozen, spellbound, a coldness sweeping through his spirit. He had witnessed something few Comanche ever had. It left him hollow and paralyzed his soul.

Beside him, Speaks No More, who had watched the demise of the Rider in horror, ran to the body of his wife. Pulling the dead woman close, he threw back his head and Dark Cloud could see tears streaming down his cousin's face. Speaks No More's mouth opened in a silent scream of sorrow, and Dark Cloud knew the white man had taken one last thing from his cousin—the death wail.

But they had not taken it from Dark Cloud.

Dark Cloud went to the burned-out remnants of his tipi, bending. He located the charred bodies of his wives and tears streamed from his eyes. A haunting sadness swallowed his heart and emotion clawed at his throat. He threw back his head, wailing the death wail. His cries rose to the sky where they dissolved among the stars. He thanked the Grandfather Above they had been spared the fate that could befall victims of the Great Cannibal Owl. They would be free to roam the lush valleys beyond the sun, not confined to wander the black nights as slaves of the dark spirits.

When the shrieks died in Dark Cloud's throat, he again loosed his knife. The grief within his spirit felt crushing, overwhelming.

He dragged the blade across his arm, slicing a bloody gash into the flesh. He felt the sting cut into the grief, but not remove it. The knife glinted with captured moonlight as he cut further slashes across his belly and legs and shoulders, praying for the Grandfather Above to free him from the bonds of his grief, wailing again, throat raw and burning, like a tortured animal. Soon the ritual ended and now he would bury what was left of his wives and fast until the grief lessened.

Dark Cloud didn't know how much time had passed, but when he stood and turned, Speaks No more had risen, and the tears had dried to tracks on his face. His cousin's flesh showed the evidence of his own grief. Gashes on his belly and forearms dribbled blood. Dark Cloud saw a look on Speaks No More's features, layered over the torment of grief, a look that questioned the things he had witnessed this night.

Speaks No More's right hand jumped to his mouth, index and middle fingers touching his nostrils, then lowering with a jerky agitated motion. Blood. The sign for blood.

Dark Cloud's brow furrowed. "What?"

"Blood," Speaks No More signed again. "There is no blood. There should be blood." He pointed to the body of his wife.

"The dark spirit sent by He Who Drinks Life has swallowed it all."

Speaks No More's face tightened. "Why has this happened?" he signed, eyes dark, laced with hate and sorrow.

Dark Cloud hesitated. "I do not know. I only know that the Great Cannibal Owl has sent He Who Drinks Life upon us for some reason."

"The white man?" Speaks No More's hands moved frantically and Dark Cloud almost lost the meaning.

He turned, gaze wandering to the distance, wondering if Spotted Buffalo Man had been visited by the Great Cannibal Owl's demons as well. A sudden thought occurring to him, he turned back to Speaks No More. "Little Waiting Woman, where is she?"

Speaks No More's gaze traveled to one of the remaining tipis; he started towards it.

Dark Cloud came slowly after him, dread in his heart. They swept aside the buffalo-hide flap, peering inside. The lodge was steeped in shadows. It gave the interior an eerie atmosphere, pregnant with the feel of death and sorrow. The dread inside Dark Cloud deepened.

On a bed of hides lay Little Waiting Woman, a girl of sixteen dressed in a deerskin dress, shorn black hair falling back from her fine dark features. She was beautiful, even in death.

Dark Cloud felt grief surge again, burn like prairie fire. He thought briefly of the white boy who planned to take Little Waiting Woman as a wife.

Speaks No More went to her and stooped, whirled to Dark Cloud, hands coming up in frantic words.

"She lives!" He signed and Dark Cloud moved closer, kneeling beside the girl. It was true, he saw: she wasn't dead as he had thought. Her chest rose with shallow breaths, but her face had turned the color of ash and her lips quivered, eyelids fluttering as if she were in the grip of a peyote vision. His gaze fell to her throat, to the twin bloodless gashes sunk deep into her flesh, and he shook his head.

She lived, yes, but he judged not for long unless the spirits took mercy on her.

"She has been left this way for a reason." Dark Cloud looked sternly at Speaks No More. "For what reason I do not know. We must ask the Grandfather Above to bring her back, take her away from He Who Drinks Life."

Speaks No More nodded, moving off with a knowledge of Dark Cloud's wants. Dark Cloud knew the magic of the spirits. He knew the ways of the shaman and their bones. If there was a chance to bring Little Waiting Woman back from the night, he would try it.

Speaks No More returned shortly, a hide bundle cradled in his arms. For the moment, their grief was pushed aside in an effort to lay claim to Dark Cloud's sister before she fell into the hands of the dark spirits.

Speaks No More set the bundle gently beside the senseless girl, untying the rawhide thongs that held it together and unwrapping it. Within lay fragments of bone and pouches of whitish powder. Dark Cloud had gathered the bones during hunting parties, the remains of what the white man called mammoths. But Dark Cloud knew better; they were the remains of the Great Cannibal Owl, who had scattered them upon the earth before journeying to the spirit world. His wives had ground some of the bones into a fine powder that held magic properties.

Speaks No More placed the bone fragments around Little Waiting Woman while Dark Cloud undid one of the hide pouches and sprinkled powder over the two wounds on her neck. The powder would suck out the evil spirits, cleanse her.

Dark Cloud uttered a low chant, mouthing the sacred words that would draw the evil away from Little Waiting Woman. He prayed the incantations would purify her, but it was up to the Grandfather Above to show mercy, save her from the night.

At last he covered her small form with a blanket of bison hide and stood. He would know shortly whether the medicine had worked, whether the Great Cannibal Owl would release her.

Stepping out of the tipi, Dark Cloud picked up his bow and set an arrow to it. He had one task left.

He walked towards the black horse tethered to the cottonwood, fury overriding his grief for the moment. The demon horse uttered a vicious throaty hiss as the Comanche leveled the arrow.

After he had finished, he went back into the tipi of Little waiting Woman and sat beside the bed of hides.

FIVE

Chris Durrin gigged his roan gelding into an easy trot across the outer reaches of his Uncle Clem's spread. The sun dropped below the horizon and twilight painted the land with hues of red, purple and shady blue.

Chris didn't mind the dusk; he enjoyed riding at night. The brisk kiss of early spring air tingled against his face, a respite from the skin-scorching heat of the long day tending herd. He could let himself relax now. The day was finished. The errant steers had been turned from the direction they'd been wandering, a small ranch bordering the Durrin property. Too many beeves had strayed over that way and not returned. Chris had his suspicions, but right now that's all they were. He wasn't prepared to confront anybody—especially a possible rustler—without proof.

Chris shifted in the saddle, drawing in a deep breath of cool spring air. He wasn't a tall man, a bit below average height at five-six, but composed of ropy cattle-forged muscle and a certain God-given talent for ranching. A squared but lean face framed gray-blue eyes that appeared permanently tinted by sadness. His high forehead already held deep creases, despite his young age.

He pushed his Stetson from his head, letting it hang at his back. The cool breeze ruffled his dirty blond hair. He found himself looking forward to a hot plate of beans and bacon when he got back to the ranch, and hitting a clean bed later on. Plenty of time to worry about vanishing cattle with the sunrise, which came all too soon to these parts.

"Them steers wanderin' impress you as peculiar at all?" came a gravelly voice from beside him.

Chris's head swiveled to the rider perched atop a cowhorse, his *segundo* at the 7HL. "Windy" McDonnell was a shade taller than Chris, built along the lines of a Comanche with squat arms, bowed legs and a deep chest. He had a ruddy complexion peppered with freckles and hair like a blazing red sunset. His nose looked flatter than it should have and tilted to the left; Chris figured that to be the result of some saloon altercation in the assistant foreman's past, though Windy had never seen fit to mention it. The remainder of Windy's features appeared too small for his large head, or perhaps his head was too large for his features. His twinkling blue eyes glittered like little marbles sunk deep into layers of toughened rawhide.

"Windy" wasn't the *segundo*'s real name, Chris knew, though damned if he recalled ever hearing it. Everyone called him Windy because once he started jawing he had a tendency never to shut up. When the cowhand had ridden into the 7HL spread five years ago, Chris had taken the notion Windy was running from something in his past. At the time, Chris figured it was none of his business to ask. After seeing Windy's skill with beeves, Clem had hired him on the spot. Chris quickly discovered Windy was worth two or three normal cowhands when it came to cattle ranching. The man rapidly elevated himself to *segundo*. What Windy might have done and was running from seemed to matter little, now. He had become Chris's closet friend, though he notched a good ten years on him.

"How do you mean peculiar?" Chris frowned, knowing, if he started Windy on something he might not hear the end of it until sunrise.

"Well, just that our stock ain't apt to wander far in that direction. Best graze is the other way. Area gets kinda rocky over there, where Shinn gots his spread."

Chris gave a small shake of his head. "Longhorns take to wanderin' for miles, though. Maybe these are just dumber than the rest."

Windy pushed out his barrel chest, which made his arms look ridiculously small, and inhaled a great breath. "Don't go makin' excuses, son. You knows what I'm aimin' at."

Chris gave an easy laugh. "Yeah, reckon I do. That don't mean I'll make it any easier for you to chew my ear off."

Windy laughed, a laugh that sounded as if it rumbled up from the bottom of a barrel. "You don't have to make it easy; I'm right practiced at it."

"You'll get no argument there." Chris smirked and turned his gaze straight ahead, waiting for Windy to go on.

"Like I was sayin'..." Windy hocked and spat. "Them steers didn't belong there, so far from t'others and on rocky land. They didn't belong there as God is my witness."

"You have a notion, I s'pose?"

"Don't be smart with me, son. You know galldamned well what I mean. Them steers were led there."

"We got no proof of that. We can't go accusin' a man on speculation."

"Speculation, hell! Them steers were led sure as I'm saddle sore! And you know Shinn was the one who led 'em. Ain't the first time, neither. I know all them beeves like each was a family member and I know some have turned up missin'. Oh, not so many, a few here and there, so nobody might take a suspicion. But I seen them wander this way one day, then *poof!* they's gone the next. Ain't seen the right number of carcasses to indicate sick or dyin' critters, neither."

"So you think they wandered on over to Shinn's spread?"

"'Wandered' ain't 'xactly the right word, but, yeah, yeah I do. What business he gots ranchin' on a piece of land like that? No rancher in his right mind would've set up on that land—'less they know they could get beeves some other way."

Chris's eyebrows arched. "Rustlin'?"

"Rustlin', damn right! That cocklebur outfit's as smelly as a two-bit whore, I'm here to tell you."

Chris considered it, seeing little to argue with. Windy had an instinct about that sort of things—anything associated with cattle in fact—and Chris felt inclined to take his word for it. But would the law? "All right, maybe I got a notion that way myself. But that still don't give us a case against the man. We might have to wait till he does cross the line before actin' on him."

"You said somethin' about Shinn lookin' familiar, if I recollect right."

Chris shrugged. "Yeah, but I ain't been able to place the fella."

"Maybe you will, 'cause somethin' about him looks familiar to me, too."

"You got a notion on that, too, I take it?"

"Damn right! And that breed he gots workin' for him...strikes me as little too cagey with a hot iron. Think he might be a brand artist from New Mex way."

"How do you know that?"

"Did me some ridin' t'other day. I saw that breed doin' some brandin'. Looked legit, but I gotta tell you, he gots a knack with a hot iron you don't see 'cept in a feller used to alterin' other folks' brands. Strike you as strange that Shinn calls his spread the Box H?"

Chris shook his head. "Not particularly."

Windy drew up, Chris reining to a halt beside him, and stepped down from the saddle. He scooched, pulling loose a Bowie knife from a tooled leather sheath. In a flat patch of dirt, he dragged the blade along the ground, forming the Durrin 7HL brand, a straight seven that formed the first vertical line of the H while the L formed the second, leaving the top of the seven and bottom of the L protruding from their respective sides. He proceeded to draw a straight line across the top, which obliterated the top of the seven, connected the upper tips of the H and ran over the opposite side an equal length. He did the same with the bottom, then joined each overhanging side by vertical lines, forming the Shinn brand, an odd Box H.

"See?" Windy looked up at Chris. "That's the Box H brand."

Chris's brow crinkled. He had to admit it looked more than a mite suspicious. "Okay, so their brand fits easy over ours. Did you see the breed alter it?"

Windy straightened. "No, can't say as I did. But it seems mighty convenient, Shinn pickin' a brand that yours could be changed to, doncha think?" Sheathing his Bowie knife, Windy climbed back onto his horse.

The things Windy said struck Chris as possible, even probable, and something about that Shinn fellow did look vaguely familiar. Chris had struggled to place him the first time he had seen him, but hadn't had any luck. He felt positive he had encountered the man before.

Falling silent, he nudged his horse forward, Windy doing the same. During their discussion, night had completely taken hold of the land. The darkness swelled, moonlight frosting the grass. Chris felt a shiver prickle along his spine.

Strangely, Windy kept quiet as well and Chris figured the assistant foreman had more than just rustling on his mind.

"You're groping for words, Windy." Chris looked at the *segundo* seriously. "Ain't like you. What's on your mind?"

"Sometimes I think you got me pegged too well, son." Windy chuckled but the sound was strained.

"In some ways..." Chris left it open.

Windy smirked. "Maybe the ways you don't are best left as such."

Chris let him off the hook. "Well, spit it out way you always do. That's the best way."

"So it is. So it is...I been thinkin'...you're about to turn twenty-seven soon. You know more about this ranch than old Clem hisself."

Chris shrugged. "Reckon."

"Pshaw! You know you do."

"What are you drivin' at?" Chris felt his belly tighten and an uncomfortable coldness creep into his being.

"Round-up is comin' and the Canadian is lowerin'. We'll be drivin' them beeves up the Western soon."

Chris gave another shrug, not sure he cared for the direction in which the conversation was heading.

"Same as every year, Windy."

"Yeah, the same...and not."

"You're beatin' around the bush."

"So I am. So I am. But see, well, you know I ain't one for a loss of words, but there ain't no easy way to say what I think I gots to say."

Now Chris felt certain he didn't like what this was leading to. Windy always came straight with him. That Windy hesitated at all, told Chris the situation was grave and Chris felt sure he knew what it was. That made it no easier to swallow.

"Maybe you should just let it go," Chris said in a lower voice, not looking at his friend. A dark feeling washed over him...something unsettling yet familiar.

Don't say it...

"No, I can't, because you know damn well how I feel about you and Clem. Ain't no secret you're like family to me. It's just that your uncle...I don't think he'll be makin' the drive this year."

Chris swallowed, Windy's words hitting him like a fist.

"What're you sayin'?" Chris had all he could do to hold his voice steady. He knew what was coming and he almost hated Windy for making him look at it.

Windy sighed, seeming to deflate. "You know, son. Your uncle looks downright sick at times. Not so much on the outside. Outside he looks healthy as a horse. But when he thinks no one's lookin', well, he sorta crumbles-like. Hear him coughin' sometimes like he's gonna spit up a lung."

Chris sucked in a deep breath, trying to steady his insides. He knew exactly what Windy was referring to. Chris had witnessed his uncle's spells himself. He had heard his uncle's wracking coughs deep in the night, had seen the older man bent double when he thought he was alone. At those times Chris tried to rationalize it, tell himself it was something that would pass, that Clem had just been smoking too many of those damn cigars of late.

He chopped the thought short as a surge of pain gathered in his heart, forcing his eyes to well with tears. Clem was fine, just a little sick. He'd get better. He had to. Chris needed him, the man who had adopted him, raised him as a son. Clem was the only family he had left.

"I can see where you're takin' it, son." Windy's face turned grim. "And I don't blame you for tryin' but you gots to face it. Your uncle's powerful ill, I figure, and—"

"Shut up!" Chris snapped, unable to stop himself or the pain-driven anger inside him. "Just shut the hell up!"

Windy frowned and Chris's face pinched, muscles knotting at his jaw, eyes growing hard. He knew he had hurt Windy, but couldn't bring himself to apologize without having his voice break and betray him.

They rode on in silence, night gathering around them like a cold velvet blanket.

He's dying...

No!

Chris shivered, heart beating thickly, nerves suddenly raw. He didn't want to think about Clem, dwell about the possibility of death.

He's back...

The coldness inside Chris grew stronger, and a notion took him there was more to it, than what Windy had said about Clem. He felt something else, in the gathering of darkness. Something...else...An external thing he could feel more than see.

Who?

He couldn't fathom what caused the feeling and at the moment had no desire to try. He was thankful when, after five minutes of strained silence, Windy spoke again. Windy never kept quiet for long and Chris suddenly felt glad for that; it pulled his mind off thoughts of the future and the dread brewing in his innards.

"What about that little squaw?" Windy strained to make his tone lighter, Chris could tell, but didn't have much success with the effort.

Chris gave an uneasy chuckle, more nerves than humor, relieved to get onto another subject.

"She's a beauty, ain't she?" Chris felt a smile pull at his lips. He saw her dark features in his mind, felt his loins stir at the very thought of holding her.

"Ah, that she is, for a Comanche. You gonna ask her to get hitched or just dip your wick forever?"

That was Windy, to the point, the way he should be. Chris again focused his thoughts on the Comanche girl, Little Waiting Woman, camped at the edge of the 7HL property with her brother, Dark Cloud, and her cousin, Speaks No More. She had reached her sixteenth birthday eight months ago, and had a smile as sweet as the spring morning air.

Dark Cloud had already granted permission for their marriage, and Clem had presented the Comanche warrior with a number of fine horses. The Comanche normally didn't trade their women to outsiders the way other tribes were wont to do; there were seldom any white "squaw men" among the tribe, but in this case it was different. Dark Cloud and Clem had become blood brothers, and Chris suspected his uncle was one of the very few whites Dark Cloud would ever consider taking in friendship. An understanding of each other's ways had existed between them since the day Clem was attacked by a bear near the river. Dark Cloud had saved Clem's life and Clem had seen to it Dark Cloud was provided with a parcel of land for a permanent campsite. Clem also supplied Dark Cloud with beef and other foodstuffs when the Indian and his family needed it. Chris had ridden out with the supplies a number of times; that was when he had first seen the young Indian woman standing beside Dark Cloud's tipi. The attraction between them was instant and Clem and Dark Cloud knew from the start where it would lead.

The smile on Chris's face widened. Since that time, Chris had discovered a number of things about Comanche marriage, some of it to his shock, but certainly to his liking.

The tribe embraced no marriage ceremony, but recognized the marriage relationship. Comanche brothers commonly shared wives, as it was symbolic of the brotherhood bond. Any adultery, however, was dealt with in a round of hard bargaining; and in extreme cases, the offender was exiled, usually taking up with another band.

Chris also learned they placed no particular restrictions on premarital sex. Commonly, the older girls slipped into pubescent boys' tipis, and initiated them into the ways of manhood. Such unions were no secret to the rest of the tribe, who looked upon them with rough humor.

"Well?" prodded Windy, jarring Chris from his reverie.

He realized he had a stupid grin on his face. "Well, what?"

"Well, when are you gonna take that little filly and get hitched? Everybody's expectin' it. Fact, me and the boys been takin' bets you'd ask her by round-up time."

Chris laughed, a little embarrassed, and shook his head. "Was figuring on waitin' till after the drive, surprising her with a ring I had my eye on."

"Phsaw! You don't need no ring. She's an Indian, for cryin' out loud! Dark Cloud practically gots you hitched anyhow since Clem gave him those horses."

"Reckon so. Reckon he wonders why I don't come and take her off his hands, but I gotta do it the way I gotta do it."

Windy twisted his head, eyeing Chris suspiciously. "You sure you ain't just gettin' cold feet?"

"What do you mean?" He sensed a deeper meaning to Windy's question, wondered what it was.

Windy laughed his bottom-of-the-barrel laugh. "Well, just that little Mexicali filly you gots over at the saloon in town."

Chris's mouth fell open. If asked, he would have sworn no one knew about that except him. How Windy had found out was a mystery.

"How do you know about that?" His voice carried an edge of anger that surprised him.

"Ain't nothin' happens here'bouts I don't know about, son. I know her name's Matalija and she's a dove at the Blue Steer. I know you done snuck off a few times to go see her."

"You must have been followin' me, then, you bastard!" Chris gritted his teeth in false anger and Windy bellowed a laugh. He really wasn't angry with Windy, more shocked he had been found out.

"Hell, somebody gots to look out for you, son! The saloon's a right dangerous place for a greenhorn such as yourself."

"Greenhorn!" A note of indignation hung in his shout. "You lowly sonofabitch!"

They laughed heartily, but Chris felt embarrassment heat his face.

"She's just...a diversion."

"Diversion, buffalo flop! You gots a thing for her. I can see it in your eyes. Admit it, son, you been wonderin' what it would be like if you could change her, make her a respectable woman. Well, take my advice, that type never changes. She's been what she's been for too long and she's done got used to it. She belongs in that life and you belong in yours."

"Yeah, I reckon you're right. But I had to see if what I had for Little

Waiting Woman was real." Chris squirmed in his saddle. "I didn't want to make a mistake and marry the wrong girl."

Windy glanced at Chris, a sarcastic half-smirk turning his lips. "You know how all-fired stupid that sounds? Don't go back to the saloon, son. You marry that little Injun filly and make yourself a good life, the kind you deserve. She's right for you. Ain't no place in your world for a woman the likes of Matalija."

Chris shook his head. "You're just a barrel of wisdom, ain't you?"

"Gots that right," Windy said smugly. "But you can count your winnin's if you take my advice."

"Like I said, she's just a diversion."

"Maybe. But don't take no chances on messin' up the real thing 'cause you gots some burr in your britches from the past. Take my word on it, it always leads to ruin." All humor had vanished from the *segundo*'s voice.

Chris clamped his mouth shut. Somehow Windy had pegged it exactly. Chris loved Little Waiting Woman, but something inside held him back from committing fully to her, something that sent him into the arms of another woman, a whore at the Blue Steer Saloon. Not that Little Waiting Woman would be particularly put off by the fact. Comanches commonly held more than one wife. But he couldn't chance hurting her in any way. She didn't deserve it. Maybe she didn't deserve him until he somehow put away those old feelings of instability that dogged him.

Windy fell silent beside him and Chris drifted with his mood, which was turning darker. A coyote howled hauntingly in the distance, another joining it in an eerie lonesome chorus. Apprehension settled cold in the pit of his belly.

He peered ahead into the moon-glazed night, across the endless fields of buffalo grass that flowed like a green ocean into The New Mexico Territory. *Llano Estacado* it was called, the Staked Plains, once the domain of the mighty Comanche, the lords on horseback, now the province of cattlemen and bawling longhorns.

At times, Chris imagined, if you listened closely, you could still hear the drumming of unshod hooves charging across the grasslands and the whoops, carefree and unbridled, of a proud and savage people.

"Sounds like horses..."

Windy's words intruded on his thoughts and he shook off his reverie. "What?"

"Said, sounds like horses, in the distance, maybe lots of 'em."

Chris peered at the older man, wondering if somehow Windy hadn't pried into his mind as he imagined the Comanche riding the Plains.

"Thought I was imaginin' them, way I do sometimes," Chris uttered, and Windy glanced at him, uncomprehending but letting it go.

"No, I heard 'em. Almost sounds like a stampede—sonofa—" Windy jerked his reins and his horse neighed in fright, but obeyed the assistant foreman's command to go to the right.

Chris yanked his own reins a beat behind, arrowing left, narrowly avoiding the longhorn that charged out of the night. His heart pounded at the near miss and he drew in a calming breath as he reined around towards Windy.

"You all right?" Chris asked in a shaky voice.

"Cripes-a-mighty! Where the hell did that critter come outta?"

Chris shook his head. "Dunno. Bolted right out of the dark for some reason."

A howl rose in the distance, sending a chill down Chris's back.

It's started...

"There's your reason, son!" Windy jutted a finger at the horizon. Chris's gaze followed, spotting a dark shape scrabbling across the grass. Another followed, two, three more after that.

"Prairie wolves!" Perplexity swept across Chris's face. "What the hell—"

"They're boogerin' the damn cattle, whole pack of 'em I'd wager."

Chris's gaze chased the shadowy forms of the coyotes, watching them cluster together, and form a sitting line across the horizon, as if—

"Chrissakes, looks like they're watchin' us!" Chris blurted.

Windy nodded, mouth forming a crooked expression. "Damn sure does, don't it? Wonder what they gots on their minds?"

"Maybe they're rabid, the whole bunch of 'em."

"Doubt it. That were the case, they wouldn't be squattin' there just a'lookin'. I'll put some men on it when we get back, see if we can't get rid of some of the mangy critters."

Chris nodded, uneasy about the situation for a reason he couldn't peg. It struck him suddenly that he had seen an increase in coyote activity 'round the ranch the past few nights, scurries of movement in the darkness, a mournful howl, but nothing particularly out of the ordinary. This gathering seemed different, somehow, as if boding something—something *evil*.

A shudder went through him and fear gnawed at his belly. His arms trembled with strain as he clutched the reins too tightly. He felt sure if he could see his hands beneath the gloves they would look as bleached as the moon.

"Godamighty, son, you're shakin' like a newborn calf."

Chris glanced at Windy, seeing his expression had turned to worry.

"You feel it?" Chris's voice came weaker than he would have liked.

"If you mean that boogered feelin' rattlin' like bones in a cemetery, I sure do. Ain't never experienced the likes."

"I have..." Chris didn't elaborate. His mind wanted to jump back, pull him into the misty black rooms of the past, to the orphanage...

No! He wouldn't let it, refused to think about it. It was over, that part of his life, over and done with and it had no connection with what he—they—felt here, now.

Did it?

"What'd you mean?" Windy's worried expression deepened.

"Nothing!" Chris snapped. "I meant nothing. Just...something's wrong. I can't tell what it is, just that it is."

"I follow you, son. We gots some kinda trouble at the ranch and it's connected with them hoofbeats, I reckon. Maybe even them coyotes yonder."

Chris's gaze leaped back to the pack of prairie wolves poised on the horizon. They set up in a clamorous volley of howls, eerie and somehow pregnant with threat.

"Ye-ah!" Chris shot his horse forward, a dull panic rising in his mind. Windy took up a beat behind, but it was only a short distance before they reined to a halt.

"Look!" Windy blurted. Chris, feeling suddenly reluctant to climb from his saddle, peered at the huge carcass sprawled in the grass before him.

Windy dismounted, tentative as he circled the longhorn corpse, finally bending next to it. Chris stepped out of the saddle, a shakiness claiming his legs. He moved over to the dead steer.

A look of disgust turned his features and a tinge of nausea pulled at his belly. The beast's throat had been ripped raw, and a hollow glazed stare stained its eyes.

"Damn good side o' beef gone," Windy muttered.

"What do you think happened to it?" Chris sucked in a deep breath. The cold fear plaguing him became nearly overpowering. He noticed himself trembling with it and forced himself to gain a measure of composure.

"Reckon the coyotes musta done it..." Windy obviously didn't believe his own words, but seemed unable to find another explanation.

"You ever know a pack of them to take down a longhorn and just eat one piece off the neck?"

"Can't say as I have." Windy gazed at Chris with a perplexed frown. "But I damn well can't think of no other reason for this."

"What about Shinn?" Chris hoped to light on a reason that would quell the shaky feeling inside, the feeling that told him he'd been brushed by evil.

"Why would he? If he's rustlin' 7HL stock, why kill this here critter? Don't make no sense. Ain't no bullet done this, neither. This critter's throat's been torn out, likely by teeth from the looks."

"Teeth? You sure?" A cold wind of dread blew through Chris.

"Yep, you can tell if you look close." Windy pointed to the steer's gored neck.

Chris had no urge to look any closer than he had already. He'd take

Windy's word for the teeth marks.

The wind of dread suddenly rose to a gale force. He backed off, turning and going back to his roan. Shoving a boot into the stirrup, he grabbed the horn and hoisted himself into the saddle.

"I don't like this one damn bit," he said, getting some of the strength back in his voice.

Windy straightened and went to his horse, stepping into the saddle and drilling Chris with a dead-serious stare. "Me, neither, and I gots the feeling this will be the least of our problems."

They kicked their horses into motion, riding only a few hundred yards before Chris reined up and circled a grassless patch of ground.

"Look!" he pointed and Windy peered down at the area, which roughly formed the charred shape of a man. Chris's gaze riveted to the spot. He had never seen anything like it.

"Looks like a galldamned body got burned up here." Windy's voice held a tinge of dark awe.

"Any fire that could have done that would have to be hot enough to set the whole damn area aflame. Besides, we'da seen it. Not even any smoke, now."

With a glance at each other, they drove their mounts towards the ranch. The closer to the house they drew, the worse the cold fear in Chris became.

It's too late...

Somehow he knew what awaited him at the ranch.

As they neared the ranch compound, he could no longer delude himself. Chris's gaze darted to the open door, and then the bunkhouse. Light spilled across the porch and onto grass, a devil of yellow with an invitation. His attention shifted to the corral, its gate swung wide, the dark bulky shape of an animal sprawled on the ground.

Other signs confirmed something dreadful had happened: damage to the pens, a few broken windows in the outbuildings, over-turned troughs and rain barrels. One sign gave him the most pause, one that cracked a cold whip across his soul: the front door of the main house hung open, oddly askew.

"Looks like whoever t'was just wanted to vandalize things, not stop the operation..." Windy muttered in a half-believable voice next to him. Chris felt thankful for Windy's words because he'd been on the way to working himself into a panic and it brought a measure of composure to his being.

"More than that," he said, tone somber.

Windy nodded. "Reckon so."

They spurred their horses to the main house, Chris leaping from the roan almost before it stopped. He crossed the veranda and halted, as if he'd slammed into an invisible wall. He stared at the door hanging by one hinge. It had been kicked open, he felt sure.

Windy stepped up beside him, gazing quickly at the damage and grabbing Chris's arm.

"Let me go in first, son." The red-headed man's eyes took on a look of deep concern.

Chris nodded almost imperceptibly and muttered something unintelligible, unable to move a muscle for the moment. Fear paralyzed him with what he knew he'd find when he entered the house. Earlier he had refused to face the things Windy had tried to tell him about his uncle; now they were being forced down his throat.

By the time these thoughts flicked through his mind, Windy had entered the dwelling. Almost in the same move, the assistant foreman came backing out.

"What is it?" Chris asked in a hollow voice. Emotion jammed in his throat and his heart pounded. A fevered look rode his eyes.

Windy grabbed his shoulders firmly, the look on the *segundo*'s face one of horror and deep sympathy.

"You gots to be strong, son. You gots to be strong. It ain't like nothin' I ever seen, I'm tellin' you straight."

"No..." Chris shook his head, the move going from slow to frantic. "No, it can't be! It can't be, Windy. Not yet—not like this!"

Windy tried to hold him back, but Chris, with a strength born of desperate hope, threw him aside. He plunged into the house, stopping short just inside the foyer. His eyes widened, shock freezing him in place.

The mutilated body of Mrs. Tulber lay at the foot of the stairs, eyes round and glassy as the dead longhorn's in the field. Horrible wounds shown on her neck and breasts, gaping raw and gruesome.

In a flicker of frozen clarity, it occurred to Chris there was damn little blood for such a brutal sight. A little had soaked into her torn dress, but there should have been more, much more.

Dark feeling fought to take over inside Chris.

Images flashed in his mind, faces, dark faces, shadowed sights and feelings from that lost time, devoured by roaring yellow and scarlet, fire and blood. Weakness gripped his legs with the stunning swell of memories. They threatened to buckle; he didn't know how he stayed on his feet. The room danced in a waltzing collage of ghosts, laughing, crying, dying. A strangled plea came from his gaping mouth. His heart felt as if it would explode in his chest.

Remember me, boy?

A voice, echoing from the spinning darkness, from the past, from hell. He mewed some sort of reply before an open palm cracked across his cheek, jerking him back to his senses.

"Chris, snap out of it! Don't let yourself go!" Windy drilled Chris with frantic eyes, but for the moment Chris could barely acknowledge him. Words garbled in his mind and his mouth closed, opened, closed again. The face, the familiar freckle- and gristle-studded face and too-small eyes with their reassuring expression penetrated his mind, drawing him back.

"It's happening again..." Chris said, freeing his words, voice shaky, unnaturally high.

"What? What's happenin', son? Tell me. Let it out."

"I...can't, Windy...I—Uncle Clem, where is he?" Chris felt a measure of control rise with his concern for his uncle. He jerked away from the assistant foreman and went into the parlor. Butter-colored light threw weird shadows across the floor and walls. The feel of death hung heavy in the air.

"Uncle Clem!" Chris shouted, seeing the older man sprawled on the floor near the fireplace. He ran to him and knelt, pulling his uncle's head up. Clem's eyelids fluttered and Chris almost screamed with relief.

"He's alive!" he shouted to Windy, who had knelt beside him. "He's goddamn alive!"

Clem's eyes opened and for a moment no recognition shown within them, only terror.

"It's me, Uncle Clem, it's Chris. Hold on. We'll get the doc and he'll fix you up just fine. You wait and see, he will." Emotion tore at Chris. He knew better. The end was a matter of precious moments. Deep gashes gaped bloody on the old man's face and blood had run from his mouth and nostrils. The old man shuddered with a violent cough and more blood bubbled out of his mouth.

"Chris..." The word came faint, a weak gurgle. "Knew I could hold on till you got back...I..."

"Don't talk, don't talk. We'll get the doc, I swear we will—get him, goddamn you!" Chris suddenly yelled at Windy, who straightened and backed up a step, startled. But he made no move to leave.

"Can't you see he's gonna be all right?" Chris went on, words turning into a frantic plea.

Windy slowly shook his head.

Clem gripped Chris's arm, fingers prying into his flesh with uncomfortable strength, and he turned his attention back to his uncle. Taking his bandanna, he wiped the blood from Clem's lips.

"No..." the older man mouthed, voice almost gone. "I gotta tell ya, boy...it was him..."

"What?" Shock slapped Chris's face. The coldness inside made him shudder. And suddenly he knew, knew the Devil had returned from hell to claim his due.

"It was Clint..." More blood ran from the older man's lips; Chris could no longer keep up with it; his bandanna was soaked with scarlet.

"He's dead, Uncle Clem. He's dead. It couldn't be him." Chris's words came out more a plea than a surety.

"No...he's...different, evil. He wants to make you suffer for what happened—" A wracking cough rattled the older man.

A sobering wave washed over Chris. Milus Clint. That was the last name he ever expected to hear, yet somehow the first. Only a demon could have done what had been done tonight, and Clint was a demon in human form.

"You'll make it, just hold on," Chris repeated, trying to convince himself of the lie.

"No, boy...I'm dead already, been dead for months...could never tell you...you seen so much...take...take care, boy. Don't let him have you...go to Dark Cloud. He can...help..." Clem's eyelids closed and his head became limp on Chris's arm.

Chris trembled with anger and hate and a flood of emotion he thought he had buried. Images from that other time threatened to push back in. He held on, he had no idea how, forced the scenes down. Tears welled in his eyes, but didn't flow. They couldn't flow. They hadn't flowed since a bastard named Milus Clint shut them off.

His trembling fingers drifted across Clem's forehead, brushing back the hair. He pulled the older man to his breast, holding him tightly, afraid to let go and face the fact that Clem was gone. *Gone.* The word thundered in his mind. Chris had known for months he'd lose Clem; he'd fooled only himself if he thought different. But their time together had been cut short and anger burned with the knowledge.

Again Milus Clint had destroyed that chance, that time together, though Chris knew it was impossible for the outlaw to be alive.

Chris held the older man for what seemed like hours, but was only minutes. He heard the soft fall of footsteps behind him, and saw Windy coming back into the house. He hadn't heard the *segundo* leave. He noticed Windy had draped a blanket over the body of Mrs. Tulber and saw sympathy on his face as he stepped closer, putting a hand on Chris's shoulder.

"Let him go, son. Let him go with the dignity he deserves. He'd want it that way."

Chris gently set Clem's head on the floor and stood, body quivery with emotion.

"I'm...sorry, son." Windy's voice was choked with sorrow. A tear trickled from his eye and he wiped it away.

"I checked the bunkhouse," Windy went on after he composed himself. "They're all dead in there, same as Mrs. Tulber. Same as that steer. I'll send for the undertaker soon as some of the other men get back from town. Best talk to the sheriff as well. Maybe we can find out who did this."

"No need for the sheriff..."

"What do you mean?" Windy looked puzzled.

"I know who did it. Clem told me before he died."

"Who?" Windy's brow furrowed, and Chris saw revenge spark in the *segundo*'s eyes.

"Milus Clint." The name tumbled from Chris's mouth like splinters of ice. He'd sworn he'd never speak that name again and couldn't even begin to put together how he'd been forced into it. Windy's expression took on a look of shock. "You know him?"

The assistant foreman nodded. "Yeah, ain't a man from New Mex way who don't. But he couldn't be the one who did this, son. No way in hell he could. He's dead."

"Yeah?" Chris's voice went distant.

"Yeah, damn right he is. Has to be. Ain't nobody who can get shot clean through the face and live to tell about it."

Chris eyed the red-haired man. "All this time, you knew, didn't you?"

Windy's gaze went to the floor, came back up. "I know some. Clem told me a bit, plus I come from the area so I heard things."

Chris uttered a humorless laugh. "I want to bury Uncle Clem here. He loved this land. It was as much a part of him as he was of it. He'd want it that way."

"Reckon he would at that," Windy agreed with a nod. "We're still gonna have to tell the sheriff and God's truth I hate to say it, but I ain't sure how many of the men are gonna want to stay on after somethin' like this."

"Then hire new 'hands. We're gonna have to get things fixed up and there'll be lots of work to do."

"Glad to hear you talkin' that way, son."

"What else is there to do?" A cynical note laced Chris's tone, as he tried to focus away from his grief.

A howl pulled him from his thoughts and coldness welled in his soul again.

"Damn varmints!" Windy cursed, on edge and pacing. "Ain't bad enough, we gots them buggers comin' 'round. I swear I'll be takin' some of my frustration out on them with a Winchester."

Chris remained silent, the spell of death wandering through him. The howling ceased and somehow he knew the coyotes would be silent for the time being. Something told him a message had been sent, that the bloodshed was far from over.

Milus Clint, if he had somehow cheated the grave, would be back.

SIX

The Dark Riders swarmed into the town of Bald Creek in a furor of
beating hooves and the onerous neighing of black horses whose eyes blazed
ebony fire. The careening steeds threw up clouds of dust and dried dung;
windows rattled. Flames in hanging lanterns jittered.

Bald Creek was a ramshackle cowtown situated a few miles from the
banks of the Canadian River. Its livelihood consisted of offering life's
dubious pleasures to trail-weary cowhands itching to spend their thirty-a-
month wages on any number and variety of sins—games of chance, whiskey,
and women with moist painted lips practiced in the art of honey-soft
whispers and dollar-a-night ministrations.

Bald Creek boasted a law of sorts. As with many cowtowns scattered
across the Plains, that law consisted of a sheriff, who, by all accounts, had his
hand in most of the illicit dealings of the Blue Steer Saloon. What law there
was, tended to be delivered by the townsfolk. Little was viewed as a trespass
of legality, except the heinous crime of rustling, which met quick justice at
the end of a rope. Whoring, gambling, drunkenness and fighting occurred
regularly with nary the blink of an eye.

It was the kind of raw town Milus Clint took to.

The town itself consisted of a latticework affair of streets, wide wagon-
rutted Main Street, paralleled by a thinner thoroughfare, joined by shadow-
clogged alleyways. Buildings, constructed primarily of clapboard, sported
false fronts. A few adobes littered the edge of town. A small cemetery with a
rickety fence flanked a white church. At that sight Milus Clint grinned.
They'd need to expand it by the time he got through with Bald Creek.

The Riders reined to a halt in front of the saloon. Dismounting, they left
their horses untethered. The beasts would not run off and no horse thief
would mess with their mounts for long. Milus uttered a choppy laugh at the
thought, recollecting an Injun horse thief who tried that stunt, sliding up to
the mount in the darkness and making sweet horse-talk. But the heathen
quickly learned he'd chewed off more than he could swallow when he stared
into the abyss of the horse's coal eyes. The last thing the Injun felt was the
black's spiked incisors crushing into his shoulder. Milus had reveled in the
horrible shriek the 'pache made as his life drained away. Then he spent the

better part of an hour laughing at the sight. He enjoyed death. It was one of the few things he could understand.

The outlaw stepped onto the boardwalk, pausing as the howl of a coyote rose in the distance. Canting his head, he listened, smiling, satisfied. He could feel the boy's pain, his anguish, and it pleased him. The suffering had commenced. It would not end until Milus saw fit. The boy had to pay for what he had done, what he had turned Milus into. And pay he would. Dearly. A debt to be collected over eternity. When the pain tore him to pieces, only then would Milus come to him, show him what true hell was like. For the boy, death would not be a comfort; it would be an endless, empty black night.

"Somethin' wrong, Milus?" Emmet asked, stepping up to him.

"Wrong?" Milus echoed, lantern light arcing across his scarred features, making them appear demonic. "Not a-tall, Emmet. Let's have us some fun with this here town. There's plenty of good whores waitin' on us to give 'em some lovin'." He laughed and Emmet joined him. The other Riders stepped down from their mounts and stomped across the boardwalk. Milus turned, gaze narrowing on Billy, who stopped, blue eyes locking on the leader.

"You know what to do, Billy." Milus's tone carried a threatening edge. "Don't muss it up this time or there won't be another for you."

Billy nodded, the cocky grin angling onto his lips. "Don't worry about me, Milus. I'll take care of her."

"See that you do." Milus spun and shoved through the batwings, the others following.

A Durham haze hung in the saloon. Bawdy bursts of laughter and loud voices punctuated the smoky air. A man with an armband banged away at a honky-tonk piano in the corner. Bargirls mingled with the crowd of cowhands, leaning over drunken men and whispering in their ears, placing their perfumed bosoms against their cheeks, running their tongues over scarlet-painted lips with lascivious artistry.

Milus scanned the women, selecting one that struck his taste, but leaving her be for the moment.

The saloon was typical as far as cowtown drinkeries went. Men playing poker and dealers sliding cards from tiger-emblazoned faro boxes clustered at the tables. Chuck-a-luck and a keno goose—a rig that dropped little numbered balls in a bingolike game—were in evidence. The redolent odors of tobacco and stale whiskey filled the air, a mix Milus had always found pleasurable. Sometimes, at times like this, he entertained the brief notion that he missed being human. Missed the old days in New Mex when he and his gang could feel the pleasure of a woman's flesh pressed against their own.

Those days were gone, he reminded himself. There was only what was and what would be. The nights, the endless trail of them, and the burning lust for revenge that filled the place within him where his soul had been.

The Riders moved deeper inside the room. Two broke off and went to a table covered with green felt to try their hands at poker.

Milus signaled with a sharp gesture of his hand and Billy angled through the tables for the stairs at the back of the room. The stairs led to an upper level of rooms in which the whores tended to the needs of cowhands. She was up there, the girl he'd come to find. She could be nowhere else, for he hadn't spotted her mingling with the crowd in the barroom. And tonight he would exact payment from Chris Durrin with her death.

He knew the boy had been with her. Milus had observed the youth carefully over the last few nights, prying into his nightmares, his pain. He'd seen the boy visit the dark Mexican beauty and the Indian girl; each would aid him in his quest for vengeance. Milus chuckled to himself, more pleased than ever with his plans.

The outlaw leader pushed through the sea of tables and sidled up to the polished bar.

Behind the bar a portly saloonkeeper was wiping out glasses and placing them on racks. Milus surveyed the rows of liquor bottles cached in a hutch beside a huge gild-framed mirror.

The 'keep flashed Milus an apprehensive look, and now that Milus thought about it, he noticed the noise of the crowd had lowered a notch as the other Riders lined up along the bar. Some of the patrons cast them wary glances. Even a few of the doves turned kohl-shaded eyes towards them. Milus was used to the looks; his scarred features attracted attention and fear; he liked it that way.

"Problem?" Milus asked the barkeep, no emotion in his voice. As the 'keep set the glass on the shelf, Milus noticed the fella's hand trembled a bit and he kept looking nervously to a spot beneath the counter. No doubt he had a shotgun located there in case of trouble. Milus almost laughed. Trouble was what he had come for and the shotgun would do the man no good.

The barkeep's lower lip moved, as if he were going to answer, but no words came out.

Milus banged a fist against the counter. "What the goddamn hell's wrong with you? I asked you a question."

"Nothing," the barman stammered.

Milus noticed the man struggling to keep his gaze off the mass of scar tissue that covered half his face.

"Somethin' 'bout my looks you don't cotton to?" Milus' cold buzzard eyes drilled the 'keep.

"No, no, not at all. It's a fine face, sir, yes it is. One of the finest I rightly seen."

"Then what's your beef?" Milus's tone became a challenge.

"Just, just that, that boy who came in with y'all, the fella who just went upstairs..."

With a nudge of his head, Milus indicated a whiskey bottle and the 'keep jumped to get it, sliding it onto the bar along with a glass. Milus swept the glass aside, sending it sliding down the bar to crash to the floor. It shattered with an explosive pop.

"What about him?"

The barkeep shot a look at the broken glass, but said nothing of it. "Just that, well, he looks a mite familiar, that's all."

"Does he now?" Milus opened the bottle and took a swig of the whiskey. He tasted and felt nothing as the liquor washed down his gullet, but the custom of drinking pleased him.

"Yeah, reckon he does. Not that I care a lick, mind you. What that young fella did was his business and he had his reasons, what with all that killin' over cattle—"

The bartender's words snapped off in a squawk as Milus grabbed a fistful of the man's stained shirt and jerked him close, then hoisted him clean off the floor. Terror swelled in the 'keep's eyes as his gaze centered on the buzzard-gored tissue and the eyes of a bird of prey. The outlaw's eyes changed, shading black, sparkling with blue-black arcs.

"P-please!" The man's voice rose, trembled. "I didn't mean nothin' by it!"

"You ain't never seen the kid before..." Milus held his voice even and the 'keep jerked a nod.

"N-no sir, I ain't never."

"Good. Makes me feel more secure that way." Milus shoved the man back and he crashed into the hutch of bottles. Liquor tumbled from the shelves, one bottle breaking. The 'keep eyed it, then scrambled to mop it up.

Milus laughed to himself, pleased, enjoying the man's fear. He could smell it, the way an animal smells its prey. At any other time he would have torn the 'keep's throat out just for the hell of it, but he had other things to attend to first.

Around the room, stares from cowhands grew harder and the noise lowered. The piano player stopped playing and slid off the bench, angling to the rear of the room and finding a back exit. No backbone on that one, Milus thought with disgust. He ignored the stares and stood, grabbed the whiskey bottle from the bartop, then tossed it to one of his men.

"Make sure you put that in my saddlebag," he said to the Rider, moving towards the dove he'd taken a shine to earlier. She backed away with nervous steps.

"What's a'matter, honey? You don't like old Milus?" A repulsive expression turned his face. She was a blonde—he was partial to blondes—

with a red sateen bodice that plunged half-way down her ample breasts, eyes shaded with kohl and coral smeared across her cheeks. Not the prettiest filly he'd set eyes on, but she'd do. She'd be a whole lot less pretty by the time he got done with her anyhow.

"I'm with someone," the dove said in a voice that carried a hint of fear. She skipped a look to a drunk cowhand sitting at the table next to her. Milus gazed at the man and the fellow gave a quick not-wanting-to-get-involved shake of his head.

"He won't miss you." Milus grabbed her arm and squeezed and she let out a bleat. At the table two other cowhands tensed, as if considering intervening, but apparently thought better of it when Milus' buzzard eyes settled on them.

"Let me go, you sonofabitch!" the dove tried to pull her arm loose, but Milus tightened his grip.

The girl had gumption; he liked that. Feisty blood tasted smoother, like good whiskey. "Yeah, I am a sonofabitch and you'll love every minute of it. Almost." He hauled her across the room and half-dragged, half-carried her up the stairs, disappearing at the top.

The other Riders selected girls and did the same.

In the barroom, noise all but stopped, only the hushed staccato breathing and subtle harmony of fear straining the silence.

Billy angled his way down the lantern-lighted hallway above the saloon, peering into the cubicles and rooms until he found the one he wanted. The straw-colored glow cast by the lantern fell on peeling red-flowered wallpaper and a soiled threadbare carpet.

He let the lopsided grin turn his lips as he stepped up to the last door. That had to be hers. She was inside and Milus wanted her dead because of some hilly-dilly link to the Durrin boy. But that didn't fit in with Billy's plans one lick. Was a shame to destroy a pretty filly like her just for nothin'. Milus could go to hell for all Billy gave a diddly damn. Before he got through there would be many more of their kind in the night, all loyal to him, not Milus. A world filled with Dead-Walkers, a place where he could belong for the first time in his life.

Billy chuckled, thinking of the one man he'd save till last, his *friend*, his goddamn friend, the no-good skunk who had ambushed him in that dark room in Fort Sumner. And the rancher, Maxwell, as well. Billy's slim fingers drifted to his chest, to the round hole over his heart. He could still feel the bullet inside him, more a recollection, he reckoned, than reality, and anger stampeded through him. No, Milus wouldn't stop him from carrying out his plans; Billy wouldn't let him.

He stepped up to the door, twisted the glass knob, then swung it open. Dim light made the room gloomy and the cloying scent of lilac saturated the air.

A woman sat at the vanity, running a silver hairbrush through her dark hair. Twists of blue lace ornamented the ebony locks, something he'd always been partial to. She looked up, her full lips working a seductive smile that rapidly dissolved into an expression of vague fear. His face wasn't unknown by a damn sight and he knew she had recognized him.

His gaze traveled down to her purple sateen bodice, to her smooth bare shoulders the color of rich olive, then to the swells of her small breasts. An appreciative look twinkled in his eyes.

Her eyes, the color of a mesa at sunset, widened and scarlet lips parted slightly.

He removed his hat and smoothed his light-brown hair and flashed a beguiling grin.

"Don't you worry none, ma'am, I ain't here to kill you." His tone came boyish and silky.

The girl reached into the top of her bodice, plucked out a derringer and shot him in the chest.

Screams shattered the hush in the barroom. Shrieks of agony, terror. Men swiveled their attention towards the stairs, mouths gaping. They sat frozen, paralyzed by the sounds and spellbinding fear. Drunken cowhands suddenly sobered, others soiled their britches.

The screams continued, rising in pitch, mixed with throaty animal sounds and the violent thud of bodies hitting the floor.

They had seen outlaw bands aplenty ride in and out of Bald Creek. The town was a haven for the lawless. Yet a certain code held sway: they came into Bald Creek, did their business without fear of the law, and as quickly hit the trail again. It was an understanding, and till now, damn few had broken it. But Bald Creek had never seen the likes of this.

The sounds of futile struggles came down, even the snapping pop of derringers, followed by *other* sounds, sounds that set their blood racing and a number of them to gulping the whiskey from their glasses.

"What in God's good name's goin' on up there?" one man asked, standing and peering at the barkeep, whose face had bleached. The 'keep shook his head and the man went back to staring at the top of the stairs.

No one made a move to go up there.

The screams died and that was almost as unnerving. They knew it was over, knew the women whom the Riders had dragged upstairs would not come down again.

Moments of heavy silence dragged by, broken at last by the clomping of boots.

The outlaw leader appeared at the top of the stairs, demon-scarred face ripe with a cruelness they'd seldom seen on a man. Limp in his arms was the body of the blonde dove he'd taken upstairs. Her eyes glared wide, unseeing, and her mouth gaped in a frozen scream. She was naked and her flesh looked unnaturally pale, as if bloodless.

The leader laughed, the sound cascading through the room, reverberating through every man like the kiss of a frigid wind.

"Reckon I'm done with her now," Milus said, eyes narrowing. "You can have her back." He heaved the girl over the rail and into the air. She seemed almost suspended a moment, a limp thing bandied about on a death-still wind. Then she dropped, body slamming into a table, which buckled with a thunderous *crack!* She sprawled on the floor, a cloud of sawdust flying up, her neck twisted at an unnatural angle. The cowhands backed away from her, most refusing to even glance at the dove.

On the landing, the Riders gathered, blood snaking from the corners of their mouths, blackness in their eyes.

"Me and the boys would like to thank you folks for your hospitality," Milus said. "Maybe we'll visit again real soon." His hand clamped onto the rail and, swinging himself up and over in a fluid animal-like motion, he leaped to the floor below. He landed with catlike grace. The other Riders came down the stairs and bunched around their leader.

At first, the cowhands backed off, giving the Riders plenty of room, then the one who had spoken to the 'keep jabbed a finger at the outlaws and shouted.

"Hell, they ain't even got guns!" The others looked, seeing the man was right, and courage gathered in their eyes. These hardcases had broken an unspoken code and that needed punishment. Their hands slapped for the Colts at their hips; few came to Bald Creek without iron.

"Folks ain't too all-fired friendly 'round here, are they?" Milus looked at each of his men. He let out a hiss and his lips peeled back from razor-sharp fangs. Blackness swallowed his eyes. He grabbed the man who had spoken, fingers curling around his throat, jerking him close. A brittle snap sounded, choking off any cry the man might have made. The outlaw leader hurled the cowhand into the crowd, bowling down two other men.

The rest, in courage born of panic, whipped out guns. A few reached for the broken table legs to use as clubs and converged on the Riders.

Shots thundered and acrid blue smoke singed the air. Lead plowed into the Riders, jolting them, but failing to hinder their approach. Bullets punched right through them, the holes cauterized with a sizzle of boiling blackness.

Behind the bar, the 'keep dived beneath the counter and came up with a shotgun. Triggering, he loosed both barrels, peppering shot into the arm and side of the Rider named Dutch. Black fluid bubbled over the Rider's wounds, sealing them. The bartender's eyes widened with the knowledge that he had just assured his own death.

Dutch, eyes burning black, hurled himself into the air, lighting on the polished bartop. Hissing, he swooped upon the 'keep, mouth splitting wide and fangs gleaming with saliva. He grabbed the barman, forcing the fellow's head back, then tore out his throat. The man went limp and Dutch heaved the body over the counter into the crowd.

A melee of shouts and gun blasts ripped through the saloon. Wood splintered as bullets and bodies slammed into tables.

Some of the cowhands panicked and retreated through the rear door. Others triggered their Colt chambers empty to no effect. The few who had grabbed clubs fared better, swinging at the Rider's heads, stunning a few. Yet when a man closed in to beat the outlaws senseless, another would grab him from behind and he would feel the piercing burn of fangs plunging deep into his neck.

The fight lasted mere moments. In the end the only cowhands left standing were the ones who had escaped through the rear door. Most of the dead had been the first to charge, or men too drunk to get away. Bodies lay splayed across each other. Glass from shattered whiskey bottles sparkled among the sawdust. Tables and chairs were collapsed and Milus reckoned he had caught a piece of luck none of the cowhands had taken a notion to stick any of his men with the shards of wood.

"Where the hell's Billy?" Milus asked, surveying the corpses. He looked to the others, p-o'd the young outlaw wasn't with them.

Emmet shrugged. "Dunno. He went up and ain't come down yet."

"Goddamn that skunk!" Milus cursed, suddenly giddy with the blood he had consumed. Some of it had been soaked with whiskey, making it all the more sweet. A comforting glow nested in his belly, despite the annoyance he felt at Billy.

A clomping of boots on the stairs attracted his attention and he turned to see Billy strolling down, that idiotic grin welded to his face.

"What took you so long?" Milus asked.

Billy shrugged. "She didn't cooperate like I figured she would." His hand drifted to the hole in his shirt, the one from the derringer shot. "Downright feisty, she was."

"You better not have mussed up." Milus' eyes narrowed, black fading to their normal buzzard color.

"She's like you wanted." A note of challenge laced Billy's voice and the youth kept Milus' gaze for dragging seconds.

Milus uttered a chopped laugh and turned to the others. "C'mon, boys, let's do this town way we used ta!"

"Sheriff might come," Emmet said, jest in his voice.

Milus chuckled. "He did. Saw him peek in during the fight then go right on out again. Guess he reckoned he'd live longer that way. Maybe he thinks we won't come back. Fact is, I've decided I like this here town. Once folks start gettin' a mite more friendly, it'll be right pleasant."

Milus looked over the room a final time, making sure no one was left alive. Stepping over a corpse, he headed across the floor and pushed through the batwings. He went to his horse, mounted. The other Riders followed, stepping into their saddles and reining around. Milus let out a whoop and spurred his black into motion.

The Riders stormed through the main street, hollering, hurrahing the town as they had in the old days. The feeling intoxicated him, made him feel as alive as he could ever hope to get.

They tied ropes to supporting beams and shot their horses forward: the beams groaned, cracked, snapped. Wooden awnings crashed to the boardwalk.

With his pearl-handled Colt, Billy triggered lead, shattering windows and punching holes in water troughs.

They kicked over barrels, tore out clotheslines and pulled down signs.

Milus flicked his blacksnake at a hanging lantern, shattering it, throwing a wash of kerosene flame across the wall of a shop.

Flames gobbled the dry boards, devouring the front of the shop in seconds, lashing at the interior until the entire establishment became a pyre. Black smoke billowed and orange flame splashed across the Riders' faces.

In the brimstone glow, Milus' surveyed the damage done and laughed. The next time they came to Bald Creek it would be in secret, in twos or threes, for food. The town belonged to him, now; it bore his mark and he would suck it dry before his revenge on the Durrin boy was complete.

SEVEN

Chris buried Clem near a stand of cottonwoods close to a stream that twisted through the 7HL land. In the daylight, shade would cover the grave. Clem had always enjoyed sitting in that cool patch; it was fitting he should have that comfort in death as well.

While Windy mumbled some words from his Bible, Chris had placed a handful of cigars atop the body.

He knew it was the burial his uncle would have wanted. Clem considered himself a part of the rich cattle-grazing land of the Plains. It was his mistress, caressing yet scolding, supplicating yet demanding. He would find peace within it, ride a trail into that realm of angels Chris had heard about in Sunday School at the orphanage.

Despondent, Chris guided his roan along the stream, tracing its winding path as it split an arroyo, meandered out the other side. He had left Windy to see to the chore of fetching the undertaker and informing the cowhands what had occurred. Chris had another duty to perform, one he couldn't leave to the *segundo*.

He headed for the Indian camp two miles away, to tell Dark Cloud of the attack on the ranch. Clem had spoken the Indian's name before he died and Chris owed it to his Uncle to honor his last wish. He supposed the motivation was partly selfishness. He needed to see Little Waiting Woman, let her hold him, ease a measure of the hurt and pain. She was the only one he wanted to run to in times such as this.

Then why do you go to Matalija? Why don't you marry Little Waiting Woman and let yourself live? Why are you so goddamn afraid?

A sigh escaped his lips. Because he was a damn fool, that's why. He loved her and that was the bottom line, and in grief he needed her more than ever. No whore at a Texas saloon could replace that comfort.

Chris' gray-blue eyes settled on the grassy terrain that skirted the banks of the stream. A somber numbness drifted over his being as his mind continued skipping back to the night's events. Guilt crept in. If he'd not taken his time returning to the ranch after turning back the cattle, if he'd stayed at the house in the first place. Perhaps Clem would still be alive and Mrs. Tulber would be scolding the britches off him in her motherly way.

He realized in an instant of soberness the fault didn't belong with him. If he'd been at the house he might well have met the same fate, but that offered little comfort.

Death. Would he ever be able to outrun it? It was always behind him, always stepping into his tracks. He saw no rhyme or reason to what had occurred tonight. No reason for the dead men in the bunkhouse or Mrs. Tulber and Uncle Clem's murders. None. No goddamned reason at all. It was brutal and it was senseless. For this particular link with death should rightly have been severed in New Mexico six years ago, when he had shot and killed an outlaw named Milus Clint.

But he hadn't killed Clint, had he? Somehow the hardcase had survived and returned for revenge.

You refused to face the past...now, it's here...

He'd spent the better part of the last few years denying the things that had happened. God knew the hurt seeped out in unguarded moments, manifesting itself in his reluctance to commit to Little Waiting Woman, in bursts of anger at the 'hands or Windy. Always he would force it away or plain refuse to think on it. Now he had no choice.

Milus Clint.

The name jangled in his memory like a rifle volley. The image of the outlaw's face rose in his mind.

Clint would be back; the outlaw wouldn't leave things undone. But before that happened, Chris had to put away his hurt, go after the hardcase, surprise him the way he had years before—and this time do the job of killing the bastard right. Chris had witnessed a powerful lot of death in his life, but he vowed he would see one more, one he would relish: Milus Clint's.

As Chris drew near the village, he turned his thoughts to the task ahead. The notion of telling Dark Cloud about Clem lay heavy on his mind. He knew the bond Clem and the Comanche shared. The Indian affectionately called Chris's uncle Spotted Buffalo Man, referring to the white man's cattle. They carried a deep understanding and respect for each other's ways. They were blood brothers.

Dark Cloud and his cousin, Speaks No More, were *Kwah-heehar kehnuh* or Kwahadi Comanches, which meant "Sun Shades on their Backs," because of the bison-hide parasols the band constructed. They were once the most vicious and feared of the *Nermernuh*, and Dark Cloud a mighty warrior, battling beside the "white Indian" Quanah Parker when the tribe fell at the hands of General Ranald Mackenzie. Their camp squatted on a tract of land beside the stream, a cluster of tipis amongst the cottonwoods with a rough corral holding over a hundred horses, the pride of Dark Cloud.

He suspected Clem had presented Dark Cloud with the animals as a dowry for the hand of his sister, Little Waiting Woman.

The camp came into view and Chris felt an acute swelling of the coldness that plagued him earlier. His hands tightened around the reins. He spied the corral with its horses and everything appeared at first glance the same as always. He couldn't peg what made him apprehensive.

His gaze shifted to the camp proper. It looked strangely deserted. Slowing, his eyes picked out little things askew that set his heart to pounding.

Among the cluster of tipis, he saw pans and utensils scattered about, as well as pieces of bones and refuge, scraps of food, Indian awls and bones picks, all strewn helter-skelter. In itself, that wasn't particularly unusual; Comanche were notorious for littering the area around their tipis. When the smell become overpowering they simply moved on.

Something's wrong...

It came to him as he scanned the tipis again: one was missing. His gaze traveled along the lodge cluster, halting at a charred circle to the right. Smoke curled from the patch and the breeze stirred ash into gray ghosts. His heart leaped, beating thick and fast in his throat. He swallowed at it but couldn't drive the feeling away.

It was unlikely the tipi had burned by accident. Comanche constructed their portable lodges of tanned bison hides fitted over a framework of slender pine or cedar poles. The shelter, flapped and ditched, could withstand violent storms and blizzards and fires were commonly banked within the twelve-to-fifteen-foot interior.

He sent his roan into the camp, sweat beading on his skin despite the coolness of the night. Drawing up, he jumped from his horse.

A movement caught his eye and he saw Dark Cloud, trailed by Speaks No More, exit the far tipi. Faces grim, set with death, they came somberly towards him.

Dread sank in Chris's belly. The tipi belonged to Little Waiting Woman. He struggled to force down the horror brewing inside him as Dark Cloud approached.

Before he could stop himself, as if it would somehow magically halt the terrible news he knew he would hear, he blurted, "Clem's dead." He clamped his mouth shut, as if the words had burned his tongue.

Dark Cloud halted, face growing darker. Chris surveyed the Comanche warrior before him, nervously noting the things he had noticed a hundred times before: Dark Cloud wore a breechcloth beneath a bare chest, which was deep and wide, tanned by countless suns. Plain moccasins made of soft chewed deerskin and buffalo soles stretched from foot to hip; they consisted of a sort of boot ornamented with beads and bits of silver. Painted blue, they were perfectly suited for horse riding. Although his short arms and legs were well-muscled, Dark Cloud's belly bulged with a slight paunch common to his tribe. Overall, his manner portrayed a dignity and a sense of pride that few men possessed or knew how to use if they did.

The Indian's chest rose with shallow breaths and his frame arched with a certain stiffness.

But Chris instantly noticed a difference in the warrior's carriage; his posture was sinking under the weight of some great sorrow. Chris's gaze locked on the slashes on the Indian's body, the signs of grieving.

He's been here...

He swallowed at the emotion welling in his throat and his gaze went to Speaks No More, whose face showed more anguish than Dark Cloud's. Speaks No More, though built along the same lines as his cousin, was a notch taller than Dark Cloud. A white scar arced across his throat, the result of a white man's Bowie knife that had rendered his vocal cords useless. He bore the same marks of self-mutilation as his cousin.

"Your words bring great sadness, Spotted Buffalo Son," Dark Cloud said at last. "He was a brother to me. I have lost much this night."

"Tell him!" Speaks No More gestured angrily, gritting his teeth at Dark Cloud. "Tell him of He Who Drinks Life and the Great Cannibal Owl!"

Dark Cloud's face showed irritation and he made a sharp sign for "No!"

"He must know!"

"He can do nothing," Dark Cloud signed back. "It is his fate."

"What's he saying?" Chris asked, finding his voice and struggling to control the turmoil he felt inside. "He looks angry."

Dark Cloud raised his hand. "He speaks of things no longer important." The Indian abruptly changed the subject. "These men who killed Spotted Buffalo Man, did you see them?"

"How did you know it was men?" Surprise chased some of the shakiness from Chris's voice.

"One of them came here. He killed my wives, Speaks No More's as well."

The news confirmed the cold dread inside Chris. The tipi had been deliberately fired by the same men who had butchered the cowhands and Mrs. Tulber, killed Clem. Chris had met their wives only in passing, but a great sorrow assailed him. More death, for him and for a people who had faced as much as they needed to face in a hundred lifetimes.

"I'm sorry," was all he could think to say, voice lowering. "Did you see the man who did it?"

"Yes." Dark Cloud appeared reluctant to elaborate but Chris had to know if it was Clint.

"What did he look like?"

Dark Cloud's words painted the man in precise detail and Chris recoiled inside. It wasn't Clint, but he felt sure the Indian described another member of the outlaw's gang who had ridden with him in New Mexico, a man called Jeters. Chris knew Jeters had escaped the posse six years ago; his body had not been found among the dead and rumor had it he had ridden for Old Mexico.

"Anyone with him?" Chris asked.

"There was no one else."

Dark Cloud was being deliberately short-answered. Chris decided to be direct. He had little choice; the Comanche warrior would never volunteer anything. "There's more to it; you're not telling something."

Dark Cloud shrugged, unperturbed. "The man who attacked this camp is dead."

Chris' eyebrows arched. A small measure of satisfaction rose inside him. "How?"

"I killed him." Dark Cloud's voice came flat and final, but Chris still sensed there was still something else he was not letting on.

"Where is he?" Chris glanced around for the remains, knowing what the Comanche did to their enemies. It wasn't pretty and he half-expected to see body parts strewn about.

"He is gone."

This time Dark Cloud's eyes betrayed him. He *was* leaving something out and irritation burrowed under Chris' skin. His nerves were raw and he figured he damn well deserved some straight answers. If Clint had returned for revenge, Chris had to know every detail, no matter how trivial, that might give him an edge.

His eyes locked with the Indian's. "What do you mean gone? You said you killed him." He let the irritation bleed into his voice, making it not so much a question as a demand.

"Tell him!" Speaks No More signed harshly, eyes narrowing with anger. Dark Cloud ignored him and his cousin grunted a disgusted sound.

"You must come." Dark Cloud turned on the ball of his foot and walked towards the tipi. Irritation fled as panic spun his thoughts to Little Waiting Woman. Dark Cloud had said his wives, as well as Speaks No More's, had been killed but he had said nothing of Little Waiting Woman. Was that what the Indian had been avoiding telling him? Dread pierced his belly with the thought.

He ran to the tipi, following Dark Cloud inside. The interior smelled of burned wood and tanned hide. Chris came up short as Dark cloud stepped aside, indicating the girl lying on the bed of hides. In the dim light Chris saw her eyes were closed and her face carried a deathly pallor. Shards of bones and small medicine bags surrounded her body.

Chris couldn't move. A flood of horrible coldness washed though him.

Jesus Christ, nooo...not her, not...her...

Chris' legs went weak, threatening to spill him, and distantly he felt Dark Cloud's hand clamp about his arm, supporting him before he collapsed. He wasn't sure whether he blacked out, for there was an instant of darkness, then a deluge of images from the past. They swirled through his mind and everything about him blurred. As quickly the scenes stopped and he saw Dark Cloud's face peering intently at him in the shivery gloom of the tipi.

He jerked his arm free of the Comanche's grasp and moved to her, staggering, legs refusing to work right. Crumbling to his knees at her side, he reached out with tentative fingers, touching her cold lips and dark features, tracing the line of her nose and brushing black hair from her forehead. He drew her towards him, pressing his head against her breast beneath which a heart no longer beat, from which no breath flowed.

Lifting his head, for the briefest of moments, his gaze settled on the marks on her neck, slashes barely visible beneath a coating of powder. He had little will to think about what they were or how they had come to be there.

He turned, looking pleadingly up at Dark Cloud, searching for anything that might provide some measure of comfort. He found none. Dark Cloud's face darkened with despair and he uttered quavering words.

"There was little life within her when we found her; the Grandfather Above was not merciful. Her spirit departed moments before you came...she whispered your name before she passed."

"My name..." Chris mouthed, taking the slight comfort he'd been searching for. It was damn little, but it was something.

I should have been here...

Again guilt swarmed over him: if only he'd come sooner, been here for her, maybe he could have reached the doc in time to help, saved her life; if only he would have married her months ago instead of waiting; if only he had done the job of killing Milus Clint right.

If only.

"Goddamn you!" he shouted suddenly and the sound filled the tipi, filled the night, filled his soul. "Goddamn you, Clint!"

He threw back his head, wailing as a Comanche would for their dead, and wailing within his heart.

She's gone...

Time dragged and Chris experienced each tortured second. Around him the gloom-coated confines of the tipi faded. He wandered, lost in some dark place, floating in an abyss of sorrow laced with strings of images filled with horror and sadness. Despair, helplessness, threatened to crush him, send him spiraling into the darkness that reached for him, into insanity.

Let go...

How comforting that would be, how releasing. A place where hope was dead, maybe had never lived. How easy. He considered letting it have him, letting the Devil pick over the fragments of his soul. Cheat Clint of whatever scheme he had in mind.

No, you can't...You have to finish it...

Something inside took over, a desperate spark of self-preservation tainted with revenge. The same thing that had pulled him back those many years ago after Milus Clint destroyed his life for the first time and Uncle Clem had taken him in.

The tipi interior focused and a chilled numbness took over his mind. He clenched his teeth, staring for long moments at the Comanche girl lying before him, her face beautiful even in death. Still he didn't cry, couldn't cry, wouldn't cry and damn Clint again for shutting off the tears.

Dark Cloud placed a hand on Chris' shoulder, urging him to rise.

"There will be great pain," the Indian said, dark eyes sympathetic. "It will not end here for you. You must face it in this time or it will swallow you as the darkness swallows the sun."

Chris nodded, uncomprehending, in no mood for Indian gibberish. He turned his gaze back to the girl.

"We will bury her as a Comanche," he distantly heard Dark Cloud say behind him. "That is the way it must be."

Again Chris nodded. He took unsteady steps from the tipi. Speaks No More gazed at him with eyes laden with compassion and a trace of anger for Dark Cloud.

Chris walked into the night, collapsing to his knees at the edge of the camp. Staring out at the stream and the arroyo farther on, he waited in hushed silence while Dark Cloud carried the body of Little Waiting Woman to a bison-hide travois Speaks No More had hitched to a pony.

Dark Cloud had dressed her in her best clothes, a buckskin shirt and long full skirt, highly decorated with beads and silver and bits of glass. The beads ran in bands down each side of her clothing, fashioned with the Comanche motif, a line of square green crosses with white square centers. In Comanche custom, her brother had painted her face vermilion and daubed red clay over her eyelids.

Without words, merely a glance towards Chris, the Indian placed the body on the travois. He walked to the right and stepped into the Comanche saddle, a pad with short stirrup straps and a thong around the horse's neck that allowed the rider to hang over the side in battle.

His dark eyes centered on Chris, who stood and went to his roan.

"Many will be buried this night," Dark Cloud told him. "Many more in the nights to come. But this will be the most painful for you. Remember that and let it give you strength."

Dark Cloud kicked his pony into motion, heading towards the arroyo. Speaks No More rode beside the warrior, face grim and gaze focused straight ahead.

They followed the twisting stream and his mind dwelled on how, in the course of a few hours, his life had been turned upside down. Clem and Little Waiting Woman were gone, and any sense of innocence that might have remained in the boy of twenty-six had died with them. No going back. He carried a man's responsibilities and guilts, and it started with burying his loved ones.

They approached the arroyo. The stream angled off to the right, snaking into the growing depression. Its sides, farther on, rose in sheer palisades to either side of the stream. Scattered caves burrowed into the walls and the rock was marbled with gaping cracks, fissures that seemed to Chris to go straight to hell.

Dark Cloud drew his pony to a stop and jumped down from the saddle. Going to the back, he stopped. Speaks No More, dismounting, glanced at a crack in the cliff wall and nodded.

Chris stepped from his saddle. As Dark Cloud stooped to lift the body of Little Waiting Woman, Chris raised a hand to stop him. He went to her, bending, lifting her from the travois. He kissed her forehead and carried her to the opening. Placing her in the crevice, as he knew was custom, he set her in a flexed position to face the rising sun. Stepping back, he peered at the dark cleft that had swallowed her.

"You'll be at peace now," was all he could to say, knowing how horribly inadequate and childish it sounded, but needing to say it just the same.

"Her journey will not be peaceful," Dark Cloud said.

Chris turned to him, a prickle of coldness creeping down his spine. "What do you mean?"

"Our legends say those who pass at night will meet with great difficulty in finding their way to the Land Beyond the Sun. I pray to the Grandfather Above her journey is smooth but it is doubtful. He will not interfere with what is to be."

"She'll find her way," Chris said with irritation in his tone. He walked away, conscious of the shakiness in his legs and the heaviness in his soul. He wasn't in the mood for one of their legends right now.

Mounting, he reined around, gazing one last time at the fissure in which he'd just buried his dreams.

"You should have told him!" Speaks No More signed, anger exploding on his face now that the white boy had gone.

Dark Cloud shrugged, expression indifferent. "What good would it have done?"

"You could have warned him, prepared him, told him He Who Drinks Life will come for him."

Dark Cloud's brow furrowed. "It would further invoke the wrath of the Great Cannibal Owl. It is no longer our concern. Death has visited and left.

There will be no further visits."

"How can you say that? Death will stalk Spotted Buffalo Son. It will destroy him as it did Tay-kan-na and the rest."

"Perhaps he has brought it on himself." Dark Cloud's voice was cold and he drew his lips into a hard line.

Speaks No More made a disgusted grunt. "You are locked in the old ways, my cousin. The old ways killed many of our people at Palo Duro; the old ways refused to bend and live in harmony with what we knew would come. It is this foolish clinging that will kill more. We owe it to him to help."

"We owe him nothing!" Dark Cloud shouted, fury storming his face. "The white man has sent our people to live in squalor and confinement. We can no longer ride the Plains and feel the wind across our chest. We can no longer hunt buffalo and taste its sweet meat. For that I should help the white man? You have forgotten where your loyalties belong."

"And you have forgotten yours!" Speaks No More fired back, hands moving swiftly and sharply. "He is the son of your white brother. You saved Spotted Buffalo Man then, why do you not save his son, now?"

"I could not even if I wanted to." A certain resignation came into Dark Cloud's tone. A distant look crossed his dark features.

"You could try. Spotted Buffalo Man gave you back the freedom the others took. His son will not take it away, but if he dies others will, and we will die, too."

"I can do nothing," Dark Cloud said stubbornly and Speaks No More cursed with his hands.

"You are a fool, cousin. I have as much right to hate as any Comanche, more than you!" He touched the scar at his throat. "Yet I will help him if I can."

Dark shook his head violently. "No, I forbid it!"

Speaks No More uttered a silent laugh. "There is no longer anything for you to forbid, my cousin."

Dark Cloud glowered and spun on the ball of his foot, stalking back to his pony. He climbed into the saddle and glanced at the crevice in which Spotted Buffalo Son had placed the body of his sister.

He let out a heavy sigh, face grim. Little Waiting Woman would not find her way to the Land Beyond the Sun. Her shade would force the white boy into facing things to which his world closed their eyes. A twinge of guilt struck him and he considered doing as Speaks No More had said, helping the white boy, though he knew it would be of little use. The boy would no sooner believe what Dark Cloud told him of the Great Cannibal Owl and the dark spirits of the night as he would have had he told him the emissary of He Who Drinks Life had perished in a swirl of black flame. Spotted Buffalo Son would call it foolish Indian superstition and walk heedlessly under the frozen moon. So what good would it do? What help would it be?

None.

The boy was on his own and Dark Cloud had only his own future to consider.

Chris rode hard into the night after leaving the arroyo. Darkness spread endlessly before him, embroidered with ribbons of alabaster and swollen shadow. The wind whipped his face, his body, but he scarcely noticed its chill. In his mind he saw her face, her smile; in his heart he felt the warmth of her touch, the caressing shivers that rippled through him as she took him inside when they made love. The sorrow was nearly too much and this time the tears almost came.

Then another emotion shook him. It roared up, a dark fire in his soul, obliterating all else.

He yanked the reins, jerking the roan short, and jumped to the ground.

Anger.

Unbridled, uncontrollable, overwhelming.

Chris raised his fists to the moon, seeing Clint's face superimposed there, a grinning, skull-like thing of bone yellow. Damn him! Damn him!

Chris shook his fists and screamed with every ounce of his hate.

"You bastard! Where are you? You goddamned sonofabitch! You want me, come for me, now! I killed you once, I'll kill you again! You hear me, Clint? You hear me? Come for me, now, you coward!"

Chris fell to his knees. A sob shuddered through his body. It surprised him. He hadn't allowed himself to experience such emotion in years. And it hurt worse than any blow ever could. Tears welled in his eyes and this time they flowed, flowed as they hadn't since he was a boy. He trembled with surges of emotion, lost in grief, heedless of the chill that swept over the Plains and the howl of a coyote in the distance. Only aware of the wrenching emptiness of regret and the bleakness of hollow tomorrows.

Deep in the black heart of the arroyo, Milus Clint poised at the mouth of a cave overlooking the stream. Behind him his men sat clustered around a fire, passing around a bottle they had snatched from the saloon in Bald Creek, playing cards and cursing. Curled about the vaulted room lay the pack of coyotes that had haunted the Plains for the past few days, their glassy ebony eyes glinting with captured firelight. All except one, the mangy animal who served as Milus Clint's eyes and ears in the night.

Milus watched the clamshell-colored moon trace its way across the coal-speckled-with-diamond sky. He smiled, through the eyes of the coyote watching the Durrin boy jump from his horse and shake his fists at an uncaring moon, through its ears hearing the boy's challenge.

THE DARK RIDERS

It was a pitiful sight and Milus laughed, harder than he had in years. His plan was working right fine. He was destroying the boy, breaking him down, and soon Milus would show him what true death was like. It was not the peace of the grave, oh, no; it was being a plaything for Eternity, with no path to ride that didn't lead into darkness. No sunlight or warmth of day, and no chance at the frail useless emotions humans saw fit to chase.

"Come for me, now!" the boy had yelled, calling Milus a coward. But cowardice played no part in Milus Clint's schemes. For soon he would accept the boy's challenge. He would come. But in his own time. And not until all the pain had been savored, all the loss and anguish had been tasted.

"Not yet, boy," Milus answered to the night. "Not yet. Not until I feel your soul drip through my fingers and I let you bleed your sorrow all over this goddamned land. Not until I've taken as much from you as you have from me. Then I'll come, boy. Then I'll come..."

EIGHT

Chris slowed his horse to a trot as he approached the main house of the 7HL ranch compound. He felt weary, leaden. Grief had sapped his strength. He had no idea how long he'd knelt in the field, sobbing in the darkness. When he had pulled his face from his hands, eyes bleary and stinging from tears, the moon had jumped a handspan across the sky, and the night felt heavy with the grave-like stillness that settled over the Plains after midnight.

He had postponed riding back to the house for another hour, afraid to return and find he hadn't somehow dreamt the whole thing, the deaths and carnage that had swept over the 7HL on the wings of a demon rider named Milus Clint.

But as he had neared the house, he knew it was no dream; it was cold grim reality.

A sinking feeling of horror settled in his belly as he looked towards the bunkhouse. Blanket-covered bodies lay on the ground in front of the porch.

He noted nine forms; eight men had been in the bunkhouse, so the extra one belonged to Mrs. Tulber. Gall burned in his throat and renewed sorrow rose in his heart. He'd miss her motherly scoldings and constant fretting, the mildly disparaging frowns she'd cast him whenever he wandered in late from his couplings with Little Waiting Woman.

"And where have you been, Master Chris?" she'd say in a higher-than-usual voice that always came touched with a suppressed chuckle.

He'd grin and look sheepish and say, "Nowhere, Mrs. Tulber. Go back to bed, now." and that would be that, except for the little sideways looks she'd cast him for the next day or so.

He'd miss that powerfully.

After dismounting, Chris tethered the horse to a hitchrail and stared at the main house. The lantern still burned within, throwing butterscotch light into the yard. A tingle of apprehension skittered along his spine, but he knew by now Windy had scrubbed any evidence of blood from the stairs, wall and floor, knowing Chris needed no reminders of his loss.

His gaze lifted to the front door, which was now closed. Windy had repaired the broken hinge.

Chris glanced back at the covered bodies, a question entering his mind: Why hadn't the undertaker fetched them yet? Surely some of the men, if not all, would have returned from town by now, and just as surely Windy would have sent one back to bring the funeral man.

Clomping steps from the far end of the veranda drew his attention and he turned his head towards the sound. Windy stood there, a grim look etched across his ruddy face, eyes drawn and watery, Stetson in hand. Windy's stubby fingers pried at the hat rim and his small eyes lowered, came up.

"You awright?" The assistant foreman's voice came low, leeched of the hardy boom it usually carried.

Chris nodded, lying. "Yeah, reckon I have to be. We still got a ranch to run. I can't let Clem down."

"You know you can count on me to stand by you, son. No matter what happens." Windy's eyes shifted and he looked uncertain.

"Earlier tonight..." Chris bit his lip to stop it from quivering. "Earlier tonight I told you the best way was to just come out with it, then I snapped your head off. I was wrong to do that, Windy. Reckon I just had no belly to admit what you said was true, or hear it stated."

"Ain't no need to apologize, son. We all gots things we want to get away from. Trouble is, them things ain't always taken with the same notion. Some of them booger us till we can't see straight. Some of them chase us down like Injuns huntin' a buffalo. Sooner or later it all comes around and we realize we should have faced it right off, before our mind gave it strength, blew it into somethin' it wasn't."

Chris sighed. "Milus Clint ain't been strengthened by my memory. He was a bastard, vicious as they come, and what he did...well, you're right about some things chasin' you down. Clint chased me down and now I gotta face him."

Windy took a few steps closer, the creases on his face deepening. "Milus Clint is dead, son. It's common knowledge in New Mex. He couldn't have been here tonight. Your uncle had to be delirious that close to death."

The assistant foreman's words got under his skin, but he knew it was a by-product of his frustration and grief, so he held his tongue. Windy didn't deserve his bitterness; Milus Clint did.

"Little Waiting Woman's dead," Chris said, voice carrying less emotion than he would have thought. His innards felt strangely frozen.

Windy's lips parted in shock and his small eyes grew harder. "What?" It was almost a whisper.

"She's...one of Clint's men hit Dark Cloud's camp, killed his wives, Speaks No More's, too...and her, though I ain't rightly sure quite how. All I know is she's gone. I just buried her."

"Galldamn, I'm so awful sorry, son..." Windy's words trailed off, as if for once he had no idea what to say, then added, "You sure it was one of Clint's men?"

"Dark Cloud described the man who did it. I recognized him as Jeters, one of Clint's old gang from New Mexico."

"Dark Cloud saw him and lived to tell about it?" A note of amazement hung in Windy's voice.

"Matter of fact, he killed him. Didn't see what he did with the body. Imagine it wasn't pretty."

Windy scratched his head and again Chris got the feeling Windy had more on his mind than he was saying.

"What is it?" Chris asked straight, a sinking feeling in his belly.

"Well, I been tryin' to think of a way to say it, but for the second time tonight I ain't able to find the words. Ain't like me, you knows, but I'm startin' to think things...well, I'll let you decide."

Chris came up the stairs and stood on the veranda. "Not sure there's much you can say that could affect me any worse than what's already happened here tonight. Can't see as how I got much left to lose."

Windy frowned out of one side of his mouth. "That may be further from the truth than you think, son..." He hesitated, gaze lowering to the veranda, coming up. He eyed Chris straight. "The men came back from town...some of 'em, anyhow."

"Some of them?" Chris felt his belly knot.

"Yeah, a few didn't make it. The ones that did are powerful scart. They said some things...well, things that sound plain loco, if you ask me, but I swear to God Almighty they didn't look as though they was lyin' or drunk enough to imagine it. I think it's best if I let them tell you." Windy nodded towards the blanket-covered bodies on the lawn. "None of 'em wanted to ride back to Bald Creek and fetch the 'taker. Can't say as I blame 'em, neither."

"Where are they?" Chris swallowed at the apprehension that choked him.

"They're in the house. Go easy on 'em; they been through hell. That much is obvious."

Chris nodded and went to the door. He paused as he entered the foyer, the image of Mrs. Tulber's body rising to greet him. The illusion left him shaky.

He went into the parlor, where eight men had gathered, some sitting, some pacing, all saddled with bleached faces and frightened expressions. They looked up at him, expectant, searching for guidance. He felt suddenly inadequate to the task. How could he guide these men, now? What could he tell them that would ease their suffering when he could not even ease his own?

"What happened?" Chris's voice came shaky and he knew it wouldn't instill confidence, but he was damned if he could do anything about it.

A man stepped forward, the one named Carter, who through some collective unspoken decision would act as spokesman for the group. The man had hair the color of adobe and a face almost the same tint. Deep furrows creased his forehead.

"We were at the Blue Steer, Mr. Durrin." Carter's lips made extra movements and Chris could hear the fear in his voice. "We was just funnin' an' all, you know, drinkin' a bit, playin' some cards, a little time with the ladies...well, there wasn't no call for what happened, sir, no there wasn't." The 'hand appeared to lose control of himself, shuddering as his voice rose and broke.

"It's all right, Carter. Go on." Chris took a few steps into the room and leaned against the sofa.

The man's gaze darted to the others, none of whom met his eyes. He seemed to bring himself under control.

"Well, just that we was all windin' down from work, way we sometimes do, when these men, musta been eight or nine of 'em, came into the Steer. Now, I'm sayin' they looked like hardcases right off, but usually they just drinks like the rest of the folks in there and leave, nice and peaceful-like. It's sort of an unwritten law in Bald Creek." Carter shook his head, shuddering again. "But these fellows, well, there was something *different* 'bout 'em."

Chris felt his groin cinch. "Different? How?"

"Well, one of 'em, he looks an awful lot like that young fella from over New Mex way, the one who was causing all the ruckus durin' that range war."

Chris's brow creased. He knew who the man referred to, but it was impossible.

"That fella's dead, Carter, killed by the sheriff in Fort Sumner. Ambushed. Hear tell it was a bullet straight through the heart. It couldn't have been him."

"Yep, that's what happened, but I swear on my mother's grave it was him. Had the same cocky grin and pearl-handled Colt...he went upstairs and never came down, far as I could see."

"What about the rest?"

Carter's eyes lowered, lids fluttering and he sucked in a deep breath. A nervous tic pulled at the corner of his mouth.

"The others went up to the bar first. Ordered whiskey just like you'd think was normal. Then the leader, he up and grabs the 'keep, says somethin' to him. Don't know what it was but the 'keep looked powerful scart."

A bolt of dread shot through Chris. "What did he look like, this leader?" He braced himself for the answer, knowing what it would be, despite Windy's contrary notions.

"Well, he was a big 'un, with long twisted reddish-brown hair and eyes like a goddamn vulture. But that wasn't the worst of it. His face, least one side, was all scarred up, just sorta lumpy and kinda sunken." Carter's eyes locked with Chris's. "It was a demon face, Mr. Durrin. I don't mind tellin' ya that. I ain't never seen the likes of it."

Chris glanced at Windy, whose face had cinched, but was shaking his head in denial. "Clint..." he mouthed, knowing it couldn't be, yet knowing it was. He could deny it all he wanted, but it wouldn't change the fact that somehow Milus Clint had escaped death six years ago in New Mexico and had returned to get even.

"It's not possible, son." Windy said it as if he were still fighting to convince himself of the fact. But the evidence was mounting. Uncle Clem had uttered Clint's name and now the ranchhand had described the outlaw. Dark Cloud had killed one of Clint's men.

Chris pulled from his thoughts as Carter's voice came again. "This fellow, he suddenly decides to take one of the doves upstairs. Then the others with him, they did the same. Things got quiet-like after they all went up, then we heard this horrible screeching, like dyin' animals, only it was comin' from the girls. After a spell, this outlaw fellow, he comes onto the landing carryin' the dove's body." The man stopped, as if stricken by the memory of the sight. He licked his lips. "I'm here to tell ya, I never thought I'd see nothin' the likes of what he did to that girl."

"Go on." Chris's voice came almost too weak to hear.

"Well, he had torn all her clothes off and her neck..." The man gulped. "Well, it was mostly gone. Looked like an animal had chewed on it."

Chris closed his eyes, took a deep slow breath, opened them. Carter had commenced to shaking and took a flask from his coat, swallowing a couple of gulps to calm himself before returning it to his pocket.

"He threw her, Mr. Durrin. Just heaved her up like she was nothin' and threw her clean over the rail. Most vicious disrespect of the dead I ever seen, even from an outlaw. Then he jumped over the rail himself and landed like a cat in the middle of the barroom. The other 'cases came down after, and as God is my witness, not a one 'cept that first kid carried a gun. Ain't never seen balls like that on no outlaw. Mostly cowards at heart, they are, but not these fellows."

Chris had to agree: most outlaws wouldn't mix it up without their irons, except possibly Milus Clint. Chris recalled the outlaw never carried a gun, or if he did never used it. Milus toted a vicious whip called a blacksnake, leaving his men to back him up with lead.

"What happened to them after that?" Chris tried to keep himself focused so he wouldn't come apart.

The man gave a violent shudder and glanced at the other men, all of whom seemed to have developed a fascination with various parts of the room or their boots.

"Damnedest thing, Mr. Durrin. This here fellow's eyes turned black as coal, only you could see little bolts of black light deep down in 'em. Like you was starin' into hell itself. Then the leader hissed."

"Hissed?" Surprise crossed Chris' face. That wasn't a trait he recalled from his previous tangle with Clint.

"Hissed, like a goddamn snake or somethin'...This next part...well, I know it sounds loco, but I swear it's true. I wasn't in my cups, Mr. Durrin, but this fellow had teeth like a goddamn coyote. Long and sharp, curvedlike. So did the rest of 'em."

Chris's brow furrowed. He didn't know what to make of the man's statement. Carter, he felt sure, wasn't lying, nor had he likely imagined what had happened. He hadn't been drunk, either. His disbelief must have shown because the 'hand stepped closer, face growing as serious as he had ever seen any man's.

"I'm tellin' you straight, Mr. Durrin. I swear I am."

"It's not that I don't believe you, Carter. After tonight I got no idea what to think. But the man you described was picked clean by buzzards. No way he could have lived through what happened." Chris' voice steadied as he fell into the comfortable role of foreman doling out orders to his men or just hearing their beefs.

"You gotta believe me, Mr. Durrin. 'Cause if you don't this fellow will have the up on you and you'll be gone 'fore you know it, just like the rest of the boys tonight."

"What happened to them?" Chris braced himself, already knowing.

"One of the fellas, can't rightly recollect which one, now, said somethin' about those hardcases not carryin' iron. Next thing I know is we's in a fight and men are droppin' like heel-flies at the end of a switch. Some got shots off..." The man hesitated, eyes pleading for belief. "But they didn't have no effect."

Chris's gaze jumped to the empty wall pegs, where Clem kept his scatter-gun, as if he had noticed something out of place on a subconscious level and the 'hand's statement had brought it to the surface.

He pushed himself away from the sofa and walked across the room. Scanning the floor, he knelt, spotting the shotgun that lay half-concealed by the chair. He sniffed the barrel and checked the loads.

Empty.

His gaze came up and traveled around the room, searching the walls and floor for evidence of where the shot had penetrated. He saw none and looked at Windy.

"It's been fired, both barrels. No sign of it hitting anything here, though. Clem must have shot whatever he was aimin' at."

Windy shook his head slightly. "If that was so, there'da been an extra body here tonight, or at least some blood."

"No, there wouldn't have been," Carter cut in. "That's what I'm tellin' you." The man's face brightened by the slim evidence Chris had discovered to support his statements.

Confusion clouded Chris's mind. He saw no explanation for it. If Clem had missed, Chris would see shot embedded in the walls or furniture. If he had hit his target, the outlaw would be dead or seriously wounded. But there was nothing and that bothered him at some level he couldn't understand.

His eyes locked with Carter's. "What you're sayin' is these men can't be killed by lead." Chris said it before he could think about how ridiculous it sounded. "Not a man on God's Earth who can't be brought down by Mr. Colt."

"Is now, Mr. Durrin. I swear to it there is. 'Cause these fellas just kept a'comin' till they butchered half the saloon. And me and the men here..." Guilt washed into the man's eyes. "We're ashamed to say it, but we ran out the back and rode straight and fast for here, never lookin' back. If we hadn't..." Carter shook again and Chris felt sympathy rise for him and the rest of the 'hands. They weren't cowards, these men. They were honest, hardworking and rugged men, full of piss and vinegar and for them to have run...well, Chris knew firsthand the effect Clint could have on a body.

"Don't blame yourself." Chris made his voice as assuring as he could under the circumstances. "If you'd stayed you'd be dead. That's how Clint works. He ain't likely to let no one live 'less he's got some purpose behind it."

"Thanks, Mr. Durrin. You don't know how much better that makes me feel. Them dead are gonna haunt me all the same for a spell. No way 'round it."

Chris took silent a moment. If it were true, if Clint had somehow survived the events of six years ago and returned for revenge, Chris had to turn it around on the hardcase. He couldn't explain the things the ranchhand had told him, but if he had any chance to get a jump on the butcher who had murdered his uncle and Little Waiting Woman, he had to do it before Clint came back for him.

He glanced at Windy, who seemed to catch what he had in mind, and though the assistant foreman didn't appear to care for it, he would not desert Chris. Chris looked at each 'hand in turn.

"I got something to say to you men." Chris kept his tone steady and dead serious. "I won't blame a one of you for takin' up his gear and headin' to another outfit if that's your mind. But there's work a'plenty to do 'round here with the sunrise, corrals to mend and horses to round up. Spring roundup and a trail drive are on the horizon, and the possibility of a rustler nipping at our flanks. Those who want to stay on got a bonus comin' to 'em. I'll need you all and extras for that, plus for what I'm about to say."

The men, tension and fear on their faces, looked at him steadily. Not a one moved nor spoke.

"I want the hardcases who came here tonight. I want them dead or linin' up for a necktie party. I aim to ride into town and see if I can't find a lead to them before they take a notion to come after me—Windy?" Chris turned to the *segundo* and the red-headed man nodded.

"I'm with you, son. I think you might be makin' a mistake doin' it so soon 'fore you've had a chance to sort things out, but I'm beside you."

Chris looked back to the men. Carter spoke up. "I'm with you, too, Mr. Durrin. What I seen tonight, well, it makes me think some things, like tryin' to do somethin' for them fellas that was kilt and maybe 'tendin' church a little more regular. I ain't a coward, sir, but I'm here to tell ya, I'm downright backass scart."

Chris nodded. "I am, too. Of a lot of things."

Another man stood from the chair and looked sheepishly at Chris. "I ain't no coward, neither, Mr. Durrin, but if it's all the same to you I'll be collectin' my pay and headin' out with first light. Got me a girl over in Amarilla and, hell, I got a whole life ahead of me. These things I seen, I just as soon forget they ever happened."

Chris moved over to the wall safe behind a picture and spun the dial until the door swung open. From a stack of greenbacks he counted out a month's pay, thirty dollars, then added another five. He handed it to the man, who tried to smile and Chris patted him on the shoulder.

"You need a recommendation you send them to me. Ain't no slight on your nerve. If I had a choice, I'd probably ride out myself." The man plainly knew Chris wouldn't, but didn't say a word.

Chris gave the rest of the 'hands a look, paid those who wanted to leave, then went to a case and broke out seven Winchesters. He handed one to each remaining man, keeping one for himself and one for Windy. He went to his room upstairs and found his gunbelt, buckled it on. He checked the Colt's chamber, satisfied, replacing the gun in its holster. He seldom carried the piece. No cowboy in his right mind worked with a heavy iron at his hip. But he was damn good with the gun, had spent hours practicing on cans and bottles in the field. He prayed he'd get a chance to put another bullet in Milus Clint, one that would bury the hardcase this time for sure.

Chris went back downstairs. Windy had already gathered the men and their mounts outside. Chris nodded to them and jammed a boot into the stirrup, hoisting himself into the saddle.

"You sure you wanna do this, son?" Windy eyed him with concern. "You seem a mite unsteady with all that's happened."

"I'm as stable as I'm gonna get. If I have a chance to nail Clint before he can get on with whatever scheme he's got in mind, I have to take it."

"Still can't see it bein' him. And that other fella, the young one Carter was talkin' about, can't see that, neither. It's like we're trailin' a bunch of ghosts."

"We damn well might be." Chris's lips drew into a tight line. Ghosts, all right, shades that had haunted him for too damn long.

They rode for town, Chris, Windy and five nervous ranchhands with more balls than any ten men. The chill air swept over Chris, making him shiver, half from cold, half from anticipation. Going after Clint gave him a focus, a direction, and he clung to it desperately. He gave no thought to what he would do if he found the hardcase, nor to the incredible claims of the cowhands about Clint's—and his gang's—invulnerability. He didn't care to; all he focused on was the outlaw leader, bringing him down; how didn't matter.

The town came into view and he slowed the horse, peering at Bald Creek as if the Devil had opened the doors to Hell and invited him in.

He's not there...

The notion struck him and he had no idea why he felt that way. But with gnawing certainty, his gut told him Clint was miles away by now, absorbed into the dark reaches of the night, waiting to strike in his own time. He s'posed he had known all along Clint had quit the town, but the slim hope of finding him had kept him steady and purposeful. He would cling to it till the last.

As a surge of determination rode his veins, he spurred his horse faster, the men following suit.

When they rode into town, they could see the damage the gang had left behind. Chris spotted shattered windows and spouting troughs, collapsed awnings and piles of clothing stamped beneath horses' hooves, broken railings and the smoking gutted remains of a dress shop.

His attention lingered on the small cemetery and the little white church next to it. He averted his gaze, uneasy. He had never cared for cemeteries and after tonight he found them even more distasteful.

He slowed his horse to a walk, Windy riding up beside him, eyes darting back and forth in their sockets.

"Looks like they left their calling card awright," the *segundo* said in a troubled voice. "Place is pretty tored up."

"Reckon I expected as much."

"Look!" Carter shouted, jabbing a finger at the Blue Steer Saloon. Their heads turned in that direction and Chris felt a surge of cold dread. Lanterns hung outside the saloon; they threw sickly amber light over a gruesome spectacle of death and the stricken faces of the men milling about. The sheriff—who stepped into the saloon—and the undertaker, Chris recognized; he assumed the rest consisted of part-time deputies and townsfolk. A few women, trembling hands held to their mouths, were crying, wandering aimlessly about. Along the boardwalk a line of covered and uncovered bodies extended to the end of the block.

Chris uttered a strangled sound. His innards felt knotted. Clucking his tongue and flicking the reins, he sent his mount towards the hitch rail. After dismounting, he tethered the animal and grabbed his Winchester, the others following his lead. They trailed him as he walked up to the undertaker. The man, a balding fellow in his early fifties, looked up at him and shook his head. His face appeared white and drawn.

"Horrible, son," he said, voice strained. "Just horrible. Never seen so many dead 'uns 'cept in a war."

Chris tried to nod, struggling to keep himself from shuddering. "I hate to make it worse, but we've got some more out on the 7HL. The killers hit there first."

"Clem?" Dread flooded the undertaker's tone. Chris knew his uncle and the 'taker had done business together and were on friendly terms.

Chris nodded, eyes fluttering closed a second, opening. "We buried him on the land. He wanted it that way."

The undertaker's brow crinkled and his eyes narrowed with a pained look. "Reckon he would. I'm sorry, son, truly I am. I'll send a wagon to collect the others."

Chris thanked him and moved towards the Blue Steer's batwing doors. He noticed the cowhands forcing themselves not to look at the shrouded bodies.

As he entered the saloon, Chris's grip tightened on the Winchester. The heaviness of death filled the atmosphere, and the room held the feeling of an abattoir. He swore he felt an odd coldness in the room, an after-feeling of the slaughter. In his mind he could imagine the bodies strewn about, throats ripped out as Mrs. Tulber's had been, and the gloating features of Milus Clint.

He scanned the few men in the barroom and went up to the sheriff, a burly fellow named Tolby with a reputation for a fast gun and a low threshold of ambition where justice was concerned. Tolby allowed most crime to flourish in Bald Creek—as long as he got his cut. Folks, who saw fit to issue the lawdog challenge tended to meet with a higher than usual incidence of back-shooting.

The sheriff normally carried a habitual expression of unconcern, but this time he looked different. As Chris' gaze met the sheriff's, he saw it on the lawman's face; the slaughter had disturbed even him. He ambled about as if he didn't know what to do, how to handle the situation.

"Sheriff." Chris stepped closer. The man looked at Chris with a semi-lost expression.

"Yeah?" Tolby's gaze lowered to Chris's Winchester, then skipped to the men with him, each armed and each concealing a panic at having to be back in the barroom. His dull eyes narrowed, a measure of bravado setting in.

Chris got right to the point. "I came here for the man who did this."

An amused look touched the sheriff's face. "You're that Durrin boy, ain't ya? Uncle owns that big spread north of here, the 7HL."

"Owned," Chris corrected, somberness lowering his voice.

The sheriff nodded, understanding. "Well, you ain't likely to find the gang who did this. They done pulled stakes after runnin' the town to hell."

"Town was already run to hell," Windy said in a sarcastic tone.

Tolby cocked an eyebrow. "Then these fellas added a double helpin' of brimstone."

"Anyone see what direction they headed?" Chris asked.

"Hell, no! If they had, they'd be lyin' on the boardwalk under a blanket, now, wouldn't they?"

"You intend to track 'em?" Chris held Tolby's gaze. The look that crossed the lawman's eyes told everything; the question was pointless.

"Best leave well enough alone, I figure. Them hardcases is gone. Hopefully they won't never see fit to come back. I'm partial to it that way." Something sparked in the lawman's eyes, something that looked suspiciously like fear. Had the sheriff seen the men who had done this? Chris was willing to bet he had. The same look of residual fear lived in the eyes of his own men.

His eyes narrowed. "You saw those men, didn't you?"

The sheriff shifted feet, gaze flicking to the floor, coming up. "I didn't see nothin'. Wasn't around when it happened. Just rode in a short spell ago." Tolby was lying and Chris knew it. It was in his manner and in his voice—he *had* seen those men.

"You lily-livered—" Windy blurted, apparently sensing the same thing, but Chris held up a hand. Sheriff Tolby glared at Windy, as if ready to go for his gun. The lawman wasn't one to push. Rumor had it he had gunned down more than one unarmed man.

"Best watch that attitude, mister," Tolby said to Windy, threat icy in his tone. Windy gave a half-smirk, unperturbed.

"Did Milus Clint do this?" Chris put it bluntly and eyed the sheriff, searching, but couldn't read the look Tolby gave him.

"Like I told you, I just rode in." The sheriff's gaze shifted to the Winchesters in the men's grips, back to Chris. "You best be careful with them things, boy. I got me enough dead men for a spell. Wouldn't want you and your bunch to go stirrin' somethin' up. Things might get touchy in Bald Creek for a spell. Folks'll be itchy. They won't need an excuse to fire at shadows." With that the sheriff moved off, heading towards the outside.

"Lyin' through his teeth." Windy looked at Chris with disgust.

Chris struggled with a heavy sense of disappointment. He had known deep down the outlaw would have cleared out before he got here, but that hadn't stopped him from building his hopes. Now, those hopes were gone and along with them probably any chance at finding a lead to Clint tonight.

Carter stepped up, nodding towards the batwings. "Windy's right, Mr. Durrin. I saw the sheriff skidaddlin' for his office when me an' the boys ran out the back. You ask me, he didn't want no part of it."

"I suspect you're right." Chris surveyed the saloon, despair welling within him. He spotted shards of broken bottles and shattered chairs and tables, but little blood, though here and there he saw a patch of stained sawdust and board. Some blood had spilled, but not nearly the amount he would have expected from such a slaughter.

His gaze traveled to the stairs leading to the upper rooms, drawn there by heavy footfalls. Two men descended, carrying a sheet-wrapped body. Chris swallowed hard, shaken by the sight, but forcing himself to move over to the men. A name touched his lips: Matalija. He stopped them, pulling the sheet back from the girl's face, a silent prayer on his lips. Relief made him weak.

It's not her...

He let out the breath he was holding and replaced the sheet. The men carried the girl outside.

"You're worried about that filly you been sneakin' in here to see, ain't you?" Windy gave a sympathetic smile and Chris nodded.

"She's just a whore, Windy, but I saw a sweetness to her the times I came here. I seen my fill of death tonight and I got no wish to see her that way, but I gotta know."

Windy nodded. "Let's go on up, then. Has to be done."

"Yeah, it does." Chris turned and went to the bottom of the stairs, hesitating, hand on the rail. He stared up the stairs, drawing in a deep breath, then went up, each step a labor.

Walking along the gloom-filled hallway, he noticed all the doors to the rooms were wide open. Stopping, taking in another deep breath and holding it, he peered into the first room, finding it empty. Moving on to the next, he discovered the reason for the screams the men had described. A dove was sprawled naked across a small table, neck gaping open as if some wild cat or bear had torn into it. Scrapes and signs of a beating shown plainly on her twisted body. Her eyes were wide open, staring sightlessly with a look of utter terror and horrible pain.

"Jesus!" Chris had to turn away, nausea welling. Bile rushed into his throat and he swallowed against it, barely managing to keep his belly down. The sight of that girl's mutilated body was one he wouldn't soon forget. One of many to be added to the list of brutal deaths he had seen tonight.

He backed out of the doorway and saw the men behind him shift feet, eyes darting, lips mouthing silent prayers. They were close to breaking; it would take damn little to push them over the edge. Feeling the same sense of instability, Chris shook his head to spare them the sight in the room.

"Stay here," he told them and not a man hid the relieved glint in his eyes.

Windy ignored the instructions and followed Chris. Each open room they came to repeated the scene of the first, or worse. Another broken body, another throat ripped wide. Again Chris noticed curiously little blood. He would have expected the walls to be painted with it. He'd seen cows slaughtered before, knew the gruesome results, and he had seen what a mountain cat could do to flesh and bone. Always a copious amount of blood was spilled. Yet he saw nary a drop here.

"Hell of a sight," Windy muttered beside him and Chris could see the assistant foreman's composure wavering.

They came to the last room. Oddly this was the only door closed. Chris stopped, unmoving and silent for dragging seconds. The pause seemed to get to Windy and the cowhand moved nervously from one foot to the other.

The red-headed man cleared his throat. "What is it, son?"

"This was her room..." Chris heard his voice sound from far away, as if it were not even coming out of his mouth. "Least it was..."

"None of them other girls...?"

"No. She wasn't among them." Although Chris found himself morbidly relieved that none of the murdered doves were Matalija, he prepared himself for the worst. His hand shook, grew damp, as he gripped the glass knob and set the door swinging inward. His heart pounded, thundering in his ears.

The soft yellow glow of a low-turned lantern filled the room. His gaze took in the surroundings, traveling from the four poster bed to the dresser, then to the vanity and small table holding a wash basin. Relief caught in his throat.

She's not here...

"Maybe there's a chance she got out, son." Windy looked plainly relieved at not finding another body.

"With what happened, I don't see how she could have unless she wasn't here in the first place."

"You thinks she was under one of the blankets outside?"

Chris shook his head. "No, all of the bodies were too big to be a woman. Reckon I was unconsciously lookin' when we rode in."

"I 'spected you were."

Chris closed the door, breathing evenly to calm himself. He and Windy went back to the men waiting at the other end of the hall.

"Might as well head back," Chris eyed his men. "Clint's gone and there's nothing we can do here that ain't bein' 'tended to already."

He got no argument. They followed him and Windy down to the street, visibly thankful to be out of the barroom and away from the bodies. Gaining their mounts, Chris and Windy turned to see the sheriff casting them a look of riddance. They reined around and headed for the 7HL.

NINE

When the ash-colored light of false dawn dappled the horizon, Chris Durrin swung his feet out of bed. He sat on the edge, face in his hands, listening to the sounds of silence and the twittering of morning birds. Their gaiety seemed somehow obscene after the events of the past night.

The gray cast brightened and a blaze of orange-red splashed the low-hanging clouds and swabbed the distant hills with color. Chris pushed himself to his feet and went to the French doors that led to the balcony. Opening them, he drew in a deep breath of brisk air. Orange-red dawn brightened into blazing yellow. The sky turned to a dome of glittering sapphire and the surrounding countryside carried a peaceful sense that belied the slaughter that had occurred just a few hours earlier.

But Chris Durrin felt no peace.

When he'd at last collapsed into bed, a bit over two hours ago, he'd not expected to sleep. What rest he did get confined itself to snatched moments in which he floated in a half-dreaming, half-waking series of shady images and ghostly pain. It would jerk him awake, leave him shaking, frightened, searching the corners of his room for things hiding in shadows.

The sunrise did little to dispel that feeling, but it was a damn sight better than darkness. With the dawn he felt a lessening of the cold apprehension that plagued him throughout the night.

Chris stared out towards the hills studded with piñon, near where the Box H had commenced operations. For an instant, his mind skipped back into the familiar pattern of worrying about the ranch and the workday ahead.

He felt strangely comfortable in that groove, but, then, he reckoned he always had. After the deaths of his parents, and his sister at the orphanage, he had forced himself to bury the aching sadness, jumping boots first into Uncle Clem's business. It wasn't easy, especially before Clem adopted him. Many times he nearly lost the battle. Finally he managed by turning his face from the past, denying it. Not completely, but enough. Why should now be any different?

It was in one respect: this time he would find Milus Clint and see to it there were no mistakes. He would see the outlaw at the end of a rope or with a bullet in his black heart.

He closed the doors and went to the dresser, atop which sat a porcelain wash basin. He splashed cool water into his face and toweled off. He dressed, then went to his bedroom door. Opening it, he stepped out into the hall.

The house seemed filled with ghosts. Honey-colored light streaked through the hall windows. Dust pirouetted within the shafts, making the hall appear spectral, eerie in ways he wouldn't have noticed before death visited this house. Everything felt different, somehow, changed: the way the light fell across the patterned rug, the way it gathered along the walls, the way the air seemed leaden and deathly still. It made him feel as if he had stepped into another world, one of gloom and sorrow, emptiness. Nothing lived in this world; nothing laughed.

He paused before the door leading to his uncle's room. It was closed and on any other day he would have heard his uncle stomping around inside, preparing for the day's chores. But no sound came from the room, now, and the ghosts seemed to thicken in the hallway.

Chris opened the door, hand quaking a bit, and peered inside. Topaz light glossed everything, the polished floorboards and unturned blankets on the huge feather bed, turned the water in the washbasin to shimmering gold. The emptiness of the room reached out for Chris and for a frozen moment he saw his uncle sitting on the edge of the bed, barrel chest pushed out in a yawn big enough to swallow a longhorn. Chris almost laughed and a smile touched his lips. He could hear his uncle's booming voice ring out: "Come on, boy! Get a move on. We got beeves to brand!"

Chris felt tears welling in his eyes and quickly stepped out of the room. He closed the door and pressed his back against it. He had damn near let his guard down. He swallowed hard. This wouldn't end; he knew it. No matter how much he immersed himself in the ranch duties, or forced himself not to think about it. The memory of his uncle was not the only ghost waiting to haunt him. There was another, that of a lovely Indian girl whom he had held in the silky darkness of the night and promised himself he would marry. Her memory would be there the next time his defenses dropped. He was even less prepared to deal with that.

He forced himself to go down the hall, legs shaky but steadying somewhat as he concentrated on ranch duties.

He descended the long staircase, heard the clangs and curses of roused men. None of the cowhands, or Windy, had wanted to sleep in the bunkhouse after what happened to the others. Chris didn't blame them. They had gathered their bedrolls and spread them about the parlor floor after pushing the furniture back.

The dining room was a flurry of activity and Chris could hear the playful curses of men setting themselves for the day's work. They were giving it their best, focusing on the routine, no one mentioning the events in the saloon.

In the dining room, on the hand-hewn table, a row of galvanized basins had been set out. Two 'hands were washing their faces and wetting down their hair. Others scrubbed their teeth with powder sprinkled on their index finger. All had dressed. From the haggard looks on their faces, Chris reckoned none had slept.

"Just in time, son!" Chris heard Windy bellow from the kitchen. He was busy scraping over-cooked bacon out of a skillet atop the cast iron stove and stirring warmed-over beans in a big pot. The assistant foreman then scooped the beans and bacon into plates he had set out on the long table. Chris devoured the meal with a voraciousness that he usually couldn't muster this early, especially for Windy's grub.

The cowhands finished their breakfast, oddly silent as they ate. Usually mornings rang with gusty laughter and good old-fashioned bitching, but the men now appeared locked in the prison of their own thoughts. They filed out to attend to chores while Chris and Windy made a half-hearted attempt at scraping the dishes clean.

Outside, the warm brassy sunlight touched Chris's face, made him feel as if his feet were on somewhat more solid ground.

An hour passed. Much needed to be done today. Men set to fixing the damaged corrals and holding pens. Carter, the outfit's best roper, took two men to go after the escaped horses. The carcasses of the dead horse and the steer in the field were gathered and burned. If a rabid animal had gotten to them he didn't want to take any chances contaminating the rest of the stock.

As the day dragged on, the air grew hot; heat waves rippled on the grassy horizon. Sweat beaded on Chris's brow and trickled down his face. It made him feel almost normal, a part of the land and of life.

Windy rode back in about noon. He had gone to a nearby town, searching for extra 'hands to hire on, coming back with five men. Windy had told them straight out what had happened, but they were men of grit and had elected to sign on just the same. It made the load easier, but it still wasn't enough. They would need extra experienced riders with the roundup approaching.

Chris turned his mind towards the upcoming cattle drive. The Canadian was receding and within another week it would be time. Twenty-five-hundred head of cantankerous beeves needed to be gathered and pointed towards the Western Trail, which angled up through Indian Territory to the railhead at Dodge City.

Chris could hear the bawling beeves in his mind, taste the dust and sweat of the trail, but the gnawing thought that Clem wouldn't be accompanying them spoiled some of his expectation. Although a dirty back-breaking business, Chris had always looked forward to and enjoyed the drive.

Windy spent half an hour helping the men set up temporary bunking in the main house parlor. Furniture was carried out and stored in one of the sheds and bunks were lined up against the walls. Chris knew it would do the men's morale no good if they were forced back into the bunkhouse too soon.

Windy trotted his horse up to Chris a short time later and eyed the younger man. His rubicund features appeared even redder from the beating sunlight; his freckles stood out like brown ink blots on cream paper.

"You holdin' up?" Windy asked and Chris felt a spike of emotion stab his belly.

"Yeah, well as can be expected, I reckon."

Windy studied him. Chris got the notion Windy was leading up to something.

"What is it?" A slight frown tugged at Chris's lips.

A hint of worry showed in Windy's eyes. "Something caught my eye, when I was on my way to town to look for men."

Chris almost chuckled "Caught your eye? Bet it was a round about path you took that just happened to meander past the Box H spread."

Windy let a grin turn his mouth and squinted. "You know me too well, son. You gots it pegged right. I just happened to ride near the Box H, and lo and behold we got ourselves a few more steers missin'."

Chris was skeptical. "Better'n two-thousand head on this spread, Windy. I reckon I don't even quite know the exact number. You couldn't notice a few gone."

"Two-thousand-fifty-three and like I told you, I practically know the stock by name. It's a peculiar facet of my memory, I reckon, but this time it was upwards of twenty gone."

"More than twenty?" Surprise turned his features and he was glad to have his mind focused towards ranch business. "But we turned back those wanderers last night."

"Welp, someone got up mighty early and lured them back. I reckon it was Shinn or that breed. With all the commotion goin' on ain't likely we would have even noticed."

"You see them beeves over there?"

"I got closer this time, saw some downright blotted brands, ones maybe they made a mistake on, plus the regular Box H. Some of them steers were mavericks, you gotta figure. I know they's ours, but I couldn't prove it. The blotted ones, well, they say a little more."

"But not enough to hang a man," Chris muttered.

"Not in your book maybe. Mine...I ain't so particular."

Chris considered it. Maybe Shinn proved just the diversion he needed to keep his mind off the deaths of Clem and Little Waiting Woman.

He gazed at Windy, a measure of confidence taking him, steeling him. "Have some of the new men go lookin' for mavericks, 'specially in that direction. We need the rest of the men on those runaway horses, but I want those unbranded steers in a holding pen by darkfall." Chris pointed to a pen with a branding chute, a narrow passageway formed of stakes and poles and a removable cross piece through which steers could be hazed for branding; he preferred that to the rope-and-take-down method practiced but some cowhands. "And tell them to make sure any others found in that direction are turned back."

Windy nodded. "I'll get to it. You want me leadin' 'em?"

Chris shook his head. "No. Just pick the best man and tell him to give the orders. Then come back here."

Windy nodded and headed towards the main house. Chris in the meantime saddled his roan, then went into the house and collected his Winchester, slid it into the saddleboot, and waited for Windy to return.

Windy came back a short while later and Chris stepped into the saddle. The red-headed man gave Chris a quizzical look.

"We're gonna have ourselves little visit with Shinn. I want a closer look at him and his operation."

"You sure you're up to that?" Windy eyed him seriously. "You went through a heap last night. You ain't had any sleep I can tell of and already you're goin' out to challenge a possible rustler. Maybe your head ain't so clear and if Shinn gots his hands in our stock he's apt to be somewhere south of friendly. You'll need your wits about you, if you know what I mean."

"I ain't a boy no more, Windy," Chris snapped, a glint of anger in his eyes. He knew Windy caught the meaning but wasn't about to be intimidated by it. "I grew up a lot with Clem and I can handle the ranch and its problems."

"Ain't sayin' you can't, son. But I am sayin' the way you're actin' ain't quite natural. You lost two people you loved last night, plus Mrs. Tulber and some damn fine men. You gots it all bottled up, the way you gots that habit of doin' and it ain't gonna get no better if you put off dealin' with it."

Chris recoiled inside, anger rising more to cover his hurt than at anything Windy had said. "I don't really need you tellin' me how to deal with my grief. We all handle it in our own way and this is the way I choose."

Windy frowned. "What I'm sayin' is I think you ran from something before and that's fine. But you can't run forever. Take it from someone who knows. I been down some wrong paths in my life and I done my best to make amends. But I know someday somethin' might come chasin' me and when it does I gotta come clean and hope for the best."

"I'll keep that in mind, but right now I got a rustler to look after." Chris shifted his attention straight ahead, indicating the conversation had gone as far as he would let it. He fought to clear the emotion clogging his throat. It galled him more because Windy was dead right. But he wouldn't let it sway his decision.

Windy let out a long sigh and reached into his pocket. He brought out a battered Bible and patted it. "Look, son, I ain't one to preach none, you know that. But there's lots of comfort in here. It's done me a powerful lot of good since a time I'd just as soon forget."

Chris eyed Windy again, saw the compassion in his eyes and some of his anger melted. "Comfort?" Chris hawked and spat. "In God? You expect me to take comfort in a God who has always seen fit to take away the folks I love?" Chris's face tightened, jaw muscles knotting. He wasn't in any mood to make peace with a God who took His vindictive wrath out in folks' lives. The Bible spoke of peace and forgiveness, yet on the same hand told of the destruction an angry God could bring at His slightest-whim.

"T'wasn't God who took them, son. You gotta believe that. T'was somethin' much darker. God didn't put us here to take things way from us, and He don't interfere with the one who does."

"You talking 'bout the Devil, Windy? That makes even less sense to me than the way folks' lives go to hell."

"I'm talkin' about darkness, son, the darkness that rode in here last night. 'Cause if Milus Clint is responsible for what happened, it was darkness that sent him. I can't tell you how I know, but Clint was a dead man six years ago and I reckon he still is."

Windy tucked his Bible back into his pocket and gazed ahead. Above the sun had slipped a few notches farther into the heart of the afternoon and a slight breeze skirted the grass. Clouds the color of clam shells hung low on the horizon and Chris wondered if it would be followed by the black clouds of a thunderstorm later on.

"We best be ridin'." Chris tried to keep the anger from his voice.

"Yeah, we best," Windy echoed with resignation. Chris knew it wouldn't be the last time his friend tried to talk to him about last night, and he dreaded the next time it would come up.

TEN

The Box H squatted on a section of the Plains broken by slow-rising hills sprinkled with scraggly grass and clumps of mesquite. It flanked the outer reaches of the 7HL, where it skirted the Canadian, cutting off the cocklebur outfit from the river in an irregular arc.

By whim of nature, the terrain on which the Box H sat had always been reluctant to support a cattle spread. But Jacob Shinn had moved in and set up shop despite the dissuasive arguments of Clem and the adjacent outfits.

Chris wondered if other outfits in range of the Box H had noticed missing cattle. He doubted other brands would be as easily changed to a Box H as the 7HL's. That led Chris to take the notion Shinn was up to more than simple rustling.

The Box H itself was a shoddy affair, small by Plains' standards. Chris spotted a couple of corrals, a handful of horses, a shed or two, plus a main house of plank. He saw no cowhands about and the few cattle in evidence seemed inclined towards 7HL grazing lands, though someone had thrown up a haphazard fence for just that exigency.

"Looks deserted," Windy muttered, slowing his horse as Chris slowed his.

Chris nodded. "Certainly not the bluster of activity you'd expect near roundup time."

"Crooked as all hell, if you ask me. Look at them steers. They're ours; I'm sure of it."

Chris's gaze followed Windy's pointing finger. He reckoned Windy was on the mark, but Chris was the first to admit he didn't have the memory for individual longhorns that Windy did.

He trotted closer to the small bunch of steers eyeing him nervously and drew up, focusing on the odd Box H brand seared into the steers' hides. If the 7HL brand had been altered, it was an expert job, but he'd heard of brand artists who could make you believe a brindle was blue.

"Could be..." Chris admitted, non-committal.

"Could be—hell! They's our cattle. I'd stake my life on it!"

The levering of a shell into a rifle chamber froze them in their saddles. Their heads turned in unison, to see a man garbed in trousers and a dirty undershirt leveling a Winchester at their back. The man stood on the porch of the plank house, dark complexion stubbled with a two or three-day growth of beard, eyes dull with alcohol. Tobacco stains spotted his undershirt and teeth, while his belly drooped over his belt line. His black hair was stringy and uncombed.

Jacob Shinn; Chris recognized him from the one time he had seen the man in town. But the recognition went deeper than that. He had encountered the man before, sometime, somewhere; he felt sure of it.

"What the hell you doin' near my goddamn cows?" came Shinn's gruff waxy voice. Chris detected a slur, along with a challenge that dared him to make a wrong move.

Chris was taken aback. He hadn't expected this. He had expected to confront the rancher, question him about cattle, put him on the defensive. Not to be threatened right off the mark. The reaction was out of line for a legitimate rancher. If Chris needed any more proof of Windy's accusations, Shinn's behavior provided it.

Chris's gaze drilled the man, trying not to let his unease show on his face or in his voice. "We're from the 7HL. We just came to talk."

"What the hell do you think you're doin' pointin' that galldamn thing at us?" Windy blurted and Chris suddenly got the impression Windy was gearing up to charge the man, despite the menacing Winchester.

Shinn squinted, peering at Windy with a mixture of anger and puzzlement. "I know you?" he asked, arching an eyebrow.

"Could ask you the same question," Windy returned in a solid voice.

Shinn nudged his head. "I seen you somewhere before. Ain't sure where, but I'll place it sooner or later—you, too, Durrin." Shinn shifted his sights to Chris.

"You know who I am?" Chris edged his horse a few steps closer.

"Oh, yeah, I know. I seen ya 'round, 'long with that uncle of your'n."

"Well, since we're all so familiar with each other, how 'bout those steers yonder? They look right familiar to me, too." Chris eyed the man intently.

"Do they, now?" Shinn's voice carried an edge of sarcasm and dull amusement. "Lots of them critters look alike, don't they? You got a name for each an' every one of 'em?"

Chris wanted to say Windy probably did, but restrained himself. Shinn's manner was deliberately obstinate, bating.

Chris's attention snapped left, as he caught motion from the corner of his eye. A man came from the back and stood at the corner of the house. The man had moved so quietly that if Chris hadn't have seen him, he would have sworn the fellow had just materialized. A breed of some sort, though not Comanche. Apache, maybe.

The man stared at them with intent dark eyes and a placid face, folded his arms.

"You real good with a hot iron, son?" Windy asked the man. The breed didn't move or respond.

"You sayin' we been rustlin' your stock?" came Shinn's angry voice. "'Cause if you are, you can just ride on back where you came from." He gestured a threat with the rifle.

Irritation pricked at Chris. He didn't like the man's surly manner one bit, but he forced his temper down. Getting angry wouldn't improve the situation—in fact, it might get them shot.

"Ain't sayin' a thing, Shinn. Just wondered if maybe some of our steers might've wandered over onto your spread. Seems we're missin' a few."

Shinn nudged his head towards the bunch Chris and Windy had inspected. "You see your brand on 'em?" The words came as much a challenge as any Chris had ever heard. The man wanted him to look over the steers and tell him the brand had been altered. Chris knew it was just the thing to provoke a bullet between the eyes.

This changed the situation. Shinn was pushing Chris, goading him for some reason he couldn't fathom. Animosity glittered in Shinn's eyes; he would plainly relish killing either of them.

Chris threw a glance at Windy, who had obviously picked up on the same thought and gone quiet.

Chris kept his voice level. "No, I don't see my brand. Your brand's on 'em plain as day."

Disappointment sparked in Shinn's eyes and Chris wondered if the man would decide to shoot them without provocation. If Shinn were siphoning 7HL stock, Chris hoped he might think twice about murder.

Shinn, appearing to think it over, backed down. "Good. Wouldn't want you to start accusin' me of somethin', Durrin." That's not what his tone said, but Chris didn't care to argue the point.

The breed watched the exchange with mild fascination, then turned and disappeared around the house. Out of the corner of his eye Chris saw him go, but kept his attention riveted to Shinn.

"You got any objections to us ridin' over your spread a little to look for our lost cattle?" Chris held back a sarcastic smile.

"Hell, you will!" Shinn blurted. "You two just mosey on back the way you came and don't veer off. I got an itchy finger sometimes and we wouldn't want no mistakes, would we?"

We would, the look in the man's eyes said plainly.

Chris shrugged and a frown touched his lips as he gathered the reins and gave the man a final stare.

"You see any of our stock headin' your way you turn 'em back, you hear? I'd hate to call in a territorial marshal or worse if it keeps up."

The man grinned a mushy grin. "I'll be sure an' do that." The words had lie painted all over them.

Chris and Windy reined around and sent their horses towards the 7HL. Chris half-expected to hear the report of the Winchester and feel hot lead plow into his back. He felt a measure of relief when none did. A few hundred yards on, he shot a glance backward, seeing Shinn had vanished from the porch and all was still again around the Box H spread.

"What do you think?" Chris asked Windy, who had been unnaturally silent since they left the Box H.

"Got more wind than a bull in green corn time! Those beeves were ours plain as could be. What's more, he wanted us to push him. I believe he'da enjoyed puttin' lead in us."

Chris nodded. "That's the impression I got. That breed?"

"Apache, I'm thinkin'. And damn good with a hot iron as sure as Shinn is a rustler."

Chris's voice lowered. "The feeling I knew him was stronger this time." Chris felt he was close to remembering, but it still hovered in the shady areas of his memory.

"Reckon I'm close to placin' him," Windy said, face grim. "Have a notion when I do I ain't gonna like it."

Chris had the same notion. "Question is, what do we do about him?"

"Find a rope, I say. We know he's rustlin' 7HL stock. Some good sturdy cottonwoods on his spread; he and that breed would look right nice decoratin' a couple."

Chris gave an uneasy chuckle, the note laced with morbid amusement.

"Maybe we should go to the territorial marshal or hire one of those range detectives."

"Bringin' in a gunfighter, which is all them range detectives is, might be more trouble than it's worth. Never liked 'em, I guess, less now..." Windy let the words trail off and Chris caught something underlying them, but didn't press it.

"What about law?"

"We bring the marshal in we better have proof 'stead of speculation."

Chris laughed. "You were ready to hang 'em on speculation a few minutes ago."

"I'm sayin' it'd be speculation in the marshal's eyes; in mine, them bastards are rustlers."

"All right, then we'll wait and see if we can find some proof."

"How?"

Chris shook his head. "Dunno, but if the number of missin' beeves gets higher, it's gonna be harder for Shinn to mix 'em in with his own stock. If his herd grows too fast, it'll look suspicious. No matter how good that breed is some brands will get botched. I'll bring the marshal in to sort it out after we find a few so we don't risk getting shot."

Windy nodded in reluctant agreement. Chris knew the segundo would just as soon wait till Shinn was off guard and sneak up with a bunch of 'hands, hog-tie him and throw him a necktie party.

"If that's what you thinks best..." Windy frowned.

"Meantime, I'm gonna head into Bald Creek and inform the sheriff of what happened with Shinn today."

Windy uttered a throaty laugh. "Won't do a lick of good and you know it. Sheriff's probably skimmin' off the operation. Wouldn't surprise me none."

"All the same, I wanna try." Chris wondered if the lie showed in his voice. He had another reason for going to Bald Creek, one that hadn't been settled last night.

Windy peered at the younger man, suspicion in his eyes. "You sure you ain't just worried about that dove and want to see about her?"

Chris stiffened. His question was answered. Windy knew. He wondered if he could hide anything from the assistant foreman.

"What if it is?" he answered with a hint of anger.

Windy let a grin oil his lips. "Hell, might do you some good at that. Ain't nothin' like a good wick-dippin' to take your mind off things."

"That ain't the reason. I'm figurin' maybe she saw something that might lead to Clint. Might be my only chance."

"That case, I'll go with you—"

"No!" Chris snapped. "Lost me enough folks last night. Ain't about to risk another."

"You can't go after Clint and his gang alone, son."

"Don't intend to. Just find a lead to him."

Chris spurred his horse into a gallop. He angled away from the red-headed man, looking back, seeing Windy continue on towards the ranch. A twinge of relief went through him. He hadn't told Windy the complete truth. He wanted to find a lead to Clint, but there was something drawing him to Bald Creek, to the dove. A feeling more than anything, one he couldn't peg exactly, but one that told him there was a reason the dove hadn't been among the others. He was damned if he knew what that reason might be, but he was determined to find out.

The first thing Chris noticed as he rode into Bald Creek was that the saloon was open. A few hitch rails had been repaired, but little other restoration was in evidence. Collapsed wooden awnings lay where they had fallen, folks walking around them as they scooted along the boardwalk. He saw activity at the cemetery, gravediggers working overtime after last night's slaughter. If Milus Clint returned to Bald Creek, Chris doubted there'd be enough room to hold all the dead.

Gaze moving farther on, Chris slowed his roan. The sheriff's office was just beyond the church. He debated stopping there; maybe he should head straight for the saloon instead. Tolby would likely be no help, but maybe the lawman had heard something by now that would put Chris on the trail to Clint. If that chance existed, Chris couldn't afford to pass it up.

He drew up, dismounted and tethered his horse to the hitch rail. He crossed the boardwalk and entered the office. It was small and sparsely furnished. A desk stood towards the left, a rickety table with a coffee pot and a few hard-backed chairs to the right. A rack on one wall held rifles and a row of empty cells to the back appeared little used; a thick coating of dust lay over the floor within.

Tolby looked up from behind his desk as Chris entered and the lawman's expression said he was anything but happy to see Chris. He grumbled a greeting and Chris removed his hat, holding it and absently fingering the band.

"Sheriff." Chris stepped closer to the desk.

"You got a good reason for bein' here?" Tolby responded, skipping the amenities. "Thought we understood each other last night."

"I understood you just fine." Chris felt anger boiling, but kept it off his face. He had to handle Tolby carefully. He'd get no information if he came at him like buckshot. "Just thought you might have heard something about the gang that came in here, where they were headed, maybe."

Tolby gave him a disgusted expression, one mixed with befuddlement. "I can't figure you, boy. You lose your uncle and half your men but you don't back off. You seen what them fellas done at the saloon and you still got a bur under your hide to find them?"

"Wouldn't expect you to understand..." Chris let the words trail off. He wanted to say he wouldn't expect a coward like Tolby to understand but a statement such as that would be enough to provoke the sheriff into killing him. Tolby looked the type.

The sheriff eyed him with a hint of anger, as if debating whether to take the remark as an insult. He folded his arms and leaned back.

"What you gettin' at, boy?"

"Ain't gettin' at nothing." Chris kept his voice steady. "'Cept I want to find those men and bring them to justice."

The sheriff bellowed a laugh. "You'd never get near them! They'd kill you dead 'fore you had a chance to spit! You must be plain loco, boy, if you think you could."

"Not loco, determined. I ain't willin' to let go what they did."

"No? Well, you should be." The sheriff stared at him and for a moment Chris thought he saw something close to respect touch the lawman's eyes. It quickly vanished.

"You sayin' you wouldn't tell me if you knew something?"

The sheriff shifted in his chair, unfolded his arms and gripped the edge of the desk. "Ain't what I'm sayin'. I'm sayin' these hombres are gone for good. They did their killin'. Now they done rode for greener pastures. I prefer it stay that way."

Was there fear in the sheriff's eyes? Perhaps. Chris saw something, but he gave up questioning the man on it. He would get nothing from Tolby on that account, but had expected as much.

"That all you got on your mind?" Tolby's tone took on a note of annoyance.

Chris moved to the window, looking out and eyeing the saloon. "There's something else. I came to report a threat."

"Threat?" Tolby looked put out. He wanted no part of anything that smacked of official business.

"Cocklebur outfit set up operations next to the 7HL, man named Jacob Shinn. Has a breed workin' for him. Some 7HL steers have disappeared and Shinn's stock is growing. I think he altered brands after leadin' the cattle over to his land."

Tolby scratched his head. "You got proof of this?" The sheriff's eyes weren't hopeful.

"No," admitted Chris, knowing that threatened to put an end to the complaint. "But today when my assistant foreman and I went to check it out, Shinn pointed a rifle at us and I damn well think he wanted to shoot us."

"Can't say as I blame him much if you was comin' up to him and accusin' him of stealin' your stock. Man's got his honor, you know."

Chris had to force himself to stifle a sarcastic laugh. What Tolby knew of honor wouldn't fill a Winchester shell. He lived by his own selfish code and others be damned. "I wasn't accusing him, but it was plain to see he thought that's what I was there for. I know he's rustlin' my stock and he knows it. The question is what to do about it."

"Well, nothin' I can do unless you got solid proof. I won't stand for no lynchin'." The threat in Tolby's voice was razor-sharp. Chris suddenly suspected a deeper motive. He turned and looked at the sheriff, whose eyes said it all: somehow he profited from whatever Shinn was up to, and that's why he wouldn't help. When Shinn sold those steers, Chris felt sure Tolby would collect a heavy tax, and in the meantime he might well afford him any protection he needed to stay in business. Chris hadn't cared much for Tolby before, but now he had a powerful dislike for the man.

Centering his gaze on the lawdog, Chris saw tension knotting the sheriff's jaw and a challenge in his eyes. He had pushed Tolby as far as he could. For now. Another time would come, he reckoned. Men of the sheriff's ilk tended to die violent deaths sooner or later and Tolby's affairs would catch up to him.

"Maybe I was wrong, Sheriff," Chris said with mock deliberation. "Maybe my steers just wandered away."

"That's the way I see it." A small measure of tension eased from his manner.

Chris smiled a false smile. "Perhaps they'll wander back sooner or later. If not...well, we'll count our losses and move forward."

"Now you're seein' straight, boy." The sheriff's posture eased further and Chris knew he had alleviated Tolby's suspicions. He turned the subject to other things.

"Didn't waste any time gettin' the saloon open, I see."

Tolby grinned. "Well, business is business, they say. Thought it'd be best if things went on as usual, so folks didn't dwell on their loss."

Best for his own pocket, Chris reckoned. He set his hat atop his head and walked to the door, pausing on a sudden thought. "You seen any sign of one of the doves over there—Mexicali gal, name of Matalija? She wasn't among the dead last night. I checked."

The sheriff laughed. "Sorry. Who knows what becomes of some of them women? Here one day, gone the next. Whores never stay in one place."

Chris let out a grunt and opened the door, disappointed. He had hoped for more, but was no closer to anything solid than he was before he came.

"Hey, careful, now, that Injun gal don't find out 'bout what you're doin'!" Tolby yelled behind him. "Could play hell with your balls! Heard them women don't cotton to no hanky-panky." A gusty laugh followed the words. Chris felt a stagger in his step. The smiling dark face of Little Waiting Woman flashed in his mind and emotion caught in his throat. Her memory was wearing at the back of his mind and he doubted he could hold off dealing with it much longer.

"She...won't mind," he whispered, and that hurt like hell. "She won't mind a bit, now." He left the office, the sheriff staring after him with a puzzled look.

As he walked along the boardwalk, the day waning, shadows lengthening, he felt a swelling depression. The sheriff's mention of Little Waiting Woman might have started it or it might have been there all along.

You can't put it off forever...

Windy was right: that kind of pain needed to be faced. Could he? Would it crush him? Is that what Clint wanted? He forced the thoughts down as the depression deepened. Now wasn't the time. He had come to Bald Creek for other reasons.

He reached the saloon, entered.

The barroom was already filled with people. The floor had been cleaned up, new sawdust sprinkled about. New tables and chairs replaced the broken ones. Bottles had been restocked in the hutch behind the bar and a new 'keep, a man Chris recognized as one the sheriff sometimes used as a deputy, stood behind the counter.

As Chris studied the room further, he noticed minute signs that pointed to last night's massacre: holes in the walls and banister where bullets had lodged, a few dark stains embedded into the floor. He noticed the absence of a piano player and reckoned they hadn't replaced the one who had either been killed or high-tailed it to safer ground. A scattering of doves mixed with the customers. He didn't see Matalija and that disappointed him. Windy was right, he could use the comfort of a woman right now, arms to hold him, even if they were bought and paid for. Sometimes a man just needed what a woman could give him, a whisper or touch, and again his heart threatened to spill over with grief for Little Waiting woman.

I miss you...

On unsteady legs, he walked to the bar, slid onto a stool. The 'keep looked at him and Chris ordered whiskey, clinking a silver dollar onto the counter. The barman poured the drink and shoved it in front of Chris, who gulped at it like a desert-parched man. He hoped the liquor would afford him a hold on his strength. The whiskey burned its way down his throat and glowed in his belly, but did little to quell the sorrow threatening to strangle him.

He noticed the barkeep eyeing him and gave the man a forced smile. "S'prised you're open," he muttered, making conversation so he wouldn't have to be alone with his thoughts.

"Sheriff said it would be best. Folks want to drown their memories, you know." The 'keep was a rabbit-looking man with slightly bucked teeth, unkempt dirty-blond hair and over-large red ears. He didn't give Chris the arrogant do-nothing impression Tolby did, more the demeanor of a man easily led or frightened into compliance.

"Those doves, there..." Chris nudged his head towards one of the girls. "New, ain't they?"

"Yeah. Not the same quality as the ones we had before, but pickin's got right slim after last night. Mostly bored widders, I reckon. Got plenty of them, now, too."

A somber tone said the man wasn't too happy about having the saloon open for business. It said he'd rather be at home, hiding out with a Springfield, but had little choice in the matter.

Chris studied the man, betting he'd get an honest answer. "There was a dove, Matalija, who wasn't with the rest last night; she in?"

The man gave Chris a funny look he couldn't read. "Uh-uh," he answered simply, as if hoping that would be the end of it.

Chris knew he had hit on something. He cocked an eyebrow. "But you've seen her?" He found his expectation suddenly building.

The man half-nodded. "Look, I can't be sayin' things 'cause Tolby wouldn't like it. You know how he can be."

Chris spread his hands. "Who's gonna tell him?"

The man appeared to consider it. "Fella, I don't want no trouble. I do what I'm told to do and that's that. It ain't much of a life, but at least it's a life, you get me?"

Chris nodded. "I ain't askin' you to betray Tolby. I just got an interest in the lady and want to know if she's all right."

The 'keep's brow furrowed. "Guess I don't see no harm in that. She came 'round late last night, after the sheriff went off and me and a couple others was finishin' up with the bodies."

Chris felt relief well. She was alive and in the brutal events that had dogged him over the last twenty-four hours that was a Godsend. "She's all right, then?"

The man's face turned with that funny unreadable look again. "Well, she kinda acted peculiar."

"Peculiar, how?"

"She wasn't walkin' too straight-like, like maybe she was drunk, only I didn't smell no whiskey on her breath. And her face, it was all palelike. Hell, she wouldn't even look towards the bodies."

Chris shrugged. "That's understandable. They were friends of hers."

"Yeah, reckon that must be it. But there was something else odd about her. She stumbled and I tried to help her, caught her arms. I swear, she was as cold as them bodies I was liftin'. An' I saw something in her eyes, like she wasn't even lookin' at me, kinda just through me. She pulled away and ran off and I was glad to see her go, I gotta tell you."

"You see where she went?"

"No."

Chris's brow furrowed and he wondered what had happened to the dove. Matalija was alive, yet something was wrong. Had she seen what Clint's gang had done? Had she escaped them? Would she come back to the Blue Steer? Or would she disappear to another town, another corner of the West, as doves were wont to do when trouble arose?

Chris downed the rest of his whiskey. He didn't feel satisfied but at least he had gotten part of what he had come for, the knowledge that Matalija had survived last night's raid. Nothing in that would lead him to Clint, but he reckoned it was better than nothing. He slid off the stool and tipped his hat.

"Something else, Mr.— " the barman said.

"Durrin. Chris Durrin. Own the 7HL north of here."

"I know it." The 'keep winced, as if what he was thinking frightened him. "When she fell against me I got me a look at her neck and there were marks there."

"Marks? What kind?" Chris felt a sinking in his belly. His mind jumped back to the tipi, to the still dead form of Little Waiting Woman and something he had taken little notice of at the time. He had seen marks on her throat, slashes covered by the powder Dark Cloud had placed on her.

"Two gashes, like she was bit by a dog or the likes." The 'keep shook his head. "Damnedest thing, but I reckon it don't mean nothin'." The man turned and went about his business.

Chris stood there a moment, a vague dread pulling at his mind, though he couldn't figure why. Were the marks connected with Clint? He couldn't see how. Yet Mrs. Tulber and the cowhands' throats had been ripped open, as if by animals.

Coyotes?

Chris doubted it. Why would prairie wolves rip out some throats and leave slashes on others? Nothing about it made sense. Maybe it was a measure of the darkness Windy talked about, and maybe he would be prey to what lived within that darkness if he didn't put it together soon.

ELEVEN

The sun sank below the horizon in a blaze of red. Distant thunder rolled and a chill rode the breeze, which slapped at the buffalo grass and shivered cottonwood leaves. Boughs creaked. The Canadian River murmured its mournful song miles away but strangely the chirping of the katydids fell silent.

Darkness swelled over the Plains. A coyote bayed, a forlorn howl, pregnant with dark promise. A second animal took up the melancholy song, another, as the pack gathered in the field. Their shadowy shapes skittered about, as if awaiting unspoken commands from the night. They would advance yards, retreat, hunching, watching, scooting forward and back again. Daggers of moonlight gleamed from their bared fangs and flashed in their black eyes. Snarls punctuated their howls.

Sitting in an over-stuffed chair in his parlor at the Box H, Jacob Shinn heard the soulless cries of the prairie wolves and fought the urge to shudder. He had heard the damn coyotes the night before, and for a few nights before that. Their incessant yowls got under his skin, the way most things did lately. He had sent that goddamn breed out with a rifle after the varmints, but the Apache had returned empty-handed, saying merely they had eluded him and he had no idea where they went during the day. He had mumbled something else, something Shinn didn't quite understand, something about darkness and some Indian spirit who brought death and life at the same time; something about the coyotes being emissaries of that dark spirit. Shinn had laughed a mocking laugh but his expression had carried a nervous edge. The breed tended to babble about spirits, when he bothered to talk at all. Hell, Jacob reckoned all along the breed had just been chewing too much of that peyote Apaches were so goddamned fond of.

Now he wasn't so sure. Because lately when night fell it came like a shroud and talk of spooks and emissaries of blackness burrowed into the back of Shinn's mind. It made him jumpier than he had ever been, even in past times when the law dogged him. That talk became somehow more believable when the sun vanished over the horizon and night held sway over the soul-gripping loneliness of the Plains. Every shadow became suddenly alive and reaching, burrowing, bunching about the house as if wanting to claw their way in, where they could swarm over him, devour him.

Jacob half-considered killing that damn Injun for putting that kind of nonsense into his head. But that wouldn't do, not now, at any rate. The Apache was the best damn brand artist he had ever laid eyes on, even though he had seen some good ones when he worked the Pecos Valley in New Mex six-odd years back.

Thoughts of the operation then brought a certain calmness to Shinn. He forced his mind from the coyotes and shadows, turning it to longhorns. The nervous edge remained but he tried to ignore it.

That boy had sand, coming to him today; and so did Windy McDonnell.

Did either of them recollect?

Shinn felt sure the boy didn't; the boy had only glimpsed him once, and Jacob had gained weight and wrinkles over the last six years. But Shinn hadn't forgotten the boy; no, he hadn't forgotten what Durrin and his uncle had done to his livelihood by settling the score with Milus Clint and ruining the best damned rustlin' operation this side of the Heaven. Shinn had been elated at his luck when he discovered the boy and his uncle had set up shop in the Panhandle. Elated and full of plans. He had settled upon a scheme that worked well in the old days, when he used to settle betwixt and between numerous spreads and lure cattle to his scraggly parcel of land. What worked then worked now and Durrin would pay his debt to Shinn.

Shinn siphoned 7HL stock ever so slowly, increasing it in notched increments until 7HL herd became Box H herd. The breed handled the brand altering. After that, Shinn made connections, through the breed, with various tribes eager to provide beef for their starving families. He was only too happy to supply it, in small lots, trading for gold and silver and turquoise and horses and Indian whores he could fence through the sheriff in Bald Creek— 'cept for the whores; them he buried where no one could ever find them.

Oh, he lost a percentage to the lazy sonofabitch of a lawman, but it was worth it—for now. Shinn felt right proud of leeching off the boy and his uncle. He saw it as the perfect give-and-take relationship: the 7HL gave him cattle and he took 'em! And with the handiwork of the breed no one could ever prove a thing.

In fact, Shinn figured he could go on and on with the scheme and no one would blink an eye at a few head of cattle turning up lost. Hell, they wandered off all the time, falling victim to disease or natural enemies. Enemies such as Jacob Shinn.

But Shinn hadn't counted on Windy McDonnell. That was a bur in his britches. He'd met Windy a time or two way back when, and he knew he faced a much greater risk of being discovered on that front. It would come to the red-headed man where he had seen Shinn before; that Shinn knew for a fact. And when it did there'd be hell to pay.

But would McDonnell tell? What was that sidewinder up to, working for the boy, anyhow? Was he running his own operation? Shinn couldn't rightly see how. It made no sense. But McDonnell posed a risk to his plans; that was all that counted.

He recollected from their brief meetings the man had an aptitude for cattle, as if he could just fix on each and every one when he led them to the various outfits Shinn had set up at the orders of...well, even if the red-haired man did remember he might not let on because that meant risking whatever plan he had in mind, too. And if McDonnell took the notion to hone in on Shinn's operation, or blackmail him, he'd soon wind up keeping company with them Injun whores.

Another howl pierced Shinn's thoughts and he jerked his head towards the door. Cold apprehension shivered through him. Swelling silence, broken only by the haunting calls of the prairie wolves, settled.

Shinn grunted and pulled a half-empty whiskey bottle from the small table beside the chair. Gulping a mouthful, he felt the liquor sear its way down to his gut and thunked the bottle back onto the table. Pushing himself from the chair, he went to the door and made sure it was bolted.

Another howl startled him; he let out a gasp. It had come from much closer this time. Too close. Moving to the window, he peered out into the night. Shadows swayed under the cottonwoods, leaves casting shapes like black demons come to steal his soul. The moon, bloated and pale, glazed the field with a bleached-skull color. He shuddered as a howl rose and fell, followed by another, then another, soon a chorus of them.

He jerked away from the window, shaking, heart hammering. He wondered where the damn breed had got off to, then recollected he had ridden into town for supplies. But that was hours ago, which meant the Apache had probably stopped off at the Steer, as he had a habit of doing.

Shinn cursed the breed, and Tolby for making it possible for the Injun to get into the place, which normally wouldn't allow heathens. He wished the damn breed weren't so important to the operation, then he could just kill—

Shinn's thoughts stopped abruptly as a scratching sounded from various points around the room—near the window, door, opposite window, back. He flicked a look at each, saw, thought he saw, dark shapes passing before the windows, indistinct forms flowing across the glass, lunging at the outside walls.

A series of throaty growls followed and Shinn caught himself muttering unintelligible words. His bladder ached, threatening to loose.

Shinn, frozen in place, forced himself to move, walked with a stiff gait to a glass-doored case and pulled out a Winchester. He checked to make sure it was loaded, levering a shell into the chamber. If those damn varmints dared come up to the house he'd damn sure have the makings of a coyote coat this winter.

Was it coyotes?

The thought stunned him. It crawled up with dark suspicions and filled him with coldness. Of course, it was coyotes. He'd heard them, hadn't he? Seen them? It had to be. What else could it be?

He had the notion all the self-convincing in the West couldn't make him accept that answer, because something else troubled him, something felt by the instinct honed all those years ago running the rustling operation. A sense for when things were plain wrong, when the time had come to pick up and move on and never look back. He felt that way, now, same as he felt six years ago when running had saved his hide as the marshal and his men closed in on the various illicit operations run by Clint in New Mexico. But he had time, then; the sense had warned him to pull up stakes before the law caught him and slipped a hemp necktie around his throat. The sense might have come too late this time. Or perhaps he had just gotten too damn comfortable and not felt it in time. It didn't really matter a lick. Because whatever caused the feeling was here, outside in the darkness, waiting for him.

Waiting?

Maybe not. Approaching was closer to it.

Don't be a goddamned fool! he scolded himself. It's only coyotes. They been comin' 'round better'n a week now and just decided to push their luck tonight. He'd show 'em what that got—and have a damn fine coat when the snows came.

It's more than that, Shinn...

"What?" Shinn blurted, spinning, jerking his rifle around, whirling another half-turn, leveling the Winchester again.

The room was empty, but he had sworn he had heard a voice, one with a frightening ring of familiarity to it. But that was impossible. The voice he thought he'd heard belonged to a dead man!

A cacophony of scratching and howls exploded from beyond the door and windows. He heard coyotes lunge frantically at the building, paws thudding against the planks, claws raking long furrows down the walls, gouging out splinters. Yipping, yowling, crashing into the house. One of the beasts slammed into the heavy door and Shinn saw it shudder. It would hold against the critters; he knew that much; no coyote was strong enough to break it down.

He'd never seen coyotes come this close to the house, become that aggressive. It wasn't goddamn normal.

He yelled: "Get the hell outta here, you sonsofbitches!" and swung the rifle to each window, then back to the door as another thud sounded there.

Everything went silent. He listened to his heart hammering, afraid to blink.

Gone?

Shinn, sweat trickling down his face and chest, stood as still as a statue, listening intently for the next few seconds. He heard no sound, as if the coyotes had just vanished.

With a deep breath, he forced himself to stop shaking and crept to the window. Almost afraid to peer out in case one of the critters leaped at his face in the glass and scared the piss out of him, he gazed out into the night.

The lawn appeared deserted. The coyotes *had* gone!

A nervous titter worked its way up from the bowels of his fear and escaped his mouth. He didn't recollect ever feeling so piss-scared—or so relieved now that the varmints had gone.

A crash snapped him around. He whirled, bleating a terrified sound as the front door-lock exploded in a splintering of wood and a rending of shattered mechanism. The door flew inward, rebounding from the wall and swinging back—stopped dead by a hand that caught the edge.

A figure filled the door and Shinn's finger jerked the Winchester's trigger reflexively. The blast sounded ear-splitting in the tiny room.

The figure at the door jolted under the impact of the .44-40 slug that tore into his chest. Then a boiling black wash sizzled across the wound, sealing it.

"Goddammit, Shinn, you're a mite fast on that trigger," the Dark Rider said, stepping into the room. Four men drifted in behind him. "Years made you rabbit-scared?"

Shinn stared, basin-eyed, mouth dropping open as the Rider crossed the room. Milus Clint grabbed the rifle barrel and wrenched it from Shinn's grip, examining it with mild interest, then tossing it onto the sofa.

Clint's cold buzzard eyes leveled on Shinn, who found his voice choked in his throat.

It was impossible, utterly impossible what he was seeing. The man in the duster standing before him had died six years ago in New Mex and that was all there was to it. Shinn felt himself edging back, pressing against the wall. Milus Clint grinned, half of his face holding the expression, the other half a hideous scarred mass, unmoving.

Clint uttered a chuckle and moved away, scanning the room, as other Riders came in, the last through closing the door behind himself, though it hung open an inch because of the shattered lock.

Clint walked to the fireplace and opened a humidor atop the mantle. Selecting a cigar, he chewed off the end and lifted the chimney off the lantern, puffing the stogy to life.

Turning to Shinn, who found himself locked in some terrified paralysis, he said "These don't 'xactly do so much for me no more." He spat and flicked the cigar into the fireplace. "Ain't a whole lot that tastes right since I died."

"M-Milus," Shinn stammered, managing to get his voice working. "H-how...?"

Milus Clint frowned out of one side of his mouth. "How ain't so important. All that matters is what is." Milus paused, looking about the room again, then centering his gaze on Shinn.

Coldness slithered through Shinn under that gaze, one he would have given his left nut to be free of. Milus Clint had always intimidated him, near the only man who could, but it felt worse, now, as if he were talking to a ghost, a demon who held sway over the darkness.

Milus wagged a finger, eyes narrowing. "Imagine my surprise, Shinn, when I came back to pay the boy and his uncle a little visit and found you here." The grin came back. "Imagine my surprise when I found you operatin' this spread, leechin' off'n his cattle. Set yourself up right nice, didn'tcha?"

Shinn jerkily shook his head, gripped by terror. "No, no, Milus, you got it all wrong, I swear. I'm legit, now."

Milus bellowed a laugh. "Legit, hell! You ain't been legit since you were born and never will be a day in your life. Fact is, I'm right glad you got yourself in business here. It fits right into my plans for the boy."

"Plans?" Shinn echoed, swallowing hard. He didn't know what Milus Clint had come back for, or for that matter how he could have survived the shoot-out in New Mex, and he suddenly didn't care a lick. He just knew he wanted no part of whatever scheme Milus had lit on. Those days were over. Shinn was his own man now.

"Always were a bit slow on the uptake, Shinn, but a damn fine rustler, I'll give you that." Milus stepped over to him and Shinn wanted recoil, but his back was to the wall.

"What you want here, Milus?" he bleated, sweat streaming down his face. He couldn't keep his voice or his hands steady.

Milus pressed his face close, thudding a palm against the wall beside Shinn's head. "I want revenge. You should know that." Milus suddenly grabbed a handful of the rancher's shirt and slammed him hard against the wall. Shinn gasped with the impact, stunned, aghast at the incredible strength the outlaw leader possessed. As Clint's gaze held his, the hardcase's eyes faded to black, like inky storms swallowing a gray horizon, blue-black bolts of lightening snapping within.

In that frozen instant Shinn saw everything in their abysmal depths Clint wanted him to see: death, the endless reaches of eternity, night upon night of emptiness. Suddenly, in sober realization, Shinn knew what a blessing death could be.

Clint's lips parted and Shinn's legs threatened to give out as he saw the curved razor fangs. His heart shuddered and his breath came in hot staggered gasps.

"W-what do you want?" The words tumbled out in a raspy whisper.

"I want you to know I'm back, Shinn. You work for me, now. You always have and you always will."

Shinn gave a jerky nod, feeling urine run down his leg.

"After I deal with the boy I might need a man who can help me out in the daylight hours...for a short spell." Clint's eyes narrowed. "But after that, I'm gonna come and give you a little gift...we're gonna be back in business just like we always was, only now no one will be able to touch us."

Shinn nodded his agreement, praying he'd have the courage to put the Winchester's barrel into his mouth and pull the trigger before that day came, but knowing deep down he was probably too much of a coward.

Chris Durrin's despair deepened after leaving the Blue Steer Saloon. By the time he climbed into the saddle and gigged his roan into a trot through town, the sun had slipped into the sea of buffalo grass and a cold wind skirted the Plains. As he rode past the cemetery a shiver of unease feathered down his spine. He glanced at the gravediggers working feverishly to bury the bodies and cover any signs of the massacre from the previous night.

Did they want to deny what happened? Bury it and never think on it again? Would that make the Devil go away? The ghosts vanish? Maybe for them. But not for Chris. Chris didn't have that luxury. Clint had not returned for the people who lived in Bald Creek; they could go on with their lives, hoping the outlaw never rode back into town. Clint had returned for him and all the denial in the world wouldn't stop the hardcase from coming after him.

The only question was when.

He had taken a small sense of hope from his conversation with the barkeep. Matalija had survived, but what exactly had happened to her? Had she witnessed the killings? Seen Clint? Is that what had caused her to act peculiar with the barkeep? Or did it go beyond that? The slashes on her neck, were they the same type as on Little Waiting Woman's throat? Did that mean a connection to Clint?

But Little Waiting Woman was dead and Matalija was not. What did that mean?

Chris had another slim hope, as he eyed the destruction left by the gang. He could follow the signs out the other end of town, perhaps discover some trace of where they had gone.

A few moments later, those hopes dissolved. The signs led into a muddle of tracks that went every which way. It was impossible for him to pick out the sets left by Clint's horses. The gang might have been swallowed by the night for all he could tell. It would take a better tracker than he to read them. He knew of only one person skilled enough to separate and follow them: Dark Cloud. But Chris had taken the notion the Comanche was unwilling to help.

He gave the search another half-hour, dismounting a number of times and searching the ground for clues, hoof imprints, twisted grass, perhaps an item that had fallen from their mounts or out of a pocket. Anything.

He found nothing, as if the gang had never existed and the carnage they had created was a part of his imagination.

Yet it wasn't his imagination. Uncle Clem and Little Waiting Woman were dead. Gone. So were Mrs. Tulber and a bunch of fine men and the wives of Dark Cloud and Speaks No More. That was real. Milus Clint had seared his brand on the Plains and he had to be hiding somewhere. Wherever it was, Chris would find him, somehow.

And kill him this time.

But if Clint were nearby, where was he holed up?

Six years ago Clint had left a trail of death across New Mexico; that trail had finally led lawmen to his camp. But in New Mexico there were places to hide, mountains and woods, volcanic caves. The Plains held only endless flatlands, broken by occasional arroyos and streams feeding off the Canadian. He gave passing thought to searching some of the canyons but that could take days and as night took hold, the chances of finding anything grew more remote.

At last he reined his roan around and headed for the ranch. As he approached the outer reaches of the 7HL spread, he heard the distant cries of coyotes. They filled the moon-frosted night and cold apprehension swelled in his soul. He caught glimpses of their dark shapes skittering across the horizon. They didn't gather as near the 7HL tonight. They tracked closer to Box H land and Chris bid them good riddance, even entertained a measure of satisfaction in knowing they'd be plaguing Shinn.

After attending to his horse, Chris went into the main house, intent on collapsing into bed. Exhaustion made his body heavy, listless. He hadn't slept since the previous night and had run on borrowed energy throughout the day. He dragged himself up the stairs, turning away offers of poker from the men downstairs and a meal of beefsteak and greens Windy had cooked up. He stopped only to gulp down a luke-warm cup of Arbuckle's.

In his room, he splashed water from the basin into his face, toweled off and fell into bed, unable to stay awake a moment longer.

Tonight he would sleep, though he knew it would be a restless slumber, disturbed by bitter memories and dark dreams.

TWELVE

"**W**hen are we gonna get out of here and have a real family?" Chris asked. His gray-blue eyes settled on the girl of sixteen sitting on the edge of the bed, sewing beads onto a buckskin shirt. His sister had learned the craft from one of the Apache girls at the orphanage and was adept at the art. Her fingers moved with surety and skill.

Chris peered up at her and frowned. He could see it in her eyes she was trying to think of something different to tell him, some other way to rephrase the words she had told him the last hundred times he had asked. He had a sinking feeling the fact was they were never going to leave the place, that no one would adopt them and they'd live out their lives here with the religious women who ran the Caring Hands Orphanage.

"Don't worry, Chris," Clara said in the motherly way she seemed to have adopted since the death of their parents. "Someone will take us in. You'll see." She said it as if she were fighting to convince herself and Chris felt his heart sink.

"No one wants us, Clara. No one wants older kids unless they need help farmin' and most of the ranchers 'round here got 'hands already for that."

Clara frowned. "You're just over-eager. You expect everything to happen yesterday."

Chris' brow crinkled. "You said that two years ago, when we first got here. How over-eager can I be?" He had her there and he knew it. She just shook her head, pretending to concentrate on her beadwork. He thought he saw her blue eyes gloss with tears but wasn't sure and wouldn't embarrass her by asking. Three years older, she was the only family he had left, sister and mother all rolled into one and he cherished her.

"What if someone comes and only takes one of us?" The question had been bothering Chris for ages now and the only way to ask was to blurt it out so it wouldn't haunt him any longer.

"Hush!" Clara said. "Don't you go frettin' 'bout things like that. I'm sure whoever comes will take us both."

"What if they don't?" Chris persisted and she shook her head, lips drawing into a thin line.

"Honestly, Chris, sometimes I think you like making things harder on yourself!"

"Ain't that." His voice lowered. "Just I worry lots." He brushed his hair from his forehead.

"You worry too much. Now promise me you won't fret over it any longer. You just keep saying your prayers and asking God and he'll send someone, you'll see."

"Sometimes I don't think God listens to me no more. Not since He killed ma and pa, anyhow." He didn't know why he said it, only that it was a way to get under her skin and he did that sometimes when he was worried himself. Clara never seemed to worry, only wait with the patience of the Saints the religious women always talked about. He knew she must have thought about it, wondered the same things he wondered about the future, but she never let her hurt or worry show and sometimes he wished she would, just once. She held it all inside and he knew that couldn't be good because it would have to burst out all at once someday.

"Chris!" Clara snapped, lips pulling into a hard line. "Don't let me hear those words come out of your mouth again or I'll have one of the Sisters take some hard soap to your tongue!"

Chris knew she wouldn't and almost smiled.

"God listens to all of us," she went on. "You know that. Just that sometimes it takes Him longer to find proper folks to take care of kids like us. He works in His own time."

"His time's too damn slow!" Chris blurted.

Clara's eyes widened. She hated it when he cussed.

"Chris..." She dragged out his name in an unspoken reprimand and he grinned. He saw a smile light in her eyes, but she kept the stern look on her face.

He turned to the window and, leaning his elbows on the sill, stared out into the wagon-rutted streets of Mascarada. Depression settled heavy in his soul and he wanted to cry, but forced back the tears.

Wandering shadows filled the street as the sun floated towards the horizon. He saw cowhands filtering towards the Matanza Saloon, weary from their day's work. He wondered what it would be like to be one of them, riding the range and driving cattle up the Goodnight-Loving Trail, to be free, to belong somewhere. Belong anywhere.

His thoughts drifted to the past and he recollected how the cold wind had slapped across the land as he and Clara headed across the Plains in a wagon bound from Missouri to Santa Fe. He remembered his parents' faces, laughing and smiling and talking all the time of a better life on the cattle ranch his father planned to stake as soon as they reached the Pecos Valley. His ma talked of how she'd decorate the house they would build and how his father would teach him to ride and rope. How to herd beeves and work the land into something they could be proud of.

But it was a dark wind that stalked over the land that day. Before he knew it, his parents were gone, killed by the consumption, and when he went to sleep at night he saw only skulls in his dreams and bony hands of Death reaching up from the darkness in his mind. He had cried, cried until he thought no more tears would come, then cried some more. Delivered to the orphanage, they were taken in by the Sisters, who looked at them with a saddled cheerfulness that he tried to convince himself was some sort of love.

In those first few months, he almost convinced himself that what they said was true. But every day he perched by the window, peering out into the bright sunlight, full of hope and promise, praying, waiting for the parents the Sisters promised him would come to adopt him some day real soon. Two years dragged by and real soon melted into near-future into someday. Now Clara told him the same thing she had told him before, but with different words, and he wished he could believe her. He knew she wouldn't intentionally lie to him, but also knew she said it as much for her own benefit as his, to hold herself and their dreams together, nurse their wounded hope.

False hope.

Shadows in the street lengthened like dark claws and the sounds of laughter and carousing grew louder from the saloon. Chris felt a smile flitter across his lips. Someday he would be like them, those cowboys from the local spreads, laughing it up and being free. He would have his own ranch and ride herd and drive cattle to railheads and have children whom he could be a father to and never leave.

Before he could stop it, a tear trickled down his face; he hurriedly brushed it away before his sister noticed.

Turning from the window, he saw Clara set her beadwork on the bed and go to a lantern, lighting it, as the room became dusky with evening. The Sisters would be calling them for vittles soon, more hard biscuits and warmed-over something-or-other. He missed his ma's cooking and the smells of supper at their house in Missouri. He felt tears well again.

A sound broke his thoughts and he swung back to the window, peered out. Hooves, lots of them, thundering in from the low hills to the west, near the Pecos.

He squinted into the encroaching darkness, trying to pick out where the clamor was coming from. At last he spotted a plume of dust. Riders, a bunch, careening towards the town. Their horses' hooves beat louder, louder, louder, and vague fear clutched his heart. He wondered why. Riders came into town often, sometimes groups of them, all 'hands from the local outfits. But something told him these weren't 'hands.

"What is it?" he heard his sister ask, suddenly beside him. He could smell her flowery perfume as she pushed her face closer to look out the window.

He shrugged. "Dunno. Looks like a bunch of riders headin' into town."

Her face tightened as she spotted them and the dull worry in him turned into budding panic.

The riders came on, tearing into town like demons on horseback, shouting, whooping, swearing. Dust billowed around the stampeding hooves of their mounts and Chris felt his panic increase with every yard they gained. He didn't know how he knew, but those men were headed here, to the orphanage.

"They're comin' here!" he blurted, seeing his sister had the same notion.

"Nonsense!" she denied, tone bloated with doubt. "What business would men like that have with the Sisters?"

"I heard somebody from one of the ranches donated some gold to the orphanage. Maybe they want it." He said it almost as an impossibility, but with the look that crossed Clara's face he realized that *was* what the men were after.

Clara pushed away from the window and grabbed a chair from a small desk in the corner, then dragged it to the door and jammed it under the knob.

Fear made his heart pound in his throat as he glimpsed the hard faces of the riders, the intent scrawled plainly on their features.

Clara doused the lantern, plunging the room into a hushed semi-darkness. She crossed the floor and grabbed him, hauling him to the bed, drawing him close and whispering for him to be quiet.

Outside the clamor of hooves grew louder, but Chris' heart pounded above it. When the hoofbeats stopped, the silence thundered in his ears.

Then shouts, curses and bawdy laughter singed the air.

A crash rang out like an explosion. The front door being kicked in! A pause followed, where a hush fell heavy as Wyoming snow. Shattered by a scream of mortal terror. One of the Sisters!

A gunshot jolted him. He let out a squeak of terror, immediately embarrassed. Clara hugged him closer, stroking his hair and he shivered, knowing the Devil the Sisters talked about had come to the orphanage.

More shots followed, more screams, punctuated by shouts and cruel bursts of laughter. Time seemed to stretch out and distort. He prayed the men would pass by this room, but that was not to be. Heavy steps sounded beyond the door and the knob rattled. A curse came from behind it.

"Find that goddamned gold!" a harsh voice yelled. Silence again. Chris forced out the breath jammed in his lungs.

The door shuddered under the shock of an impact. The chair slipped sideways an inch. Another crash of impact. The chair skidded away and the door flew inward, torn from one hinge.

The Devil poised in the doorway, grinning like a circus clown and Chris cowered in his sister's arms.

The man laughed and stepped into the room, locks of stringy hair and cold buzzard eyes showing beneath a battered felt hat. His duster flapped as he walked and Chris saw a blacksnake whip coiled at his hip. His eyes locked with the outlaw's; he saw no compassion there, no sense of humanity or gentleness. Only evil, cruelty, and he knew he was looking into the eyes of death.

"Well, well, lookee what we got here," the man said, taking another step towards them. "You look just good enough to eat!" His gaze raped Clara. Chris shuddered with the notion that took hold in his mind, a notion that told him what the outlaw intended for his sister.

"Leave us be!" Clara responded in a shaky voice. The outlaw's expression mocked her.

"That might do for him, honey, but you...no, old Milus has somethin' else in mind for you, pretty girl. You'll like it just fine."

Chris didn't know what made him hurl himself at the outlaw then, a man three times his size and weight, only that one moment he'd been filled with panic and the next his sole concern was protecting his sister from the fate the hardcase intended.

He slammed into the hardcase, but the outlaw didn't take a backward step. The man's hand flashed, clopping Chris under the jaw. Chris's teeth slammed together. Blood flowed from his lips, tasting metallic on his tongue. His head reeled. He felt himself teetering sideways, crashing into the floorboards with a muffled thump and a distant bolt of shock.

The next thing he became conscious of was the screams of his sister. They pierced the spinning clouds in his head. He forced himself to his hands and knees, looking up.

The outlaw had knocked his sister back onto the bed. He hoisted up the girl's skirt, exposing the frilly white things beneath. Climbing atop her, his hands prodded at her small breasts and his mouth slobbered across her face as she beat at his chest and shoulders with her fists to no avail.

With her nails Clara raked the side of his face and he cursed, back-handing her. She lay stunned and he groped beneath her skirt, yanking down her undergarments.

Fury erupted in Chris' mind, clearing the haze completely. He gained his feet and stumbled to the chair, grabbing it, hoisting it above his head.

The outlaw must have sensed the move, for he turned, hand thrusting up and snatching the chair leg as it descended towards him. He wrenched the chair from Chris' grip, hurling it sideways; it splintered against the wall.

Chris flung himself at the hardcase again, fists beating at the man's face.

The outlaw laughed, clamping Chris' wrists in his beefy hands. Chris kicked out, trying to rake the hardcase's shins with his bootheels. The outlaw shook him violently, brought a knee up into his groin. Vomit rose in Chris's throat, exploding from his mouth, splattering the man's shirt.

The outlaw bellowed and hurled Chris backwards. Chris crashed into the wall, dazed, unable to move.

The outlaw came at him again, and Chris felt himself lifted and thrown a second time, felt his back strike something hard yet giving, felt himself plunging through the barrier.

Glass shattered around him and he knew the outlaw had heaved him through the window. He landed in the street flat on his back, paralyzed, blood running from his mouth and nose and ears. Distantly he heard the screams and pleas of his sister; her voice wound down, trickled out, yet he couldn't get to his feet, couldn't move a limb, no matter how much he fought to rise. Nothing in his body wanted to work and he could barely feel anything, despite the pain he knew must be there.

What happened after that became a blur in Chris's mind. He heard one of the outlaws shout: "Come on, Emmet knocked over a goddamned lamp!" and knew men were scrambling from the building. Through clouded vision he saw one of them dragging a sack and knew they had found what they came for: the gold.

A man stepped over him and he stared up blearily into the cold buzzard eyes of the leader.

"See ya, kid." The leader gave a spiteful grin. "An' don't worry, I did your sister real fine." The leader bellowed a laugh and clomped towards his horse. Chris heard the muffled pounding of hooves receding into the pulsing roar of his mind. Screams sounded as townsfolk rushed towards the orphanage. He realized the roar wasn't entirely in his mind, then. Fire. The orphanage was on fire!

A coating of jittering yellow-orange glazed the semi-darkness. He saw flames shoot from the windows, claw at the evening.

He fought to move, to scream, but the blaze wavered with darkness and suddenly he knew nothing.

Chris jerked bolt upright in bed. A gasp parted his lips. His heartbeat suspended and the room took on a shivery silence. When his heart started again, it hammered against his ribs, then pulsed in his neck, throbbing, choking. He sucked in choppy breaths, fighting the residue of terror from the nightmare, the memory of that day at the orphanage. It had been years since he dreamed of it, returned to the terror-filled nightmare of his sister's death. With startling clarity everything rushed back to him, Clint and his gang, the fire. He had blacked out during the blaze and when he came to it was at the home of Clem Durrin, a rancher in the area. He awoke with a number of broken bones.

While he lay in the feather bed, a woman who told him her name was Mrs. Tulber ministered over him, hand-feeding him, washing him, until he could sit up and at last walk. No one told him what had happened in those final moments at the orphanage until he regained his strength. When Clem finally did, he told him everything, leaving out no detail. Chris had sat frozen in horror and sorrow, but he was glad Clem laid it out honest; Clem told him it was best that way if they were ever to build a relationship.

Clint's gang had stormed into Mascarada, robbing the orphanage of its donated gold and butchering all the Sisters. One gang member had apparently set fire to the place.

Within an hour the marshal gathered a posse to chase down the outlaws, but somehow they escaped into the night, leaving the town with a certain morbid amusement at the boldness of the gang. The gang had robbed before, but never with such outright contempt for the law; mostly rumors associated them with some of the rustling occurring in the Pecos Valley region.

Finally came the news Chris dreaded, had agonized over in his convalescence: his sister's remains had been pulled from the fire. No one knew whether Clint had killed Clara himself or left her to die in the flames.

Clem had seen to it she was buried proper, but that scarcely comforted the pain and loss that tore at his soul. After Clem left him alone to put his thoughts in order, Chris wanted to cry, but found no tears would come. In his mind, all he could see were the soulless buzzard eyes of the outlaw and the fear on his sister's face.

He had lost everything, everyone, his parents and now Clara. Why had God allowed that to happen? Why had He allowed Chris to live? Why hadn't He been merciful and let Clint kill him as well? Chris screamed in utter frustration and grief, realizing in that instant he would do what his sister had always done, lock the pain away and never think on it again. It was the only way he could cope; the only way he could keep from going loco with sorrow.

In the following days, his strategy worked to a degree. He found his relationship with the rancher, Clem Durrin, growing. The older man guided him, consoled him as best he could, telling him he had a home as long as he liked and would see to it papers were signed to make it legal if Chris chose to stay. Chris learned the ways of the ranch and cattle business quickly, with inbred skill. Time passed and the events at the orphanage receded further into his memory. He couldn't recall a happier day than when Clem signed those papers and became the father Chris had lost on that wagon ride across the Plains. Yet he always maintained that slight distance by calling him Uncle Clem, never pa.

Now it came down to this. The same man who had killed his sister had killed Clem and Little Waiting Women. The same bastard responsible for destroying his life in Mascarada had returned to finish the job.

Chris buried his head in his hands and sobbed in the darkness. Anger welled after a time, building until he wanted to scream with rage. He saw

Clint's face hovering in the darkness, mocking him, and he bounded from the bed, stamping across the room. He slashed a fist across the dresser top. The porcelain basin flew across the room and crashed into a wall. It shattered, shards sprinkling the floor. Fury overwhelmed him and he pounded his fists against the wall until blood ran between his fingers.

He gasped shallow breaths, fighting to get himself under control, falling against the wall and sobbing.

They were gone. All of them. His parents and his sister, Clem and Little Waiting Woman. He had nothing left except memories and a heart of porcelain, as shattered as the basin lying in pieces on the floor. Anger at Clint wouldn't bring any of them back; nothing would. Except revenge. Revenge? No, justice; justice would ease the suffering, give him the chance to find life again. To face the past.

A knock sounded and Chris' head jerked up, thoughts broken.

"You awright, son?" came Windy's voice through the door.

Chris struggled to hold his voice steady. "Go away!" He felt some of the anger remaining. He wanted to lash out at somebody, anybody.

"I heard some noise, thought there might be trouble." Windy's voice came back unperturbed.

"It's...okay, Windy. Everything's fine. I just broke a basin and cursed about it." It sounded lame but he prayed the assistant foreman would take it and go. He did. Chris heard footsteps recede down the hall.

Chris pushed himself away from the wall and went to the balcony, throwing open the French doors and breathing in gulps of chilly night air. He shivered and wept and shivered again, and at last his grief settled into a dull ache inside.

Leaning against the rail, he peered at the moon-drenched lawn and field, wondering how he would hold himself together in the coming days. What would happen if he never caught up with Clint? If the outlaw simply vanished into the night and never came back. How could he go on, knowing the hardcase was out there, killing, destroying other lives...destroying Chris from the inside?

"He won't leave..." Chris whispered, the sound melting into the night.

The notion rose in his mind as a surety. Clint had come back for something and wouldn't leave until he got it.

The thought suddenly dissolved. One moment it was there and the next simply gone. Replaced by something else that was as utterly surprising to Chris as anything that had happened in the past two days.

A strange calmness washed over him, a dark peace. He should have felt anything but that. Fury, grief, loneliness, but not peace, not some bastard tranquility.

"What's happening to me?" he asked himself, voice a ghost.

His gaze suddenly lifted to the field, as something reached out to him from the folds of the night.

Chris...

The voice floated in from the darkness, soft and caressing. It stirred his soul, his desire, though he couldn't say for sure he had heard anything at all.

I need you...

She was there, like a mirage, a rippling, distorted image standing in the moon-frosted blades of grass.

Little Waiting Woman.

The moon-glow bathed her, quivering within her image. She looked radiant, alive, but surely she was a ghost of his memory.

Yet the calmness remained at the sight of her. He felt no fear, no grief, only peace and longing, a slight clutching at his heart.

Mouth parting ever so slightly, she stood there, watching him, arms rising to beckon him. But she wasn't there, couldn't be there. She was a memory and the calmness a shadow of the things he had felt for her.

He blinked and the image melted. Moonlight shimmered on empty grass. Grief crashed back, shattering the calm spell. He shivered, at once cold and taken with the notion he was losing his mind and he'd just been shown a glimpse of insanity.

He backed into the room, wanting her more than he ever had. Legs weak, he went to the bed and collapsed. His limbs turned leaden, his heart weighted. He felt gripped by some unseen force, some specter of grief and shadow. Tears slipped from his eyes, soaking into the pillow. As the cold breeze swept through the open doors and the sounds of the night augmented, he lay there, drifting in and out of a restless slumber until the light of dawn shattered the spell.

THIRTEEN

Dawn hadn't come soon enough for Chris.

After wandering downstairs, he ignored the banter of the men and waved off Windy's offer of breakfast. The cowhands appeared in better spirits, the grisly memory of death still with them, but perhaps a little less poignant. They would carry on with their lives, the sweat and toil of the cattle business eventually cleansing their grief. They were the lucky ones.

Chris wouldn't be as fortunate. Last night had convinced him of that. In a way he neither understood nor cared to think on, he had seen Little Waiting Woman. Projected there by a fevered mind or grief, it didn't really matter. It felt as real as any night she had come to him when she was alive. The delusion left him with an aching sense of melancholy and despair.

A short time later, Chris sat in the field a distance from the main house, knees pulled up to his chest, arms wrapped around his shins, hat clenched in his hands. Hazy sunlight stung his face and a warm breeze washed over him. He gazed out at the emerald Plains and listened to the far-off murmur of the Canadian. He recollected evenings when he had sat here, after a day's work, letting the panorama fill him with a brooding peace. For all its lonesomeness the Plains at dusk could be soothing, a balm for aching muscles and a weary mind. Yet, now, something had changed, and they carried only a promise of coldness and death, of things waiting. A hell of a note, as Windy would have said.

She'll come back...

An image rose unbidden in his mind: Little Waiting Woman standing in the moon-streaked field. Yearning burned in his heart and emotion tightened his throat. His eyes glistened with tears.

For a frozen instant her scent touched his nostrils and he felt her skin pressed close to his. His fingers running through her hair, his lips searching hers, tasting every measure of her flesh.

The memory shattered and all he saw was her face in death; all he felt was the coldness of her skin; all he held were the empty promises he had given her. Grief washed over him and he buried his face in his hands, sobbing uncontrollably. It'd be all right, he tried to console himself; the pain would ease in time and he'd go on with his life. But time was a fickle bastard. It only made a body think the pain had dulled, secretly storing it away until the moment your guard came down.

His guard was deteriorating, cracking.

No, I can't let it...

If he gave in he'd be in no shape to track down Clint. He had to hold on a little longer, somehow. Just a little longer.

It hurts...

Squinting, he lifted his face from his hands. The sun's glare stung his bloodshot eyes. He drew in quavering breaths that grew steadier after a few moments.

"You really should eat somethin', son," a voice came from behind him. "Gonna be a long day without some grub in you."

He looked up to see Windy staring down at him, sympathy turning his ruddy face. Chris quickly fixed his hat atop his head and stood, looking away from the *segundo*. He couldn't let Windy see him this way. He owned the ranch, now; he had to be strong, keep things together.

You can't hide anything from Windy. You know it.

"I was just thinkin'..." His voice came out almost a whisper.

Windy took a step closer. "I knows you was. Funny thing 'bout thinkin', sometimes it helps, helps lots, lets everything come runnin' out and makes the healin' start. Other times...well, other times it just balls up your guts and makes you do things you might not do under ordinary circumstances."

"What are you gettin' at, Windy?" Chris sniffled, folding his arms against the bitterness in his heart.

Windy sighed, frowned. "Ain't hard to see you're thinkin' 'bout goin' after a dead man, son."

Chris shook his head. "He ain't dead. Can't be. You heard what the men said; they described Milus Clint. No way it ain't him."

"I knows they did. I knows they did. But it just ain't possible, I keep tellin' myself. Don't ask me how I know, I just do."

Chris eyed Windy, knowing something deeper motivated the man's words, though he was in no mood to push him for an explanation. He wanted nothing to do with this conversation as it was, but Windy made it hard to avoid; he usually got to you sooner or later.

"Facts don't lie, Windy. And the fact is, someone murdered my uncle and Little Waiting Woman and some damn fine men. And that someone's gonna have to account for it."

Windy's face turned grim. "You can't take on the gang by yourself. No one can. Hell, they probably rode clear out of the Panhandle by now, anyhow. Maybe you should just let them go—"

"Christ, you're startin' to sound like goddamn Tolby!" Chris felt a surge of anger. He was in no frame of mind to be argued out of anything he had planned. Clint was going to pay for what he had done and that was that, Windy or anyone else who tried to stop him be damned. "How can I let them go? They destroyed my goddamned life! They killed everyone I ever cared about and you're askin' me to just let things be? Turn the other cheek way it says in your blamed Bible? Jesus H., I can't do that, Windy. I can't be that forgivin'. Chrissakes, I can't even see how you could ask me to be."

Windy let out a deep sigh and raised an eyebrow. "Ain't what I'm askin'. These men deserve to be brung to justice. But you ain't gonna get no help from the law here'bouts and you can't go after so many killers by your lonesome. 'Specially these kind. Only a fool would walk into a gang single-handed. Hell, you don't even know where to start lookin' or you'da done it by now."

Chris glared at the red-headed man, fury boiling, but knew his friend was right. If he had the answers, he'd have tracked down the gang by now.

"What are you aimin' at?" he asked at last.

"I'm talkin' 'bout gettin' help, the territorial marshal, Pinkertons, whatever you want. Maybe even a posse of vigilantes, if killin' the gang is what you need to do."

Chris's voice turned stony. "You sound like you'd just as soon let 'em ride away scot-free."

"No, that ain't what I want at all." Windy's gaze dropped, came back up, centering on Chris. "Reckon what I'm tryin' to say is you've suffered enough. If you run off after those killers all hot-headed, you'll just get yourself killed. Let somebody else run them down, somebody who makes it their business. Gang that big gots to show up somewhere."

"If they don't?"

"They will. They always do. Them gangs get too big for their britches. They start thinkin' no one can hurt them, that they're somehow invincible. They get cocky and that leads to carelessness. It happened to Milus Clint in New Mex and it'll happen to these fellers. And when they're caught, if they live through it, you can be there for the hangin'. You'll get just as much satisfaction outta that as killin' 'em yourself."

Chris scoffed. "How you figure that?"

Windy's lips drew into a small smile. "I knows you, son. Worked with you a long time, now, and consider you my friend. I knows what's inside and deep down you seen enough killin' in your life. You can live with that if you let it out now. You get blood on your hands and it might be trapped inside forever. It'll eat away your innards. Soon 'nuff, the nights will seem like forever and even the sun won't look as bright. Life ain't good and it ain't long once that feelin' sets."

Chris gazed at the older man and some of his anger dissolved. Windy was right. Chris wanted justice, but he was no killer. He wanted Milus Clint dead, thought he had killed him, but at the time the hardcase had forced him into shooting reflexively.

Can you pull the trigger? In cold blood?

He felt sure he could. But living with it afterwards might be a different story.

"I don't rightly know how I'd react until after I'd done it," Chris offered meekly.

Windy nodded. "I thinks you do, son."

"I shot him once, you know, tried to kill him. I wanted to kill him for what he did to my sister."

"I know..." Windy's voice lowered. Chris stared at him, seeing a faint expression of—what? Chris couldn't tell. But he had never told Windy about the orphanage; he'd told no one except Little Waiting Woman.

"How do you know?" Chris's gaze probed the red-headed man, searching for what lay behind his eyes.

"Your uncle told me all about the orphanage and your sister..."

Chris's lips parted slightly. While it was no particular surprise Clem had confided in the *segundo*, Chris took the sudden notion that his friend was telling only half the truth.

Chris blew out a long sigh. "Clint took away the only kin I had left that day, Windy. Even after Clem took me in I swore I'd get even with the bastard someday. That day came...years later..."

Chris told Windy everything about that day, how his uncle had come to him with a stern almost sorrowful look on his face and informed Chris, then twenty, the marshal and his deputies had gotten word Clint's gang was holed up near a creek twenty miles west of Mascarada. The outlaws had grown arrogant, convinced they were invulnerable to the law. The marshal offered Clem a chance to ride with the posse; Clem, against his better judgment, made the same offer to Chris.

He recollected the sadness in his uncle's eyes, a look that understood the boy stood a strong possibility of being killed. Clem assured Chris the marshal and his men would bring Clint to justice, at the same time fully aware trying to convince him to stay behind was a lost cause.

Chris recalled the knotted feeling in his belly, the vague terror that rose with a wave of hate. He could still see the outlaw's face in his mind, hear his mocking laugh. He was afraid of Clint; he knew it. But burning hatred, the need to exorcise the demon who stalked his nightmares overpowered that fear. Nothing could stop him from going.

The marshal and his men rode out a shade past noon, Chris and Clem taking up the rear. The marshal didn't want them in the direct line of fire if something went wrong.

The sun beat on their backs; the heat was stifling. Streams of sweat ran down his face and his hands cramped as they clutched the reins too tightly. They traversed twelve miles of hard-packed trail in what seemed like moments. Time meant nothing. There was only Clint, and revenge.

The countryside meandered into low hills creased by ravines. Scrub pine and oak, stands of cottonwoods became more dense. The sun rose higher, beaming down with blistering heat. Chris grew uncomfortable, over-anxious, hate for Clint eating away at him, though he fought to remain levelheaded.

A creek suddenly loomed ahead, rushing with bubbling blue water that would soon flow red.

With a wave of his gloved hand, the marshal signaled for a halt. The men drew up and dismounted, tethered their mounts to cottonwood branches. Going the remainder on foot, the men circled out, crouching as they maneuvered into positions behind boulders or huge boles. Through a split in the fence of trees Chris could see a rickety shack with blanket awnings supported by pine poles. Men, at least twenty, milled about, some playing cards at a small wooden table, swigging whiskey, others slapping around whores they'd brought in from somewhere.

Then he spotted Milus Clint.

A burst of hatred took him and the memory of that day at the orphanage made him crazy with anger. As if possessed by some outside force, he threw away everything the marshal had planned. In blood-red relief he saw the marshal's men leveling their rifles, as well as the startled look that moved across his uncle's face, but he couldn't stop himself.

He leaped up, running, shouting: "You goddamn bastard! You killed my sister!"

His uncle lunged, trying to grab his arm and haul him back. Clem got a piece of his shirt and spun him out of step, but Chris jerked free, barely interrupting his headlong plunge into the camp.

The marshal blurted a curse and deputies sprang up, shooting. A volley of rifle fire banged like dynamite exploding in his ears. Memories from the orphanage flashed across his mind, staggering him: the outlaws thundering into town, leaping from their horses. The sound of doors crashing in under the impacts of heavy kicks. The shrieks of the Sisters and sharp curses. He heard the roar of flames, indistinguishable from Clint's laugh, and his sister's terrified screams rising above that.

The surroundings blurred, images of shouting outlaws and rifle blasts and screeching whores swirling about him.

Milus Clint's head jerked up, realization of what was happening instant and deadly on his face. His hand flashed for the coiled blacksnake at his hip.

Other outlaws leaped into motion. Colts cleared leather and came level. They jerked hurried shots at the marshal's posse, missing wide for the most part. The doors of the shack burst open and more men spilled from within, blasting away.

Neighing in terror, horses tethered to trees reared and tore free, bolting.

One of the whores shrieked as she got caught in the crossfire. A bullet, whether from the marshal's men or an outlaw, blew off half her head. She crumpled, body spasming. Chris's eyes went wide as he saw it happen; for an instant the face of his sister superimposed itself over the girl's features.

Lead whined about him and he never quite knew how he managed to avoid being hit. Slugs sent clods of dirt flying, burrowed into the ground. Plumes of dust billowed and drifted like dirty ghosts across the camp and at times it was hard to tell who was shooting at whom or what. Yet all bullets missed him. Men fell around him. Screams and curses and gunfire blistered the air, bombarding his senses, but Chris kept moving towards Clint, Winchester clenched in his bleached hands.

The outlaw's face tightened with fury but a look of self-preservation dawned in his buzzard eyes. He dived for his horse, almost reaching the frantic animal. He whirled at the last moment to see Chris descending upon him, screaming Clara's name over and over.

Clint cocked his arm, sent the blacksnake snapping out. The end took Chris on the side of his head, opening a gash on his scalp.

He reeled, pain searing through his skull, blood pouring over his ear and down his neck.

At the same instant, his finger jerked the trigger reflexively; the Winchester, partially leveled, discharged. The recoil sent him backwards, crashing to the ground. The shock dazed him, but he managed to keep his grip on the rifle.

The bullet plowed into Clint's cheek, shattering bone and mutilating flesh. A scream ripped from Milus Clint and his hand snapped to his face. Blood spurted across his groping fingers.

Chris looked up to see half the outlaw's face had disappeared, what was left a gory mask. The outlaw staggered about, screeching, clutching the whip in one hand, face in the other. He flashed Chris a look that said he'd kill him, somehow, somewhere, someday.

Clint stumbled to his horse as Chris gained his feet, bringing the rifle level again.

Clint climbed atop the frightened animal and clung desperately to the saddle, but Chris had a clear shot at the outlaw's back. He adjusted his aim...

And couldn't fire.

God, how he wanted to, but when it came down to it, no matter his fury, he wasn't a killer like Milus Clint, and even revenge couldn't force him to shoot the outlaw in the back.

He knew the outlaw would die anyway from the bullet in his head.

He lowered the rifle, watching Clint go, knowing the outlaw wouldn't make it far before life flowed out of him. All that would be left was for the marshal to recover the body.

Around him the world became deathly still. Gunfire ceased and all he heard was the groaning of fallen outlaws and the hysterical sobbing of whores. Gunpowder and dust clouds floated across the camp. A feeling of death hung heavy in the air.

All Clint's men had died, though the marshal was unable to account for four or five hardcases who had likely high-tailed it the moment the shooting started.

Only two of the marshal's men had been hit, one a surface wound; the other would have little use in his right arm for a spell, but would eventually recover. The marshal scolded Chris for almost causing a disaster, but his uncle had laid a gentle hand on his shoulder and given him a sympathetic smile. He understood and was just thankful they had come through it alive.

"I know how hard that was on you, boy. But it's finally over. You got Clint."

Chris looked out over the landscape, wondering how far the dead man had ridden. "It was an accident..." he mumbled and Clem nodded.

"Don't worry, the marshal will get him...after the buzzards do."

Chris came from the memory, eyes glossy with tears. "Marshal and his men found Clint's horse, just wanderin'. Found blood all over the saddle, but no sign of a body. Marshal figured Clint had died and fallen off along the way. Pretty easy for a body to get swallowed up in that part of the country."

Windy looked at Chris, remaining silent. Chris took the notion the *segundo* was thinking over something, looking for words to put to it, but couldn't bring himself to say whatever was on his mind.

"I felt real guilty 'bout doin' what I did to Clint, even though he was a killer. Something inside me just turned over at the thought of killin' another human being, no matter how bad he was or what he had done to me. I can't really explain it but I wrestled with it for a spell, then put it in the back of my mind, told myself justice was done and that I had nothing to feel guilty about."

"You didn't, son. It was an accident. 'Sides, you had every right killin' him. Never was a more vicious man under God's sky. But it's time to let the law work its ways. You go after him again—and I still ain't sayin' it *is* Clint—and you might not be so lucky to escape with your life."

"I don't know, Windy. Part of me says you're right, that that's the way to handle it. Another part tells me I want to be the one to put that rope around his neck and do the job right this time."

"Say the word, son, and I'll ride out and get the territorial marshal. I thinks it's the way to go."

Chris studied Windy's rough features. "Send one of the men to do it. Tell him exactly what to say and that it was Clint."

"The marshal might have some trouble with that."

Chris nodded, realizing tracking a dead man would draw more than a little skepticism from the law. "Tell him just the same. We got witnesses."

Windy nodded. "Will do."

Chris turned away and stared out across the field, mind wandering, turning over a thought.

Tell him...Maybe he can make sense of it...

"There's something else, Windy...I was thinkin' on it before you came out here and couldn't make no sense of it." Chris swallowed hard, a haunted feeling taking him. "Last night...last night I dreamt about what happened at the orphanage."

Windy's face tightened. "Figured as much when I heard the noise in your room. Had to be somethin' like that."

Chris nodded, acknowledging the assistant foreman's suspicions. "After you left...I went to the balcony." Chris hesitated, not sure how to word it. If it were just a delusion, it should have been easy. "I...thought I saw her..."

"Her?"

"Little Waiting Woman. She was just standing out here in the field and I suddenly felt so peaceful, like she had came back to me somehow and it would be all right, I could be with her, maybe forever."

Windy's face crinkled with a look of perplexity. "That ain't possible, son."

"No, it isn't. 'Cause I blinked and she was gone. But it left me feeling..." He shrugged, unable to find the words.

"You're just seein' her through your grief. She wasn't really there."

"I reckon...but she seemed so real. I swear I could have touched her."

"Be that way for a spell. You'll see her in the mirror, your dreams, all sorts of places, only natural. You loved her. Love don't let go so easy."

"No, reckon it don't." Chris felt tears threatening to spill again. He missed her more than he could put into words. "I know it sounds loco, Windy, but you figure love can reach beyond the grave?"

"In a way, I reckon. She's still in your thoughts. She lives there. That what you're drivin' at?"

Chris's lips drew into a tight line. "There's somethin' I didn't tell you about the night she died." Chris debated bringing it up; it only added to his confusion, to the unreality of what had happened, but maybe Windy could see things more clearly than he.

"What is it, son?" Windy took a step closer and put a hand on Chris' shoulder.

"I saw two slash marks on her neck, like some animal had bit her. Dark

Cloud had covered them with powder, but they still showed."

Windy shrugged. "Maybe the killer didn't have time to do worse 'fore Dark Cloud came back."

"Maybe. But when I rode to town yesterday, the 'keep told me Matalija came 'round after the attack on the saloon. He said she acted like she was drunk, but he didn't smell no whiskey on her breath. Said she had two slashes on her neck."

Windy shook his head. "This has me buffaloed. The things I seen in the last couple days ain't like nothin' I seen before. And the more I hear, the more I reckon the Devil has come to this land. Dead men and throats ripped out, bullets that don't do no damage..." He shook his head. "Somethin's come out of the darkness, son, somethin' I can't find no explanation for."

"Milus Clint is just a man, an evil man who somehow got lucky and survived a bullet in his head."

"I ain't so sure." Windy's face darkened. "No man I know of kills the way these fellas do. And to hear the men tell it, they can't be killed back. Makes me think them Injuns gots it right when they talk about evil spirits."

Chris gave Windy a searching look. "I wish I knew what to think. I wish someone could tell me."

"Some things God makes us figure out for ourselves, son. Figure this is one of 'em. Now you'd better get on back to the house and eat that grub I set for you. We gots lots of work 'round here today and I don't need you laggin' on me." Windy grinned and Chris felt his mood lighten. The *segundo* slapped Chris on the back and they walked towards the house.

Windy drew up suddenly, hand jerking up and stubby finger pointing at something in the distance. "Say, lookee that..."

Chris' gaze went in that direction. An Indian on a pinto pony sat in the field, unmoving. The breeze ruffled his long black hair and jostled his horse's mane.

"Ain't that's Dark Cloud's cousin?" Windy removed his hat and scratched his carrot-colored hair.

Chris nodded. "Speaks No More. Wonder what he wants?" As Chris said it, the Indian suddenly reined around and set his pony in motion, riding off.

"What was that all about?" Windy replaced his hat.

"Got no idea. Damn odd, though. The night Little Waiting Woman died, he seemed grieved over her and his wife, but he also looked plain angry at Dark Cloud. He kept makin' sign at him, but I couldn't tell what he said. Also got the notion Dark Cloud wasn't about to offer any help other than to bury his sister."

Windy shrugged and continued towards the house. Chris shook his head and followed him. He couldn't imagine what Speaks No More had wanted and at the moment it seemed unimportant.

FOURTEEN

With the sunset, the sky turned sooty and charcoal clouds bloated with rain surged into the Texas Panhandle. Chris hoped the impending downpour held off until after he got back to the 7HL.

After his talk with Windy, he had spent the day trying to focus on ranch chores, but his thoughts constantly wandered back to the events of the past two days and Milus Clint.

Is he dead?

Despite Windy's insistence Clint had perished, Chris saw doubt in the *segundo*'s eyes. Too many signs pointed to the dead-man's responsibility in the events at the ranch and Bald Creek—Clem's dying words, Dark Cloud's description of the outlaw's man at camp, Carter's account of the violence in town. But questions remained, plaguing him. If Clint *had* survived the bullet in his head, why wait six years to seek revenge? And why hadn't he killed Chris the night he murdered Clem? It seemed Clint had struck all around the target, deliberately saving him for last.

He wants you to suffer...

Maybe that was it. But for how long? And what then? Would Clint kill him as he had the rest? Chris didn't know. But after thinking on it, he realized Windy was right: he had to let the law go after Clint. Facing the gang alone was suicide. With the territorial marshal and his men riding shotgun, the odds were evened.

Or were they?

Clint's gang, unarmed, had overwhelmed a bunkhouse full of cowboys, as well as Mrs. Tulber and Clem, and prevailed. The outlaws had the element of surprise on their side in both cases: the 'hands had been caught defenseless, though by the looks of things in the bunkhouse some had gotten off shots. From all appearances Clem had even triggered two barrels straight into the hardcase. Yet no bodies had been left behind.

At the saloon, the story was a little different. The outlaws had slaughtered a saloon full of armed and ready men. From all accounts, the killers had taken direct shots and lived, unscathed. That made no sense. Whatever Clint was, he had to be human. Didn't he? He could die like any other man. Couldn't he? Yet how could that many heeled men be slaughtered without inflicting some damage on their attackers? After all, hadn't Dark Cloud killed one of the raiders? That proved they were simply men. Nothing more. Bandits, vicious killers, pure and simple. They had to be.

That notion was Chris's sole hope. When the marshal and his men came, they would be ready for Clint, a mere man.

Is that what you truly believe?

Chris still felt a nagging doubt. Windy's talk of darkness and evil was eating at him, and he saw too many other things that were inconsistent, puzzling: the dead steer and horse, the throats torn out, the lack of blood. Chris couldn't explain far too much of what had happened. But how could even Clint have done all that?

Something else perplexed him, though he had no clear idea why: the slash marks on Little Waiting Woman and Matalija's necks. What did those marks mean? Why hadn't both women been butchered the same as the rest, with throats torn out? Perhaps Dark Cloud and his cousin had surprised the outlaw before he was able to do that to Little Waiting Woman, but what about the dove? They'd had plenty of time to horribly murder an entire saloon full of people. Why had Matalija been left alive? Those questions needed answering before the marshal rode in.

The way he saw it, he had two choices. He felt sure Speaks No More had come to the ranch for a reason. The Indian knew something. Chris had seen it on his face that night and in his angry manner when confronting Dark Cloud. But for some reason he had decided against following through with whatever he had in mind earlier today. Chris wondered if Dark Cloud had something to do with that. Would Speaks No More defy Dark Cloud's orders, if indeed the Comanche warrior had forbidden his cousin to aid Chris? For that matter, why wouldn't Dark Cloud offer his help, since the Indian and Chris' uncle had been close?

Chris wasn't sure but reckoned he'd get little out of Speaks No More if he forced the issue. The Indian had to come on his own terms. Until that time, Chris had little choice but to wait him out.

Chris spent little time considering the second option: Matalija. He had to find her. She had the marks, yet she was alive where Little Waiting Woman was not. What did she know? Had she seen Clint? Chris reckoned there was some connection.

The only other option was to sit around and wait for death to strike. Although Windy was right, that Clint was best left for the marshal and his men, first the outlaw had to be found—and Chris damn well intended to do that much. It was a compromise he knew the *segundo* wouldn't go for, but that didn't matter. Chris made the decisions for the ranch and himself and that was that.

At sundown, coyotes gathered at the border of the property again. Their mournful howls rose in the dusk, but the creatures came only so close. Chris watched them for a spell, coldness swelling in his soul. Did they, too, have a connection to Clint? The thought was plumb loco, Chris assured himself, but right now every little thing appeared linked to Milus Clint: the coyotes, even the night itself.

It struck Chris that if he found a clue to the whereabouts of Clint through Matalija, he might throw away all sense of sanity and go after the outlaw before the marshal arrived. It would mean sure death and Chris prayed he could stay the urge, but he wouldn't let it deter him.

Chris saddled his horse, slid his Winchester into his saddleboot and rode for Bald Creek.

The Blue Steer was crowded, more so than he expected. The pungent scents of Durham smoke and redeye hung heavy in the air. As Chris made his way to the bar, the 'keep cast him a slightly concerned look.

He slid onto a stool and ordered a whiskey, clinked a silver dollar onto the counter.

After taking a gulp of whiskey Chris asked the barkeep, who still looked leery, "She come back?"

The barman frowned. "You ain't lookin' to make me no trouble, are ya? I did you a favor and I 'xpect the same."

Chris tried a smile that didn't work. "You got my word."

The 'keep studied him, apparently deciding Chris meant what he said. "Yeah, she came back all right. Last night, not too long after you left. Didn't look so bad this time, but she still wasn't right. She walked straight in and did her business, way she always does. Saw her skidaddle afore dawn."

"She come in tonight?" Chris felt a twinge of hope.

The bartender nodded. "Upstairs, only..."

"Only what?" Chris saw vague fear touch the man's eyes.

"Only it might be a good idea to stay away from her, you know what I mean?"

Chris shook his head, but a twinge of something pricked his belly, a ghost of the apprehension he'd felt the previous two nights. "Can't say as I do. Mind tellin' me what's botherin' you about her?"

"Can't really put my finger on it. She looked a mite better herself, but some of the fellers who come out of her room last night, well they didn't look so good."

"How'd they look?"

"Kinda palelike, like maybe they was feeling under the weather. They didn't say nothin', just moseyed on out and I ain't seen 'em since."

Chris didn't give it much thought. He couldn't see a connection, or a reason to alter his plans. "I'll take my chances."

The barkeep spread his hands. "Suit yourself." He moved off and Chris downed the rest of his whiskey. He slid from the stool and threaded his way through the tables to the stairs. He glanced at the crowd, townsfolk and cowhands, noting a certain strained measure to their gaiety. The doves plied their trade as if nothing had happened the other night, but an underlying tenseness existed, an unspoken fear that permeated the room.

Chris took the steps slowly, pausing at the head of the hallway. He recalled the last time he had come up these stairs, two nights ago. In his mind he saw the murdered doves, their throats torn out, their bodies battered. Weakness gripped his legs, made them shake as he started down the hall.

All the doors were closed; he had no idea if the rooms were in use. He had no desire to find out.

He reached the last door and stopped, taking a deep breath. His unease strengthened.

What will you find behind that door? More death?

Swallowing hard, he rapped lightly on the door and a voice came from within. She was here. He felt suddenly close to something he couldn't identify. Was it the hope she could lead him to Clint? Or was it something entirely different, darker? He reached for the handle, hesitating. The chilled apprehension brought on by the night swelled.

Forcing himself to grip the glass knob, he opened the door.

She sat at the vanity, carriage erect, a woman roughly his own age. Her face looked a little hard, though pretty in an innocence-lost way, spiced by her Mexican blood. As her eyes rose to meet his, he felt the immediate urge to recoil. The first time he had seen her, he thought those eyes looked like sunset on a mesa; now they appeared darker, empty, as if night had come, a dark moonless night.

Did Clint do that to her?

Dark pouches nested beneath her eyes. Her hair hung in huge loops, with curls of lace cork-screwed within. Pushed-up breasts swelled above her violet sateen bodice. Her hips were a little plump and her nose a little crooked, but it didn't detract from her overall beauty, a beauty that appeared to be withering.

Something tugged at him, a sense of compassion and perhaps more than a small degree of pity. The 'keep was right: she looked sick, paler than she should have. On his last visit, her skin was darker, creamy olive. Now its tone appeared ashen; a heavy application of make-up failed to hide its pallid quality.

Chris' gaze traveled from her face to her long throat, settling on the ghosts of two marks over her jugular. The wounds the barkeep had described had all but disappeared. Within another day they wouldn't show at all.

The dove smiled, but he saw no emotion in it, only coldness. She stood and went over to the bed, sitting on the end. Patting the mattress, she beckoned him to sit beside her. He removed his hat, fingers fumbling with the brim.

He recollected how frightened he had been the first time he visited her. He'd been with a whore only once or twice before that and his insides were all a'shake with the hungry stirring of manhood. He recalled feeling guilt as well, knowing he loved Little Waiting Woman and he was giving in to his bone-headed reluctance to commit to her. After it was over, the guilt increased. Love-making was different with the Indian girl; he knew it right then. When they coupled, he felt somehow a part of her, comfortable and completely at ease. It was only when they were apart doubts crept in. With Matalija, he felt only raw excitement and heat, forbidden pleasures without strings, worries or loss. With no love came no risk.

The dove had treated him with gentleness, at least as much gentleness he figured such a woman was capable of under the circumstances, none of the impatience of the other whores he'd visited in New Mexico. While the experience had been pleasant, it lacked the warmth and closeness he felt with Little Waiting Woman.

The thought brought sadness to him. But looking back to the dove, the feeling suddenly faded.

I can comfort your pain, but only for the moment...

Matalija patted the bed again and he felt an odd sensation of being drawn towards her, some subtle thing that reminded him of the way he had felt when he had seen the image of the Comanche girl in the field last night. Her dark eyes reached into his, beckoning him, filling his mind with shadows. A sense of detachment washed over him as he looked deeper into those eyes, those eyes...those eyes...blackness flowed over those eyes and the sensation strengthened. The edges of the room softened, burred, all but vanished, and all he could see was her. His mind clouded. He went to the bed and sat beside her.

She touched him, running her slim fingers down his arm. "You ache for another woman..." Her voice came low, husky.

Surprise penetrated his muddled thoughts. Had she read his mind?

She smiled without emotion. "I see her memory in your soul, Chris." Her fingers drifted to his face, stroking his cheek, and though the movement was gentle, unthreatening, he had the urge to pull away. A chill swept through him, rising from deep inside, from some darkness nested deep within his brains. It felt cold, her touch, so cold, as cold as Little Waiting Woman had felt in death.

"Your hands..." He wasn't sure he had spoken until she answered.

"They're cold, Chris, like the rest of me. Like the woman you love..."

"I don't understand." He gazed deeper into her black eyes and saw jagged bolts of blue-black sizzle within. His mind grew more confused. It was something she did to him, somehow, though right now he couldn't even begin to understand it. He was lost in those eyes, drowning, with little control or will of his own.

"You will understand..." She kissed him and he felt the chill touch of her lips, icily passionless. "You must never come back here."

"I..." He struggled for words, finding it suddenly difficult to breath. "...came for Milus Clint."

Her eyes narrowed. "I do not know that name." He couldn't tell whether she was lying, only that he had the desperate urge to leave her, leave this room. His senses were deserting him. The choking sensation in his throat clamped tighter. The room whirled and the pounding of his heart thundered in his ears, his thoughts. He felt himself pitch forward, hit the floor on hands and knees. Images streaked before his vision, the violet sateen of her bodice and pale olive of her flesh, the ebony of her eyes. He gasped, lungs burning, aching. Ludicrously, it struck him that he was dying for no reason and somehow Clint had stepped into his mind to cause it.

"Never come back here, Chris." Her words pulled him back and he lifted his head to see her blurred figure jittering before him. "I can't be responsible for what I might do if you return. I don't know if I can control the hunger in the last hours and I won't cause you more pain than he already has."

"Help...me..." Chris gasped, reaching out. He felt her arms beneath his, lifting him, guiding him. She pulled him across the room to double windows that opened onto an outside stairway. The cold night air slapped his face and he felt strength begin to return, but as she pulled back, he collapsed on the landing.

He couldn't tell how much time had passed, but when his head cleared he had somehow made it down the stairs to the alley that ran beside the saloon. He drew deep breaths and stumbled forward. His balance returned slowly; with each step taken he gained a little more stability.

As he peered back at the landing windows, coldness swelled in his belly. They were closed, now. He debated going back up, confronting her again. He had come to find a clue to Milus Clint and instead he had found—what?

His thoughts were too muddled to think of an answer. He couldn't even be sure of what had happened to him. One thing rang clear, however: her warning. She had warned him to stay away from her.

He paused, sucking deep breaths, fighting to regain his composure. Sounds from the saloon—laughter, raised voices, shouts—reached his ears.

Thoughts starting to focus, another thing came back to him: she had told him she didn't know Clint. He felt sure she was lying on that account. He also felt positive if he went back up she wouldn't admit as much and it would put him in some sort of danger.

Legs unsteady, he went towards the front of the saloon. Reaching his horse, he gripped the pommel, then pulled himself into the saddle. The mount beneath his legs felt more comforting than he could put into words. It was real, part of his world, and what had just happened in the dove's room was not; it belonged to that world of darkness Windy had talked about. Something told him he had just taken one more step into it.

Matalija watched the boy disappear into the darkness of the alley. Sadness wandered over her face. He was alone, tortured by loss, and she knew too well how that felt. She wondered if she should have told him what Milus Clint's man had turned her into. It would probably do little good. Clint would find the boy no matter what and that deepened her sorrow.

She had done things in her life, things she regretted and things that tainted her. She wasn't proud of them, yet somehow she had always managed to retain that small pure part of herself she could turn to in the dark hours, when she cried over shattered dreams and lost hopes. That humanness, that compassion, that guttering flame.

But Clint's man had taken that from her, hadn't he? He had stamped out that flame, turned her into something repulsive, inhuman.

But he couldn't take it completely, for seeing the pain in the boy's eyes had made up her mind. She wouldn't be part of it. She wouldn't live this way, not anymore. She wouldn't be chained to the night for eternity. And she wouldn't be responsible for causing Chris Durrin more suffering.

She was no longer alive, but even so perhaps she was more human than Milus Clint or his men would ever be.

She would see no more men, for if she did not feed within a few days peace would come and she would be free, free to sleep and turn to dust and never hurt another living sole again.

Damn Milus Clint if he thought he could stop her.

Chris rode at a canter towards the 7HL. While still confused by what had occurred in the dove's room, he grew more certain on one point: Matalija held some link to Milus Clint. Getting it out of her would prove difficult if not impossible. Going back meant suffering another bout of that mysterious spell and coming up empty again. Or worse. She had meant her warning; that was the second thing he felt sure of.

Slowing his horse, he let the coolness of the night wash over his face. He breathed deeply of the brisk air, but it did little to quell his unease. He doubted that feeling would leave as long as the sun was down, or Milus Clint was alive.

Is he alive?

He has to be...

Clouds had moved in, making the night blacker than usual. Gusts of wind slapped at the grass, made eerie slithering sounds among the blades. In the distance the howling of the coyotes ululated over the wind. A chill shuddered through him. He had ridden on nights worse than this a hundred times before; what was it about this one that seemed to cut through him, raise cold fear. The lonesome quality to it coupled with the sense of impending storm, strengthened his notion Windy was right: the Devil had come to the Texas Plains. His mind settled on things he would not have even considered possible a short time ago. As he struggled for an explanation to the killings and the experience with the dove, he wondered if grief hadn't made him loco. If he weren't simply coming apart inside and none of this was real, none of it except death.

That's what Clint wants...

Milus Clint couldn't be alive.

Milus Clint was alive.

("A darkness has moved into the Plains, son...")

Was the darkness real or imagined?

He had no answer for that question, but he found his sympathies turning towards the impossible. It was the only way to make sense of the events of the past few days.

Chris's thoughts stopped dead. A wave of coldness shook him. A roar of thunder miles off rolled across the night. His horse suddenly reared, neighing, beating the air with its hooves.

He fought the reins, muscles aching with the effort. At first Chris thought the roan had been spooked by something he couldn't see, a rattler possibly, but as he got the animal under control, he knew no snake was at fault for the burgeoning sense of fear within him. The roan merely felt what he felt.

"We bring fear, boy..."

Chris jolted as a voice sounded behind him. He urged his mount around, the roan fighting the move at every turn.

A man sat atop a black horse. Chris had never seen the likes of such an animal; barely visible in the darkness, it was huge, black as ink right down to its eyes. Yet it, and its rider, shouldn't have been there. Although Chris' attention had been focused on bringing his roan under control, he surely he would have heard another rider approach.

Yet the man *was* there. He wore a duster and a Stetson pulled low on his brow.

He's the reason for your fear...

The thought startled him, but he couldn't shake it. Something about the rider before him made a chill rise in his soul.

"Who are you?" As he spoke, Chris grabbed the Winchester from his saddleboot and leveled it.

The Rider edged his horse a few steps closer. Chris tensed, a tingling wave flowing over his scalp. The Rider appeared unafraid, despite having a .44-40 aimed at his chest.

"'Member me, boy? I rode with old Milus back when you and your uncle raided our camp. Was his second-hand man."

Judas Priest...

Chris's eyes narrowed and shock hit him. *Emmet!* One of Clint's men! Chris levered a shell into the Winchester's chamber with a jerky movement, rage overpowering him.

The Rider laughed, the sound mocking, eerie, as it dissolved into the night. "'Fore you shoot me, boy, let me tell ya somethin'. I got a message from old Milus. He says it won't be much longer 'fore he comes for you. He wants you to enjoy your sufferin' for a spell, though, so don't you go frettin' none."

"You bastard!" Chris said through gritted teeth.

"That's right, I am. But Milus is worse. Course, you done knew that. He's waited a long spell to get even with you, boy, but don't you fret none; he won't tear your throat out like them others. Old Milus, he's got somethin' special in mind for you, boy." The man giggled a high-pitched, insane sound.

"Where is he?" Chris shouted, jabbing the Winchester menacingly at the Rider.

Emmet spat. "You wanna shoot me, boy? Well, go 'head!"

Chris jammed the rifle butt to his shoulder, squinting and aiming, hands shaking from fury. His finger twitched on the trigger, but he couldn't pull it. Shooting the man would be cold-blooded murder and however much he hated Clint and his gang, he wasn't a killer. Shooting Emmet would make him no better than those he hunted. Still, it would take damn little to push him over the edge at this point.

"Do it, boy!" Emmet's voice was taunting. "Ain't you got no balls? I saw Milus screw your sis, boy! Did her up right fine!"

Rage flushed through Chris and tears flooded his eyes. Even so, he might have stopped himself from shooting Emmet then, but the Rider's hand darted for his side, brushing aside the duster flap. Too late Chris realized the move was deliberate, for the Rider carried no gun.

Chris's finger jerked the trigger. The blast rang like cannon fire. The slug tore into Emmet's chest and the Rider jolted under its impact. The shot, at such close range, should have bucked the Rider clean out of the saddle, but Emmet quickly righted himself.

"You'll have to do better'n that, boy!" Emmet shouted, half-laughing. "You can't kill old Emmet with no rifle!"

Chris didn't know what hidden blackness swept up from his being. It might have been the utter shock of seeing the bullet have no effect on Emmet or it might have been overpowering fury or fear or even a measure of insanity. But he pulled the trigger until the rifle was empty.

The slugs tore into the Rider, jarred him, but did no damage . Emmet giggled like a demon, then turned his horse and spurred it into a gallop.

Chris jammed the rifle into its saddleboot and before he could think about it bolted after Emmet.

They rode hard, miles streaking away. Chris couldn't gain any ground. No matter how hard he pushed the roan, it was never enough to catch up. Emmet matched the pace beat for beat, staying just so far ahead, as if it were some sort of game to him.

The Plains slipped away, becoming uneven as they approached the arroyo. An insane peal of laughter ripped from the Rider and Chris shuddered. Emmet was enjoying the chase, playing with him.

The ground sloped into the arroyo. Stands of cottonwoods flanked the banks of the stream that wriggled through the small canyon.

Emmet darted between the trees. Chris knew he chanced losing the Rider in the shadowy darkness. Even now he caught only a glimpse of Emmet when he reappeared at some point purposely, taunting Chris to follow.

The chase led deeper into the arroyo. Chris was forced to slow his roan in the softer sand along the bank and avoid rocks that could cause injury to his horse.

Emmet, heedless of the terrain, sped up, as if knowing the exact placement of each stone. The darkness swelled, suffused with shadows.

Losing sight of the Rider, Chris stopped. The sound of his heart drummed in his ears, the gurgle of the stream barely audible above it.

He listened for a sudden peal of laughter or hoofbeats, but heard nothing. Leaves rustled, jostled by the wind. Katydids chirped.

Edging forward along the path he thought Emmet had taken, he searched the area for at least fifteen minutes before giving in to the fact that Emmet had eluded him. It seemed impossible for the Rider to have done so. Chris should have heard something, a hoofbeat, the creak of saddle leather. Yet Emmet had vanished into nowhere.

Then a realization crashed in and his gaze flicked to the Winchester holstered in its saddleboot. He had hit Emmet point blank, numerous times—and the bullets had shown no effect! No man could have lived through that.

Had the Rider been wearing something to protect himself?

No. Nothing Chris knew of could turn a Winchester bullet at that close a range. The bullets had hit and Emmet hadn't died. Now he knew what the men had told him about the saloon fight was true. They hadn't been drunk or crazy. Neither was he, though he wished suddenly to high Heaven he was.

Dazed, Chris turned the roan and rode from the arroyo. He would have to add what had just occurred to his list of things he couldn't explain. But the incident told him one thing: Emmet had been sent for a reason. Milus Clint had just delivered word he was alive, close by, waiting in the darkness. And when he came for him, there would be nothing Chris could do to stop him.

FIFTEEN

Black Clouds boiled in the sky, scorched by great sizzling spikes of lightning. Thunder rumbled like barrels rolling over a hardwood floor. Cold pounding rain battered the buffalo grass and gusts drove rain into curved sheets. Chris listened to the storm raging beyond his window; above the downpour he thought he heard the ghosts of the past whispering to him. They told him they had moved closer, that the time was fast approaching when he would join them, to wander the night.

Ghosts or plain evil?

Maybe a bit of both.

The things Chris had seen tonight had left him shaken, confused. The walls of his sweat-and-dust workaday world had cracked and reality had seeped out. Throats torn out and men who didn't die under gunfire. Devils and demons was what it amounted to; Windy's kind of talk.

As he lay in the inky darkness of his room, Chris didn't want to believe it. He had told himself over and over what had happened earlier tonight was simply a delusion, grief-induced. He *was* going loco, plain and simple. Strain and death had broken him down.

Yet deep inside he could not make himself believe that. Despite the impossibility of it all, what had happened had indeed happened. Emmet had taken a chest full of Winchester lead and escaped unscathed. Then Clint's second had disappeared in the arroyo without a trace, without a sound.

And as rain thrummed the walls and wind wailed like banshees, the sense of the supernatural strengthened, the feeling that something evil lived out there in the wanton night. Something systematically removing everything in his life he cared about, loved, until there was nothing left.

After encountering Emmet, dime-sized sprinkles of rain pelting him, Chris had ridden back to the ranch, mood growing colder, darker. Windy had tried to question him and the men had cast him puzzled glances. He had ignored them all and headed straight to his room, falling exhausted into bed. He had lain here, staring at the black ceiling, listening to the rain beat down, for the better part of an hour, only rousting himself long enough to peel the damp clothing from his body and put on clean long johns.

Shortly after, he heard Windy rap on the door and call out, but Chris ignored him and after a few minutes, the *segundo* had gone away.

What could he say to him? That the Devil he talked about had come to the Plains, just the way he suspected? That Milus Clint was alive but unstoppable? Incapable of being killed?

Preposterous, he told himself. It just didn't happen in his world of cattle drives and back-breaking work. It just didn't happen.

Yet no amount of denial or rationalization could remove the fact that it had.

Clint belongs to the darkness. They all do...

When Clint came to collect his due, what chance did Chris have at stopping him? None, if Emmet were any indication. He saw no way to fight the Devil.

Chris twisted in bed, restless, confused. Nothing made sense anymore. Yet he needed a plan, even against the senseless. Waiting around like a steer contemplating slaughter would make it all the easier for Clint. But what could he do? What type of weapon could he use against a...ghost? Is that what Clint was? Or something worse?

No, one of them had been killed; they could not be ghosts. But just what *were* they?

Dark Cloud knows...

The Comanche. What did he know about the Riders? More than he was telling, Chris felt sure. But could he be made to talk? Or would be an easier Speaks No More target? Is that why the brave had come to the ranch today?

Another hour passed and Chris gave up the thoughts, exhaustion overcoming him and no closer to anything solid. He took slow breaths and listened to the prattle of the rain. Thunder bellowed, rattling the house; searing slivers of lightning zigzagged within the clouds' black bellies. Wind slapped the windows.

Chris' mind wandered into a half-sleep, pregnant with far-off voices and shadowy faces. A feeling crept over him, like searching dark hands, eerie, yet soothing, peaceful. He came suddenly awake, staring up at the shimmering black cotton of the ceiling.

Come to me, Chris...

A feeling pulled at him, beckoned him. He heard her voice above the drumming of the rain and wind. His eyes roved, searching the room, seeing nothing but shadowy darkness. Yet he felt *her*, and a swelling sense of utter calmness.

It's all right, now, Chris. I am here...

He should have been afraid, of ghosts or insanity, of something. Yet he felt the sense of peace strengthen. Then desire, only desire, the need to hold her again.

I am waiting for you...

Her voice in his mind again. This time he knew where it came from: beyond the window, out in the stormy night. He knew that if he got up and went to the window, she would be there in the field, Little Waiting Woman.

Chris, I need you...Come to me...We should not be apart...

Her face rose in his mind and he gasped. The poignancy of her memory invaded the sense of peace. He found himself swinging his feet out of bed, sitting on the edge, as if he had no control over his movements. As if something invisible directed him, compelled him.

Was he dreaming? Had he fallen asleep and let her memory overpower him?

No, it was no dream. He felt the cold floorboards beneath his feet; heard the rain and thunder; saw the flashes of lightning. No dream could be this real.

Was he imagining it? Yesterday he might have said yes. After Matalija and Emmet, he could no longer make absolute judgments about what was real and what was not.

He rose and went to the French doors, peering out.

Gust-swept sheets of rain whipped across the field. The water and wind-beaten Plains appeared to be an alien world, a world as starkly different from the brooding serenity of the land during the day as the peace inside him was from the horror of the past two nights.

Come to me, Chris...I have missed you...

Lightning crackled. Stark brightness washed over the landscape and swirled about the ghostly figure standing in the open storm. Her small form shone only an instant, arms rising, reaching for him, beckoning him to come to her.

Will dissolving, he opened the doors. Wind and bullets of rain pelted him, but he barley noticed. Rain soaked his long johns as he stepped out onto the balcony. He felt the icy slickness of the boards beneath his feet.

We should be together...

He went to the edge of the balcony, gripping the rail. Swinging a leg over, he let himself hang from the edge a moment, then dropped to the ground. Mud oozed between his toes. Rain plastered his underclothes to his body and water ran into his eyes, blurring his vision.

Chris, I am waiting for you...

He walked towards her, across the yard and out into the field. The same spellbound feeling he had experienced with Matalija controlled him now. He felt light-headed, the world around him fading, yet unafraid.

Lightning lit up the surroundings and thunder boomed a split second behind. He saw the Indian girl standing to his left, holding her arms out to him.

As he drew closer to her, a great wanting filled him. He felt the way he had the first time they made love, shivery with arousal and passion, a desire only she could bring out in him.

Her features shone clearly, despite the darkness. The vermilion Dark Cloud had painted onto her face ran in gory streaks. Wet specks of clay clung to her eyes. A smile touched her lips, an expression somehow colder than he remembered, yet—what? Hungry?

Her slim fingers worked at her buckskin dress and she let the top part of it fall to her waist, exposing her small round breasts. Rain splashed her dark skin, rivulets streaming down her bare front. The heat of arousal grew more intense, consuming.

(Her journey will not be peaceful...)

Dark Cloud's words thundered in his mind suddenly, nearly startling him from the spell she cast.

Lightning snaked crossed the sky, blazing white light over the land and Little Waiting Woman's form. The spell returned, freezing him where he stood.

She came closer to him, arms sliding around his neck.

His hands trembled as they moved over her slick wet skin, rounding her smooth shoulders and drifting downward to her breasts.

She pressed her body to his. Her lips caressed his face with small kisses, her tongue flicking out, probing. As her lips met his, he felt their unquenchable coldness, her chilled passion.

Her hands wandered down his chest to his groin, gently massaging. He swelled under her touch. Lips searching hers, his tongue slipped into her mouth.

Different. She tasted different, somehow. Even dazed he could tell. A flavor of moist earth, of things buried. A deadness that warned him she no longer belonged to him. Something else had stepped in and claimed possession; something that had taken all her warmth and replaced it with impersonal desire, lifeless craving.

A sudden urge to pull away took him, but quickly faded as her mouth wandered downward over his jaw to his throat. The vague fear within him whispered. But that was all. There was only compliance, surrender.

Pain stung his neck and he knew she was somehow joined to him, felt himself flowing out and darkness flowing in.

Weakness rushed through his legs and his eyelids fluttered as consciousness wavered. The rain-drenched world around him became part of him. The night was surging in, imbedding itself in his soul.

Claiming him.

Your soul is flowing out, Chris...We will be together in death as we were meant to be in life. Clint will not stop that...

Her words grew lost in the dark corners of his mind.

A coyote howled, close by, the sound startling in the downpour.

Little Waiting Woman jerked away from him, eyes flashing with blackness. Chris stared into their depths. They were utterly empty, endless and insatiable, and he saw himself trapped within.

The Comanche girl retreated, anger flashing across her face, and he saw the coyote poised there, just beyond her, mouth curled back. It snarled, teeth bared.

It was the last thing he saw before unconsciousness swallowed his mind.

The coyote dissolved in the beating rain. Arcs of black sizzled over its form, snapped within its pelt, flowed from its ebony eyes. The outlines of the creature melted away, consumed by a boiling jet mist. The mist fell inward, shaping, solidifying into the figure of a man.

The figure of Milus Clint.

"You are not to have him," Clint said in a threatening tone. Rain streamed from the brim of his hat, streaked down his duster.

Little Waiting Woman sneered. "He was mine in life, he will be mine in death."

Clint's scarred face, hidden in shadow, turned with anger. "No! I have plans for him. You will bleed his pain, no more."

"I want him!" The Indian girl's curved incisors flashed and her black eyes narrowed. "You would not let me come to him the first night, then only for a moment on the last. Now I have tasted his blood. He belongs to the Great Cannibal Owl and to me!"

Milus Clint's hand shot out, grabbing the Indian girl by the throat. He jerked her close and she struggled uselessly, trying to pry his fingers away. Her eyes widened with rage and she gasped, but she ceased fighting him, powerless in his grip.

"You live only by my whim. I can take your life whenever I please. Don't forget it, you stupid squaw. You'll obey me and leave the boy be! He hasn't suffered enough to become one of us." Milus suddenly jammed his lips to the girl's, his free hand kneading her breast. She struggled briefly then came into his arms, her hands searching his rain-soaked clothing, eyes sparking, teeth lashing. She undid his trousers, fondled him.

He pushed her to the ground, forcing her legs wide and jerking up her skirt. For an instant Clint glanced sideways, as if searching the night. He gave a low laugh of satisfaction then turned his attention back to the girl.

The Indian girl bit at his face and neck, sinking her fangs into his throat. Blood streamed out, mixing with the rain.

With his fangs, he pierced her breasts and throat, tearing at the tender flesh. The wounds healed instantly, a boil of blackness washing over them.

The girl screamed, head going back, mouth opening wide, as Milus forced himself inside her. Sizzles of black lightning arced in their eyes and flashes of lightning outlined them in stark white. Rain pelted their arching bodies and black fire flowed across their forms.

Moments later, Milus Clint threw back his head and roared into the night, spending his lust.

Speaks No More crept away in a crouch, his form obscured by the blackness of the night and driving rain. He prayed the Great Sky Spirits would not throw their bolts of light and reveal him to the dark demons of the Great Cannibal Owl. He had seen Spotted Buffalo Son nearly lured to his death by the spirit of his cousin, Little Waiting Woman. He'd been about to intervene but the sight of the coyote had stopped him. Amazed, he had watched the beast become a man of black mist and speak harshly to her, send Spotted Buffalo Son away.

It was not the first time he had witnessed his cousin's dead walk. When he had ridden to the arroyo on the previous sun, hunting food, he'd stopped at the crevice in which she had been buried. He had seen the signs she had risen, her footprints in the soft sand. Yet it should be impossible; the dead cannot walk, except in Indian legend. But Speaks No More had seen things that said it was not merely legend; it was more. Men who changed into coyotes and back again. Dead who rose. White bandits who dissolved in black fire. Perhaps he had considered Dark Cloud a fool for not accepting the new ways, clinging to the old, but he was just as foolish if he denied the old ways completely, denied what he had seen.

As the sun fell into the ground he had hidden himself in a stand of cottonwoods. Then, when as darkness swallowed the land, he could deny the old ways and dark spirits of the Great Cannibal Owl no longer. Little Waiting Woman had climbed from the crevice, turned her head towards where he hid. He was sure she had somehow spotted him, but after a while she had turned away and walked from the arroyo. He had followed, as the mist over the Plains. She had stopped just beyond the house of Spotted Buffalo Son and he had seen the boy come onto the balcony. But something had called her away that time and he had lost her in the night.

With the next sun, he had set out to the crevice to find her while she slept, but the burial place had proved empty. Had she known he would come, arrow in readiness?

Perhaps.

Perhaps not.

So he had waited, waited for the sun to plunge into the dark gray clouds, then set out for the place he knew she must come, the dwelling of Spotted Buffalo Son.

As the rain began to beat down and the sky began to roar, he had seen her, and soon after that Spotted Buffalo Son. Fear had twisted his belly as he watched her plunge her coyote teeth into the boy's throat. He'd been frozen by the sight, spellbound. By the time he finally gathered himself to act, the coyote had appeared.

The boy had been spared this night of no moon, but Speaks No More knew the next time he would not be so lucky. Speaks No More thought of the bow at his back and knew when that time came he would find his courage and prevent his cousin from taking the boy to the dark spirits. He would give her peace and send her to the Land Beyond the Sun. Tonight was not the night. There may have been more coyote demons lurking in the rainy blackness, enough to make him fail his mission.

A question came into his mind: Should he go to the boy and tell him of Little Waiting Woman? Would that make a difference? Would the boy listen? Believe? Speaks No More doubted he would. But perhaps he would try anyway, as he had come to do once before, only to ride away.

Or perhaps he would merely wait until the next moon and confront the dark spirits on his own.

SIXTEEN

The rain tapered to a drizzle as dark clouds thinned. The storm, in a whirl of fury, had spent itself like a lover. Soon the drizzle became a fine mist. Clouds parted, letting streaks of moonlight bleed through, staining the mist mother-of-pearl.

Within a cave nestled deep in the arroyo, the Dark Riders waited. A fire had been banked in the center of a huge vaulted chamber, which housed a makeshift corral to the right holding the Rider's demon steeds. One of the Riders leaned over the fence, grinning and chuckling as he fed prairie chickens and field mice to the horses.

At the back wall, the nude mutilated body of a bardove hung by her wrists from spikes pounded into the stone. Her head drooped, moans bleeding from puffed lips that stood out starkly crimson against too-white skin. Her body showed livid welts from whip lashes and patches of her flesh had been torn away by razored teeth. Little life remained in her.

Around the cave, nestled close to the fire, lay the pack of coyotes, their jet eyes ever in motion, occasional throaty growls issuing from curled back mouths.

A Rider crouched on his haunches near the pack slid a harmonica across his mouth, blowing disharmonic notes.

Milus Clint glared a look at the Rider and sneered, then glanced at Emmet. "Chrissakes, he ain't got a lick of goddamn tone since he died." Milus spat.

Emmet chuckled.

The remainder of the Riders sat on logs or bedrolls, a few playing cards, a few spiting tobacco juice at the cave walls. One hunched over a hunk of wood he had chopped from a cottonwood branch, whittling away. He shot a look to Clint every so often, amusement on his face. Milus nodded and the man set back to work, carving long ribbons of wood from one end.

Beyond the mouth of the cave Billy stood gazing out at the stream that snaked through the small canyon. Milus's attention settled on the young Rider. Emmet's did the same, a puzzled look crossing his features. Then he shook his head and peered at the outlaw leader.

"I think there's somethin' peculiar 'bout that boy," Emmet said.

Milus eyed him, giving a slight nod. "Look 'round, Emmet. There's somethin' goddamn peculiar 'bout all of us."

Emmet frowned. "What I mean is, he's always lookin' at things like he's lookin' into the past, like he's lookin' at some other life. Ain't got no head for what we're doin'. He ain't takin' no fun out of it." Emmet paused, face growing more serious. "I think he might be dangerous to us."

Milus shifted his gaze back to Billy, an unreadable look crossing his disfigured face. After a moment of silence he asked, "You booger that boy?"

"Hell, yeah! You shoulda seen the look on his face when the Winchester slugs plowed right on through me. He thought he'd a'seen a galldarned spook or the like!"

"He did." Milus's voice held no trace of humor.

Emmet chuckled just the same. "Yeah, reckon so." Milus' second paused again, as if thinking something over. "Why you want that boy so bad, Milus? Why don't you git it over with, 'stead of draggin' it out? This waitin' 'round is gettin' under my skin."

Milus' eyes narrowed. Half his face tightened. Firelight played in eerie orange and shadow over the mottled flesh. "'Cause I want him to suffer for what he done to me in New Mexico. I want his grief to tear his innards to pieces. Won't be satisfied till it does. He'll know every moment of the torment I endured and he'll know it for eternity after I finish with him."

"Why didn't you just fix him up six years back?"

"He was still a young'n then; he had little to lose, 'cept the old man. Now he has everything. I've just begun to take it away."

"That Injun girl almost mussed up your plans, Milus. You can't go lettin' her on her own no more."

"She disobeys me again, I'll destroy her. She knows that."

Emmet fell silent and Milus stared off into the distance, intent on watching Billy. He reckoned he knew what the young Rider was feelin', the longing for things that had been, the *humanness* of a man—if anyone could rightly say Milus had ever carried any degree of that in his black soul. Some folks looked for excuses when it came to men like Milus Clint, sets of circumstances that made a child play into the Devil's hands and grow up plumb wrong. But Milus knew different. Some men were just born plain bad and he was one of them. That didn't stop him from wantin' the things other folks had, the things he used to take for granted: things like sunlight and the biting taste of whiskey and the soft insides of a woman.

The Durrin boy had seen to it Milus could never have those things and for that the boy would pay dearly.

Milus' memory wandered back to the day the marshal and his men had surprised him by that creek. He indulged the reverie, something he rarely did. He and his gang had gotten too full of themselves, he reckoned, made a mistake somewhere; the law had tracked them down, bushwhacked them. He recollected feeling shock when the boy charged at him, screaming his name, shock that quickly turned to pain as lawmen followed, the sound of their gunfire like volleys of thunder. He had watched most of his men get slaughtered under the siege of lead; regrettable, but he could always find more. He would have escaped and never paid it another thought, but for Chris Durrin. The boy hadn't even known what he was doing when he charged after him. Under normal circumstances, Milus would have welcomed the situation, being challenged by a greenhorn manchild who could not have beaten an outlaw like himself even on his best day.

But Fate had intervened and a bullet had shattered Milus' face. Luck had guided the boy's hand that day, sheer dumb luck.

He had made it only a few miles before his strength deserted his hands and his fingers had slipped from the saddle horn. He had fallen to the ground, dust bitter on his tongue, mixing with the spur-metal taste of blood.

The hoofbeats of his horse dying in his ears, Milus had crawled, only making it a few feet before collapsing, cooking in his own sweat.

He recollected the blazing sun that had nearly burned his eyeballs white and the buzzards circling and swooping. They had picked at his wounded face, beaks snatching up strips of raw flesh like he would tear loose a piece of jerky. He remembered the pain.

Suddenly the pecking had stopped and through blurred vision he had looked up to see the Apache standing over him, one he had sold stolen horses to, a Mescalero. The Indian stooped, lifted him, then draped him over the back of his pony. Milus put up no resistance; he couldn't have had he wanted to. Too much life had trickled out of him.

From there forward, details became hazy.

He barely recalled entering a canyon as darkness fell. There, the Indian stopped and lowered him to the ground. A series of movements came in blurred glimpses. The Apache moved around, first banking a fire, then foraging in his saddle gear.

Milus' consciousness came and went. He caught flashes of scenes, the Apache kneeling by the creek, mixing something, then the Indian squatting next to him, prying open his mouth and forcing peyote bulbs between his teeth. Within moments the world became curiously schismed. Visions assaulted him and he felt hundreds of black beetlelike bugs swarming over his body, crawling into every orifice, choking his throat.

His lungs ached for breath and he gasped, but he couldn't breath. Darkness and firelight became marbled and he felt himself tumbling through it, into some other world. Glimpses of faces, hideous things, Injun nightmares. But in each face, some facet of his whole, like mirrors reflecting his true nature.

He was dead. He knew it as sure as he had ever known anything. This was death for him, yet somehow life, another form of it.

He passed into the realm of the night and dark spirits cycloned about him, raking him with talons of shadow, scratching away bits of his soul until they took it all. He knew he was empty inside and that emptiness would have to be filled. He sensed he had a choice. He could turn back to death and whatever fate befell the guilty, the remorseless, or he could let the dark shades enter and give him renewed life. But that life came with a price, a burden of sustenance. As long as he fed them, he would live, with certain restrictions.

Despite that, he saw no other choice. He reckoned he never had. For all he had ever understood was want and taking, and with those dark spirits he was one.

He let them in.

Milus suddenly awoke by the campfire, gasping. The Apache stared at him and Milus focused on his brown face.

"I'm...different..." His voice came distant, as if someone—*something*—else had spoken through him.

The Apache nodded. "You belong to them, now."

Milus pushed himself into a sitting position. His fingers went to his face, feeling the mud and herb plaster over his shattered features.

"It will not heal completely," the Apache said. "But it does not matter."

Milus lowered his hand, clenching his fingers, unclenching. He had power, strength he had never felt before. Inside him the night swelled.

"You did this to me?"

The Apache shook his head. "You passed on. The choice was yours. Now you are one with them."

"I'm...dead?" Milus looked at his hand. It was true; he felt different, somehow, but not dead. He couldn't be dead. He was sitting here, talking to the Injun. Wasn't he? Dead men didn't talk to the living.

"If I'm dead, that means no lawman can harm me, Injun. No one can!" Excitement rose in Milus Clint's voice and he stood, an insane laugh tumbling from his lips. Blackness swarmed across his buzzard eyes, arcing with blue-black streaks. His lips curled back and razored fangs glinted with firelight.

"You are what the Apache call 'Dead-Walkers', what the few white men who know call 'Dark Riders'. The dark spirits have been summoned and have drained you, then filled what remained. To keep them you must fill their need."

Milus, black eyes glittering, orange firelight swimming over his mutilated face, turned towards the Apache. "What the hell do you mean by that?"

The Apache peered straight at him. "You must feed them. You will learn that quickly or be destroyed. You will drink of the blood and suffering and fear of others."

"Hell, I always done that!" Milus grinned. He liked the way he was, dead yet alive and indestructible.

"You are not invulnerable," the Apache said, as if reading his thoughts.

"Whatta you mean, Injun?" Anger lashed Milus' tone and he grabbed the Indian, hoisting him to his feet with the strength of a grizzly. "I'm dead, ain't I? You said so. Ain't nothin' can kill a dead man."

"You cannot be killed," the Apache said unperturbed. "But you may be destroyed."

Milus' gaze narrowed.

"There are laws, even for the darkness. You may never again gaze upon the face of the sun, for its rays will turn you to dust. You are vulnerable to the rules of nature and Indian weapons, the same as any man. Do not cross running water, for it will purify you; do not touch fire, for you will burn as any other."

Anger twisted Milus' face. "What the hell-damnation good is that? That's just like being alive—worse, for chrissakes!"

"You will discover powers in exchange. The white man's weapons will no longer destroy you. You will have power over those humans you choose, the ability to bend their will. You will be one with the creatures of the night, the coyote, the owl; they will be your eyes and ears. There is more and you will learn as the dark spirits judge fit."

Milus cocked his head. "Now, that's better. Reckon that makes bein' dead right more appealin'." Milus thought about it and plans formed in his mind. Some of his men, the ones holed up in the shack, had likely escaped. "Can I make others like me? Tell me!" He jerked the Apache close, black eyes boring into the Indian's brown ones.

"Yes, there is a way, a choice. When you drink their blood, you can fill them with dead-life or destroy them. The spirits will teach you."

"Why you doin' this, Injun? I sold you some horses and beeves, but never gave you no deals. Why help me?"

"I did not help you. I cursed you."

In that instant, Milus Clint knew the Indian had spoken the truth. He was cursed. For eternity.

He laughed, the sound insane and echoing through the night. Then he tore out the Apache's throat.

After, he walked to the creek, watching its babbling path for long moments, snakes of moonlight reflected and swept away within. He balled his fists and screamed at the sky, feeling intense hunger swarm over him.

Nights passed and he learned, as the Indian said he would. The Dark Spirits taught him everything, from initiating other Riders, to shaping into creatures of the night or black mist. These gifts he kept to himself, telling the men only as much as he deemed necessary. Sharing power was never his strong suit.

In time, he had learned to live with the night.

Milus' mind focused on the present and burning hate for the boy gnawed at him. He had learned to live with it, yes, but he had never learned to forgive or forget. Chris Durrin would know what it was like to be imprisoned by the night, to be a slave to it. To be a Dead-Walker. But that was yet to come. For now his rage would be spent another way. Milus looked at Emmet. "Tell Billy I want to see him."

Emmet gave Milus a puzzled look, but gained his feet and went to the mouth of the cave.

"Ever just want to ford a river again?" Billy asked Emmet, as the Rider walked up to him.

"Ain't never gave it a thought." Emmet rubbed his chin.

"We can't do it no more, Emmet." The lopsided grin came onto Billy's face. "Hell, we didn't know we couldn't till Sanders ran into one chasing an Injun gal and got plain washed to pieces. Milus never told us. Can't see no sunrises, neither, and we can't run no beeves 'cross a river. We ain't never gonna be able to."

Emmet shrugged. "Don't see how there's much need to, Billy."

"No?" Billy gave Emmet a blank look. "You don't think so?"

"Big ol' pain in the ass goin' 'round 'em, now, but I can live with it."

"Don't know if I can, Emmet." Billy turned back to the stream. "I want to ride herd again, way I did in New Mex. I want to do the things I use to do, feel the sun on my face and smell the new grass and taste the trail dust."

"Better put that talk away, kid. If Milus hears it..."

"Milus ain't got nothin' to say about it, far as I'm concerned." Billy paused. "He hides things from us, Emmet. Things he wants to keep for himself. But I find out and he ain't got the power he thinks he's got."

"That's blasphemy, kid."

"Yeah? We're blasphemy, you know. Ain't no Bible God responsible for us. But we still got a choice to make it different. I'm takin' that choice."

Emmet shook his head. "He wants to see you, Billy. It'd be best if you didn't take that attitude with him."

Billy's face flashed a puzzled look, then he grinned wider. "Does he, now?"

"Yep, told me to fetch you."

"Tell him to wait."

Emmet frowned. "Don't see that's such a good idea, kid. He'll be right peeled if'n you don't come."

Billy stared into the distance, laughed a mocking laugh. So Milus wanted to see him. The time had come as Billy had known it would. Welp, now was as good a time as any. Billy had his mind and his plans made up and they no longer involved Milus Clint. He turned and walked into the cave, Emmet watching him, thoughts transparent. Billy knew Emmet figured he didn't carry a lick of sense, but the second was wrong. Billy did have sense and it was time he started using it.

"What took you so long after you went up to the whore's room the other night?" Milus eyed the young Rider, little emotion on his mottled face.

"Whatta you mean?" A slight look of concern crossed Billy's blue eyes and Milus felt pleased by it. He had grown dog tired of that goddamned grin and cocky attitude.

"You didn't come down till we was ready to ride. You musta been doin' somethin'. One whore ain't no problem."

"Just took me longer to get done with killin' her, is all."

"'Cept you didn't kill her, Billy." Milus' eyes went black. "You left her like us."

"No, I swear I didn't, Milus." Billy's eyes took on deeper concern. "She's dead, just like you wanted."

Milus gained his feet, stepping closer to the young Rider. "She's dead, awright. But not the way she should be. Did you think I wouldn't feel her, Billy? Did you think you could get away with somethin' like that? She's one of us. The Durrin boy even went to her last night; Emmet saw him. You could have mussed up my plans real good, boy."

"Just thought it would be better if she was like us—"

"You ain't s'pose to think, goddammit! You're s'posed to listen. I'm goddamn tired of you goin' off half-cocked and doin' whatever the hell you like."

Concern suddenly vanished from Billy's eyes, replaced by anger and cocky challenge. The lopsided grin hit his lips and he jabbed a finger at the leader. "I don't give a diddly goddamn what you think, Milus. You been so goddamn wrapped up in your own revenge you can't see the big picture. I want to make the whole world like us, so we can live again, least part ways. You want to goddamn exterminate ever'body and leave us nothin'!"

"What the goddamn hell are you jawin' about, boy? The world ain't meant to be like us. We're meant to prey on 'em. Take what we want. The weak got to perish, feed the strong."

Billy shook his head. "You're plumb wrong, Milus. We can all live in the night, be the way we used to be."

"You gone goddamn soft in the head, boy? It ain't never gonna be that way."

"You ain't the law with me, Milus. You can't control me way you do rest of these sheep. I know there's things you ain't told us. We got powers you keep hidden. I'm leavin'. You can have your revenge, but I'm gonna have me more than that. I'm gonna have life!"

Fury blazed on Billy's face and he started to turn.

Milus' hand darted for the whip coiled at his feet, snatching it up. With a sweep and jerk of his arm, he snapped it. The flayed end took Billy in the back of the head, sending him reeling. Milus laughed.

"You ain't goin' nowhere, boy, 'cept straight to hell!"

"You sonofabitch!" Billy leaped at the outlaw leader before Milus could snap the whip again. He slammed into him, forcing him backwards but Milus brought his fist around in a hammering blow that sent Billy sprawling.

"You ain't got enough in ya to whip me, boy! Even Dead-Walkers got an order of authority."

Billy pushed himself up and charged recklessly at Milus. The hardcase sidestepped, arcing a blow into Billy's temple and the younger outlaw crashed into the stone wall.

The Rider with the harmonica stopped playing and the outlaw whittling looked up, watching with mild interest. The rest observed the brawl with strained humor.

Milus closed in on Billy, knocking him sideways with a knife kick to the groin. Billy crawled on hands and knees along the cave floor. Black fluid dribbled from his mouth.

Milus motioned to the men and two Riders grabbed Billy's arms, hauled him to his feet, then dragged him from the cave.

Milus nodded to the man who'd been whittling and the Rider held out the branch piece he'd carved into a sharp stake. Another stake lay at his side. He scooped it up and gained his feet.

Filing out of the cave the Riders followed the men dragging Billy to a stand of cottonwoods. They forced him against a huge tree. One jerked up Billy's right hand, pinning it against a thick branch. Milus took a stake from the whittler and stepped up to Billy.

"You wanted to see the sunlight, Billy, well, now you're gonna get you're wish." Milus cocked his arm, bringing the stake back, then hammering it forward. The wood pierced Billy's wrist, plowed through flesh and bone and burrowed into the branch. Billy's face twisted with pain, but he gritted his teeth, remaining silent.

Milus motioned for Billy's other arm to be held up and he took the second stake, driving it through Billy's left wrist into the tree.

Milus stepped back. He stared at the young outlaw, whose face showed spite, not fear. Grabbing the blacksnake, he lashed at Billy just short of twenty times. The young outlaw groaned, slumping, suspended by his wrists from the cottonwood. Gored lashes across his face and chest dripped black.

"There you go, boy." Milus gritted his teeth. "Let me know what it's like to be human again..."

Milus spun and disappeared back into the cave. The other Riders glanced at Billy with pained looks mixed with fear, then followed the leader in. Emmet glanced at the beaten outlaw and walked towards the cave.

"Emmet!" Billy screamed.

The Rider turned. "Sorry, Billy. Told ya not to push him. Ain't nothin' I can do for you now."

The night sky lightened with gray streaks of false dawn. The grayness crept over Billy's face and he turned his head towards it. He no longer feared the coming of daylight. In fact, he welcomed it, because it meant an end to the longing, to the loathsome thing he had become.

He felt the heat rising within him, crawling across his flesh like fire ants. Stinging, biting, devouring.

The sky split with shafts of blazing orange-red and Billy cursed Milus Clint and hoped to hell the boy named Chris Durrin would somehow learn the truth in time to destroy Milus, this time for good. But he saw little chance of that happening.

One thing Billy did know: he would see Milus again, sometime, in Hell, and he would be waiting for him.

Shafts of light wandered over the arroyo walls, slinking across the ground until they reached him. He gritted his teeth, peering for the first time in a year at the glowing yellow face of the sun. It was his last vision and that was just fine with him.

Sunlight struck him dead-on.

Black fire burst from Billy's face. It sizzled across his features, swallowing them. Ebony flame skittered through his hair, over his clothes, swarming, gulping. He became a pyre of crackling black fire, plumes of inky smoke billowing, then subsiding.

In moments, nothing remained but the stakes hammered into the branches and the singed outline of a body on the tree.

On the ground, at its base, lay a pearl-handled Colt.

SEVENTEEN

Chris awoke with a start, sitting bolt upright in bed. Morning sunlight shined through the windows in blazing streaks of yellow. The glare stung his eyes and it took a moment for them to adjust to the brightness. His sight focused on the room, seeing the double doors leading to the balcony were wide open. Rain had soaked the floorboards and a crisp chill filled the room. His heart pounded with vague unease, something left over from the darkness, though he wasn't sure at this point what it was. He wondered how the doors had gotten open, how he hadn't heard them blow in or the storm wailing into the room. Had *he* opened them? Something murky in the back of his mind told him he had.

Why?

What had happened during the night?

The vague unease strengthened. A sudden rush of images brought a mixture of feelings: fear, sorrow, wanting. The images came dark and out of focus, just out of reach. Every time he tried to grasp one it melted away, though in its wake it left...*something*. A feeling of emptiness, utter and eternal, a sense of complete loss.

His breath caught and his heart pounded harder and when he held his hands in front of his face they were trembling. *Judas Priest!* He was shaking for no reason. He drew deep breaths, letting them out slowly, struggling to calm himself. After a few minutes his heart slowed and the residual fear eased, but the feeling of emptiness remained.

Something touched you last night, something evil...

Swinging his feet out of bed, he sat on the edge, face in his hands. Suddenly aware that his undershirt was clinging to him, he felt his long johns then the sheets; they were damp; he'd been sleeping in wet clothes. How had they gotten that way? Had he gone out into the rain? How else would they have gotten wet?

His head began to throb. All evidence pointed to him having gone out into the storm, yet he couldn't recollect having done so.

Chris gained his feet, legs shaky as he walked to the French doors and closed them. He fell against the wall, nausea twisting his belly, exhaustion making his muscles rubbery. He lifted his head to peer out into the sunlit field and the ghosts of the night swirled among the sparkling blades of wet grass.

Little Waiting Woman...

She had been there, hadn't she? Calling to him, reaching out. Was that why he was wet? Was that why the doors were open?

Had he gone to her?

A sudden rush of longing told him he had, though the memory was hazy. But what had happened after that?

He couldn't recall.

For a second her image formed in the glare, a creature of sparkle and desire, as quickly dissolving, leaving only glittering streams of sunlight. The field was empty, steam rising from it as the day heated.

Nothing threatened him in daylight, did it? Nothing called out to him or waited. Only in darkness. And with the night the memory would return fully, the haunting.

Pushing away from the wall, he went to the dresser and splashed his face with water from the stainless steel basin Windy had brought up. His head rose and he stared at his battered reflection in the mirror. Puffy dark pouches nested under his eyes; his features carried a drawn look and his cheeks were sunken. Three days' worth of stubble peppered his face; his lips were cracked and his skin appeared unnaturally sallow.

A bolt of apprehension went through his belly as his gaze locked on the specter of two marks on his throat—the same type of marks he had seen on Little Waiting Woman and Matalija!

Flashes of images whirled in his mind at the sight. Beating rain and darkness; bastard passion and pain and her mouth at his neck—

Gone.

The images vanished and only his reflection remained, the reflection of an empty man.

The sounds of the men downstairs preparing for the day filtered into his mind, bringing him back to the present. The room swelled with light as the sun climbed higher in the sky and a small measure of strength returned.

Shaking himself from the spell, Chris located a spare set of underclothes and dressed. He made his way downstairs, legs steadier with each step.

The men had filed out to start work, but Windy stood in the dining room. Chris saw a plate of beans and bacon set out for him, but he wasn't hungry. He waved it away as Windy indicated the plate, opting for a strong cup of Arbuckle's instead; the coffee was scalding, but he barely noticed, gulping it. Windy watched him drink, a look of discontent on his ruddy features.

"Son, you gots to keep your strength up. You look like hell warmed over."

"I can't eat, Windy...I'm fine. Not hungry, is all." His voice held little conviction.

"Don't look none too fine. You know better'n lie to me. I always see through it."

With a burst of anger Chris swept his arm across the table, sending the plate flying. Beans splattered the wall and floor. He glared at the *segundo*. "I said I didn't want it!" It came out a shout and he didn't know why he felt such fury, only that he did and couldn't stop it. Some dark part of him wanted to fight, to shout. He felt ready to explode inside. He shook his head and went for the door, stepped out into the bright morning.

He heard the shouts and laughter of the men hard at work and it did nothing to calm him. In fact the normalcy might have made it worse, pointed out the impossibilities concealed within the darkness.

He breathed deeply of the steamy air, fighting for some sort of control over himself. He'd never felt this unstable, even after his sister's death. He remembered feeling anger then, at Clint, at himself, and guilt damn near every waking moment until the day they tracked the outlaw down. But it was focused fury; he was angry at *something*. This felt different. He felt furious at hidden things, veiled evils that lurked in the shadows of the night, things that by all rights couldn't be real, couldn't be alive. But they were and there was absolutely nothing he could say to himself to convince him otherwise now. Clint and his men were dead, yet alive; Little Waiting Woman was buried yet standing outside his bedroom last night.

"Tell me what's happenin', son," Windy's voice came from beside him suddenly. "You're lookin' like you're comin' apart and I know you gots plenty of reason for it. But keepin' it balled up inside don't help a lick."

Chris's breath staggered out and he shook his head. "I don't know, Windy. I don't know what's happening. I think I'm going loco. I've been seein' things that make no earthly sense to me."

"We all been seein' 'em, that's a fact. You can't let it make you jiggered or you'll only give Milus Clint an easier time of it."

"I saw one of his men last night, the one called Emmet," Chris blurted before he could stop himself. He suddenly needed to let it out before it ate him alive.

"What?" Windy stepped closer, boots clomping on the porch.

"He rode up behind me. Never even heard 'im. He said Milus would come for me soon."

"Then Clint's still in the Plains; he didn't pull stakes..."

"That ain't the half of it. I got to feelin' kinda strange after I went to see Matalija, like she worked some sort of spell over me. I got all faint and the next thing I know I was ridin' back to the ranch. When Emmet rode up, he goaded me into shooting him, pretended to go for a gun, 'cept he wasn't heeled."

"He's dead?" Windy asked, doubt in his eyes.

"I emptied the whole goddamned rifle into him, Windy. I swear I did. Point blank range. Couldn't have missed him. But he swallowed lead like it was nothin' and rode off. I couldn't catch up no matter how hard I rode. Chased him into the arroyo and he just vanished into the night. It ain't possible, but it happened."

Windy took a deep breath, too-small eyes sinking further into the gristle surrounding them. "That just goes along with what the men said about the saloon fight, son. You ain't loco, 'less they are and that ain't likely."

"Then tell me what happened. Tell me somethin' that makes sense. What makes a man take that much lead and live? What makes a dead man come back to life and a woman rise from her grave?"

Windy squinted. "You seen her again?"

"I think so. Last night. Can't recollect for sure."

Windy nodded. "Thought as much. Found you curled up on the veranda. Me an' one of the boys carried you to your bed. You was mutterin' her name, insistin' we leave the windows open so she could come."

That confirmed it for Chris; he had been outside, seen her. His hand drifted to his throat, to the ghost marks there. "I did see her..." It came out almost a whisper.

Windy frowned, leveling his gaze on Chris, eyes serious. "Been thinkin' it over, son, but what I gots to say sounds loco. If you wants to hear it..."

"I'm a lot more ready to believe it now then I was three days ago. A lot more ready to believe just about anything." He looked at the *segundo*, a haunted look in his eyes.

"Them Injuns in New Mex, them Mescalero Apaches, they gots a legend 'bout dark spirits that walk in the night. What I heard was kinda vague, mostly campfire stuff, but maybe there's somethin' to it."

"Tell me."

"Well, just that the medicine man of the tribe would find someone at death's door and force him through some sort of ceremony that made him part of the night. I heard 'em called Dead-Walkers, or Dark Riders. Never believed a lick of it. Always reckoned it was some of that peyote vision stuff them 'paches shovel out. Now...well, I ain't so sure—because Milus Clint died that day you shot him."

Chris's gaze drilled the red-headed man, who seemed on the verge of saying more. He saw pain and doubt in Windy's eyes, more than he had ever seen.

"I thought Clint died," said Chris. "I heard some men escaped from the cabin; maybe one of them found Clint and helped him." Even as it came out of his mouth he didn't believe it.

"No, son. None of them helped Milus." Conviction came in the *segundo's* voice.

"How do you know that?" Chris felt his belly knot as a surety overrode his confusion: Windy knew more about Milus Clint than he had told. The thought suddenly chilled him.

"I wanted to tell you last night, son, after it came to me where I'd seen that Shinn fella before. But after findin' you on the veranda I couldn't."

"What are you sayin', Windy?" Chris felt anger strengthen for a reason he couldn't pinpoint.

Windy drew in a deep breath, his body tensing. His gaze dropped to his boots, then came back up again and he shifted feet. "I know why Shinn looked familiar and why none of the men back at the shack could've helped Clint. I seen Shinn in New Mex, when he was handlin' Clint's rustlin' end of the operation, one of the ones who was, anyway. See, son, I done some things, then. I ain't proud of 'em by a damn sight. I done some things that would've got a man hung. By all rights I should have died that day you and the marshal came for Clint."

Chris's eyes narrowed. "Christ..." He tensed, a chilled wave sweeping through him. Beads of sweat broke out on his forehead and the muscles to either side of his jaw balled.

"I was havin' some thoughts about quittin' Clint's gang even then, but the marshal made up my mind that day 'fore I could. You see, I was in that shack when the marshal raided Clint's camp. Me an' a few other men, Emmet included. We hightailed it out the back and rode for Santa Fe. *All* of us. Not a one went back for Clint, though we saw him ride off, bleedin' like a sonofabitch. We knew he wouldn't make it and we knew if we got caught, we'd hang. I did a lot of thinkin' after and realized what I did was plumb wrong. This helped me." He pulled the Bible from his pocket and held it up. "This helped me realize I had to make amends for the things I done, the things Milus Clint had done. So I came to your uncle and signed on with the 7HL, aimin' to do the best I could at makin' sure that debt was paid."

Fury boiled in Chris's veins. The memory of the orphanage shook him. He saw the riders thundering into town, up to the building, their faces shadowed but obvious. One of the riders...*Shinn!* That's where he had seen the man, riding with Clint's gang all those years ago. Only a glimpse, but it had burned into his mind. He knew Windy was right and it angered him even more.

His vision blurred with a crimson haze. The man before him, the man he called his friend, had been a part of the gang who had destroyed his life. It didn't matter that Windy had gone honest and that they had shared so much. Nothing mattered except venting the rage and that Windy had belonged to Clint's gang. Chris had something solid to focus on, now, not fleeting feelings and darkness. By damn he would.

"You sonofabitch!" he screamed and Windy's eyes bled with pain. "You goddamned sonofabitch!"

Chris lunged at the *segundo*, swinging this fist in a clubbing arc.

Windy made no move to defend himself. He stood solid, eyes pained yet resigned to what was coming.

A heavy *crack* sounded as Chris's knuckles collided with Windy's jaw, sending the assistant foreman stumbling backward. The *segundo* crashed into the wall. His body vibrated with the impact.

Chris hurled himself at the man, bloodlust in his eyes. He swung again and again and still Windy made no move to fight back. The *segundo* took the blows in silent resignation, blood flowing from his lips and nose, until he finally collapsed on the veranda, battered and bleeding and gasping.

Windy looked up at Chris through puffy, half-closed eyes. Through the fury in his mind, Chris could barely see the man who had been his friend.

"I knew this day would come, son..." Windy said, breath ragged, words halting. "I knew I'd have to tell you one day and you'd have to get it out of your system. I can't change what I did, only pray you can accept it and know that I meant it when I said I was your friend. Still am."

"Get out of here, you bastard!" Chris took a threatening step towards Windy, grabbing his shirt and hoisting him to his feet. He hurled the man across the veranda. Windy barely kept his feet.

The assistant foreman looked back at him, pain from his soul outshining the pain of the beating.

"There's a lot of talk about forgiveness in this book, son," he said, holding out his Bible, which he had managed to hold onto. "Don't rightly expect you can forgive what I done, but I hope you'll try. You'll need to if you want to beat Clint this time."

"I see you anywhere again, I'll kill you..." Chris's lips drew tight. Tears flooded his eyes and raw anger melded with bitter loss, the loss of a close friend. His entire body shook and his lungs burned.

With a defeated expression, Windy nodded and shambled off. Chris watched him saddle his horse and ride out, not looking back.

He didn't move from the porch for long moments. He stared in the direction Windy had ridden. As he watched the settling dust, the pinpoint of motion Windy had become in the distance, Chris felt something die between them. The trust he had built with this man over the years, the camaraderie and closeness. Gone, in a heartbeat. He wouldn't have thought it possible that Milus Clint could take anything more from him than he already had. But the outlaw had taken something else—a friend. And Chris would not forget that when the time of reckoning came.

The neighing of a horse pulled him from his thoughts. He turned and looked behind him to see Speaks No More in the field, sitting atop his pony.

The Indian seemed to be observing him, sitting stone still in the saddle. How long had be been there? Long enough to see the fight with Windy? The Indian's face turned in a frown and he reined around, riding off in the direction of his camp.

Chris stared after him, a sudden need for action, any action, overtaking him.

He saddled his roan and mounted and with a sharp kick spurred the animal towards the Comanche camp. This time he wouldn't let the Indian off the hook. If he, or Dark Cloud, knew anything about Clint, Chris would force it out of them. And in his frame of mind, he didn't care if he had to kill one of them to do it.

EIGHTEEN

By the time Chris saddled up and lit out after Speaks No More, the mute Indian had already put a couple of miles between them. But it didn't matter. Chris knew where he was headed: back to camp.

Chris drove his heels into the mount's sides, urging the roan into a full gallop. A burst of adrenaline pumped through his veins. Muscles tightened with every jounce of the horse, jolting his entire body and rattling his teeth, but he paid it little mind. All that mattered was focusing on something, giving his anger a direction. And Speaks No More and his closed-mouthed cousin made perfect targets.

How could you betray me?

His mind still reeled with the knowledge Windy had been part of Clint's gang. The assistant foreman was more like an older brother than a friend and the betrayal stung like hell. While he realized he had let his temper get the better of him in the beating he'd administered to the *segundo*, the disclosure couldn't have come at a worse time. Throughout the carnage caused by the outlaw leader, Windy had been Chris' last supporting beam; he had no one else to lean on. With Windy gone Chris's fragile structure of denial threatened to collapse.

You should have let him explain. He's been your friend a long spell, but you gave up on him just like that...

Judas Priest, maybe he *should* have listened with his head instead of his fury. The *segundo* had been as close to him as any man and no matter what he had done Windy deserved a second chance, didn't he? He'd stayed beside him all this time and had never once done anything to indicate he hadn't gone honest. But rage made Chris need to strike out at something—someone—solid. Windy had given him that opportunity. The Comanches would be next.

You can't take it out on him or the Indians. They aren't responsible for your pain—Clint is.

Windy's face rose in his mind, chasing a twinge of regret. Then Clint's face shattered that and all he saw was the man he despised, the godless monster responsible for murdering his loved ones; all he saw was the face of a demon, no longer a man, who promised to come for him and deliver him to the darkness. In some way, in the past, Windy had been part of that. A spike of horror made his belly drop: had Windy been present the day Clint's gang raided the orphanage? Or had he joined up with the gang leader after? If Windy had participated in the slaughter at the orphanage...

Chris might forgive anything else. But not that. Despite the friendship they had shared.

As he searched his mind, it occurred to him Windy had never once let on about his past crimes. The *segundo* had lived his life above reproach, seldom even joining in the good-natured if bawdy pastimes of poker and whore-bedding with which the other cowhands saw fit to unwind. Windy had always been there for Chris, nearly as much as Clem. His work and reputation were spotless, the past was the past. But how could Chris accept that? He couldn't. Not now. Not when the image he saw in his mind was that of Windy running from the shack the day the marshal raided Clint's camp.

Suddenly another face rose in his mind: Shinn's. Another link to Clint. Was the rustler a tie to the gang's past—or to its present? That was something Chris would have to determine. And when he did, God help that sonofabitch.

But first he had the Indians to contend with.

Dark Cloud and his cousin knew more than they were telling. Chris felt sure of it. Chris reckoned Speaks No More had been on the verge of revealing it twice in as many days. Perhaps he would have if not for the confrontation he'd witnessed between Chris and Windy. It didn't matter. If Speaks No More knew something of Clint and the madness that had swept into the Plains, Chris would force him to tell.

The grasslands tumbled off into a stream-laced depression that sloped into the arroyo. The camp came into view and as Chris approached he saw Speaks No More dismount and sprint into a tipi. The campsite had been cleaned up, to the extent that a few pots and pans had been gathered and set to one side. The burnt-out remains of the tipi hadn't been touched. Chris reckoned it wouldn't be. The Comanche would consider the area tainted, forsaken by their good spirits, haunted by their dark ones.

He slowed his roan to a trot. His heart beat thickly as he stopped and dismounted. The tipi flap flew back and Dark Cloud came towards him, Speaks No More a step behind.

Rage overtook his manners. As he came forward, Chris jabbed a finger at the Indian warrior, who seemed unperturbed. "You're gonna tell me just what the goddamn hell's been happening!"

"I do not know what you speak of." Dark Cloud said it evenly, but a twinge of emotion tightened his face. His dark eyes narrowed and Chris had to fight the urge to throttle the answer out of him. He wanted to, God, he wanted to. His nerves felt gritty with frustration and anger. It would not take much to make him snap, though in his worn condition he realized he had little chance physically against the stocky warrior.

"You know, goddammit! I saw him—" He stabbed a finger at Speaks No More. "—in the field yesterday and today. He came to tell me something. I think he wanted to tell me the other night but you stopped him. I think you know a hell of a lot more about what's going on than you've told me!"

Dark Cloud cast Speaks No More a disparaging look. "I forbade him to interfere. He refused to listen."

The admission took the last of Chris' control. Dark Cloud would not be intimidated into telling what he knew; the admission was as far as it went. In a burst of fury, Chris flung himself at the Comanche, swinging a fist, yelling.

Dark Cloud moved faster than Chris would have thought possible. The Comanche sidestepped the blow easily and Chris hurled past the Indian, sprawling on the ground face-first. Under any other circumstances it would have been comical, a rank amateur tactic deserving laughter. Yet under these circumstances it only infuriated Chris more.

Dirt clogged his mouth and dust stung his eyes. He spat and pushed himself up, scrambled to get into a position to throw another punch.

He never got the chance. Dark Cloud's moccasin-clad foot filled his mouth and ringing pain splintered across his teeth. The gunmetal taste of blood mixed with dirt soured his mouth and he spat a brown-red stream.

His head reeled from the blow. The world streaked across his vision. He crawled forward, trying to regain his senses and get to his feet. He made it part way up when a brown fist cracked into his jaw, sending him flying backwards and down again.

Chris lay there, stunned, gasping. A loud hum throbbed in his ears.

As his eyes focused, the glare of the sun stung them and he blinked, arching a hand over his face. He swiped at the dirt-coated blood running from his lips. He considered struggling to his feet for another try at the Comanche, but the fury-driven energy had drained out of him.

He looked up to see Dark Cloud extending a hand. Chris spat another stream of blood and dirt and waved off the Comanche's help. Climbing shakily to his feet, he glanced at Speaks No More, who gestured angrily at Dark Cloud.

Dark Cloud nodded. "Little Waiting Woman has risen." Little emotion touched the Indian's tone.

The revelation confirmed what Chris already knew about the girl he loved. That Dark Cloud admitted to it fit perfectly with the Indian's make-up. Chris knew, despite the beating he'd taken, he'd gained Dark Cloud's respect. Few men would face the Comanche unarmed and Chris, in fury, had. Now it was Dark Cloud's turn to offer compensation.

"You've...seen her?" Chris's voice came out gravely.

Dark Cloud shook his head. "No. Speaks No More saw her walking in the night; he saw her come to you."

Dark images flashed in Chris's mind: he saw her standing in the field, rain bathing her, lightning caressing her body. It was true, all of it. The Comanche had seen her, too.

At once relief and horror coursed through him. His legs trembled and he felt as if he would collapse again. His mind fought to grasp what had happened, what she had become. He touched the ghost marks on his neck and coldness swelled in his soul. She had died. He knew death when he saw it. He had buried her in the crevice in the arroyo. Yet she lived, somehow, for he had seen her, touched her, felt her in his soul. She was dead, yet alive.

Like Clint.

Chris' lips parted but no words came out. He couldn't begin to understand the meaning of all that had happened—*how* it had happened, only that in some bastard way it fit in with Clint's plan of revenge.

"Why?" Chris mumbled.

"She has been sent back by the Great Cannibal Owl...for you."

"She wants...to kill me?" Chris felt his heart burn. He refused to believe the young woman he loved was capable of that. Yet she no longer belonged to him. He knew that. She belonged to the night, to a devil named Milus Clint.

Dark Cloud shook his head. "No. She would have killed you the first night if that was what she intended."

"Then why? Why would she come back?"

"I do not know. You shared a bond in life, perhaps in shadow death it is the same. Or perhaps there is another reason, one known only to He Who Drinks Life."

Clint knows; he damn well knows. It's part of this somehow, part of him.

"I saw Milus Clint as good as dead, yet he's back. What in God's name is he?"

"The man you call Clint is no longer. What remains of him is only the evil he was in life, an emissary of the Great Cannibal Owl: He Who Drinks Life, that which descends in the dark to devour men. He seeks revenge for some deed done him in life. You have brought him upon us."

Accusation and reproach hung in Dark Cloud's tone. He blamed Chris for all that had happened; that was clear. Yet at the same time, Chris saw something in the man's eyes that said that blame went deeper, condemned him and his race for the subjugation and humiliation borne by the entire Comanche nation.

Chris returned the accusation with anger. "Why didn't you tell me before?"

"Would you have believed in dark spirits then?"

Chris shook his head. He reckoned the Indian was right but it did little to take the sting out of the fact that Dark Cloud had hidden the truth from him.

"I did not think so." Dark Cloud looked smug and Chris despised it.

"I'm listening now." He glanced at Speaks No More, who looked at Dark Cloud and gestured.

"Tell him!" he signed.

Dark Cloud nodded. "Apache call them Dead-Walkers; white men call them Dark Riders, the few who know of their existence. The dark spirits of the Great Cannibal Owl took He Who Drinks Life between the world of life and the world of death. An Apache shaman guided the black spirits to him. They filled him and now he fills them. He took the others with him, made them as he. They walk the night for eternity, drink the life from the living. Feed on suffering and fear and blood."

Chris's mind went back to Mrs. Tulber and the ranchhands, then to Little Waiting Woman and Matalija, the marks on their necks. He swallowed at the sorrow the images rose in his throat. "Why do they...mutilate some and not others?"

"They choose whom they make as they are, whom they wish to wander the nights of eternity."

"Their victims become like them, the ones not torn up?" Chris' hand drifted to his neck, the marks.

"When the moon moves from there to there—" Dark Cloud pointed at the sky, drawing his finger sideways a few inches; Chris estimated the time to be between two and three hours. "—they walk again. Death cannot hold them."

Chris's heart beat thickly with each word. "You knew she would rise, didn't you?"

"I did not know for certain. I prayed the Owl Bone Magic would save her, that the Grandfather Above would show her mercy and lead her to the Land Beyond the Sun."

Chris' head dropped and he stared at the ground. A week ago he would have called Dark Cloud's beliefs foolish; things like that simply didn't exist in the gritty workaday world of cattle ranching. Now...now he knew they were true. Clint was dead, yet alive, as was Little Waiting Woman. And Clint's revenge wouldn't be complete until he destroyed Chris.

Chris could no longer wait until the territorial marshal and his men arrived. They would ride straight into their deaths if he did. No, whatever he had promised Windy, and himself, was worthless, now. He had to somehow find Clint and destroy him.

You'll have to destroy her, too...

The thought froze him and he drew in a deep breath to control himself. He forced the thought from his mind. If he dwelled on it he would have no chance against Clint. Maybe that was Clint's ace; if so, Chris couldn't let the outlaw play it.

"I have to find Clint, kill him. But I saw Winchester slugs swallowed by one of his men like they were candy. You killed one. They must have weaknesses."

"Your white man's rifle will not harm them. He Who Drinks Life is protected by the shaman magic against your weapons of death. Perhaps if the damage was much...I do not know for certain."

"Just what the goddamn hell *will* hurt them? There has to be something."

"They are vulnerable to whims of nature. They fear the cleansing light of the sun, for it will destroy them. They do not fear fire, but may be trapped in a circle of burning flame. This is the way of some tribes. They will burn as any man."

"The first night, in the field, near a mutilated longhorn, I saw the shape of a man burned into the ground..."

"Swallowed by black fire, the poison of their dark souls. Something killed him."

"Only way that could have happened was if a longhorn gored him."

"They have dominance over the creatures of the night, the coyote and the wolf, the bat and the owl. They may become as them. Your Spotted Buffalo belong to the day, as do the morning birds and bear. They are equal to the night animals as is natural."

"You means whoever gets who first?"

Dark Cloud nodded almost imperceptibly.

"You must help him!" Speaks No More gestured sharply at Dark Cloud.

The warrior's brow creased and he held up a hand. "No. Spotted Buffalo Son must face He Who Drinks Life on his own. The dark spirits are angered at him, at the white man."

"I ain't askin' for his help," Chris said to Speaks No More. Chris was surprised how much bitterness came out in his tone. "Dark Cloud and my uncle had their obligations; guess that don't extend to me."

Dark Cloud glared at Chris. "There is nothing more I can do."

"Didn't rightly expect there would be." Chris turned, disgust on his face and anger in his heart. While on one hand he accepted what Dark Cloud had told him about Milus Clint, the rational side of him still fought it. However he felt a flicker of satisfaction. He had gotten what he came for: an answer, at least a partial one. Clint was no longer a man and Chris would have to face him on his own before the outlaw had an opportunity to complete his plan. Resolve gave Chris a respite from the insanity he'd felt creeping over him. He would find Clint before Clint found him.

He went to his roan and mounted, peering back at Dark Cloud.

"How'd you kill him, the Rider who raided your camp? At least tell me that."

THE DARK RIDERS

Dark Cloud turned and walked back into the tipi and for an instant Chris thought the Comanche had simply chosen to ignore his question. But a brown hand whisked back the flap and Dark Cloud came back out, holding up an arrow. With a snap of his hand, the Indian flicked the arrow to Chris, who caught it.

Dark Cloud said nothing, staring a moment, then went back into the tipi.

Chris looked at the arrow, then shoved it in a saddlebag and nudged his head at Speaks No More, who nodded back.

Reining around, Chris rode for the ranch. He had something now and for the moment it was enough.

NINETEEN

The sky melted from blood-red to violet to onyx. Stars glittered and bone-colored moonlight glazed the Plains. Coyotes banded on the horizon. Clint was out there, waiting in the night.

The dusk filled Chris with dread. He had watched the sun set from his bedroom balcony, had seen darkness gather over the land, had felt it grow at the edges of his soul. As if it consumed everything real, everything natural and living.

You bastard...

He wondered what Clint would do next and if he could hold together under the assault. When would Clint come to finish the job? Tonight? Tomorrow night? Would the outlaw simply swoop down on him before he found a way to fight back? Or would he have time to develop some sort of strategy against the demon outlaw?

The uncertainty was the hardest part, the waiting. Chris's resolve was shaky and the past few days had left him little strength with which to fight. Clint had gotten the upper hand on Clem and Little Waiting Woman, as he had that day at the orphanage. Both times no one expected him to come.

But Chris knew Clint was out there and that it was only a matter of time. Chris knew what Clint was:

A Dead-Walker.

An Apache legend.

Yet a reality, one Chris was forced to accept.

You beat him five years ago...

But that was luck, sheer and blind. He needed more now. He could not charge blindly into the outlaw's camp and expect to come out alive.

The marks on his neck suddenly throbbed, pulling him from his thoughts. He touched them. A trickle of wetness. He looked at his fingertips, rubbed them together.

Blood.

His blood, seeping from the wounds.

She'll come tonight, not Clint. She'll come and you'll be helpless and this time...

He stared out at the moon-glazed buffalo grass, half-expecting to see her, but the field was empty.

A swell of laughter and voices from the downstairs reached his ears and he knew what he had to do next. He could risk his own life, but not the lives of his men. He pushed away from the rail and went into his room, closing the window doors. Going downstairs, he went to the parlor. The cowhands looked up at him, going silent as they noticed the somber look on his face.

Chris summoned his resolve. "I got something to say to you men, but I want you to understand, depending on what happens in the next few days, you all got a job here later on."

Carter stood from the bunk on which he was sitting. "Sounds like you're cuttin' us loose, Mr. Durrin. We're willin' to stay. We all know the risk involved."

"No, you don't exactly," Chris said earnestly. "The gang who rode in here the other night, the outlaws you saw at the saloon, are going to come back."

Carter's brow bunched. "You can't be sure they will, Mr. Durrin. Likely they skidaddled. No use in 'em stayin' 'round these parts."

Chris almost smiled. "They didn't go anywhere. The leader, Milus Clint, wants to get even with me for what I did to him in New Mexico. He won't leave till he does. I don't want any of you men here when he comes back, because you'll just end up like the others."

"How you figure on dealin' with him yourself? We saw what his gang did at the saloon. Ain't no way one man, no matter who he is, can best him if'n a whole barroom couldn't."

Chris shrugged. Carter was right and he had no answer for the man. He didn't know when Clint would make his final move and what weapon he could use against a dead man when he did.

"I don't know, Carter. But I know whether you're here or not, it won't change things none. He'll come and with y'all gone it'll mean just that much less bloodshed."

"If you reckon that's best, Mr. Durrin, I'll accept it. I gotta tell ya, I was plumb scared they would come back, though I told myself a hunnert times they wouldn't."

"I ain't askin', I'm tellin'. I want you all out of here tonight. In an hour, no more."

Carter nodded, the look on his face one of resignation tinged with relief. The men set about fixing their bedrolls in silence. Within an hour, the room was empty and the receding sound of hoofbeats echoed from the distance as they rode off.

It was done. Chris knew he had to turn the men loose, for their own protection. He couldn't risk their lives any more than he already had.

An ominous silence fell over the big house. Amber light from the lamp washed the parlor in an eerie glow. Only the staccato howls of the coyotes broke the stillness. Coldness and vague fear crawled through him as he stood frozen in the room.

Minutes dragged and suddenly he thought he could hear his uncle's laughter, then the whisper of Little Waiting Woman singing to him in the night. A breeze scratched at the window. Lamp light flickered from a draft; shadows jittered.

Forcing himself from the spell, he fetched his Winchester and loaded it, then set it against the wall near the parlor window. He knew it would be of little use, but the very act brought a measure of comfort to him.

Milus Clint wanted Chris to suffer. Well, he had. More than any man ever should. But Chris saw nothing else Clint could take from him and maybe that give him an edge. Clint had destroyed Chris's life a second time; that couldn't be changed. But there was still more to it, something else the outlaw had in mind. What was it?

He wants to make you like him...

The thought jolted Chris. With a surety that came from some unknown place inside he knew that was the remainder of Clint's scheme. The outlaw was feeding on Chris's anguish, suffering, but that wasn't enough for him. He wanted Chris to share his fate, to be trapped in the darkness. That had to be it. Chris had inadvertently created Clint that day the marshal raided the outlaw's camp; Dark Cloud was right to blame him in that respect. Chris had drawn the killer to the Plains.

But that was as far as it went, as much fault as Chris would accept. Now, the blame rested solely with Clint and Chris refused to pay any further price. The hardcase would never complete his revenge, one way or the other. Chris eyed the Winchester: that was his escape if things fell in Clint's favor. The thought gave him a fleeting sense of security. Clint would never change him into one of them; Chris would die before that ever happened.

But that decision would come later.

A coyote howled. The sound echoed through the room, somber and threatening.

He's taunting you, goading you...

It was a mistake to feel secure in any way. It would only shift the advantage back to Clint. He could not make the same mistake the outlaw had, could not let himself become arrogant. Too much was at risk.

He won't let you kill yourself. He won't let you escape that easily...

With the thought, anger swelled and he embraced, thankful for it because it overrode his exhaustion. He could use anger; it was a way to keep going, to fight.

You bastard...

Fury overcoming him, Chris stormed across the parlor and threw open the door. He walked out into the night, crossing the yard and going into the field.

He balled his hands into fists.

"Where are you?" Chris shouted at the night, fists trembling and bone-white. "Where are you, Clint? You coward! I'm calling you out, you sonofabitch! I've had enough of your games. You can't hurt me anymore, you hear me? You can't hurt me!"

Chris waited, unsure what he expected to happen. The breeze gusted, whipping the grass flat. The moon bathed him in cold indifferent light. The coyotes fell silent, as if mocking him.

"I'm not afraid of you, you bastard! I'm not afraid! You took everything I had. You can't take any more. You hear? I killed you once, I'll kill you again!"

Fury spent itself like a shooting star and night crashed in around him. Clint would leave his challenge unanswered because it suited his end.

He felt suddenly defeated. Carter was right: how could he expect to best Clint when a saloon full of men had failed? When Clint wasn't even human? He wasn't equipped for it. It wasn't part of a cattleman's world; it was part of a nightmare world, one in which Chris didn't belong.

Words and rage were useless. Clint couldn't hear him. No one could hear him.

The silence deepened. No katydids, no night creatures, only the shushing waters of the Canadian in the distance.

Then, something else...

A calmness swelled over him and he suddenly knew what was happening. He *had* been heard; his challenge had been answered, but not by Clint directly.

He whirled to see the figure of Little Waiting Woman standing behind him. Her dress top hung at her waist, flaps jostled by the breeze. Frosty light caressed her skin, her small breasts, her pale face. Blue-black hair snatched shivers of starlight and an emotionless smile painted her lips.

Come to me, Chris. Tonight we shall be together.

Her voice caressed his mind, making him shiver with wanton feelings. It drew him to her opening arms.

A thought flashed in his mind: maybe he was wrong, maybe there *was* something else Clint could take away from him. And maybe she held it...

Speaks No More rode out of camp as the sun fell, despite the disapproval of Dark Cloud. He dug his heels into the Pinto pony's sides, urging it into a faster gait. He rode in the direction of the ranch house.

He had argued relentlessly with Dark Cloud for the last few hours, but his cousin had remained stubborn, refusing to budge from his position on the matter of the white boy and his fate. Speaks No More had grown weary of listening to Dark Cloud's flimsy excuses of angry spirits and dark justice against the white man. Speaks No More knew as well as any the white man's capacity for destruction and savagery; they had cut the words from his throat with a Bowie knife. But that was long ago, when the Comanche still ruled the Plains. Those were the old days and the old ways. Dark Cloud still clung to them, and he would perish because of them, as had many *Nermernuh*. But not Speaks No More. If Speaks No More were to perish, it would be with dignity. He would not wait until the dark spirits found him.

He saw no way to stop the progress of the white man. Dark Cloud should have realized that as well as anyone: the warrior had fought at Palo Duro when Mackenzie crushed the Comanche. Even their bitter enemies, the Apache, would soon learn it was useless to resist the loathsome spirit the white man called Manifest Destiny. There was no use fighting it any longer, but Dark Cloud was a stubborn fool.

He Who Drinks Life would surely destroy Spotted Buffalo Son, forbid him to enter the Land Beyond the Sun and defy the Grandfather Above. Then Spotted Buffalo Son would wander the night, an emissary of the Great Cannibal owl. He would drink the life of the innocent, and soon the night would be full of black spirits and dead men. Dark Cloud and Speaks No More would perish just the same.

Speaks No More could not let that happen, even if he must kill Spotted Buffalo Son himself, to spare him the fate of Little Waiting Woman. But that was yet to be seen. Perhaps Spotted Buffalo Son would discover the strength he needed. If not, speaks No More vowed to be ready.

Speaks No More had another reason for helping the boy. The dark spirits had taken Speaks No More's wife. They had also taken Dark Cloud's, yet his cousin seemed to ignore that. The warrior was content grieving in the old ways, the maiming, fasting, wailing. Speaks No More was not. He never would be. He abided by them, yet he would deal with the awful sadness in his heart in another manner—by tasting the nectar of revenge.

Last was the matter of Little Waiting Woman. She would not find peace while the Great Cannibal Owl forced her to wander the night. Speaks No More knew that. So he vowed to send her to the Land Beyond the Sun. Tonight. Tonight he would find the courage to free his stricken cousin.

Before departing camp, he had strapped his bow to his back, filled his quiver with true-flying arrows. After watching his cousin with the white boy last night, he knew she would return to him, despite what He Who Drinks Life had told her.

Speaks No More brought the Pinto to a halt many yards from the house. He let the breeze flow across his bare chest and stir his dark hair while his eyes narrowed, searching the night. He could feel them in the darkness; the evil spirits were close. Perhaps he was already too late?

Coldness swelled in his heart and belly. Vague fear of the old legends troubled him, despite what he told himself, that his arrows would destroy the dark spirits where the white man's rifle bullets would not. Black ghosts seemed gathered all about him, brushing his flesh, making him shudder. He dismounted and crept through the grass, dread growing stronger as he drew nearer to the ranch house.

As he came within yards of the spot he had last seen Little Waiting Woman and Spotted Buffalo Son, he summoned his courage. Crouching, he waited, and unlimbered his bow.

A short time later, he saw Spotted Buffalo Son come from the house. He was yelling something, raising his fists to the sky. Speaks No More knew it would not be long now...

Chris saw emptiness in her black eyes. Endless depths of despair, loneliness, corruption. He was looking into the soul of the night itself; there was no sunlight, no warmth, no compassion. A thought told him this was what nothingness, utter and complete, looked like, and in that instant he knew the girl before him was no longer the one he had known, loved. She was merely a shell with no soul except that of the darkness, a representation of life. But, despite that knowledge, he couldn't stop himself from going into her opened arms. As if the emptiness had reached from her and filled him, filled the hole left by sorrow and grief.

At his neck the marks throbbed, trickling blood. His blood rushed through his veins, leaving him weak, helpless. His hands came up as if of their own volition, sliding over her shoulders. Her flesh felt cold, lifeless. Her features remained emotionless, like a face from the grave, and her eyes arced with blue-black light.

Yearning swelled within him. His mind clouded, reeled. Her cold lips pressed to his, searching, tasting, possessing with each kiss. Her hands drifted over his shoulders and he stood frozen, lost in her spell. Her mouth moved over his cheek, tongue flicking out.

I need you, Chris. We must be together. I came back for you...

Her voice whispered in his mind, black angels. It was a thing of need and of hunger instead of passion. He tried to focus on its emotionless quality, pull himself free, but his thoughts slipped away when he met her eyes.

Join me in the night. It will be ours. We can be together always...

"Yes..." he whispered, head lifting to expose his throat. Beads of blood swelled from the marks and she licked them up. The marks pulsed with burning pain, inviting her, aching for her.

Her lips drew back; curved razor fangs glinted with saliva and moonlight.

Something within him surrendered and he waited for the piercing of his flesh. She would drain him, join him to her and he wanted it in that moment, more than he wanted life and sunlight, love and warmth. There was only wanton desire, bastard passion.

A dull *thuck* pierced his dazed thoughts and he felt her jolt against him, then jerk back. The spell shattered as if he had plunged off the edge of a canyon and hit bottom. He staggered under the wrenching emotion that tore their souls from one another's. His eyes widened in horror as his vision focused on her.

Little Waiting Woman's head thrust back and a hiss escaped her lips. Her incisors, stained with scarlet, shown in the pale light. Black fluid snaked from the corners of her mouth and she tore away from him, body shuddering, going limp.

She crumpled to the ground, black eyes lightening momentarily to their normal brown. She lay still and Chris dropped to his knees beside her. The point of an arrow protruded from just beneath her left breast; it had plowed through her chest after entering from the back. He gazed up, tears flooding his eyes. In a blur he saw the pain-stricken face of Speaks No More peering down at the Indian girl. The Indian gripped a bow with bleached fingers. He shook his head, lips parting in mute apology.

Chris turned back to the Indian girl. Little Waiting Woman struggled to move but her body seemed drained of all its strength. Her lips quivered as she made a plaintive strangled sound. As Chris pressed his ear close, he heard her words.

"Forgive me..." Then black fluid bubbled from her mouth, cutting off anything further she might have said. Her eyelids fluttered closed and her head fell back. As Chris looked on, stunned, black flame sprang from her body, dancing over her flesh, sizzling, devouring. She dissolved in ebony fire. At last only the outline of her body seared into the grass remained.

Chris forced himself to his feet, looking back to Speaks No More. The Indian's face was fraught with sorrow and sympathy, but also an expression of surety that he had sent Little Waiting Woman to find peace.

"No!" Chris shouted at the Comanche. His mind filled with rage and pain. She had come back to him, only to be taken again. He had lost her to the grave twice. No man should ever have to face that. In a flash he realized Clint had delivered an answer to Chris' challenge, proved he could still hurt him in ways Chris could not begin to imagine.

With the look in Chris' eyes, Speaks No More scrambled back, panic crossing his face. Chris, insane with grief, lunged at him, grabbed his arms.

"You killed her!" he heard himself scream, as he shook the Indian. "You killed her!"

Speaks No More's face twisted with fear and Chris wanted to kill the man, might have had he possessed the strength to do it. But he had nothing left. His muscles deserted him and he fell to his knees again, sobbing uncontrollably as he buried his face in his hands.

The breeze gusted, scattering her black ashes to the wind. This time she was truly gone. The night was filled with the sounds of emptiness and the screams of what might have been.

When he looked up, Speaks No More had gone and the moon had jumped a handspan across the sky.

There's nothing left...

He gained his feet, legs unsteady, and stumbled back to the house, throwing open the door, leaving it that way. Seeing the rifle poised against the wall, he considered for long moments putting the barrel into his mouth and depriving Milus Clint of his victory. Did he have the courage to pull the trigger? To face his own death after he had run from so many others?

The Winchester was a way out. It would give him victory over Clint. Wouldn't it?

Whether from uncertainty or lack of nerve, he hesitated. His gaze came away from the rifle. He staggered to the cabinet at the corner of the parlor, falling against it, sliding down along the wall as his strength failed and tears burned down his face again. He pulled open the cabinet door, finding an Orchard whiskey bottle Clem kept for guests. Gripping the bottle, label blurry before his vision, he uncapped it and took a pull. Liquor seared down his throat and he nearly choked on it, coughing out half a mouthful. It ran over his chin, soaked his shirt.

Her face appeared in the darkness before him and he reached out to touch it, but it dissolved. Another ghost. Tears flowed harder.

He was lost, now. No direction or hope, only pain and hurt and indecision. Clint out there, a Winchester in here.

So easy...

He gulped at the whiskey a second time. The liquor went down smoothly, filling his belly with warmth. Another drink.

Do it...escape him...

When a third of the bottle was gone, the room began to swivel around him and resolve filled his mind, courage. He would spit in Clint's face, leave him empty-handed if another goddamn Dead-Walker was what he wanted.

You can pull the trigger...

Yes, yes he could. He could put the barrel in his mouth and pull the trigger and all the pain would vanish instantly.

Courage filling him, he tried to get to his feet, intent on collecting the Winchester, but his legs refused to work right. He thudded down, the world streaking with darkness and scratches of lamplight.

A low snarl pulled his senses temporarily into focus and he saw a coyote hunched in the doorway. The beast, lips curled back and fangs bared, peered at him with black eyes. Chris stared back, almost uncomprehending, then his eyes narrowed.

"G'on, you sonofabitch!" he shouted, hurling the whiskey bottle. "Get outta here!" The bottle bounded from the doorframe, shattering on the tile and splashing whiskey. The coyote bolted into the night.

It was the last thing Chris remembered before unconsciousness blackened his mind.

Speaks No More rode like the wind towards camp. In his heart, he felt a great sadness for the white boy and for Little Waiting Woman, though he knew she, at least, had found peace. She was free to journey to the Land Beyond the Sun, and despite Dark Cloud's arguments, he would be glad as well.

But there was more to do. Speaks No More realized that as soon as he had put an arrow through Little Waiting Woman's heart. The white boy had little left with which to fight. He would make easy prey for He Who Drinks Life. He needed help and Speaks No More would give it to him. He owed it to Spotted Buffalo Man's memory and honor. As well as the honor of the Comanche people. He Who Drinks Life would not stop once he took Spotted Buffalo Son. Speaks No More and Dark Cloud would surely perish next. The disease would spread and eventually it would reach the Comanche reservation. It was a matter of foresight and self-preservation, something the True People had shown far too little of in the past.

Speaks No More would have to find He Who Drinks Life and send him back to the dark spirits. Dark Cloud would have no choice.

But how would he find He Who Drinks Life?

Apache legend said the Dead-Walkers were active only at night. In the daylight they must seek shelter from the sun's face. That would be the best time to find He Who Drinks Life. At night the Dead-Walkers were too strong, too dangerous, surrounded by others of their kind. He Who Drinks Life would not be taken so easily as Little Waiting Woman, if Speaks No More could isolate him at all. He cursed himself for not taking advantage of his opportunity on the previous night, when He Who Drinks Life had come for Little Waiting Woman. That had been the time to destroy him. But Speaks No More had let his courage run as sap from the tree and lost his chance.

Regret served no purpose now. There was only tomorrow and opportunity.

Where would the Dead-Walkers sleep during the sun? The place had to be dark, protected. In the vast openness of the Plains he saw only one place that would provide such sanctuary: the arroyo. The Dead-Walkers had to be somewhere in the arroyo. He knew caves existed there, deep openings that went forever through sheer stone walls. The sun never penetrated beyond their yawning mouths. He would begin there, with the first light of dawn, find their camp and destroy them. He would bring plenty of arrows.

A piercing coldness suddenly swarmed over Speaks No More, stopping his thoughts dead. Beneath his legs, the Pinto pony staggered in its gait and neighed. The animal felt it as well.

He reined the horse to a stop. The Pinto danced nervously as he patted its neck, seeking to calm it. The coldness swelled, coming from all around him, squeezing him, crushing him. The presence of the night was close, too close. His heart pounded and he knew at once that tomorrow's sun, for him, would never rise.

A snarl snapped his attention to a spot diagonally ahead of him. A coyote hunched in the grass, snout trembling as it bared its fangs and growled. Its black eyes shined with arcs of blue black—and death.

At the corners of his vision, Speaks No More saw other dark shapes, moving, never still. They circled his horse, darting in just so close, then out again.

The Pinto neighed in panic and he squeezed his legs tight about its belly but it was too late. The animal reared, beating the air with its hooves. Speaks No More struggled furiously with all his Comanche skill to hold saddle as the horse danced sideways. It humped its back and shot straight up like a spring uncoiling.

Speaks No More's hands whitened as he twisted the reins to no avail. He managed to hold on briefly, but there was no way to calm the spooked animal, not with the coyotes snapping at its legs.

The Pinto bucked and kicked, reared and neighed and spun about. Speaks No More's hands wrenched loose from the reins and his legs jerked from the saddle. He was suddenly falling backward, the horse no longer beneath him. He hit the ground on his back with jarring force and lay there, staring up at the sky, the glittering stars, stunned. The Pinto bolted, its hoofbeats receding into the night.

When his head cleared, Speaks No More pushed himself up, gaining his feet, legs shaky. His gaze flicked about, eyes widening.

Four coyotes surrounded him, cutting off any path of escape. He doubted he could have outrun the creatures even if he had the chance. As they peered at him with black eyes, fear froze him to the spot.

One of the coyotes, the largest, issued a low growl and he knew it meant his death. Panic broke the spell and he spun, intending to run, despite the odds against escaping.

A coyote darted sideways, countering him. When he whirled back to the front, the large coyote had vanished and a man stood before him, duster rippling in the wind, moonlight prying at the hideous mask of a face beneath a battered hat.

"You were watching us last night..." the man said, voice low and accusing. His dark eyes sizzled with blue black arcs. "I let you. I knew you'd kill her and bring the boy deeper pain. Now you're useless to me."

Speaks No More cringed at the expression that turned half the man's face. It was the face of the darkness, of evil and legends. It glared like a black skull and he knew the reflection was that of his own death. He no longer had to find He Who Drinks Life; He Who Drinks Life had found him.

"What's a'matter, Injun? Coyote got your tongue?" Milus Clint laughed. The sound echoed over the fields like the gibbering of skulls.

Speaks No More spat at the leader in contempt and defiance. If He Who Drinks Life killed him, he would not have an easy time of it.

He feigned bolting in one direction, another, still another.

All the coyotes had become men, and each parried his moves perfectly, blocking retreat.

Speaks No More let out a strangled squawk, despite his resolve. His hand swept for the bow at his back, but as he brought it forward, the man-demon in front of him uncoiled a long whip from his side. The whip cracked. Deep pain burned into the back of Speaks No More's hand. The bow flew to the ground. In a heartbeat, he considered lunging for it, but the thought died in his mind.

The whip cracked again. A stinging gash opened on the Comanche's face. A fist hammered him between the shoulder blades, knocking the wind from his lungs and throwing him face first to the ground.

His head lifted and he saw the leader's boots before his eyes. His gaze traveled upward, stopping at Clint's disfigured face.

The leader stooped, grabbing Speaks No More's arms and hoisting him up as if he were a sparrow. The outlaw hurled him backward and Speaks No More crashed to the ground on his back for a second time, stunned, unable to move.

The Dead-Walkers converged on him and he felt darkness swarming in, cutting off the starlight, the moonlight.

His life.

TWENTY

The boy had every right to throw him out. Damn right he did! What had he expected, anyway? For Chris to welcome his admission with open arms? For him to just automatically embrace him with forgiveness? After what Clint had done to him? Wasn't likely.

Windy downed a mouthful of whiskey and grunted. He sat at the bar at the Blue Steer, feeling a glow commencing in his head. It eased the pain he felt from Chris kicking his britches off the 7HL, as well as the paining lumps and bruises from the beating the boy had laid on him. He usually didn't drink, not no more, anyhow, not since he'd left Clint's gang—what was left of it—and set himself on the straight trail. But tonight was a special occasion: he was celebrating the loss of a friend.

"You deserve it, you old sidewinder," he mumbled, face pinching. "You galldamn deserve it."

It was too much to ask for Chris to forgive him, wasn't it? To accept that his friend had ridden with killers, killers who had murdered his sister and uncle. Understanding was the best Windy could have hoped for, but that was lost, too.

Windy's head swooped, settled. The redeye was hitting him fast. He reckoned he rightly didn't give a damn. Everything he lived for was tied up in the 7HL. The ranch had been his salvation in a way, a chance to right the wrongs of the past and for a spell he had done it. Although he knew he would have to tell the boy eventually, he always put it in the future. The future had come too sudden-like and under the worst circumstances. Judas Priest, he never expected Milus Clint, or whatever he had become, to return. Clint should have been buzzard bait. Now Clint had the Devil on his side. Perhaps he always had. With the condition young Durrin was in—well, hell, even in peak shape Chris would prove no match for the likes of Milus Clint and the darkness that had claimed him.

"He needs me there," Windy muttered. "More than ever." But Chris had promised to kill him if he laid eyes on him again. Maybe that's what a man like Windy McDonnell deserved after all; he'd out-run the noose for a spell and figured God had actually granted him the opportunity to make amends and undo the past. But maybe God had never really listened and maybe it was time for a reckoning.

What was it Chris had said about the past chasing you down? Hard to recollect, being full up with redeye, but maybe it applied just as well to him. The past had found him, the way he always suspected it would, but it had found him at the wrong time and Chris would have to pay the price for it. Milus Clint would kill the boy, maybe worse.

Didn't that just beat all?

"What could you do, anyhow?" he asked himself. He was no match for what Clint had become, either. But he reckoned he was a good deal more stable than Chris Durrin at this juncture; he hadn't suffered the way Chris had. He had lost a good friend in Clem Durrin and some fine 'hands, but his grief didn't run as deep. He could handle it with the help of the Good Book tucked in his pocket. Chris didn't have that to lean on. Chris hid the pain away, hoping it would never show its face. But inside it destroyed him and that, Windy reckoned, was what Clint counted on. Whatever Clint had become, he fed on that, sucking the soul out of young Durrin so he could just waltz right in and fill up the empty space with darkness.

Windy didn't want to see that happen. But what choice did he have? He couldn't very well go back to the ranch and even if he did he'd never get through to the boy. Chris was like to fill him full of Winchester spit before he got a word out. The Durrin boy was no killer, but men did uncharacteristic things when their grief got the better of them.

"'Nuther?"

Windy looked up, focusing on the barkeep, who peered at him with a furrowed brow and an unspoken question.

"Yeah, reckon," Windy muttered, not caring. Hell, what was one more?

As the barkeep poured the drink, Windy watched him, then flipped a silver dollar onto the counter. While the barman seemed on the verge of saying something else—now that he thought about it he had caught the man throwing looks his way every so often—he appeared to decide to swallow it.

"You gots somethin' on your mind?" Windy prodded, in no mood for small talk for one of the few times he could recollect.

"Well, just—you're that Durrin fella's friend, ain't you?"

"Used to be. Not so sure anymore. Not so sure 'bout nothin'. What of it?"

The 'keep frowned, appearing to debate something and Windy felt a prickle of irritation.

"Look, whatever you gots to say, just say it. My patience is a mite strained right now." Windy's too-small eyes sank farther into his head as his eyes narrowed.

The barman swallowed. "Hell, I don't want me no trouble with the sheriff so you gotta keep this 'tween you and me..."

Windy nodded. "Ain't likely to give Tolby nothin' but a one-fingered

Injun sign."

A slight smile came to the 'keep's lips, but quickly faded. "That Durrin fella, he come in here askin' 'bout one of the doves, Matalija. Went up to see her. Seems like he was worried 'bout her."

Windy's face crinkled. "What about her?"

"Well, she's been actin' right funny since, even 'fore that, maybe. Thought he might like to know."

Interest sparked in Windy's eyes, clearing some of the gauze from his mind. "Maybe he would. Why don't you tell me?"

The bartender hesitated, thinking it over, then went on. "She ain't been takin' no men up to her room since the first night she come back after the killin's. And she's lookin' downright sicklike. Never see hide nor hair of her durin' the day, neither. Always used ta."

Windy shrugged, unable to see where it was leading. "Seems like lots of folks, 'specially a dove who survived the other night, might act that way after what happened."

The 'keep paused and Windy knew there was more to it.

Windy grinned. "Like I said, I ain't gots a likin' for Sheriff Tolby if'n that's what you're worried about. Nothin' you tell me will find its way back to him."

The barman nodded, a note of relief touching his features. "If it did I wouldn't be long for this here world. Don't reckon I want to come along his bad side."

"You ain't gots to worry about it with me." Windy's tone was honest, reassuring. "I'd just as soon see Tolby run over by a stage."

The 'keep's mouth slid back and forth and he licked his lips. "Them fellas who came in and killed all them folks the other night, I think they been back."

"What?" A startled expression hit Windy's features. He felt as if someone had just told him the Devil was in his parlor, waitin' on him with a contract.

"Well, ain't seen none of 'em myself, but a few other women been showin' up in alleys and such with their throats tored out. Killed just like them others. Plus some ain't showed up at all."

"How long has this been goin' on?"

"Last two nights, I reckon. Undertaker's even taken to burnin' 'em, now. He thinks those boys might have spread some disease or somethin', like rabies. 'Sides, cemetery's plumb full up."

"Don't s'pose Tolby's looked into it?"

The 'keep scoffed. "Reckon he'd rather not. These ain't fellas he can shoot in the back."

"Why you riskin' your hide tellin' me this?"

The bartender shifted feet. "Reckon it's 'cause I'm piss scared, more than

I am even of Tolby. No one in Bald Creek'll lift a finger to stop these boys if they decide on ridin' back in and doin' more killin'. Maybe your friend will; he's got the look of a fool in his eyes...maybe you do, too."

The barman sighed and suddenly moved off, busying himself with wiping out glasses. He apparently had nothing more to say and Windy puzzled over the statements he had made. When Clint raided the town the first night, he had made no pretense of hiding himself. Now, he, or his men, were sneaking in to kill or abduct women. Perhaps the outlaw had not worried about it the first night because he had the element of surprise on his side. Now, maybe he figured he stood some risk of being discovered before he could complete the task he had come back for: revenge on Chris Durrin. Discovery and confrontation past the first night wouldn't fit into his plans of tearing Chris down piece by piece, would it?

Windy figured it wouldn't. And maybe if he told Chris that information they could find a lead to Clint by watching the town until they spotted one of his men. Then they could follow him. It might be the boy's only chance.

Windy pushed his whiskey back and stood. He felt a measure of unsteadiness from the liquor. He glanced at the 'keep, who was over-wiping a glass, then at the barroom proper.

He crossed the room, intending to leave. He would take the chance of going to Chris, accept whatever risk it involved. If there was a way to repay the boy for the past, that was it.

Halfway across the room, he stopped, turning and looking at the stairs. A notion hit him. The 'keep had mentioned something else besides the continued killings—the dove, Matalija. Was she involved in this somehow? He wondered if the dove could tell him more than the 'keep. She had survived the carnage of the other night and Chris had mentioned the marks on her throat, like the ones on Little Waiting Woman and the ones Windy had pretended not to notice on Chris.

Did that mean she had come in contact with Clint? One of his gang?

To Windy's mind that's exactly what it meant. But was she for them, or against? He saw a connection, but couldn't figure quite what it was. It might prove risky going to her if she worked for Clint. It might prove deadly. But if it meant a lead to the outlaw, he had to chance it.

Windy headed for the stairs. With the alcohol making his legs heavy, the climb seemed endless.

When he reached the top, he steadied himself, peered down the hall, remembering the slaughter of the other night. He shuddered and went to the room Chris had told him belonged to the dove. Taking a deep breath, edgy for some reason he couldn't pinpoint, he rapped on the door. A voice beckoned him in and dread settled in his belly.

He closed the door behind him and stood with his hat in his hands. A dark-haired woman sat on the edge of the bed, looking up at him with haunted, hollow eyes. He could see why Chris had come to her: she was pretty in a hard way, prettier than most doves he had seen, likely had been more so in the past. Because the barman was right: she looked sick in some way. Her face appeared drawn, starkly pale. Her cheeks were sunken and black pouches nested beneath her eyes. The flesh above her sateen bodice was like bleached olive. Her hair carried no sheen; even the bright lace that adorned the huge loops did little to beautify the lusterless strands.

She sat, fingers digging into the edge of the mattress, as if she had all she could do to hold herself upright. In Windy's opinion, the dove didn't look long for this world.

His gaze traveled to her throat. He saw no marks in the pale flesh and he wondered what that meant. He wondered what it meant for Chris, too. The boy was owl-headed if he thought Windy wouldn't mention the marks the next time he saw him.

"Ma'am," Windy muttered, having a hard time keeping the shocked expression on his face. He hadn't expected the dove to look so fragile, so...vulnerable. It wasn't what he was used to where whores were concerned.

"You don't approve of what I do, do you?" Her voice was steady, telling him she wasn't as close to the end as he had thought.

"Ain't my place to judge that, ma'am. I ain't gots a clean past and dung don't fall so far from the steer. I'd be a hypocrite if I told you different."

She gave him a wan smile. "You came here about Chris Durrin?"

Surprise jumped onto Windy's face. It quickly gave way to suspicion. He wouldn't let the dove lull him into a false sense of security. Too much besides his own life was at stake.

"How'd you know that?"

"Why else would you come here? I'm not seeing men. I told the 'keep that. I told him to keep them away, tell them I was sick."

"Well, you're right. I did come here hoping you could help him."

Sadness wandered into her eyes. "There's nothing I can do. I told him never to come back here. If he does he will die."

"You know that for sure?" Windy's brow knotted. If she was in with the gang, now was the time she would lie to him.

"Clint's men came into town the past two nights. I feel them when they come. The way an animal can sense fear, I can sense them. I'm little more than that, now, you know."

Windy shook his head. "'Fraid I don't understand, ma'am."

The wan smile again. "You don't have to. All you have to know is they will see Chris if he comes to Bald Creek and tell Clint. Clint will come for him then, because he'll be afraid I'll lead Chris to him."

Windy moved deeper into the room. In the sallow light from a low-turned lamp, her skin looked almost transparent. He swore he saw the blood running through the blue veins on her cheeks and forehead.

"Then I reckon I need your help more than ever. I was plannin' to go to the boy, but he might not give me the chance to tell him what you just told me. You could get to him, tell him what you know. Please, ma'am, the boy's suffered enough already. If he gots a chance against Clint, give it to him."

"No." Matalija averted her eyes. "I've done all I can."

"How can you say that? The boy outright told me he saw somethin' different about you, different than in the rest of the gals in this place. Said he saw a sweetness 'bout you."

She laughed, the sound hollow, condemned. Her gaze lifted to meet his. "I used to think so, too. When I had dreams, hopes. But those died when I came to this town, became what I am. Maybe he saw that, saw a reflection of a little girl's dreams, but that was...before Milus Clint. Now, I feel nothing but the darkness that reaches for me, pulls at me—you know what it is to lose everything? Everything when you thought you already had nothing?"

"Reckon I do. But I also know what it feels like to gain somethin' back 'cause you pick yourself up after a mule's kicked you in the teeth."

She uttered a spiteful chuckle. "Look at me. Look at me! Can't you see I'm empty? Can't you see there's nothing left inside me anymore?"

Windy nodded, compassion gripping him. He saw the loneliness in the dove's eyes. The lost hope. He'd felt that way himself a time or two after leaving Clint's gang. "You do look sick, ma'am. But that ain't because you don't care."

Her eyes locked with his. "You don't know what we are. We're not human; we're less than that. We need blood to live. Did you know that? It sustains us. We hurt others just to survive. One of Clint's men made me like them. He wasn't supposed to, but he did, and damn him for it." Her lips curled back and her razored incisors shown plainly in the gloom.

Windy's eyes widened. Fear glittered within them. He took a step backwards, despite himself. "You, you're one of 'em..."

"Don't be afraid of me." Her voice lowered to almost a whisper and she stood. Her eyes faded to black, then to their normal color. "I'm not like Clint. He lives off suffering more than blood. He cherishes the very act of killing, torturing. He cherishes death, destroying what lives. It feeds the evil within him and makes him more than the rest. I won't be like that. I won't spend eternity looking at the night."

Windy recovered a measure of his composure. He believed her. If she had intended to kill him, he'd be dead by now. While he had come prepared to find she was part of the gang, he hadn't expected what she'd become and would have made easy prey. No, she was telling him the truth. She hated what Clint's man had made her; it showed plainly in her eyes, and she saw fit to put an end to it.

"You want to die, don't you?"

A thin smile came to her lips. "I already died. I want to be dead. I told the 'keep not to send any more men, because without them it's only a matter of days before I grow too weak to even seek shelter from the daylight. The sun will find me, then, and I'll be thankful for it." She moved to the window, opening it. "You must leave and help the boy yourself. I can do nothing for him, now. Milus Clint has claimed him. If you are truly his friend, you'll go to him and kill him before Clint does, save him from the fate Clint intends. Save him from being like me."

Windy frowned, knowing he had nothing further to gain from staying. She had made up her mind. Nothing he could do or say would change it. Forcing her was out of the question.

He cast her a last look and climbed through the window. After going down the steps to the alley, he paused in the darkness as a sense of hopelessness washed over him. Maybe the dove was right. Maybe he had no hope of stopping Clint, only of saving the boy from his fate by killing him.

He didn't care for that notion a lick. There had to be some other way. His hand drifted to the Bible in his pocket and he held it over the book. If he ever needed guidance he needed it now. There had been times in the past when he swore he'd heard God whisper in his ear, but as he prayed now he felt an odd silence in return. Maybe he was on his own this time, maybe he had asked too much in the past and the burden lay solely in his hands.

"You're just confused and a little drunk," he reassured himself, but it did little to dispel the hopeless feeling in his gut.

He moved forward, reached the mouth of the alley and stopped. Across the street and down a block a light glowed from the sheriff's office. Windy noticed a couple of horses hitched to the rail out front.

A noise from the office caught his attention. The door rattled open and Sheriff Tolby stepped out onto the boardwalk, another man following him. With a feeling of hate, Windy instantly recognized the second man: Jacob Shinn, the Box H owner!

Windy's small eyes narrowed until they appeared non-existent. Tolby slapped Shinn on the shoulder, uttered a gusty laugh.

Windy retreated from the mouth of the alley, cloaking himself in shadows and watching the two men speak to each other. The words were low and he couldn't make out what they were saying, but even from this distance Windy saw something about Shinn had changed. The rancher looked edgy, boogered. His gaze kept flicking around, as if expecting something to jump out of the darkness at him.

A realization stopped Windy's thoughts: two horses were hitched to the rail—Shinn's and—

Before he completed the thought, he heard the drawing back of a hammer and felt the cold metal barrel of a gun jammed into the back of his neck.

"Walk towards them!" a voice commanded. Windy knew then whose horse was tied with Shinn's—the breed who worked for the Box H.

They moved out into the street and the sheriff and Shinn's heads came up in unison. Their gazes centered on the *segundo* and he felt any remaining whiskey haze clear from his mind. He stopped before the men and again he got the impression Shinn was afraid of something. Tolby, on the other hand, looked mildly amused.

"Well, well, lookee what we got here." Tolby's voice came out a half-chuckle. Shinn muttered a curse.

"Found him across the street in an alley, watching you," the breed said, shoving Windy a step closer.

"Good thing you had the Injun watchin', ain't it, Shinn?" Tolby said smugly. He turned and went into his office, coming right back out, rifle in hand. "I'll take 'im." Shinn flashed the sheriff a look that said he knew what was going to happen.

"You shoulda kept your nose outta it, McDonnell," Shinn said. "We had a nice little operation goin'. You shoulda respected the old days and kept out of it."

"I'll see you on the end of a rope," Windy's eyes narrowed.

"Only one you'll see at the end of a rope is yourself—if you're lucky!" Tolby's voice was jeering and he gestured with the rifle, indicating for Windy to move inside the office. Windy glared a look at Shinn, who shook his head and went to his horse, the breed following.

The sheriff herded Windy inside and shut the door. The sound of retreating hoofbeats drifted in from the street.

"You ain't so smart, now, are you, McDonnell?" Tolby cocked an eyebrow. "You and that Durrin kid shoulda known better'n to keep poking around."

"You plannin' on hanging me?" Spite steadied Windy's tone.

"Hangin' you, *hell*, no! Way I see it, you're gonna try an' escape. Naturally I'll be forced to stop you." The sheriff moved suddenly, jerking the rifle around and up.

Pain exploded in Windy's temple as the butt crashed into his skull. The room tipped. He stumbled backward, legs going every which way.

He crashed into a rickety table, which buckled, sending the coffeepot flying. Brown liquid splashed the wall.

Windy went down, head reeling, thundering. He barely felt the shock of slamming into the floor. Through the roar in his ears he heard the sheriff bellow a laugh.

"Shouldn'ta tried to escape, McDonnell. Just makes it harder on yourself!" The butt swooped towards Windy's head again and pain cracked across his teeth as it took him full across the mouth. Blood spurted from his mashed lips and tasted gun-metal bitter on his tongue. His whole lower face went numb.

But the blow had peculiar effect on him. It cleared the cobwebs from his mind. Everything took on a stark sharpness. He knew the sheriff intended to beat him until he was half-dead, then shoot him in the back of the head, the way he had done other "criminals".

If that happened, Clint had Chris and this town, and he would go on killing with no one to stop him. The thought galvanized Windy and he peered up at Tolby with hate in his eyes.

"Come on, McDonnell! Git up! Give it some fight!" Tolby's yells mocked him. "You been workin' cows too goddamn long! You gone downright soft!"

Windy's gaze flicked to a table leg that lay nearby, then back to the sheriff.

Tolby came at him again, just as Windy started to gain his feet. The rifle butt arrowed towards his head. Windy jerked his head sideways and the butt shrieked past, thudding against the wall.

With a sudden lunge, Windy snatched up the table leg. He brought it up with all his strength. The leg bounced from the side of Tolby's face.

The sheriff squawked, stumbling backward a step, but managing to retain his hold on the rifle.

Windy jumped to his feet and moved before Tolby could set himself again. His legs were shaky but he brought the move off. He had to: his life—and Chris'—depended on it.

The sheriff whirled, swung the rifle. A frantic look leaped into his eyes as the *segundo* charged at him.

Windy deflected the rifle with the table leg, but Tolby, panicked, managed to jerk it back before Windy could set himself to take advantage of it. The rifle butt smashed into his upper arm. Pain shot down his forearm and the leg suddenly dropped from his grasp as his fingers went numb.

He barely knew what occurred next. He lunged, somehow, one hand working, and got his fingers wrapped around the rifle frame. They struggled, going backward. Windy slammed into the wall, but kept a death-grip on the rifle.

Tolby fought to turn the muzzle towards Windy's chest. Windy raked a bootheel down the sheriff's shin. Tolby bellowed, his strength faltering an instant. Windy took advantage of it.

He forced his finger onto the trigger and got his numbed arm halfway up under the barrel. Throwing himself forward in a last ditch attempt, he squeezed the trigger as the barrel turned towards the sheriff.

Tolby suddenly realized what was happening and tried to push back.

A blast shattered the silence. The rifle bucked in Windy's hand. For a moment he wasn't sure whether the bullet had plowed through him because he felt liquid running down his front. He expected pain, searing pain, but none came.

Tolby's grip slackened and Windy released the sheriff. The liquid came from Tolby. Blood. The bullet had plowed through Tolby's chin and exited the top of the lawman's head, burying itself in the ceiling.

The sheriff crumpled to the floor and Windy stared in a daze at the dead lawdog. He hurled the rifle to the floor, suddenly repulsed by it, then stumbled from the office into the cool night. Gasping, he felt nausea well in his gut.

He saw damn little choice for himself, now. He doubted anyone would miss Tolby and even Shinn might be glad to be rid of him. But the Box H man knew Windy had stumbled onto their rustling connection and something would have to be done about it. Windy knew from his association with Clint's gang, Shinn would be quick to back-shoot him. That meant he had little time left to get to Chris. The risk no longer mattered.

Standing at the mouth of the cave, Milus Clint laughed. The sound filled the night like the howl of a coyote. Things were going right fine in his estimation. He'd damn near broken the boy tonight and soon he would swoop in for the kill. He felt Durrin's suffering, felt it feeding the darkness within him, engorging it. He'd entertained a fleeting worry that the boy would take his own life, but through the eyes of the coyote he had seen that wouldn't happen. Durrin still nursed a spark of life—one fanned by the misguided thought that he would somehow destroy Clint.

A fool.

Milus would never let that happen, not this time. And he would find a way to stamp out that remaining spark before he turned the boy into one of them.

"There's a chance you won't be able to control him once it's done." Emmet's voice suddenly came from beside him, breaking his thoughts.

"Huh?" Milus looked at him, face emotionless.

"Couldn't control Billy. The Durrin boy might be set to destroy you once he's like us. Ain't no tellin' what a crazy kid like that'll do. I seen that last night when I let him chase me."

Milus grunted. "I know exactly what he'll do, better'n he knows himself. I sent Jeters in to get Billy; that's why he turned bad. I'll take care of Durrin myself. He won't be able to defy my orders...that'll make his torment all the more complete.

"Hope you're right..."

Milus glared at Emmet and Emmet shrunk back, knowing better than to push him. Durrin would learn that as well.

Milus stepped back into the cave. Riders sat around the fire, which cast an orgy of orange and shadow across the walls. Some played cards while others sat laughing and gulping whiskey that had no effect. The coyotes lay curled about, eyes constantly in motion.

Milus went to the back of the cave where a nude girl hung from ropes tied to stakes driven into the stone. A different girl, one in a line of many. She had been beaten and across her chest and throat strips of flesh had been chewed off. Milus lifted her head, gazed into the glazed empty eyes and let it flop back down. The men had been feeding off of her for the better part of the night, but Milus had restrained himself, focusing solely on Durrin. Now the urge for blood had grown overpowering. The Indian hadn't been enough, divided between five of them.

He turned to Emmet, who looked up from a whiskey bottle he was coddling.

"This one's had it," Milus said, indicating the girl. "Send Dutch and Bartlett to fetch another, one of sturdier stock his time." He chuckled.

Emmet nodded, gesturing to two Riders, who led their horses from the cave.

TWENTY-ONE

When the pinto pony returned riderless to camp as the sun chased away the night, Dark Cloud knew Speaks No More had perished at the hands of He Who Drinks Life.

Tightness gripped his throat and bands of sorrow clenched around his heart. He prayed his cousin had gone to the Land Beyond the Sun and not become as Little Waiting Woman, a Dead-Walker. He felt pain at his cousin's death, but selfishly the pain was mostly for himself. He was completely alone now, a lost spirit of the Plains. Anger rose at that as well, bitterness that everything had been taken from him. How could the gods give a man so little and take it all the same?

He encouraged the anger, for it pushed aside the biting grief. He had warned Speaks No More not to interfere with the vengeance of the Great Cannibal Owl. He had warned him to let the white boy face the darkness alone. Spotted Buffalo Sun had brought it on himself. What right did his cousin have to ignore the warnings? What right did he have to defy the Great Cannibal Owl's vengeance? What right did he have to die and leave Dark Cloud with nothing more than the cries of memories on the wind?

Dark Cloud dropped to his knees, balling his hands into fists. The anger smoldered and the grief rushed back. He lifted his head and wailed at the sky, voice echoing to nothingness in the night.

Dying.

He pulled the knife from its sheath and poised it above his wrist, hand trembling and eyes filling with tears that didn't flow.

The old ways. What good were they? Would they bring Speaks No More back, or his wives or Little Waiting Woman? Would they stop the emissaries of the Great Cannibal Owl? Did they matter at all anymore?

He let the knife fall from his grasp, choosing to forgo the ritual maiming as he recalled Speaks No More's words. Perhaps he was too confined to the old ways—they had let him down. They had left him with emptiness in his hands. Could he blame Speaks No More for that? Could he blame the white boy?

The sun climbed above the horizon, orange-red splashing the ground like blood.

After dragging moments, the heaviness of grief burdening his soul, Dark Cloud lifted his knife, watching bloody sunlight glint within the blade for an instant, then sheathed it. He gained his feet. He had duties to perform and he could not allow his pain to delay him from the tasks. He would mourn later.

He set about securing a travois to his horse. Mounting, he glanced at the camp, a question plaguing him: what did he have now? Was there truly something left or was it all emptiness? He had the freedom his brothers on the reservation did not, but freedom was better appreciated when shared. What did emptiness care of freedom? It only mocked him, showed him the lifeless corners of a land once teeming with the pounding of buffalo hooves and the hunting cries of the Comanche. Mocked him with lonely howls of coyotes and the soul-stealing voices of the dark spirits. He no longer belonged to the Plains. Perhaps he had not for years, but it had been easier to cling to the old ways than admit it.

Dark Cloud wondered briefly if the white boy felt the same way. Had he not lost as much? Suffered as much? He had seen Spotted Buffalo Son's haunted eyes as he placed Little Waiting Woman in the crevice.

Dark Cloud had his answer. He truly had nothing but the man he was, a fool set in his old ways and dying legends.

Dark Cloud set out in the direction from which the pinto had come, towards the ranch house where he knew Speaks No More had intended to go. He would find his cousin's body if there were anything left of it and bring it back for burial.

Then Dark Cloud would decide his own fate.

The first thing Chris became conscious of was someone forcing his head under water. He had no idea who—or why, for that matter—only that someone had a handful of his hair and he was kneeling, doubled over a trough.

The someone jerked up on his hair and his face came out of the water. He coughed a stream of dirty, bug-filled liquid. His eyes stung as bright sunlight hit them. With a sudden panic that his attacker was trying to drown him, he struggled to fight the man—it was a man, judging from the strength, but the dunker forced his face into the water again. Chris choked on a mouthful and felt his sinuses burn as he breathed water.

To his surprise, the dunker brought him up and let him go. Chris, braced by his elbows, collapsed against the trough in a spasm of coughing. A pounding commenced in his head. Brilliant sunlight blinded him, jabbing slivers of pain into his skull. He gasped, coughed, fought to steady himself. His eyes came open, as quickly closing as glare intensified the pounding. In a glimpse, he realized he was out near the barn; he'd been dunked in the rain trough. The storm of two nights past had topped it off and Chris had the impression he'd swallowed a good bucketful. What he hadn't swallowed he was wearing. His hair and shirt were soaked.

"Hell of a way to wake up, ain't it, son?"

Chris's head snapped up. "You sonofabitch!" he yelled, coughing. He squinted, forcing his eyes to remain open a crack, despite the glare. The fuzzy features of Windy hovered above him.

With a burst of strength, he flung himself from the trough and arced a fist at the *segundo*. Windy sidestepped easily and Chris sprawled on his belly in the dirt, getting a mouthful. He spat repeatedly, trying to clear the grit from his mouth. Anger surged in him for the man he'd promised to kill if he ever saw him again.

He struggled to push himself to his feet, but his legs refused to hold him upright and he fell back to the ground. He felt arms jammed under his, hoisting him up. Windy dragged him towards the house and there wasn't a hell of a lot he could do about it but cough and cuss.

"Door was open, son," he heard Windy say through the hammering in his brain. Chris was too weak to resist as the *segundo* hauled him across the veranda into the house. "You're lucky Clint didn't pick last night to come along and finish the job he started. He'd had easy pickin's with you all laid out that way. I found you out cold on the damn floor early this mornin'."

Chris swore a reply and Windy bellowed his barrel-chested laugh.

Chris let himself go limp, feeling Windy alter his grip. That's what he had hoped for. He heaved out with all his strength, breaking free and stumbling towards the Winchester propped against the wall. Coming up with it, he swung it around.

For a moment, he struggled to focus his gaze on the red-headed man, whose image wavered in front of his eyes. It was no easy task but he managed to jerk the rifle level. He was satisfied he could still hit his target if it came down to it, blurry or not.

"I told you I'd kill you if you came back!" Chris said through gritted teeth, fighting a wave of nausea. His belly wanted to climb up his throat and his senses threatened to reel. He had all he could do to keep the Winchester steady; the barrel shook despite his efforts.

With a jerky step forward he jammed the muzzle against the *segundo's* wide chest. His hands trembled and his finger twitched on the trigger.

"You can do that, son. I probably deserve it for all I done back when. But you ain't a killer and you were my friend. What's more, I think you still are."

Chris squeezed the frame tighter, hands bleaching, but his resolve withered. A thin line of sweat broke out on his forehead, a single bead tricking down his face.

I can't do it...

He lowered the Winchester.

Throwing the rifle to the floor, he collapsed onto the couch, face in his hands.

"You took a chance coming here, Windy," he said when he at last looked up. He could see the *segundo's* concerned face more clearly now.

A certain smugness pulled a smile onto the assistant foreman's lips. "Reckon I did. But it's one I had to take. I owed it to you for what I done. 'Sides, I knew you couldn't shoot me when it came down to it. You might kick my tail outta here again, but figured not before you heard what I had to say."

"If you were wrong?"

A touch of humor came into Windy's voice. "Don't think I'd take the chance of leavin' that thing loaded, do you?" Windy nudged his head at the Winchester and grinned.

Chris felt a renewed twinge of friendship towards the man. He had missed him, he had to admit. When Windy was around Chris had someone to lean on, someone to pick him up and set him straight, the way he always had. But one thing tainted all that had gone before with the man, one thing that stood in the way of them ever being close again.

"I gotta know something, Windy..." Chris's voice trembled. A sudden quaking throttled his entire body. It took him a moment to get it under control.

Windy's face went serious. "I wasn't with Clint's gang when they killed your sister, son. I swear to God's word I wasn't. I joined up with them a spell later and I was never involved with no killin's, though I knew he done 'em. Reckon I told myself if I wasn't along I wasn't responsible. Ain't that way, I know, but it helps me live with what I was part of. I took care of most of the rustlin'—that's how I know Shinn."

"I'm sorry, Windy, for what I said and did. I should have given you a chance." He meant it. He had acted out of misdirected anger and now he regretted it. Years of friendship and trust could not be so easily erased and he figured he had come damn close to losing the only person left in his life he cared a damn about.

"Ain't no need to apologize. You been through hell and it's gonna get worse."

Chris tried to stand, fell back onto the couch. Windy frowned. "We gots to get you cleaned up, son. Clint ain't gonna let this go much longer."

Chris looked up. "I saw her die again, Windy. Little Waiting Woman. I saw her die again last night."

Windy nodded. "She musta been made one of 'em, same as that dove you gots at the saloon."

Chris's eyes widened. "Matalija..." he whispered.

"She don't look so good, son. She ain't long for this world and it's by her own choice. She was made into one to them and she don't care for it a lick. She told me if I was your friend I should kill you, now, before Clint came and made you one, too."

Chris' eyes hardened. "That why you came here?"

Windy moved to the window, looking out then turning his back to Chris. "No, I came here 'cause I ain't so ready to give up on you yet. We could ride outta here, buy us some time—"

"*No!* I ain't runnin' from him! He'd just find me wherever I go. He's part of me, now. I can feel him somewhere inside. He won't be satisfied till he takes his revenge."

"Suit yourself, son. Call me a fool, but I'll stand by you way I told you I would."

"I sent the men away. You could go with them..."

Windy shook his head. "Like I said, figure I owe you, son. At the least, your uncle gave me a chance at makin' a new life and there ain't nothin' else for me, now."

Chris caught the hint of bitterness in Windy's voice. "You ain't tellin' me something, Windy. I can hear it in your voice even if I can't see your goddamn face straight."

Windy gave a humorless laugh. He told Chris of overseeing the meeting between Shinn and Tolby, and how the sheriff had tried to kill him—and the results of it: the sheriff had taken his own bullet.

"Ain't likely anyone will grieve for him," Chris said when the *segundo* finished. He felt no remorse for Tolby himself. "But Shinn..."

"We'll deal with him after we get Clint."

"We gotta find him first. Maybe Shinn knows how."

Windy shook his head. "Ain't likely. Reckon Shinn came here with his own agenda. Doubt he knows Clint's back. If he does, Clint sure as hell wouldn't leave him in plain sight if'n Shinn knew where to find him."

"Then we're stuck waitin' on Clint to make his move. I don't like it."

"Maybe we ain't. 'Keep in Bald Creek told me some things..." Windy explained all the man had related about the continuing murders and disappearances. "If them Riders are sneakin' in, it must be 'cause Clint don't want to take the risk of being found before he comes after you. He ain't gots the element of surprise no more."

Chris scoffed. "Way I see it, he don't need it. He's too powerful."

"Maybe. But it might mean he gots some weaknesses. If we can figure out what they are..."

"Dark Cloud told me some of them, but I can't see how they'll be of any use." Chris recounted what the Comanche had told him. "He killed a Rider with an arrow. Neither of us can shoot one straight so it won't do us a lick of good."

"No, but maybe somethin' like it, if we surprise him."

"You figure we could go to Bald Creek and wait for one to ride in, then trail him back to where they're holed up?"

"That's what I had in mind, son. Then we can wait till the territorial marshal and his men get here. It's the only chance we gots."

The day trickled by for Chris. He lay on the couch a good part of it, recovering his strength and letting the thunder in his head subside while Windy forced beans and bacon down his throat. He had hope now, a small measure of it anyhow. It helped push the horror and pain of the past few days to the back of his mind. He knew before he could even hope to deal with what had happened that he had to track down Clint and see him dead. There was no other way. He had nothing to lose.

Except your soul...

No, he would see to it provisions were made for that. If he failed to get Clint, he would take his own life, or have Windy do it for him—before he became a Dead-Walker.

The sun splashed the hills with blood-colored light. Chris got up, going to the window. He watched the day fade to evening, dread swelling. The coldness returned to his soul. It told him he had no right to hope, not with all the tragedy that had come into his life. Any chance he had against a monster like Clint was a long shot.

Shadows stretched across the lawn, swaying menacingly. Every dark patch seemed to reach for him, carry some monstrous intent. He had never considered darkness to be living thing; he did now.

A coyote howled in the distance and he shivered. He could feel Clint out there, a part of the night. "You sonofabitch," he whispered. "Where are you?"

He turned away from the window as Windy came into the room. A tense look passed between them. It was time. Chris picked up the Winchester, reloaded it.

"Ain't gonna do no good, son."

Chris nodded. "Reckon I know as much, but I'll take it just the same."

Windy tried a weak smile. "Don't mind tellin' you I'm powerful scared. Got no desire to die just yet, but the odds are with it."

"I think I died when Clint took Clem and Little Waiting Woman. And someone once told me dyin' in the soul is worse..." He smiled thinly at the red-headed man and moved towards the door.

With a great sadness in his heart, Dark Cloud watched the sun run from the night. He had found Speaks No More's body shortly after setting out in search of it. It had been mutilated far beyond that of Speak's No More's wife. Dark Cloud had gently lifted the remains into the travois and brought the body to the arroyo, burying it close to the place where Little Waiting Woman had been laid to rest. She had risen, but Speaks No More would not. He Who Drinks Life had seen to that. Little remained of Speaks No More after the dark spirits had finished, less after the buzzards had filled their bellies.

Dark Cloud passed the day in grief, fasting, chanting the old songs and dwelling on the future. Nothing eased his sorrow, unburdened his heart. Nothing would remove the haunting spirits of despair. He had begged to the Grandfather Above for relief, but none had come.

It was after that he had reached his decision.

No longer did he have a place here. The Plains held emptiness for him, now. No longer would the Comanche ride with the wind and no longer would they feel the victory of the buffalo hunt. The land was tainted with the evil breath of the Great Cannibal Owl. No Comanche would be at home there again. There was only the reservation and some small respite from loneliness, but that would come later.

Many times during the day had the white boy's face entered his mind. Dark Cloud now understood Spotted Buffalo Son, felt as he did, alone and barren inside. Dark Cloud had been wrong to blame him for bringing the dark spirits. They had come on their own; the Great Cannibal Owl had chosen to strike his wrath on Dark Cloud's family, as well as Spotted Buffalo Son. Speaks No more had been right to say it would not end with the white boy's death. The dark spirits would spread across the land if they were allowed to exist in this world. Dark Cloud knew he had to help the white boy defeat them or his cousin's death would be in vain.

The dark winds told him He Who Drinks Life would come tonight. There was no reason to delay and Dark Cloud had felt the coldness sink into his bones as the sun set and the coyote moaned. The dark spirits were close. He could feel their breath, hear their sighs. Perhaps they would come for him as well, but he would not wait for them. He would go to the boy, help him, die as the warrior he had been, riding proud beside Quanah Parker into the hell canyon. If he went down in defeat, he would perish with iron in his blood and courage in his heart. His was the true soul of the *Nermernuh*.

Dark Cloud went into his tipi and gathered what he would need. First came his arrows of seasoned dogwood, buzzard and owl feathers fastened to their shafts with glue boiled down from the horns and hooves of buffalo. He examined the flint warheads, chipped with crudely barbed edges to pull the flesh of its victim inside-out if removed. A Comanche could loose twenty arrows in the time it took a white man to reload a musket ball and tonight Dark Cloud would see to it they flew fast and true.

The warshield with its magic powers came next: fashioned of carefully laminated layers of the toughest bison hide, shaped to a convex surface and packed between with furs, it could turn an arrow or lance or even a musket ball at fifty yards. His fingers drifted over the magic symbols painted upon it. He touched the bear teeth and bits of human hair attached to its edges, the signs of a mighty warrior.

After he had gathered his weapons, he took care to dress himself for the battle. He greased his long straggly locks with bear fat, strands parted along the top of the scalp and braided to either side. He decorated the braids with bits of silver and beads and glass. Next he drew broad black stripes across his face and forehead; black was the color of death and tonight there would be death a-plenty.

Last he lifted his war helmet, a thing he had thought he would never place proudly on his head again. The headdress, grimmest of the Plains, was made of bison scalp, the great thrusting horns of the bull retained. As he placed it on his head, he felt its comforting heaviness and almost smiled. For a last time he would give himself to the old ways. For a last time he would be a warrior, not the white man's dog.

Strapping his bow to his back, he left the tipi. He mounted his pony and peered off into the darkness and at the cold face of the moon. Digging his heels into the pony's sides, he set off for the ranch house. Yes tonight Dark Cloud would ride proud and high. Tonight he would be *Nermernuh*.

"You're lettin' the boy go too long, Milus," Emmet said, gazing at the leader, who stood at the mouth of the cave. Within the vaulted room, the Riders waited, hunger growing, gnawing, acute. The girls they had dragged back from Bald Creek the previous night were useless, now, used up within a couple of hours.

"I'll decide when he's suffered enough." Irritation pricked Milus' voice.

Emmet peered at him, looking disgusted. "You let things go too long six years ago, Milus. The marshal's men found us then."

"They ain't gonna now, are they? We're too powerful for them this time. They can't touch us here in the night."

"That boy collects himself and comes over us durin' the day things will be powerful different, doncha think?"

"He won't." Milus looked out into the night and for the first time a glimmer of indecision came into his cold buzzard eyes. He had been sure that Injun girl's second death would destroy Durrin emotionally, but he sensed something amiss. He should have felt the boy's pain more, should have been satiated by it. But that wasn't the case. He sensed guttering strength in Durrin and that troubled him. The dark spirits within him were restless, clamoring to be freed. What had gone wrong? He wasn't sure, but he couldn't give it much longer before he was forced to change his tactics. He had grown too full of himself six years ago; he wouldn't allow that to happen again.

"He won't..." Milus said again, as if to reassure himself.

"He might. The boys saw the whore again last night, when they rode into town. She was up in her room and that ranchhand of Durrin's came out her winder. They woulda got 'im, but for him gettin' caught by that waste of a sheriff and Shinn."

Milus considered it. The dove was a possible problem. He had known it the moment he sensed her rising, becoming one with the night. Now she might have told Durrin's man about the Riders; that posed a risk.

"You might have a point, Emmet. She's one of Billy's loose ends. Shoulda seen to her 'fore now. Tell Mace, Dorsey and Clade to go get her. Bring her back here. We might as well have us a bit of fun with her before she gets fed to the coyotes." Milus paused, considering further. "You go with 'em, make sure nothin' gets mussed up. They don't need to do no thinkin' on their own. After that we'll see 'bout gettin' after the boy."

A new strength filled Chris as he and Windy tethered their mounts to a rail a few blocks from the Blue Steer Saloon. The seed of hope had grown. If they could follow a Rider, trail him to Clint...

It wasn't much to grab hold of, but it was something. Chris reckoned he'd be no good if he let go of that hope—he'd be giving Clint exactly what he wanted.

"What if one don't come in?" Windy suddenly asked.

Chris eyed him. The *segundo's* face was fraught with tension and a shade of doubt. "Don't want to think about that."

"Me neither, but now that I think on it we're takin' as much a chance as we would waitin' for him at the house. How do you trail a galldarn spook, anyhow? They're used to the night. We ain't."

Chris shrugged, resolve wavering. He kept silent as they went down the boardwalk. He knew what he had to do, no matter what the risk or odds. Clint would come for him one way or the other; he wouldn't sit around waiting for the hawk to pounce.

A certainty gripped Chris: tonight, he would find his lead to Clint, or Clint would find him. He didn't know what gave him that surety, only that when the sun rose tomorrow morning one of them would be dead. Chris' hand drifted to the Colt at his hip.

"Promise me, Windy, that if Clint gets us you'll kill me before he can turn me into one of them. I can't live that way. I can't face eternity lookin' at the goddamn night."

Windy glanced at Chris. "You do the same for me, son. I got no wish to be wanderin' the night like some damn Injun spirit—what the hell?"

A rumble of hooves caught their attention.

They spun, Windy's arm jerking straight out, pointing towards the end of town.

Four Riders appeared, barely visible in the darkness. They came fast, on coal-black horses, like the horsemen of the apocalypse in Windy's Bible. A chill shuddered down Chris's back and dread froze him. It was mesmerizing in some morbid way, their approach, the way a snake is spell-binding to a mouse. Dark Riders, demons on horseback, shades of the past. His mind jumped back to the day at the orphanage, when he had first seen Clint's gang ride in.

Windy's pulling on his arm brought him back to the present.

"We mistimed it bad, son! They seen us and they're headin' our way!" Windy yanked Chris along, picking up the pace. Chris stumbled after him.

Chris' mind reeled with the sudden turn of events. He had planned to track Clint, get the jump on him, but any chance of that was crushed. The Riders had spotted them and now they would finish the job Clint started before he got a chance at the outlaw.

"Why ain't they sneakin' in this time?" Chris yelled. "They rode straight in!"

"Have the notion they came for your dove, son. Probably one of 'em saw me with her last night and figured she was a risk. Soon as they spotted us they decided to throw caution to the wind!"

Behind them the Dark Riders devoured the distance. The thunder of hoofbeats grew louder and the street filled with whoops and shouts of outlaws.

Chris and Windy reached the saloon and dived through the batwings. Inside voices and laughter stopped dead. Heads swiveled towards them.

"Get out!" Chris yelled, waving his arms frantically. The patrons gawked at them and the 'keep shot them a worried look.

"Riders!" Windy bellowed. "The ones from the other night! They're comin' right behind us!"

That did it. Men jumped from their seats and doves' faces went white. The 'keep grabbed a shotgun from beneath the bar and bolted for the back door with the rest. The room emptied. Tables flew over as drunk cowhands crashed into them, fell, scrambled up again. One of the doves shrieked, kept shrieking. The sound suddenly died as she was jerked through the door by a cowhand. The room went ominously silent.

Chris heard the Riders bring their horses to a stop outside the saloon. He and Windy stood frozen in the middle of the room, listening to the clomp of boots crossing the boardwalk.

A voice called out from the landing. They looked up. Matalija stood leaning against the rail, looking down.

"Up here!" She waved them on and Chris didn't need to think about it. He and Windy reached the stairs just as the first Riders piled through the batwings, stopping just inside the doors.

"Make it easy on yourself, boy!" Emmet shouted. "Old Milus might have mercy on ya if'n you do."

Chris ignored him, continued going up. Matilija, with a measure of effort, pushed herself from the rail and staggered along the hall. They followed, catching up. She looked weak, about to drop. They each grabbed an arm and helped her forward.

When they reached her room, they dived through the door and slammed it shut. Windy shoved the vanity in front of it, then a small table and chair.

"Ain't gonna do much good but it beats doin' nothin'!" Windy yelled.

They could hear the sound of boots on the stairs.

"Go!" Matalija said, pointing to the window. "I'll hold them off as long as I can."

Windy started for the window and Chris grabbed the dove's arm. She seemed too weak to resist.

"I ain't leavin' you to them!"

"It doesn't matter, Chris." She tried to pull away from him. "I won't live through this anyway."

Chris ignored her, pulling her to the window. Windy had already gone out. "I ain't got time to argue the point." He pushed her out, then climbed through.

Behind them, the heavy thuds of men kicking at the door sounded. A crash. The vanity overturned and men flowed into the room.

Chris and Windy, the dove between them, descended the stairs and made their way through the alley.

A Rider appeared in front of them.

One had stayed behind. He blocked their exit and within a moment the rest would come up behind them.

"Ain't nowhere to go, boy!" the Rider said, laughing. "Might as well not fight it."

Chris swung a fist at him, hurling Matalija towards Windy in almost the same move. The Rider took the fist full across the jaw and didn't flinch. He grabbed two handfuls of Chris's shirt and flung him around.

Chris landed with a jarring thud in the street, air knocked from his lungs, teeth slamming together.

"Told ya it ain't no use, boy!"

Chris pushed to his hands and knees, head coming up to see the Rider take a step towards him. He scrambled to his feet, stumbled in the direction of Windy and the girl, both of whom had come into the street. The shouts of the other Riders sounded from the alley.

They ran, Chris and Windy pulling the dove along.

"You can't hide, boy! You might as well give in!"

The other Riders came from the alley, walking towards Chris and Windy.

"He's right, son." Windy said. "Ain't nowhere to go they can't get us. We're done for."

"The church!" Matalija pointed to the white building a short ways down the street. "They won't go in there. Their evil won't let them."

"She may have a point, son." Windy peered at Chris, then at the dove. "Hope you're right about that, ma'am."

"Not much choice." Chris's face turned grim. "They'll get us anyhow."

They crossed the street, the Riders closing in, and climbed the steps. Matalija suddenly pulled back.

"I can't go in!" She said, fear on her face.

"You said it yourself, ma'am," Windy said. "Their evil won't let them enter. You ain't evil. You proved that by helpin' us."

Matalija started to object but they had no time to discuss it. Chris hauled the struggling dove up the steps with Windy's help. They went into the church, slamming the door behind them.

The Riders stopped just beyond the building. Anger crossed their faces. Chris heard muffled curses.

"Looks like she's right," Windy said, peering out a window. "They're out there starin' in like lost steers." Windy paused, brow crinkling.

"What's wrong?" Chris asked.

"One of 'em's headin' off."

Chris looked out. He saw Emmet walk back down the street to his horse and mount. Reigning around, the Rider spurred off towards the Plains.

Windy looked at Chris. "Reckon he's goin' to fetch Milus?"

Chris nodded. "Has to be." They turned away from the window, gazed at the dove. A nervous look darkened her face as she glanced about.

"Told ya it'd be awright, ma'am," Windy said in a soothing tone. "Reckon God don't care who you are if you ain't hurt no one."

She looked at him, a thin smile coming to her lips. "First time I been in a church in a long while. Was gonna be a Sunday School teacher once..." Her voice trailed off and she seemed to slip into her thoughts.

"Come on out, boy!" A voice boomed from the street. "Save yourself the beatin' Milus is gonna give ya!"

Windy's face turned darker as he peered at Chris in the gloom of the church. "Hell of a note, son. They can't come in and we can't go out."

"Maybe there's a back way outta here..." Chris said without much conviction.

Windy cocked an eyebrow. "Would it matter? Where in the hell we gots to go? Ain't likely we'll get to our horses 'fore they get us, and even if we did Milus ain't gonna let it go no further, now."

Windy was right and Chris felt his heart sink. Any hope he had fostered of burying Milus Clint for good deserted him. They were trapped with no way out that didn't lead straight into the hands of the Dark Riders.

"Guess we wait till sunrise, then..."

"Then what?" Windy asked, looking at the dove then back to Chris.

Chris shrugged. He wished he knew.

Dark Cloud halted his pony in front of the 7HL ranch house. Peering at the dark building, a glimmer of confusion showed in his eyes. Perched atop his pinto, bathed in moonlight and shadow, the Comanche warrior made a fearsome figure. The horned buffalo helmet and black streaks painted on his face made him look like an avenging devil, as equal to the minions of the Great Cannibal Owl as any warrior had ever been.

Dark Cloud studied the house, dark eyes roving, searching for the slightest movement, hint of life. He saw only the creeping of the shadows, heard only the whisper of the leaves on the grass, the snorting of the horses in the corral and the singing of the night creatures far off. A coyote howled and his lips turned into a grim frown.

Spotted Buffalo Son had gone. The ranch was deserted except for the white man's buffalo in the holding pen and the horses in the corral. Was he too late? Had He Who Drinks Life already taken Spotted Buffalo Son? If not, where would the boy have gone? He would never run from He Who Drinks Life; Dark Cloud was sure of it. That was not the boy's way. He had the courage of a Comanche. If not Dark Cloud would never have allowed a union between him and Little Waiting Woman. But if the emissary of the Great Cannibal Owl had come for him, Dark Cloud would have seen the signs.

Dark Cloud's attention jumped to the distant horizon as the sound of hoofbeats carried over the wind. His eyes narrowed. A Rider appeared, a black speck careening across the Plains. One of them, Dark Cloud knew: a dark spirit, a Dead-Walker. The Rider continued on, coming from the direction of town, heading in the direction of the arroyo, miles distant. He felt little surprise, as that would be the most likely place for them to hide during the day.

The Rider was oblivious to Dark Cloud, who remained motionless against the night, watching. The Rider grew smaller, vanishing into the darkness. The sound of hoofbeats faded.

Gone.

If the Rider had come from town, that meant the boy had likely gone there as well. Dark Cloud dismounted, gaze searching the ground as he walked, hunched, in a widening arc. He found the signs of horses having ridden away from the ranch, older tracks he attributed to a number of men, Spotted

Buffalo Son's men, Dark Cloud guessed. They had ridden away with the last sun. He found fresher tracks, two horses; they had ridden away a short while ago. The tracks headed out across the land, towards town and Dark Cloud knew he was right: the boy and one other had gone there.

Dark Cloud went back to his pony and mounted, a sense of urgency overtaking him. He could see what was happening. The boy had gone to town for some reason, where, Dark Cloud felt sure, a Dead-Walker had seen him. The Rider would reach his camp shortly, bring He Who Drinks Life, and the boy, if not dead already would perish.

If the boy had gone to town, Dark Cloud would as well; that's where his battle lay. He wondered what the white men there would think when he rode in, garbed for war. It was a risk. They might decide to kill him. But maybe it didn't matter. He would fall as a true Comanche, in battle. If he must die, it would be with dignity, on his horse. That was the way of the *Nermernuh.*

TWENTY-TWO

A lantern shattered the church window.

One of the Riders had fetched it from where it hung outside a shop and hurled it through. Glass splintered with a tremendous jangle and rained to the floor. The lantern sailed on through, hitting a pew and exploding, splashing kerosene across the bench and floor. The kerosene caught instantly and tongues of flame leaped up.

"Looks like they ain't fixin' to wait for Clint!" Windy yelled, backing away from the flames. Chris and Matalija edged close to the door. The heat was already scorching, reddening their faces.

Yellow-orange light outlined the worry on Chris's face. Clint's men had cut off their less-than-hopeful options. It boiled down to two choices: burn alive or walk straight out into the hands of the Riders.

He shot a glance at Windy, then Matalija. Windy's small lips had set in grim lines.

"Maybe that back way is our only hope, now. Ain't much, but it'll buy us a few seconds." Windy's voice held little confidence.

Chris gave a nod but remained silent. His slim chance of hope had faded to nothing. For all practical purposes, Clint had won. If they went out that door, the Riders would hold them until Clint arrived to complete his revenge. That left Chris no choice.

"I'm stayin'," Chris said. "I won't let Clint make me one of them."

"Son, I know what you're feelin' but maybe God'll be with us—"

"With us?" Anger shaved an edge on Chris' voce. "For chrissakes, we're in a church and He ain't with us!"

"Son, it ain't the time to argue religion or politics. We do and the choice won't be ours at all." Windy nudged his head in the direction of the back door. A narrow aisle led to a small anteroom housing the rear exit.

Flames had snaked across the aisle, lashing up the wall in great wavering sheets, devouring the dry wood. The way was searing but passable if they went single file, though in another moment it wouldn't be.

Chris nodded to Windy, nerves raw. Windy was right. They had to try it. If the Riders caught them, Chris still had the Colt at his hip. He wouldn't hesitate to swallow a bullet and it was preferable to burning alive.

His shout rose above the crackling of flames. "All right, let's go—"

Matalija screamed as another lantern sailed through the stained glass window. Shards of glass shattered in a rain of captured firelight. The lantern burst with an explosive belch and a bundle of flame flashed across the aisle. It blocked the anteroom and back exit.

"Godamighty!" Windy blurted. "Looks like they thunk it out this time!"

They scooted back, throwing their arms in front of their faces against the heat, which had become blistering. Smoke billowed, choking their lungs. Breathing grew difficult, each gasp a chore.

Chris and Windy exchanged looks. While no words passed between them, each knew the other's thought: burning to death was a horrible way to die. Chris had seen a horse perish that way in a barn fire and he would never forget it, but it came with a question: was it worse than living forever in the night?

"Dyin' this way's better'n what Clint gots in mind, son," Windy said, as if reading Chris' thought.

Chris' hand slid over the handle of the Colt at his hip, lingering on the warm metal. He eyed the assistant foreman and Windy gave the slightest of nods. The fire wouldn't take them. A bullet or smoke suffocation would finish it first.

Chris' hand fell away from the Colt. They had another few minutes, and he would cling to them, though he couldn't have told anyone in that moment why he wanted to live. Perhaps it was something about Clint winning that goaded him, perhaps it was some deeper inbred desire for survival. The reason didn't matter, it just was.

In a few moments, everything he had ever been, every hurt he had ever suffered would perish. There would be nothing more. No one to mourn him, to grieve for him, nothing left behind but an empty cattle ranch and ghosts, and Shinn would probably take that. Any trace of the Durrins would be wiped from the Plains. Forgotten.

Chris suddenly found himself praying the God in Windy's Bible was true, that something better existed beyond death and his family, Clem and Little Waiting Woman would all be there waiting for him. It provided scant comfort, but it was all he had and a flashing thought told him it was a damn poor time to suddenly discover religion. But coming face to face with your own death did things to a man. While the death of loved ones sometimes robbed you of your faith, a man's own death sometimes strengthened or provided you with it.

He pushed the thoughts aside, a sudden constriction in his lungs making him cough. Tears ran from his eyes by the time he got it under control.

Through blurry vision, he saw Windy had moved to the window. Chris edged in beside him and Matalija moved backward, the glow of flames flickering across her ashen face. It held little expression now, except, possibly one of vague contentment. The look said she had resigned herself to her fate, was almost grateful for it.

Outside the Riders paced in front of the stairs, gazes locked on the church door. Chris heard their bursts of laughter and jeers rise above the crackling roar of the flames.

"They're lickin' their chops!" Windy said in a burst of coughing.

"Looks like we'll be disappointing them and Clint." Chris's voice came low, but steady. There was a slight solace in knowing he would cheat Clint out of his revenge. It was damn little after all Chris had lost, but he would hold it as his dying thought.

A blood-chilling wail ripped through the night.

The cry came sudden, challenging, and Chris jolted at the very unexpectedness of it. It ululated through the street like a demon call, echoing from building walls as if it had a mystical life of its own. Their gazes jerked in the direction from which it had come.

A figure materialized out of the night, a fearsome silhouette on horseback with great thrusting horns. A thing that matched the demonic wail that preceded it. But with the sound something rose in Chris, something he couldn't immediately pinpoint, but there nonetheless, like a glint of gold in a pan of river sand.

"What the Sam Hill is that?" Windy blurted, brow furrowing.

Chris gave a slight shake of his head. "Maybe the Devil decided to come personally..."

Windy shook his head suddenly, expression brightening. "Comanche devil! It's Dark Cloud. He's wearin' a Comanche war helmet!"

Dark Cloud was a grim sight indeed as he drove his pony forward. The Indian careened through the dusty street, yipping and shrieking a challenge. Clouds of dust and dried dung swirled up around him. The horse's galloping hooves churned up clods.

The Riders jerked around in unison, momentarily perplexed by the sight of the charging Comanche

In the next instant, their looks melted from perplexity to cold realization. Chris could see the evil looks on their faces. They had planned this time, thinking out their steps after trapping Chris, Windy and the dove in the church, but they hadn't expected what came after them now, and were taken utterly by surprise. Clint had made a mistake and the result of that error was hurtling down upon them.

Dark Cloud drew within a hundred feet of the Riders and suddenly dropped to the side of his horse. One leg hung looped over the pony's back as he angled himself into a position where he used the horse's body as a shield. In almost the same movement, Dark Cloud unlimbered his bow and drew back an arrow. Comanche warriors were masters of the art of firing from beneath the horse's neck while hanging over the side.

The first Rider stared with a dumbstruck expression at the arrow that seemed to have magically embedded itself into his chest. His shock was short-lived. Black fluid spurted from his gaping mouth and nose. It bubbled from around the arrow. Black flame jiggered over him, bursting suddenly from everywhere on his body. It burned violently, but only for a moment. The flaming Rider fell to the ground, dissolving into dust.

By that time, Dark Cloud had loosed two more arrows. The first struck a Rider in the neck. The Rider squawked, making choking sounds. He yanked the arrow out; it tore free with a chunk of flesh. The wound gushed back fluid. Flinging the arrow aside, he staggered forward, clutching at the gouting hole.

The second arrow plowed through the third Rider's shoulder. He jumped back, pulling frantically at the arrow as black fluid boiled from around its shaft.

Dark Cloud careened past the outlaws, hoisting himself into a sitting position and yanking on the pony's reins. Slowing the pinto, he whirled it around.

In the church, Chris and Windy had moved to the door. Fire ripped across every wall, through aisles and over pews. Great black clouds of smoke billowed from burning wood and varnish. Timbers creaked; flames roared and snapped. The building structure was rapidly weakening, would collapse around them in the next few moments. If they didn't get out immediately, Dark Cloud's help would be for nothing.

"Let's go, son!" Windy yelled. "The Indian gave us a chance!"

Windy yanked the door open. Chris started through, stopped. He looked back to see Matalija had not come forward. She gazed at them with a vacant yet peaceful look.

"No!" Chris yelled, realizing what she intended.

"I'm staying, Chris," she said, moving backward. "I won't live like them. I don't have to now."

Chris made a move to go after her, but Windy grabbed him, wrapping his arms around Chris' chest and hauling him through the door. Chris struggled, but had little strength left.

"Let her go, son! She wants to die."

"We can't leave her in there. I can't leave her..." Chris' yells turned to a sob, as Windy pulled him out into the comforting coolness of the night air. He coughed, throat clogged with smoke. Sweat and tears streamed down his face.

"It ain't your choice, son; it's hers. It ain't like your sister."

Chris stopped struggling. He knew the *segundo* was right. As Windy set him free Chris turned to see Matalija for one last time. She gave him a thin smile and stepped into the flames.

His sister had been given no choice in dying in the orphanage fire, and despite what Windy said, Matalija had not been given a choice, either. Clint had forced her into the flames as sure as if he had been there to push her himself. His hate for Clint renewed as he watched the fire engulf her. He turned away, unable to bear the sight any longer.

The sound of hooves took his attention from the dove. Dark Cloud's horse charged towards them, the Comanche again hanging at the side of his pinto.

The two wounded Riders tried to scatter. Unsuccessfully. They went in opposite directions, but Dark Cloud was prepared for the move.

An arrow skewered the first through the chest before he made it halfway across the street. He froze, as if suspended in motion, then exploded in black flame, disintegrating.

The other reached the boardwalk, jerking short as Dark Cloud's arrow plowed though his back. He reeled backwards off the boardwalk, crashing onto his back in the street. The arrow snapped off in his body. Within seconds, ebony flame devoured him.

Dark Cloud came upright in his saddle, pulling back the reins. He turned the pinto, trotted up to them. Chris peered at the Comanche's black-streaked face, hard eyes. He said nothing, giving a slight nod. No words were needed.

"Better get a move on, son." Windy nudged his head towards the Plains. "Clint ain't gonna waste no time gettin' here."

Dark Cloud gigged his horse along the street and Chris and Windy ran for their horses. Behind them, the church gave a shudder. Beams groaned, snapped. The building collapsed and a pyre of flame shot into the night. Chris couldn't help thinking of the woman inside.

After reaching their horses, they mounted, reined around and started forward.

They made it only a hundred feet before drawing up short.

Five men on black horses met them at the other end of the town. For the first time in six years, Chris confronted the maniac who had murdered his sister, his uncle, Little Waiting Woman, God knew how many others. His breath caught as his gaze locked on the mutilated face of Milus Clint. He saw the effects of the rifle bullet from the day the marshal's men had cornered the gang in New Mexico, saw the damage exacted by lead and buzzards, shadowy beneath the battered flat hat. Clint stared back with a smug expression.

The spell was broken nearly instantly as fury exploded within him. He was the Devil, Milus Clint. He had been six years ago and six years before that. And he was more so, now. A soulless reflection, no trace of humanity left within his cold buzzard eyes. He was responsible for every nightmare tormenting Chris since that day at the orphanage, every buried shred of grief and pain. And now they were face to face and the circle would close. He tensed, intending to rush the outlaw, fury overpowering reason.

"Don't, son!" Windy shouted. "You'll get yourself killed right off!"

The words barely penetrated. All the hurt and suffering rushed out, as if it were a dam dynamited by Clint. A bloodhaze clouded his vision.

Milus Clint's smug expression turned into a half-leer.

"You knew I'd come for you, boy." The outlaw's voice stayed even, emotionless. "Where's your balls, now?" Milus gestured and the other Riders dismounted, walked towards the three men, Emmet in the lead.

The sudden whine of a loosed arrow came from beside Chris. A glance told him Dark Cloud had fired and was resetting for another shot. The shaft plowed into Emmet, stopping him in his tracks. The Rider gaped in surprise and black fluid sprayed from his mouth. His eyes, flashing black and wide, rose to Dark Cloud, then his eyelids fluttered.

"Goddamn..." Emmet mumbled, the word liquidy. He pitched face forward, thudding into the dust. Black flame burst over him. In seconds all that remained was his charred outline in the street.

Before the other Riders could react, Dark Cloud plucked another arrow loose. The shaft shot towards Milus Clint.

Clint's arm shot up, snatched the arrow out of mid-flight. The half-leer widened and in nearly the same move he reversed the arrow, hurled it back at Dark Cloud. The Comanche jerked sideways but not fast enough to avoid it completely. The flint arrowhead buried itself in his shoulder and he dropped the bow. Blood ran from the wound. Wincing, he snapped off the shaft so it wouldn't flop about and cause more damage and pain. To pull it out would mean taking a chunk of flesh and muscle and risk bleeding to death.

"It ain't that easy, Injun." Clint nodded to the three Riders on the ground, all of whom had frozen with the first arrow fired. "You'll need more than that to stop me. I ain't so easy to surprise no more."

Chris' gaze flicked to Dark Cloud, Windy, the Riders, Clint. He had damn near let his hate get the better of his judgment and Dark Cloud had seen it. The Comanche had averted it by acting immediately. Otherwise Chris would have charged Clint and that would have given the outlaw exactly what he wanted. The Comanche had given Chris a chance and he wouldn't squander it. With another glance at Windy and Dark Cloud, he communicated a silent intent. He yanked the reins, kicking the roan's sides and letting out a "Yah!" The horse skipped sideways, bolted. Windy and Dark Cloud followed a beat behind.

They plunged into a side street, shadows swallowing them. Slowing to maneuver in the darkness, they angled their animals through the street with as much haste as was safe. A twisted ankle would end their escape in a heartbeat.

Behind them Chris heard Clint shout an order that sent the Riders in pursuit.

The three men came out onto a parallel street, fifty yards ahead of the Riders. Light from hanging lanterns made the going faster and they kicked the horses into a ground-eating gait.

The town fell away. They rode hard across open land, wind slapping at their bodies. Hooves pummeled the grass flat, swallowed the miles. Chris wondered if escaping the Riders made a difference. He felt sure Milus was playing with them, letting them think they had gotten away before moving in for the kill. The Riders' horses were fast, faster than anything Chris had seen, and they had little head start on them. It was all part of Clint's game, something to make revenge taste all the sweeter. But even at that Clint wouldn't let it go too far. This time he wouldn't let arrogance set him up the way it had six years ago.

Chris had only a minute or two at the most to think of something once they reached the ranch. Then it would be over. But how could they fight Clint, now? How could they hope to win when a saloon full of able-bodied men had perished like flies?

The ranch came into view. Shooting a glance backward, Chris knew he had misjudged the time they had. A minute or two had been too generous, for the Riders were already in sight on the horizon. They were closing amazingly fast.

Chris reined up near the house. Windy and Dark Cloud drew up beside him.

"We ain't gots no time, son!" Windy's voice held something as close to panic as Chris had ever heard out of him.

The Riders cut the distance in half. They heard the rising thunder of hooves beating in time with their pulses. Chris shot a glance at the Riders, then at Windy and Dark Cloud.

"We gotta slow 'em, somehow, till we can figure out what to do." His words came in a gasp.

"How?" Windy asked. "They'll be on us in another half-minute!"

Chris' belly plunged and sweat streamed down his face. They were out of time and had no defense against the outlaws. Mind racing, Chris's gaze swept over the grounds, desperately seeking anything they could use as a weapon. He saw nothing—

The holding pen! A thought flashed and he remembered the first night Clint had come to the ranch, the dead steer and blackened outline of a Rider in the field.

In the pen, the unbranded steers shuffled nervously, bawling. Chris leaped from the roan and raced for the pen. Reaching it, the Riders fifty yards away, he threw aside the chute bar, then kicked open the corral's gate. He ran back to his horse and yanked his Winchester from the saddleboot. Levering a shell into the chamber, he triggered a shot before Windy could get a word out.

The blast spooked the already boogered longhorns. Steers bawled, panicked, and Chris yelled behind the shot.

The longhorns flooded into the chute in a wave of rippling muscle and blind fear. Bleating cries filled the air and log rails gave as the steers fanned outwards, bolting into the night.

The Riders, within twenty feet of the ranch, suddenly yanked on their reins, scrambling to reverse direction and get themselves out of the way of the stampeding cattle.

They didn't have the time. A sea of frightened longhorns charged straight into the men. The black horses fell first, as beeves canted their blocky heads and scooped rapier horns, skewering them. The mounts exploded in black flame. The Riders found themselves suddenly with nothing beneath them and fell into the charging wave of cattle.

The first Rider was impaled on a horn; the steer carried him twenty feet before the Rider burst into a bundle of ebony fire. The remaining Riders touched ground but had no time to run. Horns gouged into them and they fell, trampled beneath the beating hooves. They perished in black flame.

Windy let out a whoop of joy. "Yee-hah! You got 'em, son!"

Chris stared transfixed at the bolting longhorns as they scattered into the night. They would keep running for miles and Chris prayed he would be around to worry about getting them back.

Windy gripped his arm. "There's only Clint left, son. We can find somethin' to get him with. It'll be three against one!"

Chris's gaze lifted to the horizon. A chill swept through him and he let out a long breath. He could feel Clint. Feel him coming. Feel the darkness approaching. The time for running had passed and now there was merely the reckoning, debts due.

The mournful howl of a coyote rose in the night, as if in answer. Milus Clint had returned for Chris and he would not go away empty-handed, despite losing his men.

Chris would be here to meet him.

Chris turned to the other men. "You and Dark Cloud get the hell outta here, Windy." His voice was worn but firm.

"What in God's name you talkin' about, son?" Windy's too-small eyes held a puzzled glint.

"Just what I said: you two ride on out and don't stop. Clint's coming for me and I'll face him on my own."

"You're talkin' nonsense, son. You can't—"

"I have to, Windy. I had to since the day he came to the orphanage and murdered my sister. You come back here during the day tomorrow. If I ain't here...well, don't waste no time high-tailing it as far away from this place as you can and don't leave no trail."

Windy's gaze searched Chris and he knew the *segundo* could read him, see the resolve in his eyes. Chris needed to face Clint on his own if he ever expected to face the pain the outlaw had caused him. It was time to meet the past dead on instead of running from it. And he wouldn't risk anyone else close to him.

"'Fore you go, build me a branding fire near the barn and do it quick."

Windy nodded, sighing. "What you gots in mind?"

Chris frowned, sadness to his expression. "Something Matalija let me know when she died..."

Windy gave a puzzled look, but quickly set about building a branding fire next to the barn. Dark Cloud watched in silence, showing little evidence of the pain he must have felt from the flint arrowhead buried in his shoulder. The bleeding had stopped but the wound would have to be tended to soon.

Chris went to one of the sheds, located a tin container of kerosene and a 7HL branding iron. He set the iron beside the fire, which Windy had quickly coaxed into a roaring blaze. Chris lugged the container into the barn, came out a few seconds later, then placed the iron in the flames.

"Get outta here, now, Windy," Chris said, tone hard. Windy nodded, went to his horse and mounted. "Dark Cloud needs that wound fixed up," Chris added, eyeing the Comanche, then Windy again. "Best see to it."

Windy nodded, face grim. "You take care, son. I'll be prayin' for you."

A humorless laugh tumbled from Chris's lips. "Maybe this one time I could use just that."

Windy and Dark Cloud rode away, the *segundo* throwing numerous worried looks backward.

Chris wasted no time. He ran back into the barn and grabbed the tin container, dribbled the kerosene in a rough circle on the barn floor. He splashed the walls and hay bales, then climbed the ladder leading to the loft and dumped kerosene up there as well. He threw open the loft doors. Carrying the tin, he went back down the ladder. After setting it on the floor and securing the back doors, he went to his horse. He pulled loose his saddle, slapped the roan on the flank, shouting. The horse galloped away. He fashioned a lasso and walked to the back of the barn. Whirling the lasso above his head, he let it fly, roping the beam protruding from the wall above the open loft doors. He wanted an escape route, though he doubted he would get the chance to use it.

If he had to die to get Clint, he would do it.

He walked back to the front of the barn, closed one of the doors, then went to the branding fire. He paused, looking into the distance.

He saw him, now. On the horizon, riding for the ranch. Clint seemed in no particular hurry, his shadowy figure bouncing lightly in the saddle, coming at a steady yet somehow threatening pace. The outlaw knew Chris was waiting for him. He had no need to hurry; he judged the result to be inevitable, Chris reckoned. That was Chris' sole chance, that arrogance that had led to the outlaw's downfall the first time.

Dread swelled in his belly as he stared for another moment at the approaching Dark Rider, the monster who had shattered his life, murdered his loved ones. Hate rose up, filling him with bitterness and fury. Flashes of the orphanage, Clem and Little Waiting Woman struck his mind.

"C'mon, you sonofabitch..." he muttered. Another few minutes, that's all it would take. Another few minutes and he would stand face to face with everything he had locked away in his mind. Face to face with a nightmare. Face to face with death.

He scooped the glowing iron from the fire and went into the barn to wait.

Milus Clint rode into the compound at a trot. His buzzard eyes scanning the area, a half-grin pulled at his face as he spotted the fire. Chris could see the expression plainly from where he stood in the center of the barn, near the loft ladder.

"Durrin!" Clint shouted. "I know you're here, boy! You can't hide from me. Give yourself up and I'll make it easy on you. I'll kill you fast!"

Chris kept silent, watching Clint through the open door. The fury in him brewed. The iron glowed orange in his hand. He knew when Clint looked into the barn he would see it.

Milus Clint dismounted, saddle leather creaking. He strode forward, looking about. Chris saw the outlaw's gaze suddenly stop at the barn. He had seen the open door, the glowing iron. Good. Now just to step inside.

Clint came towards the barn. His grin widened and the fury in Chris strengthened.

"C'mon, you bastard...come inside..." Chris said through gritted teeth. Clint obliged, pausing at the door and looking in. He entered, halting a few paces in front of Chris.

"I've waited a long time for this moment, boy. You made me into what I am. I aim to return the favor."

Chris fought to keep his composure. If he gave into his anger now, all would be lost.

"You made yourself, Clint. Through your hate and evil. I had nothing to do with it."

Clint bellowed a laugh. "Do you know what it's like to be imprisoned by the night? Worse than any hell-hole jail cell in New Mex, even worse than hangin'. You wouldn't have been there the day the marshal raided, I wouldn't be like this." Clint took another step forward. "It ain't all bad, though. I got more power than I ever dreamed existed. Ain't no one can stop me, now. I can take life same as I always could, 'cept now I can give it, too, way I aim to give it to you."

"You took your revenge by makin' me suffer. That's all you get." Chris held up the iron.

Clint scoffed. "You plan on brandin' me to death, boy? You'll need more than that to hurt Old Milus"

"Reckon I won't." Chris tossed the iron sideways.

It sizzled as it hit the floor and Milus Clint laughed. The laugh died in his throat an instant later.

The glowing end of the iron hit the kerosene Chris had spread around the barn. The fuel ignited with an explosive *woof!* Flame leaped from the floor, scooting across the contours of the rough circle. It surrounded them, blocking the doors with a wall of fire.

The conflagration spread outward from the circle, following trails of kerosene. Walls burst into flame, crackling, snapping, popping. The blaze whisked across the boards and heat singed Chris' face. Orange-yellow light played across his set features. For the first time, a thin smile of confidence and satisfaction came to his lips.

Clint's head swiveled and a look of sudden comprehension flashed across his face.

"You got too full of yourself six years ago, Clint," Chris said, no emotion in his voice. "You got too full of yourself now. You should have made sure you finished me off when you killed my uncle."

Clint whirled, left, right, looking for a way out, finding none. What Dark Cloud had said about the Dark Riders being confined within a circle of fire was true. And just as surely the flames would kill Milus Clint as they would any man. But Chris couldn't take the chance of Clint somehow escaping. He had to finish the outlaw.

He leaped to his left, doubled and came up with the tin of kerosene. Clint turned to him, grasping his intention instantly and lunging.

The outlaw moved faster than any man or creature Chris had ever seen. Before Chris could set himself, Clint grabbed him and hurled him around with the strength of a grizzly. Chris fought to keep his hold on the tin, swung it in a jerky arc and splashed the hardcase with kerosene.

Clint wrenched the tin from Chris's grip, hurled it aside.

He jerked Chris close. Chris' boot heels barely touched the ground. Clint's lips curled back from curved razor fangs. It reminded him the man he faced was no longer human and he had gotten overconfident. Clint was faster, stronger, deadlier than any man could be and Chris had little chance of escaping the barn with his life. Yet that didn't matter—as long as Clint burned, too.

He looked into the outlaw's eyes, saw them shade to black, sizzling with arcs of blue-black light. Chris saw death reflected in those eyes, death and something inhuman, compassionless, evil.

Clint hurled Chris as if he were a child. He crashed to the floor, stunned by the impact. He had little strength remaining and the blow damn near finished what was left.

As he struggled to push himself up, the room spun. Around him streaked ribbons of yellow-orange. The interior was ablaze, walls crawling with flame. The sickly sweet stench of crisping hay was acrid in his nostrils. Black genies of smoke billowed up, choking his lungs and stinging his eyes. He coughed, pain spiking his chest. His eyes ran with tears and his throat felt tight and parched, his tongue thick and dry. It wouldn't take the barn long to burn to the ground and less time for the smoke to strangle him.

Beams creaked under the terrific heat. Exploding pops sent sparks spiraling, catching more hay bales afire.

Flames crept up the loft; another moment and the hay stacked up there would catch, blocking hiss retreat. If he didn't get up the ladder soon, he wouldn't ever.

He struggled to reach his feet but the crack of a whip and a spiking pain across his face sent him down again. He had taken his eyes off Clint only for an instant, but it was enough time for the outlaw to unlimber his black snake. Chris' fingers went to his cheek; blood trickled from a gash running nearly to his ear. His blurred gaze rose to meet Clint's.

Clint brought the whip back again. "We're *both* gonna die here, boy! You ain't getting' away. I'll see you burn the way your sister did!"

Clint snapped the whip and a gory slash appeared on Chris' jaw. He barely felt the pain. With the mention of his sister, fury surged through him. It gave him strength, temporary but blessed.

He scrambled backward on hands and knees, trying to get out of the way of another lash. The whip cracked; a stinging gash appeared on the side of his neck.

The smoke had become suffocating. Chris gasped for air. Heat blistered his face and hands. Sweat streamed down his face and his fury-driven strength began to fade.

"You're a damn fool, boy!" Clint shouted. "You could have lived forever!" Clint cocked his arm for another whip strike.

It never came.

With a tremendous *crack!* a ceiling beam snapped in half, crashing down in front of the open barn door. Sparks exploded, fiery rain. Planks tumbled from above and a wall of flame sprang up from the debris.

Milus Clint paused, looking to the beam then back to Chris, who was crawling towards the loft ladder. The outlaw leaped, sailing through the smoky air ten feet to land before Chris. A hiss escaped his lips.

Chris tried to move back, but flames stopped him. Their heat singed his back. His mind reeled, searching for a way to escape Clint, reach the ladder. Beyond the circle of fire, flames had reached the base of the ladder; soon they would devour it. And Clint blocked his way. Even if the outlaw hadn't, Chris knew he wouldn't make it. Clint was too fast, too strong.

Something at the corner of his eye caught his attention: the branding iron. The 7HL end lay within the flames, the other end sticking out but probably red-hot.

"There's no where to go, Durrin!" Clint shouted above the roar of the flames. "It's over. You'll die with me, but not before I have the pleasure of eating you alive!"

Clint's fangs gleamed with reflected sparks of firelight, dripped with salvia. He lunged at Chris.

A beat before, Chris moved, throwing all his strength into the effort. Chris would accept death by burning, but not by the outlaw responsible for destroying his life.

Clint came down on top of him, stopping Chris in mid-motion. Chris' hand trust out, fingertips touching the end of the iron. Pain shot through his fingers as the iron, superheated, seared his flesh. He gritted his teeth, curled the iron into his hand. It was agony but the thought of Clint winning made him hold on.

Clint hoisted Chris to his feet, pressing his mangled face close. His mouth opened wider, fangs glinting, as he forced Chris's head back to expose his throat.

Chris made a last desperate swing of his arm and Clint laughed at the puny effort.

But it was enough. The iron hit Clint's chest, sizzled. For an instant the 7HL brand burned through the outlaw's shirt and seared its outline into his flesh. Then the kerosene Chris had splashed on the hardcase ignited. A bundle of flame swirled over Clint.

The outlaw shrieked an inhuman sound and stumbled wildly back, releasing Chris. Flame wrapped itself around him. He gyrated, a creature of flame and smoke. Shadows of blackness swept across his melting face and black fluid boiled over his form, but as quickly as the damage was repaired, fire ate away the new flesh. It consumed Clint too fast, devouring his flat hat and hair, duster and clothes, flesh and bone.

Chris wasted little time watching the outlaw. He was sure Clint was done for.

He could no longer breathe; the smoke had become too thick, choking. He reeled, faint, lungs burning. He gasped, swallowing more smoke. Where he had held the iron was a raw paining welt.

He struggled to hold his breath, staggered forward. The outline of the loft ladder was barely visible through the smoke and tears stinging his eyes. Flame was all around him, surging up from spots on the floor. Timbers snapped, crashing down. Sparks showered him, biting into his reddened flesh.

He avoided the fallen beams more out of instinct than plan. At any second one might come crashing down on him and he would perish with Clint.

Throwing his hands before his eyes, he blundered through the flaming circle and to the burning ladder.

Something grabbed him from behind, spun him around. Clint! The outlaw was a hideous spectacle of charred flesh, hairless, naked, blisters of blackness bubbling over him. Black eyes penetrated Chris' soul and he could see the black spirits damning him.

"*Judas Priest...*" he mumbled.

"Not...that easy...boy!" Clint's mouth didn't move and the voice that came out wasn't even remotely human. He pulled Chris back towards the center of the barn. Chris had little strength to resist.

Clint let go suddenly and Chris stumbled back in shock. He saw the point of a lance jutting from Clint's chest. The outlaw staggered, black fluid gouting from his wide-open mouth. Chris had no time to see where the lance had come from.

He half-stumbled, half-fell against the loft ladder, struggled to pull himself up with every ounce of his remaining strength and will. The ladder was red-hot and pain shot through his already-blistered hands. He gasped, inhaling a deep gulp of smoke and choking. His lips were cracked, tongue swollen. His muscles quivered, threatening to give out.

The ladder began to tremble, creaking as it started to pull away from its fastenings.

Three rungs.

He could barely hang on. The ladder inched outward. If it pulled loose, now...

With a primal yell he hauled himself upward. Muscles shook, aching, pain ripping through every joint.

Two rungs.

His head swam and blackness crept along the edges of his mind. The roar of the flames receded into the background, replaced by a lulling thrum. Death was calling to him and he wanted to let go of the ladder, fall back into the inferno. Be swept away...comforted.

One rung.

Now. Let go. Give in to the call. It would be so easy...so easy...

The ladder collapsed beneath him!

His legs were suddenly hanging in midair. He distantly felt the wrenching shock of his arm jerking taut as he gripped the edge of the loft. His fingers began to slip and he didn't know why he held on, what force inside made him cling desperately to life. His consciousness wavered.

Let go...let go and be warmed by the flames, free of the past and sorrow....Just let yourself fall free...

His fingers slipped another fraction.

He could hold on no longer. He gave a last desperate attempt to pull himself up onto the loft, but his muscles refused.

He let go—

A hand clamped about his wrist. He felt himself rising, being lifted. An angel, maybe. A red-headed angel with a barrel chest. The angel hoisted him into the loft and across his shoulder. Through stinging blurry eyes he saw ribbons of flame reaching for him, reluctant to let go of their prey.

Through the clamor in his brain he heard the red-haired angel shout something about holding on and felt himself whisked from the heat into the cool night air. He clung to the angel with what little strength he had. In fits and starts the angel was taking him down, down, down the rope he'd left hanging outside the loft doors.

Close to the bottom, the rope snapped and they plunged the remaining five feet to the ground. Chris tumbled onto the grass, unable to move, staring up at the dark sky. He felt two sets of hands grip him, pull him away from the barn as the entire backside of the structure began to cave. The flaming wall came down with a great crash and a ball of sparks and smoke exploded into the air.

The angel lifted him again, then eased him down. Water rushed over him and he realized the angel had placed him in the rain trough.

It was the last thing he knew before blackness swallowed his senses.

The world focused around Chris. At first he saw merely a lighter shade of blackness. It turned into vague images, objects. Every inch of his body was in agony and the pain helped bring him further awake. He lifted his head, seeing worried faces swim before his vision, Windy and Dark Cloud bending over him.

"You gots some pretty bad burns and sucked in a lot of smoke, son, but you'll live, though for a spell you might wish to hell you hadn't."

Chris struggled to form words; his swollen tongue and parched throat made it difficult, but he managed to speak in a hoarse whisper. "I...told you...to go..."

Windy bellowed a laugh. "You should know me better'n that by now, son. I wouldn't let you face the Devil alone."

Chris turned his head to see the barn had collapsed. The beams were ash and cinder, now, flames licking up occasionally, spent quickly. Thick smoke poured from the wreckage, but the breeze whisked it across the Plains in charcoal clouds.

"Clint...?"

Windy nodded. "He's gone, son. Dark Cloud got him with that lance and the whole damn barn fell on him, least what was left of him."

Milus Clint was dead. For good this time, but Chris felt no sense of elation. Only emptiness, longing for those who had been taken from him.

But even that was mercifully short. Blackness drifted across his mind again and he let it take him to a world without pain, without grief, without sorrow. A world without Milus Clint and Dark Riders.

TWENTY-THREE

Three days later, as false dawn splashed gray light over the Plains, Chris stood looking out across the land. He had never felt as glad for a sunrise. His face and hands carried the scars of the fire, though the burns weren't as serious as Windy had thought. Chris would wear the bandages for some time to come and it hurt like hell, but it was a small price to pay for destroying Milus Clint.

He glanced at the charred remains of the barn. Occasionally, smoke spiraled up and Chris thought the wisps seemed like Clint's dying breaths escaping into the light. Occasionally, an ember snapped like Clint's dying curse. Occasionally, feelings of deep remorse and sadness overtook him as he remembered the loved ones taken by the monster who now lay beneath the rubble. Occasionally, he recollected the woman he longed for, the woman he'd made love with in that barn.

He took a deep breath of crisp morning air, lungs and throat still tender, lips still stinging. He watched the sun blaze over the horizon, glossing the field with gold and for an instant it almost seemed like old times, rising to greet the new day with Clem, looking forward to the night with Little Waiting Woman. The chill dissolved and the sun warmed him.

It was over. That's all that mattered. Milus Clint was dead, though his legacy of sorrow would live on, maybe for the rest of Chris' life. That was something yet to face. He wondered if he could ever fully confront the loss he'd suffered. It would take time, maybe more than he had. But a door had been opened and he'd damn sure step through it. He would confront it in bits and pieces, wouldn't let the past poison his insides any longer. He couldn't bring his loved ones back but he could at least begin to remember them with a small degree of peace and go on, as they would want him to do.

"You awright, son?" he heard Windy ask, coming up beside him.

"Yeah, I reckon. Just glad to see the sun, is all."

Windy let out an easy laugh. "Feel that way myself. Had me enough of the darkness for a spell."

Chris, taking another deep breath, fixed his gaze on a spot in the distance. "Don't know if I can ever face all the death, Windy. At least not enough of it to be happy again."

Windy frowned, folding his arms. "Seems that way now, but in time it won't so much. Hurts have a way of bleedin' themselves of their poison once they've been lanced—and Clint, he was lanced." The *segundo* gave a barrel-chested laugh and Chris found himself smiling at the man's bad joke.

His face grew serious again. "Seems like only emptiness out there, Windy." Chris nudged his head at the Plains. "Inside, too."

"You own the 7HL, now. Clem would want you to go on with it, I know he would. And I ain't goin' nowhere. I can round the men back up and we'll have them cattle up the trail to Dodge 'fore you know it. Trail drive's just the thing to take your mind off, well, what happened. When you get back you'll find yourself more steady and ready to start comin' to terms with the past. Take it from someone who knows, sometimes it's a damn sight harder to run and know it's only a pace behind you than it is to turn around and kick it in the britches!"

"I'll miss her, Windy. Especially when we get back from the drive and I think about how I would have asked her to marry me then. I'll miss them all." A tear slipped down his cheek and Windy placed a hand on his shoulder, gently squeezing.

A noise behind them drew their attention. They turned to see Dark Cloud mount his pinto. The Comanche nudged the animal towards them. Windy had dug the arrowhead out of Dark Cloud's shoulder and bandaged the wound after dowsing it with whiskey to keep infection from setting in. The Indian had spent the last few days recovering.

"You can stay," Chris said, looking up at the Comanche with a thin smile. "You got a place here, same as you did with my uncle"

Dark Cloud gazed at the endless expanse of the Plains, sorrow bleeding onto his face. "No, I no longer have a place here." He reined around and dug his heels into the pinto's sides. Chris and Windy watched him disappear into the ocean of buffalo grass.

"Reckon he'll head to the reservation?" Windy asked.

Chris nodded. "It's all he has left and it ain't a hell of a lot for a man like that."

Windy frowned and moved off, leaving Chris gazing out across the land. Chris felt sorry for the Comanche but knew he shouldn't. Dark Cloud wouldn't want his pity, only his respect—and he already had that. He felt a bond with the Indian, each suffering as much, losing as much. In one respect it was worse for the warrior; at least Chris had a place to belong, a home.

Windy returned, leading Chris' roan, as well as his own horse. He handed Chris the reins and Chris cocked an eyebrow.

"Rounded him up while you was recuperatin'. Time you climbed back on a horse, son. Reckon we might ride over thataway..." Windy nudged his head east and realization struck Chris. They had one seed left, didn't they?

"Got some ranch business to 'tend to, don't we?" Chris's face went grim.

Windy nodded and slapped the rope coiled on his saddle. "Reckon we gots some justice business to 'tend to." The *segundo* mounted and Chris followed suit, knowing it would be the first step towards dealing with the past. He noticed Windy had slipped the Winchester into Chris' saddleboot, as well as one into his own. Windy had told him the territorial marshal had shown up during the time Chris was unconscious, the day after Clint's death. There had been little need for him by that time and the man and his deputies had ridden away, shaking their heads and cursing about it being a damn waste of time coming. Windy told Chris the marshal hadn't believed a single word about Clint and was familiar enough with Tolby not to give a damn what had happened to him. The 'keep had taken over as sheriff and declared Tolby's death an accident. Past that point, the marshal wouldn't hear a lick about rustling.

They gigged their horses towards the Box H.

They approached the ranch cautiously, eyes alert, but saw no sign of movement. After trotting up to the main building, they dismounted, grabbed their rifles. Shinn would not catch them by surprise again.

Windy skirted the side and edged up to the wall behind the front door. He knocked, pulling back.

"Who's it?" a slurred voice sounded from the interior. Chris glanced at Windy, who shrugged. Fear laced the man's question, along with drunkenness.

"It's Chris Durrin, Shinn!" he yelled. "We got ourselves some business to finish. Rustling business. Get out here!"

The door rattled open and Shinn, face twisted with anger, came through the doorway like a lion, waving a rifle menacingly. "I told you—"

The click of Windy levering a shell into the chamber of his Winchester stopped Shinn in mid-sentence. The cocklebur rancher's eyes shifted to the *segundo*, who leveled a rifle at his back.

"Be obliged if you'd just drop that," Windy said, stone in his voice. "We ain't askin' nice this time, neither. We know who you are and what you been doin'."

Sweat dribbled down Shinn's face and he licked his lips, looked nervously at Chris. He seemed to be considering shooting his way out of it, though, even half-drunk he realized it was certain death.

Chris brought his Winchester up and Shinn hesitated, then dropped his rife.

Windy stepped to his horse and unlimbered the coil of rope from the saddle.

Shinn's eyes widened. "Christ, you're gonna kill me anyway?"

"Anyone else here?" Chris cut in, jabbing the Winchester at him.

"Just the b-breed, in the bunkhouse," Shinn stuttered. A wet patch appeared at his crotch. He suddenly blurted: "He's the one who done it al! Changed your brands! I didn't have nothin' to do with it, no sir! Said he'd scalp me if I said a word. I swear, Durrin!" Shinn started to blubber and Chris realized this wasn't the cocksure man he'd dealt with the other day. Something had changed the rustler and Chris felt a twinge of sympathy.

"You weren't singin' that tune the other night, when you handed me over to the sheriff," Windy said. "Hold him here," he added to Chris and walked towards the bunkhouse.

Windy roused the breed from his sleep and prodded the Apache next to Shinn.

Chris peered at the breed. "He says you're responsible for the whole thing."

The Apache looked at Shinn and a humorless smile touched his lips. He looked back to Chris. "I changed the brands, that is all."

"Figured as much," Chris said. "You weren't part of Clint's gang; that fact saved your life. I'll leave you to the law."

The Apache nodded, something next to relief glinting in his eyes.

Shinn fell to his knees, pleading. "No, please...don't—"

"You were with Clint the day he killed my sister." Chris' voice came low, final. "This is for her..."

While Chris covered Shinn, Windy went to a cottonwood and strung a noose, then led his horse beneath the rope...

ABOUT THE AUTHOR

Howard Hopkins lives in a small Maine seacoast town and has written twenty-seven westerns under his penname Lance Howard, the latest of which saw print in December, 2006, titled, *Nightmare Pass*. In addition, he's written six horror novels under his own name as well as comic book scripts and articles for various publications, both on and offline. Please visit his webpage at: www.howardhopkins.com. Also visit his My Space page and blog at www.myspace.com/yingko2.

Also by Howard Hopkins...

Grimm
The Nightmare Club
Night Demons
Dark Harbors
Pistolero

Lance Howard Westerns...

Blood on the Saddle
The Comanche's Ghost
Blood Pass
The West Witch
Wanted
Ghost-town Duel
The Gallows Ghost
The Widow Maker
Guns of the Past
Palomita
The Last Draw
The Deadly Doves
The Devil's Peacemaker
The West Wolf
The Phantom Marshall
Bandolero
Pirate Pass
The Silver-mine Spook
Ladigan
Vengeance Pass
Johnny Dead
Poison Pass
Ripper Pass
Nightmare Pass
Hell Pass

www.ingramcontent.com/pod-product-compliance
Lightning Source LLC
Chambersburg PA
CBHW030518020726
47494CB00004B/1149